Daughter

of the
GOD-KING

ANNE CLEELAND

sourcebooks
landmark

Published by Sourcebooks Landmark, an imprint of Sourcebooks, Inc.
P.O. Box 4410, Naperville, Illinois 60567-4410
(630) 961-3900
Fax: (630) 961-2168
www.sourcebooks.com

Library of Congress Cataloging-in-Publication data is on file with the publisher.

Printed and bound in the United States of America.
VP 10 9 8 7 6 5 4 3 2 1

For Sarah's mom, who adopted a wide variety of delightful children; and for all others like her.

Chapter 1

H attie Blackhouse was aware that she had—regrettably— something of a temper, and that this trait often led to impetuous decisions that were not always thought out in a rational manner. Fortunately, because she had lived a solitary life in the Cornish countryside, few had experienced either her temper or her impetuosity, and she had thus far avoided embarrassing herself in public. Until now, of course.

"Have you a card of invitation?" asked the respectful under-footman. He asked in English, which meant he had taken one look at their clothes and concluded they were either impoverished refugees or English, as the Parisian ladies around them were very much *à la mode*.

"We do not," she replied evenly, and lifted her chin. Now that she saw how grand it all was she conceded that it had been—perhaps—not the best idea to show up here at such a place uninvited and that she may indeed wind up as a public spectacle, but she had no one to blame but herself. Her old governess—the traitorous Swansea—had been a gentle, indulgent woman who had only interfered that one time when Hattie had taken a crop to the gardener's boy after he tied a can to the Tremaine dog's tail, and even then the distraught governess had apologized for curbing Hattie's impulse to beat the boy soundly, but the gardener was a good one and good gardeners were apparently few and far between. I must remind Robbie that I did a good deed for Sophie, Hattie thought as she squared her shoulders on the threshold of the Prussian embassy. I have a feeling he may not be best pleased when I make my appearance; but truly, coming here seemed such a good idea at the time, and I was sick to *death* of being exiled in Cornwall.

"Perhaps we should have sent a card 'round to your fiancé, first." Bing's tone was dry and deferential, but Hattie was given the uneasy feeling that Bing was well aware this was all a hoax. Even more reason not to tell her freshly minted companion that she had shoved an intruder down the back stairs of their Parisian townhouse less than an hour ago. Although the jury was still out, Bing seemed the sort of person who may have felt it necessary to notify the *gendarmes*, and Hattie didn't have the time, just now; she was going to confront Robbie—another traitor in what seemed to be an unending list.

"I'm afraid we haven't any calling cards, Bing; and we are gate-crashers of the first order."

"Very well," said Bing, unruffled. "It is a good thing I am armed, then."

Hattie hid a smile as they stepped forward in the line to be announced at the ambassador's *soirée*—fortunately it hadn't been a ball, as Hattie didn't own a ball gown. Truth to tell, she didn't own anything suitable for a Parisian *soirée*, either, but this was the least of her concerns; as she was preparing for this outing at her parents' townhouse, she had heard a noise coming from the back stairwell and after flinging open the door, had been astonished to confront an intruder, equally astonished in beholding her before him. On instinct, she had shoved him as hard as she was able and he had tumbled backward down the stairs as she slammed the door shut and bolted the lock. A burglar, she assured herself; someone who thought the place was still empty and who was unaware that they had lately taken up residence. Although he hadn't seemed like a burglar and had stared at her in such an odd way, as though he was seeing a ghost.

She moved forward another step, frowning in distraction. She hoped Robbie was here at the embassy, as she may have need of reinforcements—there was the other man lurking on the corner of the street yesterday, also. For pity's sake, it was as though no one had ever seen a girl from Cornwall before, and her clothes were not *that* bad, surely.

"Hathor," Bing prompted under her breath, and Hattie brightened to bestow a smile on the footman at the door, resplendent in his livery. The man looked over her head for parents or presenters—no hard task as she was rather short in stature—and then seemed surprised to behold no one there. But Hattie had successfully shoved the intruder down the stairs, and buoyed by this thought, she announced with confidence, "I am Miss Blackhouse; I am here with my companion, Miss Bing."

Understandably nonplussed, the footman inquired in a discreet tone, "You have no card of invitation, mademoiselle?"

At this juncture, Bing, who was tall and spare and very correct, offered in a shocked tone, "Perhaps you do not recognize the name, my good man. This is Miss *Blackhouse*, the daughter of the famous Blackhouses; the ambassador will be thrilled she has chosen his *soirée* over all the others."

Although she was half inclined to laugh out loud, Hattie made an attempt to look famous as the footman's eyes widened and he quickly passed her along to the host after murmuring an apology. "Miss Blackhouse and her companion, Miss Ding."

3

"*Bing*," Hattie interjected impatiently. "Miss *Bing*."

But her correction was swallowed up in the reaction of the Prussian ambassador, a large, rather burly man with a gray goatee and an impressive array of medals displayed along his blue sash, which was itself impressive due to his girth. "Miss Blackhouse," he exclaimed in astonishment, and lifted a monocle to his eye. "Welcome—why, indeed; welcome."

Hoping that the footman was paying attention, Hattie took his hand with a sense of relief that she was not to be shown the door, and then was forced to stand as he clasped her hand in both of his with no indication he would release her anytime soon. "The tomb of the god-king's daughter," he pronounced in tones of deep emotion as the candlelight glinted off his monocle. "An amazing find—it quite takes one's breath away. Tell me, do your parents know the identity of the princess as yet?"

Another fervent Egyptologist, she thought with resignation; she had met his type before and unfortunately they were thick on the ground nowadays, with everyone mad for all things Egyptian and the world's fancy being caught by the tombs currently being uncovered in the Valley of the Kings.

"I believe not," she equivocated. Best not to mention that she rarely heard from either of her negligent parents; her information instead was gleaned from the local newspapers—or Bing, who was well informed due to her late brother. Reminded, Hattie offered, "There does seem to be a curse, though." As soon as she said it, she inwardly winced—she was thoughtless to mention it in front of poor Bing, who still wore mourning black.

But Bing did not falter, and added, "Indeed; several lives have been lost under unexplained circumstances."

4

The ambassador's eyes widened and he glanced to those still waiting in the receiving line, clearly torn between his duties as host and his burning desire to buttonhole Hattie and quiz her about this fascinating bit of information. He called out, "Monsieur le Baron; your aid, if you please."

Hattie turned to meet the newcomer, tamping down her impatience. She had used her connection with her parents to crash this party and it was only fair that she pay the piper for a few minutes before she went off in search of Robbie. He wouldn't fail her, although she fully anticipated a dressing-down later in private. Hopefully it wouldn't be as bad as when she'd gotten lost on the Tor back home—and *truly*, that had not been her fault.

The baron was revealed as an elegant, silver-haired man who approached with his hands clasped behind his back. "Yes? Might I be of assistance?"

With barely suppressed exultation, the ambassador introduced him to Hattie. "Baron du Pays, my dear." And then, with a great deal of significance, "Monsieur le Baron, if you would entertain Miss Blackhouse while I attend to my duties here—she brings the latest news from the excavations."

The baron could be seen to go quite still for a moment, his gaze fixed upon Hattie's, until he found his voice and bowed over her hand in the elegant manner known only to Frenchmen. "*Enchanté*, Mademoiselle Blackhouse." The pale blue eyes then fixed upon hers again with an expression she could not quite interpret—assessing, or calculating, or—or something. "I was so fortunate as to have met your parents once; extraordinary people." He looked up to a companion, who approached to join him. "Monsieur Chauvelin, come meet Mademoiselle Blackhouse."

But Hattie was astonished to recognize her former

intruder, and coldly riposted with a great deal of meaning, "I believe we have already met, monsieur."

She could hear Bing's soft intake of breath at her tone, but the man only shook his head and gravely disclaimed, "I do not recall such a felicity, mademoiselle."

"If you will excuse us," Hattie said with a curt bow and then turned away, a surprised Bing in her wake. In her abrupt movement, she met the eye of a man who appeared to be watching her from the side, although he quickly turned away and melted into the crowd. He appeared to be a civil servant of some stripe; his manner unprepossessing, his dress understated. But something in his bearing—his cool assurance, perhaps—belied his appearance and made her wonder why he watched her. This is a very strange sort of *soirée*, she thought; in Cornwall we may not be *à la mode*, but everyone certainly has better manners.

"Do we seek out Mr. Tremaine, Hathor?" Bing walked along beside her as though her charge had not just snubbed two distinguished gentlemen for no apparent reason.

"We do, Bing. And I am heartily sick of the tedious god-king and his equally tedious daughter."

"As you say," Bing replied.

Robbie was tall, and so she quickly scanned the assembly, looking for his blond head and wishing she could whistle for him. In the process, her gaze rested upon the self-assured civil servant, who had managed to stay parallel with her despite the crowded quarters. Lifting her chin, she gave him a quelling look just so that he was aware she was on to him, and then at long last spotted Robbie's form at a small distance in the crowd. He was surrounded by a group of people, and bent his head for a moment to listen to a blond woman, who was trying to speak to him over the noise of the throng. "I see him, Bing—and not a moment too soon. Come along."

But before she could squeeze in his direction, Hattie was confronted by the Prussian ambassador himself, who gallantly handed her a glass of punch and indicated he would like to speak to her in a quieter corner. Short of pulling her hand from his and pushing yet another one bodily to the floor, she had little choice but to comply, and followed him to a less-crowded area near the windows, taking a quick glance to mark Robbie's location in the process.

"Did you enjoy speaking with Baron du Pays, Miss Blackhouse? He is the French vice-consul in Egypt."

"Oh—is he indeed?" It wanted only this; Hattie had probably launched an international incident by her snub, but surely a vice-consul shouldn't be consorting with burglars. As if on cue, the vice-consul came over to join them, although this time he was not accompanied by the aforesaid burglar, which was just as well, as Hattie may have felt it necessary to dress him down and she was *truly* trying to control her temper.

With an air of extreme interest, her host crossed his arms over his bemedaled chest and rocked back on his heels. "If you would, Miss Blackhouse, tell me more of the curse; could it be the wrath of the ancients, visited upon those who disturb their legacy?"

"One can only wonder," Hattie replied, as diplomatically as she was able. She barely refrained from muttering a curse herself—one that Robbie himself had taught her. How anyone could believe that lifeless objects could be "cursed" was beyond her comprehension, but the superstitious were a stubborn breed and—apparently—could be found at the highest levels of diplomacy, which told its own tale. She glanced sidelong at Robbie, and saw that he was conferring with the self-assured gentleman who had been watching her; Robbie then lifting his head to glance with surprise in her direction. Which was rather strange; why would the gentleman know that it was Robbie she sought out? Bing surreptitiously touched her elbow to draw her attention back to the conversation, and with an effort, Hattie pulled her gaze back to the ambassador's magnified eye.

"...and the tomb with no clue as to the princess's identity. Extraordinary."

For two pins, Hattie would have asked why any rational person would feel this topic was of the least importance, but so as not to embarrass poor Bing she attempted to refocus; after all, the ambassador was her host and she should not allow Robbie to think she was incapable of deporting herself in diplomatic circles. Although it was a dull group, truth be told, and it was hard to believe the intrepid boy next door had willingly chosen this sort of life. "It is believed she was the daughter of some famous pharaoh," offered Hattie vaguely, stealing a glance toward Robbie as he made his way toward her. Oddly enough, he had the blond woman in tow—she was quite old—at least thirty, if she was a day. Perhaps the woman required his support due to her advanced age.

"Seti," murmured Bing behind her in an undertone.

"The Great Seti," added Hattie smoothly. "The god-king; presumably her father."

The ambassador leaned forward, his expression avid at having gleaned such an intriguing scrap of information to tout to his fellow aficionados. "Indeed? And have your parents discovered why a princess's tomb was found in the Valley of the Kings? The only female to be found—most unusual."

At this juncture, Robbie arrived and greeted her with astonishment. "Hattie, by all that's holy—however did you come to be here?" As he turned to explain their acquaintanceship to their host, Hattie realized she couldn't very well confess that she had come to Paris for the express purpose of trying to convince him to marry her, and with this in mind she retreated to a less-crazed explanation. "I came to visit my parents, Robbie."

The reaction to this disclosure was a rather heavy silence, with the baron lowering his gaze to the floor and Robbie's expression suddenly shuttered. Hattie looked from one to the other in surprise, but was forced to acknowledge the blond woman with Robbie because she offered with a doubtful smile, "Here—in Paris? But I recently left your parents in Thebes."

"Did you indeed?" Hattie was very much afraid her tone may have indicated her displeasure at having been shown to be equivocating, not to mention it was of all things annoying that this too-tall blond knew more about her parents than she did. She hastily added, "I thought they would be here in Paris, instead; I meant to surprise them, you see."

The baron took the opportunity to interject, "A coincidence; I have recently journeyed from Thebes, myself."

Again, there was a tense silence in response to this observation and the woman did not acknowledge this remark with even a glance in his direction. Hattie, alive to the undercurrent, wondered why they had all converged upon her when they didn't seem to like each other very much and half-hoped for an open quarrel so that she could use the opportunity to speak privately with Robbie. Not to mention the self-assured gentleman was now standing at the vice-consul's back, pretending to converse with a woman wielding a flirtatious fan even though Hattie was well aware he was eavesdropping on their conversation. Why, every man jack on the premises appears to be prodigiously interested in my doings, she thought with surprise; it is all very strange.

The ambassador informed the newcomers, "We were discussing the latest Blackhouse discovery—the tomb of the god-king's daughter."

"Extraordinary," agreed the baron. "Indeed, the artifacts uncovered include the sacred sword *Shefrh Lelmelwek*—the Glory of Kings, bestowed by the gods on the pharaoh himself."

Hattie didn't need to look at Bing to feel her companion's surprise. It appeared the vice-consul was indeed lately come from the excavation at Thebes, and he was very well informed. Bing's brother had indicated in his letters that the discovery of the mythical sword was a well-kept secret.

With an attitude that bordered on the rapturous, the ambassador looked to Hattie, wide of eye. "Such a mystery! How could such a wonder have been bestowed upon a mere female? And how could she have warranted a tomb in the Valley of the Kings?"

Hattie did her best to come up with an answer, wishing she had paid more attention when Bing was speaking of such things. "We must suppose that she performed some extraordinary service so as to be a heroine in the eyes of the Eighteenth Dynasty."

Bing made a small sound behind her that indicated Hattie was mixing her dynasties again—but honestly, who could keep them straight? It was three thousand years ago, for the *love* of *heaven*. But correction was to come from the blond woman, who announced in an indulgent tone, "Seti was Nineteenth Dynasty, I believe."

Curbing an urgent desire to make a cutting remark, Hattie recalled her circumstances and subsided. "Yes—yes I am sorry; I misspoke." She then caught the self-assured gentleman's gaze upon her again and realized he was amused. Why, he is *laughing* at me, the wretch; I should spill my punch on him, just to show how little I appreciate being the object of his amusement—or being exposed as ignorant in matters Egyptian. The man turned away as Hattie sipped her punch, thinking that this was an odd sort of party—and Robbie was making no effort to have a private word, which was perplexing in itself; if nothing else, he should want to take her aside to give her a bear-garden jawing for surprising him in such a way.

But he had his own surprise that, as it turned out, would trump hers. Robbie turned to the woman in warm approval, and pulled her hand through his arm. "Madame Auguste knows a great deal about the excavations—she lived in Egypt for years."

"No more," she laughed. "Now I will be an English-woman."

"England's gain," offered the ambassador gallantly, and sketched a small bow.

With a smile that bordered on the patronizing, the woman addressed Hattie. "Only think, Mademoiselle Blackhouse, we shall be neighbors, you and I."

With dawning horror, Hattie found she was having trouble putting together a coherent thought. "Is that so?" she managed, and almost dispassionately noted that she could now hear her heartbeat in her ears—never a good sign.

"Wish me happy, Hattie," Robbie revealed with his easy smile. "Madame has agreed to marry me, and I am the lucki-est of men."

Chapter 2

With a discreet movement, Bing removed Hattie's cup of punch from her nerveless hand—apparently afraid her charge would drop it or perhaps even throw it—but Hattie was made of sterner stuff and with a monumental effort, righted her ship and pinned a smile to her lips. "Why, that is wonderful news. My best wishes, Madame."

"A whirlwind romance," the baron observed, and there was an edge to the comment that made Hattie slide her gaze to him, wondering if the baron was winding up to throw a cup, himself.

"And a timely one," the woman riposted with a touch of rancor, her eyes narrowed.

The ambassador was nothing if not a diplomat, and hastily turned to Hattie before blows could be exchanged. "Do you enjoy your stay in Paris, Miss Blackhouse?"

Paris is *hideous*, thought Hattie. Aloud, she managed, "Very much—although we are just arrived, and have still to settle in."

"Will you meet up with your parents in Egypt?" The slight smile was not reflected in the baron's unblinking pale eyes and Hattie again had the sense there was an undercurrent whose import was lost upon her—Lord, but this was a joyless group—and Robbie as joyless as the rest of them, despite his genial mien; she knew him better than most.

"I'm afraid my plans are as yet unformed," she replied vaguely. Even if she had any sort of plan—which she did not—Hattie would not have confided in him, having lately decided that men should not be trusted. Very lately.

"May I assume that you stay here in town, mademoiselle?"

Hattie wondered for one horrified moment if the baron thought to call upon her, then decided she was misinterpreting the situation—the man was old enough to be her father, for heaven's sake. "Yes—we stay at my parents' townhouse off the Rue de Rivoli."

"Perhaps you will allow me to provide an escort on those occasions when one is needed." The vice-consul tilted his head slightly to the side in Gallic supplication.

Good God, she thought in alarm—the old *roué* is indeed going to call upon me. "That would be delightful," she replied politely, and wished him away. For reasons she could not name, she took a quick glance to ascertain the whereabouts of the self-assured gentleman and saw that he no longer held his position behind the baron, but was aligned along the wall at a small distance, viewing the crowd with an air of disinterest.

"So—you have been to the tomb itself, madam?" To add insult to injury, the ambassador had apparently decided that Hattie was a less-than-satisfactory source of information, and so now appealed to the blond usurper. "You must tell us what you observed."

"I understand it is cursed," Hattie offered in a brittle tone. Robbie, long familiar with the warning signs, shot her an admonitory look.

"There are many secrets in the Valley of the Kings," the woman replied with an air of defiance as she clung to Robbie's arm. "One can understand why the former emperor was *fascinant*." Hattie was vaguely aware that Napoleon had fought a battle in Egypt but it seemed of little relevance now as he no longer held sway there—or anywhere else for that matter—being safely secured in exile on the Island of Elba. A good riddance, she thought; even though she had been tucked away in the wilds of Cornwall she was aware that the Congress of Vienna was trying to determine how to reassemble the shambles that the French emperor had made of Europe. Robbie had abruptly left home—being attached to the British contingent in some unexplained way—and so had set in train this series of events that had resulted in Hattie's current humiliation on the floor of the Prussian embassy in Paris. When you thought about it, the former emperor had much to answer for, the wretched tyrant. And it didn't help her frame of mind to admit she had thought no further ahead than meeting up with Robbie and living happily ever after—although it appeared that this plan was now in as much a shambles as was Europe after Napoleon.

With a thoughtful air, the baron crossed his arms and considered the floor for a moment. "I suppose Napoleon saw his own actions through the prism of history, and tried to incite a comparison to the pharaohs—at least in the minds of his followers."

"And he is now relegated to the dustbin of history." The Prussian ambassador emphasized the words with unabashed relish.

The baron tilted his head in acknowledgment. "*De vrai*; but say what you will, he did have a rare talent for inspiring his followers."

But even this tepid praise could not be borne with equanimity by Hattie's host, who drew his bushy grey eyebrows together in extreme disapproval. "He had a talent for causing a great many casualties—and destroying lives. Bah! They should have executed him forthwith—one such as he will never be contained on Elba—it is sheer folly."

Impressed by this impassioned speech, Hattie reassessed her opinion of the ambassador—he was much more palatable when he wasn't fawning over the long-dead princess.

"We must not speak of war; the ladies will disavow us." The baron turned to Hattie yet again with a polite smile. "Mademoiselle, could I interest you in a tour of the Tuileries tomorrow, if the weather holds?"

Before Hattie could scramble for an excuse, Robbie interjected, "I must claim priority, Monsieur le Baron; allow me to catch up with my old neighbor while I give her a tour of the British embassy."

Perversely, Hattie found she was inclined to cut the ground from under Robbie's feet as a turnabout, and turned to Bing. "Have we any plans tomorrow, Miss Bing?"

Without hesitation, Bing prevaricated, "We do have several cards of invitation—"

But Madame Auguste interrupted to tug playfully on Robbie's arm in mock chagrin. "*Mon cher*, tomorrow we must meet with the curé about the wedding—have you forgotten?"

"After we meet with him, then," he reassured her with a smile, fondly placing his hand over hers.

This seemed rather ominous to Hattie, who felt compelled to ask despite her better judgment, "The wedding is imminent?"

"Friday," replied the woman, who then added graciously, "You must come—please."

"I would be delighted," said Hattie, and then bestowed a dimpled smile on the group. "If you will excuse me for a moment?"

After taking her leave, Hattie retreated to the ladies'

retiring room, only barely resisting an impulse to stalk because she couldn't shake the uneasy feeling that there was more than one pair of eyes watching her. "Well, Bing; that did not go at all as expected."

Bing offered ready sympathy, bending her taller head down to Hattie's. "I am terribly sorry, Hathor, and I can easily see why you were misled; he certainly doesn't seem a jilt."

But Hattie was compelled to come to Robbie's defense, and so confessed, "It is not as bad as it appears, Bing; we were never engaged—I said it only so you would make no protest about the trip."

"Ah," said Bing without real surprise. "You cannot be blamed, but I confess that I have always wanted to travel, and any excuse would have done."

Despite everything, Hattie had to smile at her companion's unflappable mien. "I will keep that to mind, then." As soon as they passed into the privacy of the retiring room, Hattie paused and let out a long breath. "There is something very odd going on, did you see?"

"I did," Bing agreed.

"And Robbie—" Hattie frowned, and shook her head. "I can't imagine what he is thinking—it is very unlike him; he is not one to fall head over heels."

"Sometimes—sometimes young men fall prey to older, more *experienced* women." Bing said it delicately, so as not to make an innuendo that might shock her charge, but Hattie disagreed, and shook her head. "Not Robbie, Bing; he is not one to be enthralled in such a way. Something strange is afoot—did you see how they were all barely civil?"

"The French and the English are rivals in Egypt," Bing

suggested. "Perhaps a quarrel erupted over there that has carried over here."

But Hattie was not willing to speculate, and instead decided to take action. "I'll not endure another minute, so I am going out the window, Bing. Pray exit discreetly and meet me around the back."

Bing considered this for a moment, her arms crossed across her bony chest. "We are on the second floor, I believe."

Hattie strode over to lift the casement with a jerk and peered outside, the cool evening air like a balm on her overheated face. "There is a wisteria vine—I will contrive."

Bing stepped to the window after Hattie, slinging her reticule over a shoulder. "I shall follow, then."

Hattie paused, one slippered foot over the sill. "There is no need, Bing—only come around and meet me below."

"I will come—I climbed many a vine with my dear brother."

Smiling at the reference, Hattie relented. "All right—in honor of Edward, then."

"Somewhere, he is very pleased." With an efficient movement, Bing hoisted up her black skirts, exposing practical white-thread stockings. "Perhaps I should go first in the event I am needed to catch you."

Much on her mettle, Hattie assured her she would not fall and within a few moments was clambering down the vine, skillfully testing the branches as she went. She was a first-rate climber stretching back many years and indeed, some of her best climbing adventures had been performed at the side of the newly affianced. The fact that she wore a full plethora of petticoats scarcely slowed her, and in a matter of minutes her uncertain mood was much improved—there was nothing like making a daring escape to lift one's spirits.

Easily outpacing Bing, Hattie reached the vine's trunk and

determined there were no more branches upon which to gain a foothold. There was nothing for it—she would have to leap down for the remainder. As she steeled herself to jump, a voice floated up: "Allow me to be of assistance, mademoiselle."

Hattie knew who it was without looking, even though he had never spoken to her. "If you would," she replied calmly. She felt a hand beneath her foot, and then leapt outward, her slipper in his hands as though he was helping her down from a very tall horse.

Mid-leap, he caught her at the waist and then placed her carefully on the ground. She looked up into the face so close to her own and noted that his neutral expression was belied by the lurking gleam in the brown eyes. His face was rather appealing—the nose slightly curved and the brows darker than his hair.

"I thank you." She stepped away from the hands that lingered on her waist.

"A lovely evening," he commented, as though the situation was the merest commonplace. He spoke English but his accent was French.

"Hathor?" Bing's voice floated down. "Is someone there?"

"Not to worry," Hattie called to her. "It is merely—"

"Monsieur Berry," he supplied.

"—Monsieur Berry," she concluded. They stood in silence for a moment and watched Bing's careful descent. "You mustn't peek up her skirts as you did with me."

"I was unable to resist," he replied, unrepentant. "Such an opportunity cannot be passed by."

She could not restrain a chuckle, but shook her head. "I am in no mood to banter with you, my friend."

"I am aware—I was afraid for a moment it would come to blows, upstairs."

Hattie glanced up at him, chagrined. "I had to retreat—she outweighed me by a stone."

But the gentleman met her eye and rallied her, "Never—I would wager my last penny on you; you have not her weight but you have guile—always the advantage."

Laughing, she felt immeasurably better, and raised her face to his. For a second he stilled, an arrested expression in his eyes. Ah, she thought. The mask slips a bit—and he thinks me charming, despite himself. There was little time before Bing landed, so she asked a direct question. "Who are you that you follow me about?"

He did not miss a beat. "I must speak with you."

"No need to skulk, then," she chided him. "I so dislike skulkers."

"I must speak with you unobserved," he amended.

Arching a brow, she shot him a look. "Unobserved by whom?"

"Ah, your companion *formidable* alights." He moved to assist Bing, who was understandably a bit flustered by his attentions.

Hattie bent to brush the leaves off Bing's skirt while Berry stood at a discreet distance. "Don't ask," Hattie said under her breath.

"I wouldn't think of it," replied Bing in the same tone.

"May I call for a *haquenee*?" asked Berry, making a gesture toward the street.

"If you would," Hattie agreed, thinking the situation a farce and very much in keeping with the tenor of this miserable, miserable evening.

Hailing a horse-drawn transport, he recited her address to the driver without asking her for it, which put him on the receiving end of another assessing glance. As he handed Bing into the conveyance he turned to Hattie. "I will call on you tomorrow, if you will permit."

"To what purpose?"

"It is important you do not leave before I have spoken to you."

Hattie shook her head slightly in bemusement. "Why on earth would I retreat? I cannot allow Robbie to think I am crushed; I am not such a sap-skull."

He ducked his chin at her, his eyes gleaming in amusement. "You are forthright."

"And you are a master at avoiding questions you'd rather not answer—it appears I am no match for you in guile."

He teased her with a charming smile, his teeth flashing white in the darkness. "Come, come—such modesty; you are the god-king's daughter, after all."

Surprised, she met his eyes to find his gaze suddenly sharp upon hers. The gentleman did not appear crazed—he must have misconstrued a chance comment. "You misunderstand—the new tomb contains the remains of the god-king's daughter."

"Your pardon," he said, and bowed.

Chapter 3

On the carriage ride home, Hattie frowned out the window, thinking over the odd and convergent events of the evening. "I will need to purchase some new clothes." Unspoken was the desire to have something rather low in the décolleté, as she had an impressive figure for one so petite and had noted that she'd best look lively—the Frenchwomen she had met thus far were very well turned out, and he seemed like the kind of man who would take notice of such things.

"That's the spirit, Hathor," offered Bing with approval. "One need only inspire second thoughts."

With a guilty start, Hattie realized they were speaking at cross purposes and pulled her attention back to Robbie's strange situation. "It does defy credulity, Bing—I am certain his parents know nothing of this engagement. It seems so unlike him; and to have chosen such a woman—"

"Infamous," agreed Bing. "There is no choosing between you."

"I am unlucky in love," she teased. "Recall that I lost the curate, too."

"Well then; I wash my hands of the sterner sex," pronounced her supporter with equanimity. "Although the Baron seemed rather *épris*, if I may say so."

Hattie shuddered. "I'd as lief retreat back to Cornwall— whatever is he thinking?"

"May-December," sniffed Bing. "A shame we cannot arrange to switch with Mr. Tremaine."

Hattie chuckled and decided that all in all, she was not as devastated as she should be with the ruination of her latest plan to escape her dull day-to-day existence in the Cornish countryside. The only child of world-renowned Egyptologists, she had spent a solitary childhood because her parents were more often in Thebes than in England, digging around in the sand and in the process catching the imagination of their countrymen, who were looking for any distraction from the never-ending war. Chafing at this state of affairs, Hattie had grown up to be independent-minded and scornful of the restraints imposed upon young females, although there was little point in challenging authority as there was little authority exerted over her in the first place. Fortunately, her tendency toward recklessness had been tempered by Miss Swansea, Hattie's gentle governess who was more friend than mentor and had dutifully remained at her post even after Hattie reached the august age of eighteen years—her parents apparently unaware that this milestone had been achieved.

Longing to travel and see the world, Hattie had secretly cherished the hope her parents would send for her once she reached adulthood, but the invitation—unfortunately—was not forthcoming. In a fever of impatience, she decided it was past time to arrange her life to her own satisfaction and that satisfaction necessarily was to be found somewhere beyond the rugged Cornish countryside—Hattie knew herself for a restless soul.

To make matters that much worse, Hattie was almost

painfully envious of the boy next door, who was attached in some way to the Diplomatic Corps and was often called away for assignments that he spoke of only in the vaguest of terms. After careful consideration, it seemed that the most likely avenue of escape would be to convince him that she would make an excellent helpmeet, and so to this end, she embarked upon a campaign to marry Robbie.

After mulling it over, Hattie had concluded that the best strategy for presenting oneself as a marital prospect to someone who had never considered one in such a light was to procure a rival suitor. However, as her acquaintanceship was limited, she was forced to settle upon the local curate as the appropriate stalking horse, even though he was some fifteen years her senior. Although she felt a stab of guilt at using him in such a way, she assuaged her conscience by reflecting that at his age, he held no interest in romance, anyway.

In this, however, she was mistaken. The curate readily accepted her invitations to tea but sat and shyly contemplated Miss Swansea, who blushed with eyes downcast under his scrutiny. Looking from one to the other, Hattie foresaw the failure of her plan with good grace and reassessed her campaign. Before she could come up with an alternate, however, she was forced to absorb the double blow of losing Miss Swansea to matrimony and losing Robbie yet again, when he left suddenly without even saying goodbye, leaving Hattie to bedevil his father into admitting, with a bland expression, that it had something to do with the Congress, and he wasn't expected back any time soon.

Into this inauspicious situation Bing had arrived, hired by her parents to replace Miss Swansea. Bing's brother Edward had been an Egyptologist employed by Hattie's parents but he had been killed in a cave-in—an unfortunate occupational hazard. As Edward had been supporting his spinster sister, the Blackhouses offered Bing the post as Hattie's companion and so solved two problems at once.

It soon became apparent that Bing was a bluestocking of the first order and intensely interested in Egyptology; therefore it came as a severe blow to the new arrival to learn the Blackhouse manor contained no artifacts and that the only offspring of the famous couple had little interest in anything remotely Nineteenth Dynasty. Fortunately for Hattie, however, she had little difficulty in convincing Bing that they should visit Robbie in Paris—Hattie had read that the Congress was in recess and the city was quite festive as a result. There were plenty of funds at hand to undertake such a journey—Hattie's neglectful parents had nonetheless seen to it she had the means to live very comfortably—and with a companion in tow, it was the perfect excuse to have an adventure and at the same time, meet up with Robbie and convince him she'd be no bother if he'd just *please* marry her. Unfortunately, it seemed that someone else had convinced him first and she was left with no other immediate plan than to acquire a decent dress and discover who this Berry person was—hopefully in that order.

With a rattling stop, their hackney arrived at the townhouse and Hattie took a careful assessment of the street corner, where she'd seen a gentleman lurking earlier—not to be confused with the gentleman she had shoved down the stairs or the gentleman who had helped her down from the vine; that she was the focus of attention seemed evident, and she needed to keep her wits about her. The reaction this evening—even from Robbie—had been very strained when she mentioned her parents, and since she was of no interest in her own right, it must have to do with them.

Rather than allow them to exit the vehicle themselves, the hackney driver leapt down with good humor and handed them out, remarking in heavily accented English that it was a fine night. He wore a muffler over the lower half of his face even though it was a warm evening, and Hattie wondered if he had pockmarks, poor man. "How much do we owe, please?" She was not well versed on how much things should cost in France, and hoped he didn't mean to take advantage, pockmarks notwithstanding.

But as she opened her reticule to bring forth a coin, another man burst forth from the shadows and dashed toward them, cutting Hattie's reticule from her wrist and pulling it roughly from her arm as he sped past—all in the flash of a few seconds.

"Halt," called the driver in outrage, then hastily to the women, "Wait here, *mesdames*—I will pursue him."

With another shout, the driver took off after the cutpurse, leaving Hattie standing beside Bing for a moment in stunned surprise. "Heavens; are you injured, Hathor?" asked Bing.

"No, but he'll have little to show for his troubles and it serves him right—he should have guessed that you would be carrying the lion's share of the funds." Hattie said the words a bit absently—she had noticed that the driver shouted at the cutpurse in English although both men were—ostensibly—French.

Bing suggested, "Perhaps we should enter the house; I cannot like the idea of remaining out here exposed, and he may come back once he realizes he chose the wrong victim."

"Yes, let's go in." Hattie was uneasy herself, thinking over the mystery of the English-speaking hackney driver who had been commissioned by the self-assured Monsieur Berry.

But the evening was not yet over, as the gentleman whom

she had seen lurking earlier in the day took the opportunity to approach them as they mounted the steps. He was well-dressed, and did not appear intent on robbery—although Hattie decided she was past being surprised, anymore. "Mademoiselle Blackhouse—if you please—"

But apparently Hattie was not quite past being surprised, because Bing drew a small flintlock pistol from her reticule and aimed it square at the gentleman. "Halt or I will shoot."

The man paused and held his hands out to his sides, looking every bit as surprised as Hattie by this turn of events. "Your pardon, madam; I must speak with Mademoiselle Blackhouse—please."

"Speak, then," said Hattie, stepping down a step toward him and instinctively judging him harmless. "What do you know of all this and why have you been watching the house?"

His pleading gaze fixed upon hers, he spoke in a low, intense tone. "You must return to England. It is very important that you go back to your home, mademoiselle."

This was completely unexpected and indeed, seemed to take the opposite tack of every other person of her Parisian acquaintance. "And who are you?"

He hesitated. "I stand as your friend. I promise you this, Mademoiselle Blackhouse."

"Were you sent by my parents?" This seemed the only explanation, but how her parents were made aware so quickly that Hattie had kicked over the traces and bolted for Paris was a mystery—she hadn't known herself, three days ago.

Once again, the man hesitated, and then glanced over his shoulder. "I can say no more. But it is not safe for you here."

Hattie drew her brows together. "Why is this? Surely you must see that I need further explanation—what is this all about? Why is it not safe?"

"Please, mademoiselle; return to your home." He fingered his hat brim, and then added, "And you must tell your English friend nothing—nothing at all." Retreating a step, he bowed a formal little bow. "I bid you good night." Returning his hat to his head, he turned and began walking down the pavement at a brisk pace.

"How very odd," Bing remarked as she returned her weapon to her reticule.

Smiling at this understatement, Hattie agreed, "Yes, let's go in before yet another one accosts us. Tell me, Bing, have you ever had occasion to shoot anyone?"

"I've never had occasion even to fire," Bing confessed. "But as a single woman I feel I must take precautions."

"You must teach me," said Hattie as she unlocked the door. "Then I could shoot Robbie; or better yet, Madame Auguste."

"Don't forget the Baron," suggested Bing as they were greeted by the maidservant, who took their wraps. "And the cutpurse."

"Good God, there will be no one left in the city at this rate—and I've only been here a day. I suppose I could spare this last gentleman, who has very good manners and apparently acts as a Cassandra-at-the-gate, giving ominous warnings. Perhaps he is worried about the so-called curse." This, actually, was not a bad theory, as there seemed no other with which to work.

"Edward always said that superstition was a crutch for the fearful."

Hattie smiled as they crossed the parlor, their steps muffled on the thick rug. "He was a wise man, then, and I must bow to science. But good God, Bing; even you must admit these are strange and untoward events."

Bing ducked her chin. "Indeed; I suppose you will have mixed emotions, Hathor, when you meet with him tomorrow."

"Yes—I wonder what it is he wants," Hattie answered absently as she mounted the stairs, unaware that they spoke at cross purposes yet again.

Chapter 4

The following morning, Hattie's childhood companion in misdeeds beyond counting presented himself at the door, his easy smile belying the trace of wariness in his eyes. So, she thought as he embraced her in a bear hug—there is more to this tale than there appears; fortunately, I know how to winkle it out of him.

"Hattie—Lord, you are a welcome sight. I am sorry I did not have the opportunity to speak to you at length last night."

She decided it would be best to turn the subject away from her abrupt departure from the Prussian embassy, and instead introduced Bing. "Miss Swansea married the curate—did you hear?"

Taking her elbow, he escorted them to the waiting carriage. "I did; at long last the man screwed up his courage—my mother had despaired of him. And she wrote that Sophie finally had her pups—another big litter."

Hattie arched a dark eyebrow as the driver opened the door for them. "Then I am relieved, Robbie—I was worried that all communication between you and your mother had failed for some reason."

There was a small pause while Robbie bowed his head in acknowledgement. "I have been remiss; unfortunately, there has been little time to correspond—I must bring her up to date."

"Ensure that she has her smelling salts about her, first," Hattie teased as he handed her into the carriage.

With a grin, Robbie didn't make an attempt to demur as he settled in the seat across from Hattie and Bing. "It *is* rather startling news, isn't it?"

Hattie was feeling immeasurably better, now that she was able to gauge him without the annoying Madame Auguste clinging to his arm. It seemed to Hattie—who knew him better than most—that he was not particularly enamored of his bride-to-be. There must be some other explanation for this hastily patched-together betrothal and for whatever reason, he didn't wish to reveal it. As the carriage rattled along over the cobblestones, she was suddenly given pause, aware that there was perhaps a ready explanation for such a hasty marriage. Impossible, she thought in distaste—at her age, the woman was nearly beyond child-bearing. Still, she had best tread carefully; Robbie may be honor-bound to marry her and if this was the case, Hattie had no choice but to support him—and support his poor mother, who would certainly need it.

With this possibility in mind, she did not press him but spoke of the news from home and other inconsequential matters until they arrived at the British headquarters in Paris. After crossing the threshold of this august building, Hattie and Bing were introduced to several gentlemen who were attached to the embassy in some manner—and who eyed her discreetly as she walked past. They must have heard about the contretemps last night, she thought, her color high, and wished she hadn't been so gauche; she didn't want to embarrass Robbie—although he seemed to need no help in that department. Honestly, men were so stupid, sometimes.

Unaware that she was casting aspersions upon his judgment, Hattie's escort led the ladies around the facilities, explaining that everyone's time was currently consumed by the negotiations surrounding the Congress of Vienna—even though progress was very slow as a result of everyone's trying to take advantage and no one willing to cede an inch.

Hattie had followed what news she could find and could only agree—the post-war meetings were like one of those children's games where you threw all the cards in the air and everyone ran and attempted to catch as many as they could; it would be a while before Europe was stable again, before new boundaries and alliances could be established.

With Bing trailing discreetly behind and out of earshot, Hattie decided she would no longer allow him to avoid the subject—after all, someone had once told her she was forthright—and she observed, "How lucky that you can be spared long enough to be married, then. Will your parents attend?"

After a moment he replied, "It is rather short notice, unfortunately."

The equivocal answer made her wonder if perhaps he wanted to present his poor parents with a *fait accompli* for fear they would disapprove of his bride; it seemed a valid concern, the bride being a bit long in the tooth. "Is it…" She paused delicately. "Is it the same situation as the Postmaster and Miss Harding?" Even Cornwall had its share of scandal, human nature being what it was.

Shocked, Robbie chastised her in a low voice, "Hattie, for God's sake—"

"You won't speak of it," she defended herself. "You should be happy, and you're not."

"No—it is not a marriage of necessity and you should

not be speaking of such things," he retorted, annoyed. "Honestly, Hattie."

"I am trying to help," she insisted stubbornly. "How did it happen, then?"

He offered a bit stiffly, "I met her when I was in Egypt, last month—"

"*You* were in Egypt, too?" Now it was Hattie's turn to be shocked; apparently everyone was visiting Egypt, willy-nilly, whilst she was sequestered away back home with as little to do with herself as the *stupid* princess in her *stupid* tomb—it was beyond all bearing and she resisted an urge to stamp her foot, knowing it would only cement everyone's bad opinion of her.

"—and we decided to marry on the spur of the moment."

She eyed him, waiting, but he volunteered nothing further and refused to meet her eye. "Well then; I see," she offered in a tone that conveyed the exact opposite.

He flashed her a conscious glance but would not elaborate. "Look, it's complicated and I don't want to quarrel with you—not today."

Contrite, Hattie took his arm, recognizing the unspoken message that he was upset and she shouldn't press him. "No—of course not, Robbie; I shouldn't be teasing you. Tell me instead about Vienna, and how important you are."

Willing to change the subject, he began to describe the diplomatic maneuvering at the Congress and Hattie listened, asking an occasional question and allowing her attention to wander. She glanced around at her surroundings, appreciating the sense of purpose that emanated from all the people around her. I do much better when I have a purpose, she realized; I think that was the problem at home—I had no purpose to my life, so I created an artificial one, which really didn't suit me at all. As she looked up at Robbie's profile, she congratulated herself on this self-discovery. Growing up, his generous parents had included the solitary child on the neighboring estate in all their family doings—it was they who had given her the nickname never used by her parents—and so it was only to be expected that the affection she felt for Robbie was sisterly, and not at all lover-like. She nodded as her escort continued to speak—she truly wasn't paying much attention—and couldn't help but think that it was just as well her campaign to attach him had failed miserably. It was not meant to be, she thought with little regret, and couldn't help but remember the feel of another man's hands lingering at her waist, and the sensations engendered thereby. Distracted, she realized that Robbie was awaiting a response from her. "I'm sorry, Robbie. What did you say?"

"There is a gentleman here who would like to speak with you for a few minutes, Hattie. I'm afraid it's rather important."

Such was the state of her thoughts that Hattie's heart leapt for a moment, thinking she was no sooner to think of Monsieur Berry then he was to magically appear. However, instead she entered a small office that contained a rather serious grey-eyed man who rose to take her hand. "Miss Blackhouse."

She noted that he gave no name, and she also noted with a shock of recognition that the attaché who closed the door behind her was the erstwhile cutpurse from the night before—she had only a glimpse of his face as he turned to leave, but Hattie had a very good memory, which had always been one of her strengths. Suddenly wary, she sat with Robbie across the table from the grey-eyed man as Bing was asked to wait outside. I cannot like this turn of events, she thought as she clasped her hands in her lap; but at least I will *finally* learn what is going on, although I imagine the explanation will not include the reason why the British embassy wanted to steal my reticule.

The other man's gaze met hers in all seriousness. "When was the last time you heard from your parents, Miss Blackhouse?"

It was a strange question—Robbie was certainly well aware of her parents' tepid interest. "I hear from them occasionally," she answered cautiously. "Why?"

"Anything of late?"

Something in his tone made her search his face, her brow knit. "What has happened?"

He paused, the expression in the grey eyes grave. "Apparently no one has heard from them in a long while."

Dismayed by the innuendo, she reasoned slowly, "And because you are concerned, you must not think it the usual case when they are at a dig and do not communicate for weeks at a time."

"I fear for their safety," the gentleman confirmed with a nod. It seemed to Hattie, though, that he was watching her very closely and didn't seem all that distraught, given the subject.

Robbie, on the other hand, offered gentle sympathy as he reached to cover her hand with his own. "I am sorry, Hattie."

There was a pause while they allowed her to assimilate this alarming news, but her mind instead leapt to the theft of her reticule, as well as the mysterious gentleman's warning to return home, which was in stark contrast to Monsieur Barry's warning not to leave until she had spoken with him. "I see," she said rather inadequately, and stalled for time, carefully wary.

"Nothing has been verified," the grey-eyed man continued. "But it does not look well."

There was another pause in the conversation and Hattie

did nothing to fill the silence, thinking instead about Robbie's unexpected betrothal and his sincere sympathy, beside her—she knew him too well to pretend he did not fear the worst about her parents. She wondered for a moment if the two events were connected in some way—he was certainly not behaving like a bridegroom on the cusp of marriage—but this seemed implausible. On the other hand, *everything* seemed implausible from the moment she had first set foot in this *stupid* country.

When the grey-eyed man spoke again, the topic seemed anticlimactic, given their previous discussion. "Did your parents come often to their residence here in Paris?"

Hattie looked at him a bit blankly. "Yes—they do." She deliberately used the present tense in contrast to his use of the past tense. "They come to Paris to arrange for exhibitions at the museum."

He persisted, watching her carefully, "Your parents own no other property in town?"

"I'm afraid I have no idea," she confessed. "They did not discuss such things with me."

Almost diffidently, he continued, "Do you know if they had a strongbox—something in which they kept important documents?"

Bemused, she shook her head. "A strongbox? No—I've never known of such a thing." She made a slight gesture toward Robbie. "Although Mr. Tremaine can verify that I was not in their confidence, so it truly doesn't mean much." Unbidden, she remembered the mysterious gentleman's warning to tell Robbie nothing—which seemed ludicrous; she would trust Robbie with her life. Except for the persistent and annoying fact that the British embassy had apparently decided to steal her reticule. Lifting her chin, she demanded, "What is this about? Why this interest in their property?"

"It is unclear what will happen with their estate."

Hattie could not quite keep the edge from her voice. "It has not yet been established that my parents are dead—or has it?"

Reacting to her tone, Robbie ducked his chin in the apologetic gesture he had made since they were small children and squeezed the hand he held. "Sorry, Hattie; we are thinking of your welfare—how you will go on if they continue missing."

Hattie abruptly rose to her feet, and the surprised gentlemen hastily rose also. "Please keep me informed of any further news, and I thank you for your concern." She could sense the men exchange a glance as she turned on her heel to go, but she had decided, sitting there, that she was not to be trifled with. Apparently there was a connection between Robbie's work at the Congress and her parent's work—although no one wished to tell her what it was and indeed, the basis for any such link was unclear; her parents had little interest in anything less than three thousand years old, after all. In any event, she had heard her fill of equivocations, and was leaving.

Chapter 5

On the carriage ride home, Robbie made a mighty effort to coax Hattie out of her temper and was largely successful, only because Hattie had resolved on a course of action, which always tended to calm her down. "I'm sorry if I was rude, Robbie, or if I've made trouble for you, but I thought he was rather rude to me in the first place."

"He's not one to be accommodating," Robbie disclosed with an apologetic shrug. "I am dashed sorry you heard the news in such a way, Hattie; my fault—I should have broken it to you myself."

At Bing's glance of inquiry, Hattie apprised her of the unsettling silence from her parents, but Bing, as was her wont, did not become distressed and instead reminded Hattie that it was not so very unusual, after all. "Edward always said they were all-consumed; particularly when they came across a new find. I have no doubt they are not aware they have raised alarm, and will soon reveal another extraordinary wonder to the world."

But Hattie was not convinced by this pragmatic advice, having gained the impression that the grey-eyed man was not to be trifled with in his own turn. She asked Robbie, "Is the gentleman your superior? He did not mention his position."

"In a manner of speaking." Robbie offered a rueful smile. "He's rather a hard taskmaster, as you can imagine."

"He can't be worse than the Irish schoolmaster, I'll not believe it." The conversation then turned to a lively reminiscence of that gentleman's short but memorable tenure at the Tremaine manor while Hattie noted well that her lifelong friend was not going to tell her what he knew about her parents and this very strange situation. All the more reason for Hattie to keep her plans close to the vest, and so she carefully avoided any inquiries about why the British authorities were so interested in her Egyptologist parents or why Robbie was to marry a woman he never bothered to mention. When she had a chance to have a private word with Bing as they took off their hats back at the townhouse, Hattie asked quietly, "How well do you speak French, Bing?"

"Passably," Bing responded, considering it. "I couldn't write a book."

"I would like to sail for Cairo as soon as possible, and I'd like you to slip away and book passage while I distract Mr. Tremaine in the parlor."

"Certainly; it seems the best course to take, given the circumstances." Without a blink, Bing began buttoning up her pelisse once again.

"Don't mention it to anyone, please."

"I wouldn't think of it," her companion replied, and exited toward the kitchen.

Robbie was standing at the bow window with his hands clasped behind his back as Hattie joined him and called for tea. He held out a hand, and with easy familiarity, she placed hers in his. "I'm wretchedly sorry about all this, Hattie—shall I take you for a tour of the city, to take your mind off it?" He brought his other hand to cover hers, and regarded her with a warm and rather tender expression that was very unlike his customary casual treatment.

"Will your fiancée come along?" Mainly, she asked just to discomfit him; *someone* should make an effort to mention the poor woman.

But he was not to be thrown off in his attempt to sweeten her up. "I believe she is otherwise occupied—it would be just you and me."

"And Bing," Hattie reminded him—just to make it clear she was no longer in short skirts, tagging along behind him. She wondered what he was about, making up to her like this, and was curious enough to resist an impulse to cuff him; instead awaiting his next move with interest.

"—and Bing," he agreed, smiling. "Lord, it is good to see you, Hattie—you remind me of home, and of a simpler time."

"A bit too simple for my taste," she admitted. Robbie dropped his gaze to finger her hand, and Hattie wondered if she would have the wherewithal to spurn an advance if he proceeded to make one. She was not to find out.

"Mademoiselle Blackhouse; forgive me if I intrude." Berry stood at the entry to the parlor, completely at his ease. "The door was open and there was no servant."

For whatever reason, Hattie did not believe him and allowed her skepticism to show in her glance as she introduced the two men. There was no answering gleam today; instead the Frenchman's expression was politely correct. "Tremaine? Then you must be the gentleman who was in Thebes—the neighbor to Monsieur and Madame Blackhouse."

"Indeed. And you are—?"

Hattie awaited the reply with interest, thinking it unlikely they were to hear the truth, but with a small bow, the visitor explained, "I was the Blackhouse agent in Cairo."

While Hattie endeavored to hide her astonishment, Robbie addressed the man with renewed interest. "Yes;

we—the British consulate—we were trying to reach you, to discover if you could cast any light on their whereabouts."

She could see from Berry's expression that he was not best pleased that Robbie had already raised the subject of her missing parents, and for a moment his enigmatic gaze rested on her face with a trace of concern. "If you do not mind, monsieur, I should discuss the matter in private with Mademoiselle Blackhouse."

If Robbie were a dog, thought Hattie, he would have bristled. "I assure you I am in Miss Blackhouse's confidence."

But the other man seemed discreetly perplexed. "Indeed? Last night at the Ambassador's reception I did not have such an impression—"

It was masterfully done, and the subtle but barbed reminder of the contretemps involving Madame Auguste made Robbie press his lips together and curl his hands into fists as the silence stretched out. Recognizing the warning signs, Hattie hastily stepped in. "Robbie, I should speak to Monsieur Berry and discover what he has to relate."

Thus dismissed, Robbie could only bow over her hand with as much grace as he could muster, shooting her an admonitory look that only annoyed Hattie to no end. Who was he to admonish her—with all his talk of strongboxes and attempts to turn her up sweet—the non-forthcoming thiever of reticules. "Good day," she said firmly, and watched his reluctant exit.

She turned to face Berry, who was doing only a fair job of hiding his own annoyance. In a completely different tone than he had used with Robbie, he pronounced with scorn, "There is a man who seeks one wife too many."

"How many have you?" The words were out before she could stop them.

"None." He turned his head to meet her eyes, and there was a long moment while time seemed to stand still as they faced one another, their gazes locked. Hattie was able to hear her heartbeat in her ears for an entirely different reason than the usual, and finally broke the silence. "Then I suppose you are not the best judge of how many is too many."

"As you say." He nodded a bit stiffly.

Ah, she thought—he is unhappy he let the mask slip once again but he cannot help himself, it seems. The knowledge was exhilarating, and she had to resist a strange and compelling urge to place her palms upon his chest. Take hold of yourself, she thought in alarm, and turned aside to break the spell. "Shall we be seated in the parlor so that I may hear your news?"

"Or the garden, instead," he suggested politely. "It is a fine day."

As it was now threatening rain, she concluded he was concerned they would be overheard, and willing to humor him, she walked toward the French doors at the back without demur. "I have no chaperone at present, but I promise I will not try to compromise my way into becoming your first wife."

But his guard was now firmly in place and he would not be teased. "As you wish, mademoiselle."

Hattie led him into the small, walled garden in the back that featured a wrought-iron tea table and two chairs alongside a flower bed. As he pulled out her chair, she noted he was once again dressed in understated clothing and not from the finest of tailors. Nevertheless, Hattie had an impression of strength and assurance that could not be concealed by subterfuge—that he was merely an agent for her parents seemed unlikely. Another mystery—and I've only been here a day, she thought as she allowed her gaze to dwell on the fine set of his shoulders. He was perhaps thirty, she guessed, and if he was indeed unmarried it was not for lack of opportunity, despite his efforts to hide his light beneath a bushel. Resolving to appear older than her years, she folded her hands in her lap and wished she had thought to bring a wrap as it was turning quite cool.

Berry sat across from her and began in a low tone, "Did you bring any servants from England, mademoiselle?"

Hattie blinked, as this seemed an unlikely opening. "No, we hired them from the local service. Should I fear poison in my soup?"

In response, he met her eyes in all seriousness. "You must be cautious—particularly in what you say when they are about."

This comment made her reply in a tart tone, "There seems little point; I obviously know less of what is going forward than apparently everyone else in Paris."

But he would not be goaded, and said only, "That is as may be, but others suspect you hold secrets; therefore you must be careful."

"I am already aware—the British arranged for my reticule to be snatched last night." She wasn't certain why she told him, except that she wanted to show him she was not a complete fool.

"Yes," he replied as though this was the merest commonplace. "And then you were approached by the Comte deFabry."

Hattie digested the interesting fact that despite being some sort of clerk, Monsieur Berry was very well informed. "Is that who it was? He never mentioned his name but he seemed rather harmless."

"What did he say to you?"

Once again, Hattie was answering questions without

obtaining any answers in return—this was how things were done in France, apparently. She countered, "Why—do you think he is not as harmless as he seemed?"

"I cannot know," he explained patiently, "until you tell me what he said, mademoiselle."

This seemed irrefutable, so she complied, as best she could. "He kept apologizing," she concluded. "He was very polite and deferential."

"I would ask that you not speak with him any further."

Exasperated, she pointed out, "I imagine he would say the same thing about you, and I have no reason to obey either one of you. What has happened to my parents?"

If she thought the bald question would discomfit him, she had misjudged her man. "They were last known to be at the new tomb in Thebes, making an inventory of the excavations. Other than that, I have very little information—even from those who assisted them with logistics. They have literally vanished without a trace."

Her brow knit, Hattie stared at him and tried to assimilate this bleak assessment. Berry held her gaze with his own level one, a trace of sympathy contained therein. Made uneasy by its presence, she pointed out, "I often have no communication from my parents for months on end."

"No one knows this better than I," he agreed. "However, for three months they have been unaccounted for."

"Three months?" Hattie tried to hide her dismay. They wouldn't willingly be away from the site for that length of time—it was indeed as everyone thought; something was very wrong.

Berry tilted his head in apology. "I visited your home in England and found that you had traveled here. It caused a delay, which is unfortunate."

She hated to say the words but found she was compelled. "Do you believe they are dead?"

"I fear so."

Dropping her gaze for a moment, she regarded her hands in her lap. "I see." She wasn't certain how she felt—she hadn't known them very well, after all. On the other hand, it was one thing to feel an orphan and another to actually be one.

"I am so sorry," he offered. "I was hoping you may be of assistance. Have you any information? Did they inform you of their plans?"

"No," she responded, her gaze raised to his again. "They did not."

He persisted, leaning forward, his expression intent. "Was there any recent correspondence? Any items entrusted?"

A silence fell, and into it Hattie asked, "What is it you were searching for, upstairs?"

Chapter 6

I f Hattie expected Berry to disclaim, she was to be disappointed. "It is their house," he pointed out in a reasonable tone, "and I am their agent."

They regarded each other across the table for a long moment. You are a foolish, foolish girl, she chided herself, to be taken in by this so-capable gentleman. "What color are my mother's eyes?"

"I don't know what you call it," he replied as though the question was not unusual in the least. "*Vert-brun*; green with brown. *Hazel*."

"It is the same word in English." And it was true—her mother was pale and attractive in the best English tradition. Vain about her skin, she was always swathed in hats and veils when in the sun. Hattie's eyes, by contrast, were so dark as to seem almost black. "And my father?"

"I don't remember." Indicating with a gesture, he raised a hand. "He is missing the little finger from his left hand."

This was true—it was crushed by a cornerstone, years ago. "What did my father call my mother?"

"Neph," he said immediately.

The knot in Hattie's breast dissipated. The nickname was an abbreviated version of Nephthys, an Egyptian goddess who was notoriously unfaithful. Her parents' sense of humor—along with everything else—stemmed from their only passion. It seemed unlikely Berry would know these details unless he had indeed spent considerable time with them. Feeling an inappropriate stab of envy, she asked, "Did they ever speak of me?" Horrified, she wished she could pull the words back; the last thing she wanted was to appear pathetic before this man.

"They were very fond of you," he replied gently, neatly avoiding an answer. Ashamed of her lapse, she didn't press the subject, but instead felt very young as she turned her gaze again to the hands folded in her lap.

"Hathor; an unusual name."

She sensed he was trying to ease her embarrassment and so she rewarded him by pulling herself together and rendering her best dimpled smile. "My friends call me Hattie."

The gambit was not successful as Berry's expression became distant and he asked with austere formality, "Would you know where your parents kept any important items, mademoiselle—items they were reluctant to part with? Perhaps a safe on the premises, either here or in England?"

She did not respond immediately, thinking that it was almost amusing—he was setting up a mighty resistance to the attraction that leapt between them, the intense awareness that made him lose his train of thought while the breath caught in her throat. "I imagine you know the answer better than I—I hope you locked the door behind you in Cornwall."

An appreciative gleam of amusement appeared in his eyes—they were such a pleasing shade of brown, light with golden highlights. Recalled to the fact that she had just received bad news, she tried to temper her thoughts.

There was a small silence as thunder could be heard in the

distance. "Mademoiselle Bing approaches," he noted, and rose to his feet.

Hattie turned to behold the welcome sight of Bing bearing a woolen shawl—Hattie had been trying not to shiver and thereby spoil this promising *tête-à-tête*. "Thank you, Bing. Monsieur Berry acts as my parents' agent in Cairo; in light of the unsettling news, he has come for a visit."

Bing cast a skeptical eye at the gathering clouds but made no comment, depositing the wrap across Hattie's shoulders. "Then you will have much to discuss. I shall ring for tea and leave you to it."

Amused, Hattie made a mental note that Bing had apparently determined Berry was more friend than enemy, although Bing was not aware this guest had his own shortcomings—burglary being among them. "I think not, Bing—it looks to rain."

But Berry was not to be hinted indoors where there was a danger of being overheard. Instead, he addressed Bing in a deferential manner. "Mademoiselle, my inventory of the Blackhouse effects listed some items which unfortunately I cannot lay hands upon. It would be useful to know if these items actually exist—I would not like to think an unscrupulous person could take advantage of the current situation. I understand your brother was Monsieur Edward Bing."

"Indeed," Bing verified with a nod.

"I am sorry for your loss," the Frenchman offered in all sincerity, but there was a slight undercurrent to the words that Hattie could not quite like. "Did he ever send you anything from the site?"

"Oh, no," Bing disclaimed immediately. "Edward was not one to keep anything for himself; he strongly believed the artifacts belonged to the world and the appropriate place for them was in a museum—although many others disagreed, and sold them privately."

"A dedicated man," agreed Berry in a respectful tone. "Would that there were more like him."

Bing admitted, "That—and it was important not to displease the local authorities by smuggling away the treasures; after all, the site could be shut down."

"But I thought the British controlled the sites," said Hattie in surprise. "My parents certainly seemed to go wherever they wished."

"No—not the British; at least not as yet," Bing explained to her. "A viceroy named Muhammad Ali has taken the lead on regional matters since Napoleon's forces left—but you are correct in that it is only a matter of time before the British reestablish authority in the area. Unfortunately, it is a difficult situation in Egypt—there are treasures to be seized and the French, the British, and the locals are all vying for power over the excavations."

"You are well informed, mademoiselle," observed Berry with open approval.

Bing's lean cheeks turned pink with pleasure. "I followed my brother's doings quite closely, monsieur."

Hattie added, "It was Edward who found the *Shefrh Lelmelwek*—the Glory of Kings. Did you hear of it in Cairo? It was hidden inside an ordinary unguent jar."

"A very significant find," Berry agreed. "Word of the discovery spread very quickly."

I must be paranoid, and seeing a mystery behind every bush, thought Hattie as she eyed him narrowly; but it seems to me there is a certain constraint in his voice when he speaks of the mythical sword, and when he speaks of poor Edward, also. But before she could quiz him on the topic, Berry asked, "By chance, did Monsieur Bing refer to an engraved golden disk—perhaps not very large?" He indicated the small size with his fingers. "It is one of the missing artifacts."

Bing shook her head with regret, obviously sorry to disappoint her new admirer. "Minor gold items are vulnerable to theft—Edward often decried the work of the tomb raiders."

"There is also an item that is described as a 'senet board,' but I am not certain what is meant."

Bing was more than willing to enlighten him, being an authority on all things entombed. "It refers to a game board, rather similar to a chessboard, which would be played in the afterlife."

"You know of no such item?"

Bing shook her head again. "I fear one can only assume the worst if an inventoried item is missing—the black market is thriving, unfortunately."

Conceding, the Frenchman spread his hands. "It is fortunate most of the artifacts are accounted for, then." He turned his head, listening. "Someone is at the door."

Bing rose to investigate and Hattie immediately pounced on him. "What do you know of Edward's death?"

"Leave the door to your chamber unlocked, tonight," he directed.

A bit taken aback, she stared at him for a moment until Bing claimed her attention from the terrace, calling out, "Hathor, Baron du Pays has come to call. Shall I bring him out?"

It wants only this, Hattie thought in annoyance as she stood to address Bing—for two pins she would send the wretched vice-consul to Elba to keep company with Napoleon. "The rain approaches—it would be best to reconvene in the parlor, I think." Turning to relay the invitation to Berry, she discovered that he had disappeared. A quick glance around the small yard revealed no clue—he was gone. It seems he wishes to entertain the wretched baron as little as I do, she thought with resignation, and headed indoors.

Chapter 7

As the rain came down outside, Hattie was compelled to
endure the prescribed half-hour visit with their distinguished guest, her only consolation being Bing's small nod in
answer to her look of inquiry that indicated that her companion
had indeed booked passage away from this god-forsaken city.
The baron was all solicitous attention—polite and charming in
an old-world way—but Hattie found him off-putting with no
explanation for her reaction. "You are too kind," she said for the
second time, responding to his offer to drive out to Versailles.
She meant it literally, but she could see that he interpreted the
comment as a young girl's proper sentiment in reaction to his
generosity, and was well pleased. Fortunately, the gentleman
wasn't to know that by this time tomorrow she would be away
from this place, and from everyone's opportunings.

With a proprietary air, the Frenchman continued, "I
understand you have seen little of the world and I will be
delighted to change this unfortunate circumstance—the Sun-
King's palace is one of its wonders."

"Ah, yes—the Sun-King," nodded Hattie, at sea.

"Louis XIV," interpolated the ever-helpful Bing. "An
extraordinary ruler."

"Similar to the god-king, Seti," Hattie offered so as not to
seem completely ignorant.

The vice-consul was so taken with this comparison that Hattie feared for a moment he would embrace her on the spot. "Exactly," he smiled, his pale eyes gleaming. "My dear mademoiselle—you are very discerning."

"That I am," she agreed, and wished she could discern him taking his leave.

But it was not yet to be, and her visitor continued to regard her with an expression of warm approval. "History records the great men—men who leave a blazing legacy in their wake, *chère* mademoiselle; they are few and far between and we are indeed fortunate if we are given the opportunity to serve such men."

From all reports, it did not seem he referred to France's recently restored Bourbon king and she entertained a suspicion that he spoke of the now-deposed emperor, who was England's greatest enemy. This seemed in bad taste, and so she steered clear of the subject by offering in a neutral tone, "I suppose it must be exciting to feel one is participating in historic events."

"We live in extraordinary times, mademoiselle; and history has not yet closed its books."

This said with an air of suppressed exultation that Hattie found incongruous, and so she tentatively agreed, "Yes— the congress has yet to come to a conclusion and I suppose France's future is a bit uncertain."

At this remark, he lowered his gaze and a small smile touched his lips. "*Pour la gloire*, mademoiselle."

It occurred to her that he hadn't mentioned the one subject that—one would think—should be foremost in his mind, and so she ventured, "As the vice-consul in Egypt, I imagine you are aware that my parents are missing."

Immediately he raised his eyes to hers, his expression

apologetic. "I did not mention it, mademoiselle, because I was not certain you knew of this and I felt it was not my place. Please accept my sincere assurances that everything possible is being done to find them."

"Yes; I spoke with their agent, and it was he who told me the unfortunate news." Hattie watched to see if this man was aware of the other, but he easily acknowledged, "Yes, Monsieur Berry; a very capable man, and well known to me. He is *dévasté*, of course, but he holds out hope."

Now, that is doing it a bit too brown, thought Hattie, who then realized that—in truth—no one seemed very *dévasté*; instead everyone seemed much more interested in the elusive strongbox. "They also have a solicitor in Cairo, I understand. Would he be of use?"

The baron pressed his lips together in subtle disapproval. "He is a native man, with a tendency to be belligerent, as is in keeping. We can expect little cooperation from such a one; instead he will be looking to feather his own nest."

"That is indeed a shame," offered Hattie with barely concealed impatience. "One would think everyone involved would be eager to cooperate, instead of working at cross purposes."

Her ironic tone, however, was apparently lost on the man who seemed to suddenly remember his initial purpose as he leaned in again to touch her hand. "You are without protectors, at present, Mademoiselle Blackhouse. Allow me the honor of standing in, as the occasion arises."

"You are too kind," Hattie reiterated. "I shall indeed count on your support, as well as that of Mr. Tremaine, from the British embassy. You may not know that we are long-time acquaintances." This last to remind him she was not exactly friendless.

This time, the baron smiled a genuine smile that reached his eyes. "Ah, yes; Monsieur Tremaine and his unexpected bride."

His tone was slightly derisive, and Hattie could feel her color rise until she remembered that this gentleman and Madame Auguste seemed to have a rancorous relationship, based upon the barbed conversation at the embassy *soirée*. Seeking to turn the conversation, she observed only, "Mr. Tremaine was always full of surprises."

The older man nodded, the gleam still in his eye. "*Eh bien*; I believe he sees himself in the guise of a shining knight—the widow having been so recently bereft."

"Was she?" Hattie knew she shouldn't be gossiping about Robbie but was unable to help herself. "Monsieur Auguste having passed away recently?"

"Murdered by footpads in Cairo," the vice-consul replied, smoothing a sleeve. "Most unfortunate; it left your parents in an awkward situation."

Hattie blinked. "Was Monsieur Auguste involved with my parents?"

Her visitor lifted his cup to sip his tea. "*D'accord*; he was their liaison with the Ministry of Antiquities."

There was a small, rather shocked silence as Hattie and Bing assimilated this unexpected connection. "Do you think…" ventured Bing.

Disclaiming, he set his cup down and shook his head. "No, no—there appears to be no connection to the Blackhouses' disappearance; a random crime, only—there are violent elements in Cairo as there are in any other large city, and your parents were in Thebes at the time. Nonetheless, the deplorable act has made it all the more difficult to mount a search for your parents." He reached across to touch Hattie's hand again. "Rest assured, it is my only priority, and no resource will be spared, mademoiselle; I stand at your service."

"Thank you." Hattie forgot to tell him he was too kind, as instead her mind was occupied by this news of yet another unexplained death—assuming her parents were dead—and everyone's extreme determination to bedevil her. Perhaps there was something to this curse business, after all.

As if on cue, the distinguished Frenchman asked in a serious manner, "Are you aware where your parents kept their strongbox? Perhaps it would contain information helpful to the search."

"I haven't a clue," confessed Hattie. Thinking to forestall him, she added, "And I do not know if they had any other properties."

"A pity." He raised his head to smile indulgently, although the expression in the pale eyes remained unreadable. "Nevertheless, I shall see that you are well taken care of." To her dismay, his gaze rested discreetly on her breasts for the barest moment.

"You relieve me no end," Hattie assured him in a brittle tone, and wondered if it would provoke an international incident if she pushed the old lecher out the door. She refrained from putting it to the test, however, and at long last she stood with Bing at the window to watch his elaborate carriage draw away. "Behold my new beau, Bing."

Bing crossed her arms. "One of several, it seems."

Hattie gave her companion an arch look. "Come now, Bing; if you refer to Monsieur Berry, I believe he is more your beau than mine."

Bing made a wry mouth and turned from the window. "I can see what's before me."

Secretly pleased with this insight, Hattie merely replied,

"Then see to it we have no more visitors, if you please; I am beginning to believe there is something to this curse, after all."

"Nonsense," said Bing. "Merely an unfortunate sequence of events—save one."

Smiling at the addendum, Hattie turned to mount the stairs, unwilling to confess to Bing that she was expecting yet another visit from the same.

Chapter 8

H attie dithered on the horns of a dilemma—what did one wear if one were expecting a gentleman to make a clandestine visit to one's bedchamber? Under normal circumstances, of course, the answer would be obvious but these were not normal circumstances as the gentleman in question did not seem bent on seduction. Hattie allowed her gaze to rest on her bed, and wondered what her reaction would be if such an attempt were made. I don't know if I would mount much of a resistance, she admitted to herself—this was exactly why girls should be chaperoned within an inch of their lives.

Unthinkable to entertain him *en dishabille*—although her nightdress was very pretty and she would very much like to show it to him—she finally decided she would wear her day dress, and hope Bing did not make a visit to her chamber or that the upstairs maid would not think it strange she had asked for no assistance this evening. Affecting a causal air, she announced that she would read in her room after dinner and bade Bing good night, sitting up with a candle while the house gradually settled into silence. I hope I haven't long to wait, she thought, as she re-arranged her skirts yet again; I've had a tiring day, between all the dire warnings and various attempts to pry information from me.

Sometime after midnight, when the candle had burned low and Hattie had left the book open on her lap to rest her eyes, she awoke with a start to behold Berry standing before her.

"Oh," she said, and sat up straight, feeling at a disadvantage. She wondered how long he had been there.

"Be easy, mademoiselle," he whispered as he crouched down before her. "I must speak with you."

"So you keep saying," she whispered in return, a bit crossly. "Speak, then." She noted that he wore a dark workman's coat. His skulking uniform, she thought—he excels at it.

"What did Monsieur le Baron have to say?"

She considered this for a moment. "I expect an offer at any time."

He looked up into her face, the angles of his own accentuated in the illumination of the single candle. "I must be serious, I'm afraid."

But Hattie quirked her mouth. "I *am* serious—it is the most annoying turn of events, I assure you."

This surprised him, she could see, and he lowered his gaze, thinking.

"Am I an heiress?" This had occurred to her as a likely explanation for this sudden interest—hers was a name that was venerated in certain circles and if her parents were indeed no longer alive, there were those who would leap at the chance to marry into the Blackhouse legacy. Indeed, the Prussian Ambassador would probably be the next to haunt her doorstep.

"I know not," her visitor admitted. "But I imagine you would be the executrix of your parents' estate—I was unable to obtain exact information from their solicitor in Cairo."

"You spoke to him?" she asked, suddenly alert. "The Baron spoke to him also, but does not seem overly fond of him."

The gentleman made a small sound of annoyance in his throat. "A most unhelpful man."

"I imagine," Hattie ventured, "that he is not supposed to give out information, given the circumstances."

Berry refrained from comment, and thus reminded, Hattie ventured further, "I understand that Madame Auguste's late husband was connected with my parents' work in some way—through the Egyptian government."

"Yes," he agreed, and offered nothing further, which was maddening but to be expected; he gave little away, this self-assured gentleman, which made it all the more interesting that she could sense he was wrestling to resist the attraction between them—wrestling and not necessarily succeeding.

In a steady voice, she asked, "Tell me honestly; do you believe I am in danger?"

"No," he said immediately and looked up into her eyes. "No, mademoiselle, you are not in danger."

Almost apologetically she pointed out, "The comte who gave me the warning last night seemed to think so—and there are a great many corpses piling up. It does give one pause."

The brown eyes were intent upon hers and she could see that he was wrestling again, an undefined emotion simmering just below the surface. "You will not be one of them—my promise on it."

That she apparently now had a champion was much appreciated, and so she smiled upon him in the soft candle-light. Immediately, his expression became shuttered and she could sense his withdrawal. His mighty resistance had been raised again, and truly, it was just as well that one of them was resisting this magic; she was already regretting that she had not worn her pretty nightdress. To cover the moment she teased him, "You shouldn't pour the butter boat over Bing—she'll be expecting an offer of her own."

He bowed his head in amused acknowledgment. "Mademoiselle Bing is very capable, I think."

"Indeed she is. But she does not think Edward's death was anything more than an accident, while you apparently do."

He hesitated, weighing his words again, so she chided with a hint of impatience, "For the love of heaven, monsieur; you expect much from me but give little in return."

The rebuke seemed to have the desired effect and he relented. "Yes, I believe there is a connection; that his death was not an accident."

"But you don't think there is a curse, do you?" In the quiet darkness of night, the idea seemed less fantastic.

"No; but there are those who would encourage such thinking."

"Who?" she asked, her brows knit. "And why? Who are you, exactly?"

Bending his head for a moment, he touched her hand, quickly. "I am afraid I cannot say. But if you know anything of these matters, Mademoiselle Blackhouse, you must tell me—and tell me immediately. You must withhold nothing." The brown eyes were raised once more to hers, the timbre of his voice very serious.

Hattie nodded, serious in her own turn. "I understand."

There was a pause while it seemed to Hattie that he awaited a full confession. As she did not give him one, he continued, "I would ask that you be wary of Monsieur le Baron."

"Readily. Do I fend him off with my hatpin?"

But he would not joke, and chose his words carefully.

"He may contrive a situation where you would have little choice but to accept an offer."

"Not with me, he won't."

Despite himself, he smiled. "Nevertheless, be wary, if you please."

She assured him she would do so, and then felt a small pang at the realization she would avoid all such problems by stealing out of town tomorrow. She wondered at Berry's reaction, and then consoled herself with the certain conviction—unless she had completely misjudged the situation—that she would see him again, and sooner rather than later. "Now, if you don't mind I do have a question, if you will condescend to give me an answer."

"*Cela fait trembler*," he teased in mock apprehension, the planes of his face softening in the candlelight as he gazed up at her.

"Why did you refer to me as the god-king's daughter last night? Since you have worked with my parents, you couldn't have confused the meaning." Try as she might, she hadn't been able to come up with a plausible explanation.

He answered easily, "Your likeness was used to depict the princess."

She stared in confusion. "I'm afraid I don't understand."

Tilting his head, he explained, "It was your parents' idea. After the find, there was a great deal of publicity—it was astonishing that a nameless princess would be buried in the Valley of the Kings. A fanciful likeness was printed up and distributed—it bears a resemblance to you."

"Oh," she said, rather pleased and surprised by the implied compliment. "I see."

"You were not aware of this, it seems."

"No. But my parents always loved a good jest."

He dropped his gaze for a moment and she remembered that her parents were missing and presumed dead, and she probably shouldn't be making light of the situation by flirting with their very appealing agent—who was no more a clerk than she was the stupid princess.

As though coming to the same realization, Berry brought all flirtations to a close by rising to his feet and she rose with him, her heart beating in her ears; half hoping he would attempt an advance and half hoping he would not, as she was not certain she would make a whole-hearted attempt to thwart him.

He bowed his head to whisper, "Lock the door after me, if you please."

She nodded, not trusting her voice as she followed him to the door. Just before he slipped out, he turned and put a finger under her chin to lift her face to his. "You must make me a promise, mademoiselle," he said in a low voice, his face in the shadows.

She waited, nearly suffocating on a pleasurable precipice.

He leaned in and spoke in a tender tone. "You will not look upon Monsieur Tremaine in such a way."

Blushing hotly, she ducked her chin and closed the door on him with a firm click, hearing a soft chuckle as she did so.

After washing in the now-tepid water and climbing into bed, Hattie lay with her arms behind her head and contemplated the soft moonlight coming in through the window—she had much to think about. Her parents paid little attention to their only child but there had always been the conviction that this circumstance would change—that as soon as she was old enough to help them in their life's work she would be summoned. Now it seemed the summons would never come—and despite their failings, they were her parents and didn't deserve to die, unmarked and ungrieved in a foreign land.

She twisted a dark ringlet around her finger and thought about her three visits this day, and the general misapprehension that she knew the location of the all-important strongbox. Robbie had not behaved as though he were a man about to be married. The Baron believed her an heiress and was apparently hoping to secure a fortune by fair means or foul. Berry claimed to be her parents' agent in Egypt, yet he did not know that Hathor was the name of a prominent Egyptian goddess. He also had searched her house uninvited and had locked horns with her parents' solicitor, and—if she were guessing—it would not be beyond the realm of possibility to believe that he was some sort of spy; it would explain his penchant for doing whatever he wished even though he had adopted the *persona* of a clerk. This led her to draw a similar conclusion when it came to Robbie and his grey-eyed superior; try as she might, she didn't see how the diplomatic doings at the Congress of Vienna could have instigated this hotly contested search for her parents' strongbox. Something untoward was going forward, and whatever it was, apparently it was dangerous; many were dead and the Comte—whatever his name was—had urged her to flee back to England with all speed.

Pulling gently on a fine chain she wore around her neck, she withdrew the golden disk that was suspended upon it. Frowning in concentration, she contemplated the unintelligible markings engraved upon the disk for the thousandth time. I have no idea whom I can trust, she thought. And so I will trust no one.

Chapter 9

"We sail upon the *Sophia*, which will depart from Le Havre on the tide day after next." Bing was thinking about practicalities as they sat for breakfast the next morning, Hattie a bit heavy-eyed from her late night. "Do we fold up our tent and depart without comment, Hathor? Will you miss Mr. Tremaine's wedding festivities?"

"With great pleasure." Hattie buttered her bread with more force than was necessary. "And for the record, the gentleman was disinclined to discuss the event, and turned the subject at every opportunity." The two women exchanged a significant look in the manner of women everywhere who predict a mismatch, and a small silence fell as they continued their repast. A bit guiltily, Hattie realized that she would have to tell Bing *something* of what was going forward—although thus far she'd been an exemplary cohort—and so she decided to speak only in cautious generalities, for the time being. "I know my parents had a solicitor in Cairo—a Mr. Bahur—and given recent events I think it is important that I meet with him in person."

Bing nodded. "Certainly understandable—I imagine he would want to speak to you, also; one may presume he awaits instruction."

Hattie thought about what Berry had told her. "Do you think I am the executrix, then?"

"I have no idea, I'm afraid, but it is another reason to seek him out; if you are not the executrix you will need to speak to whoever is fulfilling that role."

"I suppose I shall need to draw upon their funds." Hattie had never considered such mundane matters in the past, mainly because she'd never gone anywhere nor done anything remotely interesting.

But Bing shook her head slightly in disagreement. "Your accounts are yours outright, Hathor—to draw upon as you wish. This was made very clear to me."

Thinking on this, Hattie smiled at her companion and reflected without rancor, "How strange that they were so generous with their money but not with their attention."

"I shall say nothing on the subject," said Bing, and pressed her lips into a thin disapproving line before she took another bite of dry toast.

But Hattie was not one to dwell on the past—particularly now that the future seemed to hold a hint of promise, given the glimpse of that simmering emotion—and replied, "Come, now, Bing—they were bringing the wonders of the ancients to the world and I—well, I would have been underfoot. And," Hattie teased her, "I would never have met you, else. Promise you will not up and marry some no-account suitor, as did Miss Swansea."

"I'm afraid I am not the marrying kind," Bing disclaimed with her slight smile.

"Well then, this will be as close to an elopement as we'll come, I imagine. I'd rather not trust the servants with our plans, so please pack a few essential things discreetly—we'll need to purchase more appropriate clothing once in Cairo, anyway—and we'll hire a hackney and be well away before anyone has a chance to plague me further."

"I cannot blame you for your caution, Hathor. It does seem…" Bing paused, her thin wrists resting on the table. "It does seem that there are powerful forces at play."

Hattie was reminded that Bing was no fool, and was obviously drawing her own conclusions. "Yes. And I cannot like the feeling that I am playing blind man's bluff while everyone else refuses to give me *an inch* of useful information."

"And you mistrust the British authorities." The statement hung in the air, a hint of a question contained therein.

Hattie could only reply with all sincerity, "I'm afraid I do, Bing; I have good reason, believe me."

Her companion seemed satisfied with this assurance, and returned her attention to her tea and toast. "Then it is settled. I have always wanted to see Egypt, and quite look forward."

The bell rang, and Hattie looked up in surprise as it was too early for morning calls. She heard a man's voice—not Robbie's—and then the maid came in to announce a visitor who was revealed to be the grey-eyed man, Robbie's superior. That worthy did not stand on ceremony but strode directly into the breakfast room, his hat in his hand and his expression grave as the women hastily rose. "Miss Blackhouse, Miss Bing—please forgive my intrusion but I am afraid I have unsettling news."

"Robbie?" asked Hattie in alarm.

Contrite, the man paused and held out a reassuring hand. "No—I am sorry to have alarmed you but instead it is Mr. Tremaine's fiancée—I'm afraid there has been a terrible accident."

Hattie stared at him, and then realized she was not, after all, very much surprised. "Madame Auguste? Why, what has happened?"

The gentleman's gaze did not waver. "I am sorry to report she has met with a fatal accident; Mr. Tremaine has asked that I fetch you to the embassy so that you can support him at this time—"

Hattie interrupted with a touch of impatience, "Can you not tell us what has happened?"

Their visitor shook his head in a regretful disclaimer. "I do not know the particulars, Miss Blackhouse. But Mr. Tremaine has urgently requested your assistance."

Hattie found it rather ominous that the man wouldn't tell her, even though she would bet her teeth that he knew exactly what had happened to Robbie's wretched bride—and it didn't help that she felt a bit remorseful for being so short with the poor, doomed, aged woman. The British must be worried that Hattie was next on the list of victims, despite Berry's assurance that she was in no danger; otherwise there was truly no reason for this exigency—or for this particular man to come fetch her—if her only role was to comfort the bereaved. Unless, of course, they wished to torture her secrets from her in the embassy basement, and the British usually frowned upon such procedures—or one would think, anyway. In any event, she wasn't going to allow the gentleman to think she wasn't aware that he was prevaricating, and so she bluntly concluded, "You must believe that I am in danger, then."

She could hear Bing's soft intake of breath at such plain speaking, but their visitor only bowed his head in acknowledgment. "All the more reason to come to the embassy, miss."

"Of course; we will come, then." Hattie turned to Bing. "Do you have any mourning bands, Bing?"

Bing shrugged her spare, black-clad shoulders with regret.

"I am afraid not, Hathor, as I remain in full mourning for my dear brother."

Hattie turned to the grey-eyed man and said briskly, "If you would allow me step into the draper's for a moment on our journey to the embassy—it is just up the street—I can purchase mourning bands for poor Robbie and myself."

The grey eyes regarded her without expression. "Perhaps such a purchase can wait—"

But Hattie quirked her mouth, and interrupted candidly, "I was unkind to the decedent on the one occasion when I met her, and so I feel obligated to show every consideration, to try to make up for it. I don't want Robbie to feel I do not share in his sorrow."

As expected, the gentleman assented, having little choice in the matter. "Very well, then."

As the women fetched their gloves and hats, Hattie murmured to the hovering Bing, "Stand ready; we are going out yet another window. Bring along the passage vouchers."

"Do we leave out the back?" asked Bing in tone that indicated she was willing but uncertain of the success of such a tactic.

"No—I imagine they are watching the house to make certain no one seizes me before they do. Good God, Bing; was there *never* such a place for dark doings? City of Light, my eye. Come with me and stay close."

With all appearance of complicity, they accompanied their escort to the waiting carriage, Hattie noting with a quick glance that the embassy driver was the same as the hackney driver from the first night—which came as no surprise whatsoever. "Poor Robbie," remarked Hattie aloud. She meant it, too—it would be embarrassing to act as chief mourner when one had hardly time to act as bare acquaintance. "Did Madame Auguste have family in Paris?"

"I am unaware," replied the gentleman as the carriage began to move.

Knitting her brow, Hattie watched out the window for a few moments as the city's inhabitants stirred to life. "We must purchase mourning cards, also, Bing. We can send the announcements to those who must be informed—Robbie never had a good hand."

"Very good," agreed Bing. "He will no doubt be too upset to think of such things."

Hattie sat back in the seat, counting off tasks on her fingers. "Yes—we'll speak with him, and discover what needs to be done, and how many cards will be needed. Perhaps we'll have to help make funeral arrangements, also, although I have no idea how such a thing is handled over here—I imagine she was Roman Catholic."

"We shall see," Bing assured her. "Every propriety must be observed."

"Here we are at the draper's," the grey-eyed man announced as the carriage pulled up to the curb. With a deferential air, he added, "I will escort you ladies within, if you don't mind."

"Of course," said Hattie, who then added with an amused sidelong glance, "I am counting on you to stand the ready, on account of my reticule having been unaccountably stolen."

"Say no more, Miss Blackhouse," the other assured her in a wooden voice as he handed her down. "I shall be honored."

"Have Robbie pay you back," she suggested.

"No need."

"You are very kind." I shouldn't bait him, she thought, but I cannot allow him to believe I am as stupid as he thinks.

Once within the shop's interior, Hattie sized up the two women within and approached the younger. "We will need blacks, I'm afraid," Hattie explained in French, and began walking to the back of the shop where, in the time-honored tradition of draper's shops, there were rolls of all variety of fabrics, stacked high on tables and shelves.

The girl assumed a sympathetic expression, her pretty mouth drawn down. "*Quel dommage*, mademoiselle."

"That's as may be," replied Hattie, who walked behind the stacks and straight toward the back door—she thought it best to strike quickly, whilst her keeper was carefully viewing the street out the front window. "Say nothing," she whispered to the surprised girl with a smile. "I go to meet my sweetheart, and *mon oncle* disapproves."

"Ah! *Oui*, mademoiselle," the girl answered, and lingered behind the stacks, looking self-conscious, as she watched them slip out the door.

"Quickly, Bing; we'll find a hackney on the next street up; I'm afraid we will have to lie on the floor for a time."

"Certainly," said Bing, and gamely lifted her skirts with both hands.

Chapter 10

A nd so in two days' time Hattie stood on the deck of the *Sophia*, holding her hat on her head with one hand with her face turned into the wind, thrilled to feel the ship skimming along the water. The trip across the Channel from Southampton had been her first sea voyage—her first voyage of any kind, truly—and she had enjoyed it immensely. "It is so glorious, Bing—small wonder sailors never want to come home from the sea."

Bing, however, was pale of lip. "I believe I must go and lay abed, Hathor."

Hattie turned to her usually steady companion with concern. "Are you ill, Bing? Allow me to assist you."

But her doughty companion was embarrassed by such a show of weakness and refused all offers of aid. "There is no need, Hathor; it has been my experience that a short nap and a citrus drop will set me to rights." In dignified retreat, she then made her way down the companionway stairs to their cabin.

Turning her face back into the breeze, Hattie listened to the hissing of the water as it sloughed off the hull and breathed in lungfuls of sharp, tangy air as she leaned against the ship's railing. They were headed to open sea and the water became rougher, the ship dipping in the troughs more dramatically as she closed her eyes and licked the salt spray from her lips—glorious, she thought, removing her hat so that she could feel the sun on her face—she definitely did not have her mother's aversion to the sun. They had laid low, both on the trip to Le Havre and then at the inn, staying indoors and out of sight in the event the British or the Baron or even the mysterious Comte tracked them down, but in the end the ship was away with none the wiser, and Hattie celebrated having the sun once again on her face and the exultation of having outfoxed her pursuers. Indeed, her only regret was that there would be no further opportunities for post-midnight *tête-a-têtes* with Monsieur Berry, but she consoled herself with the sure knowledge that he would turn up again, if for no other reason than to plague her about the stupid strongbox, which was apparently of great interest to everyone still left alive in all this.

"Mademoiselle."

She would know his voice anywhere, and in utter astonishment she jerked her chin down to behold Monsieur Berry, standing respectfully at a small distance. Rather than gape at him, she pulled herself together and warily waited, the realization that he was one step ahead of her and two steps ahead of the British making her heart sink. I hope I have not been an idiot, she thought; but I suppose if he wished to do me in, he has already had plenty of opportunity to do so. On the other hand, the fact that he was here unannounced could not be described as anything other than ominous, and it was past time she brushed the stardust from her eyes.

He had not approached, as though aware that she needed time to process this unlooked-for development. "Please do not be angry; you will come to no harm at my hands—my promise on it."

"Why are you here?"

"Why do you travel to Cairo?" he countered.

But she would win this round. "My parents are missing, if you will recall."

He took a tentative step closer, watching for her reaction. "You do not understand many things, mademoiselle; and you take a very foolish risk."

But this was the wrong thing to say to Hattie, who retorted hotly, "A greater risk than staying in Paris, where I am besieged by men who seek to beguile my supposed secrets?"

He slowly shook his head in denial. "I cannot speak for Monsieur Tremaine, but I do not attempt to beguile you, mademoiselle."

This was so patently untrue that she replied with a full measure of scorn, "I beg to disagree; Robbie has never arranged to meet me in my chamber after midnight."

But apparently he disliked being chided every bit as much as she. "Come now; you nurse a grudge because I would not kiss you."

Her face flooding with color, Hattie was so shocked she could not even make a furious rejoinder. "You should go," she managed, holding on to her temper only with an effort.

"No, I will not." He stepped close and put a hand on her arm, bending to look into her face. "Look—I am sorry. I shouldn't have said it."

"You are no gentleman," she bit out, wholly embarrassed, which made her all the angrier.

"Forgive me; I was unkind."

Placing her palms over her eyes, she took a deep breath. You need to calm down, she thought, or you are going to cry, and that will not go well at all.

His voice continued next to her ear, the timbre quiet and

sincere. "Hattie, these are dangerous people—allow me to keep you safe." His use of her name did get her attention—his accent resulted in an emphasis on the second syllable that she found very pleasing, despite everything. She lifted her gaze to his, and saw that he was very serious, his eyes searching hers.

"Please don't be angry—it is for the best, believe me." He did not retreat behind his usual formality; for once his manner seemed genuine, and she found it more disarming than if he had made a dozen pretty speeches. "Allow me to help you."

Hattie fixed her gaze on his cravat, and even as she was aware that she shouldn't trust him an inch, she couldn't seem to help herself, and so complained in a tone that unfortunately sounded rather childish, "I would ask that you were more honest with me; I am heartily sick of mysteries."

"I cannot be honest with you. But I can protect you."

Surprised, she lifted her gaze to his and digested his comment, both parts equally alarming. "I thought you said I was not in danger."

"That was before I knew you were leaving for Cairo on your own."

"No longer—we have been commandeered," she riposted with some heat.

"What was I to do? You would not tell me of your plans."

There was a hint of accusation in his voice that told her he was rather hurt by this, and hearing it, she took pity on him. "It is nothing personal, you understand; I don't know who to trust."

"You can trust me," he assured her without hesitation.

She arched a dark brow in skepticism. "Can I? Who is it you work for, truly?"

There was the barest pause. "I cannot say," he replied. "Because I will honor your request that I be more honest with you."

"Oh—I see." This was surprising, and seemed to indicate a softening of his attitude. "Have you lied to me before?"

"Yes," he admitted in the same even tone.

Assimilating this admission without taking offense, she confessed, "I would like to have a turn at being mysterious—but I have no secrets whatsoever."

"It is a burden, sometimes." He met her eyes and she had the impression he was referring to their rendezvous in her chamber—when he infamously would not kiss her—with a hint of apology, which was very much appreciated.

She sighed. "I wish I knew more about all of this."

"It is best that you do not, Mademoiselle Blackhouse."

Quirking her mouth, she observed with regret, "I was 'Hattie' for a moment, but now I am demoted to 'Mademoiselle Blackhouse' once again."

He smiled, the wind blowing his hair about his forehead—she had to clench the railing to refrain from smoothing it down for him. "*C'est cela*; I do not wish to offend again—you are fearsome when you are angry."

"Then keep that to mind, and do not cross me," she teased.

Still smiling, he seemed disinclined to bring their conversation to a close and leaned against the railing beside her. "You enjoy the sea."

"Very much—although this is my first real voyage." Equally disinclined to move away, she cast about for something to say in return. "Where in France do you hail from, monsieur?"

He shook his head with regret, and glanced down to her. "I cannot say."

She stared at him in surprise. "Because it would be a lie?"

He gave an ironic little nod. "*De vrai.*"

Knitting her brow, she met his gaze with amused exasperation. "Heavens; making an effort at honesty is rather complicated, apparently."

He glanced out over the sea, the smile still playing around his mouth. "I have never made the effort before, so we shall see."

So mesmerized was she that she didn't notice the approach of the ship's captain until he cleared his throat, standing beside her. "Miss Blackhouse." Captain Clements was a bear of a man, whose ginger hair was grizzled with gray and whose manner was that of a lifelong seaman; unrepentantly bold and brash of manner. The shrewd gaze behind the spectacles shifted for a moment between Hattie and Berry, and she found herself blushing and hoping everyone aboard had not been an interested spectator to their quarrel.

"I trust you find the accommodations to your liking."

Shading her eyes, she assured him, "Very comfortable, Captain. Thank you for taking us on such short notice."

The captain leaned on the railing to her other side, which forced her to turn her back upon Berry; she noted the men did not speak and wondered if perhaps they were at odds. He continued, "I must confess I have followed your parents' work with great interest and so I was very pleased to find your name on the manifest, Miss Blackhouse; do you make the trip to visit them often?"

With a mental sigh, Hattie girded her loins for yet another discussion about the tedious princess. "No, sir; this is my first visit to Egypt."

"Is that so?" The captain met her eyes in surprise.

"I did visit their exhibition at the British Museum once,

in London." She didn't want him to think she knew *nothing* about her parents' work—although it did seem that Bing was much better informed and Hattie wished for a moment she was still present, so as to feed her a few lines.

With a faraway gaze, the captain considered the vast ocean stretching away before the ship. "Yes—it was a unmitigated triumph; why, I can recall when they electrified the world when they discovered the Temple of Amon-Re at Abu Simbel—I can think of no other find that garnered such attention."

Pleased that she knew at least one fact, Hattie disclaimed, "I was not yet born, I'm afraid."

"And this latest—the unknown daughter, lying in state in a place reserved only for pharaohs. An amazing mystery."

"Indeed." And then, because Berry was listening, she managed to dredge up yet another fact so as to sound semi-informed. "A mystery which hopefully will be solved—I believe there is cautious optimism that the hieroglyphic language on the tomb can be translated, now that the key has been discovered."

"The Rosetta Stone," agreed the captain with a nod. "Napoleon had his uses, I suppose."

Fearing that they were going to stray into yet another tedious conversation about the deposed Emperor and his place in history, Hattie hastily noted, "I should check on Bing—she is unwell, I'm afraid."

The captain doffed his hat with good humor. "A pleasure to meet you, Miss Blackhouse; I hope you will join me for dinner this evening."

Hattie smiled her acceptance. "Thank you—on behalf of myself and Miss Bing." If the captain thought she'd dine with him unchaperoned she would disabuse him of this notion.

With a nod to Berry, the other man strode away with a well-pleased air, and Hattie knew a moment's qualm that she would be simultaneously fending off flirtations from the captain whilst trying to encourage them from Berry, which would make for a trip as complicated as Berry's resolve to be more honest with her.

Berry sketched a bow. "*Au revoir*, mademoiselle."

"*Au revoir*, monsieur." While she regretted the captain's interruption of their conversation, she consoled herself with the fact there would be plenty of opportunities to speak with Berry—hopefully at length—during the course of the journey. With this happy thought in mind, she made her way to their cabin to find Bing asleep in the upper berth. Moving quietly so as not to wake her, Hattie settled in on the edge of her narrow berth and took a moment to review the conversation on deck. Berry had resolved to be honest with her—it seemed that their passionate argument had resulted in a shift in their relationship; an understanding of sorts. Nevertheless, she vowed that she would never again appear to be inviting his advances—she had learned a very humiliating lesson.

Bing stirred in her sickbed. "Do you remain well, Hathor?"

Standing to address her suffering companion, Hattie took a thin hand in her own. "I'm afraid I do. I am almost ashamed."

"Nonsense. Once I am over the initial discomfort I shall recover, never fear."

"Is there anything you need? Or do you long for me to leave you alone?" It had occurred to Hattie that a sickening chaperone was not necessarily an unadulterated evil.

"I am only concerned that I fail in my duties to you— there are rough seamen aboard and your presence may evoke a reaction."

"Now it is my turn to say 'nonsense' to you, Bing; I had

a pleasant conversation with the captain up on deck and am perfectly comfortable." Best not to mention that the captain had the look of a man embarking on a flirtation. "He would like us to join him for dinner."

"Excellent," Bing intoned weakly.

Eyeing her doubtfully, Hattie offered, "If you'd rather, Bing, I will cry off and tell him we will accept his invitation tomorrow."

"I shall be recovered," her companion insisted. "It is merely mind over matter."

"The spirit may be willing, but the flesh is green around the gills," Hattie pointed out gently. "I'll not contribute to your demise; the tiresome god-king's daughter has already inspired an alarming mortality rate."

From her prone position, Bing sighed, one hand resting on her forehead. "Even if we do not discover your parents' fate, we shall see their affairs settled—there is that."

"Yes. And speaking of which, I will now astonish you and inform you that Monsieur Berry is aboard."

"Is he?" Bing contemplated the cabin's ceiling for a moment. "That is indeed astonishing."

"Not a coincidence, I imagine. Keep your pistol about you, if you please."

But Bing drew a breath, and turned her head toward Hattie. "I can't imagine he means to do you harm, Hathor."

"So he says; but we would do well to be very wary, Bing; at least until we understand what is afoot." Mainly, Hattie was trying to remind herself of this, as she was half inclined to return to the deck forthwith and search him out again.

"I will be wary, Hathor, but I must admit that it will be useful to have a gentleman at hand."

Agreed, thought Hattie, who was nothing if not honest.

Chapter 11

H attie and Bing made their appearance at the captain's
table as planned, Bing having righted herself by sheer
force of will.

"You must give me a signal at dinner if you feel too
unwell to continue," Hattie instructed in a low voice as they
approached the captain's quarters in the stern. "I will make
an excuse."

"That is kind of you, Hathor, but will not be necessary,"
Bing replied with a show of vigor as she wrapped her black
Norwich shawl more tightly around her angular shoulders.
"I daresay I am much improved."

Dubious, Hattie put hand firmly under Bing's elbow. "Use
the word 'prodigious' and I will know it is time to depart."

"Very well," said Bing, testing it out. "I hope the captain
does not serve sausage, for fear I will make a prodigiously
quick exit."

The captain's quarters were relatively spacious compared
to the other cabins, and featured a row of small-paned windows across the stern. Hattie was envious; she couldn't be
comfortable enclosed in a small, windowless space, which is
why she was determined to find whatever excuse she could
to avoid spending time in her cabin. Featured at the cabin's
center was a dining table complete with a candelabrum

that was secured to the table by pegs; a servant was in the process of lighting the candles and nodded to them as they entered. Dressed in a formal suit of clothes, the captain greeted both ladies and gallantly complimented Hattie on her good looks. "You must stay hidden away from the crew or you will incite a riot—it is not often the *Sophia* carries such fetching cargo." He bent to bestow a lingering kiss on her hand.

"Is the ship named after your wife, perhaps?" Hattie asked in an innocent tone, teasing him.

Laughing in appreciation, he steered her to the table. "Minx. The *Sophia's* the only wife I have. At present," he amended gallantly.

Hattie accepted the proffered glass of Madeira from the servant. "And like to be the only one; a sea captain is a poor candidate for a husband, one would think."

"Never say so," he disclaimed as he saw Bing seated. "And I have half a mind to marry post-haste, for no other reason than to prove you wrong."

She laughed, enjoying herself as they began their repast. "I shouldn't criticize; I would not blame you for sailing whenever the opportunity arises, Captain—I enjoy it very much. My poor Bing, on the other hand, finds the sea disagreeable."

"Not the sea," Bing corrected her with a faint smile. "Only its movement."

"I am sorry for it," the captain said to her with ready sympathy. "My cook concocts an excellent remedy—I shall call for it." He turned and gave a brief instruction to the servant.

Sensing that Bing was embarrassed by the fuss, Hattie reclaimed his attention. "How long have you captained the *Sophia*, sir?"

"Not so very long, actually; after the Armistice I traded in my seventy-four for a frigate; I find that the route to Cairo is particularly lucrative."

Hattie nodded, well aware that England was mad about all things Egyptian ever since the end of the last century, when Napoleon had first explored the area. Indeed, it was one of the reasons her parents could afford their expensive passion—there was an avid interest and therefore an unending supply of wealthy backers willing to fund the Blackhouse efforts.

Their meal was surprisingly good, but on second thought, Hattie decided that Captain Clements was a man who did not stint on his pleasures. Bing's restorative proved to be a dark, viscous liquid contained in a small glass, which her companion dutifully sipped as the meal progressed. It did appear to bring more color to her cheeks, and Hattie suspected that alcohol served as its base ingredient. I must ration my Madeira, she thought, else we will both be tipsy and there will be no one left to hold the captain at arm's length. She asked him, "How long will you stay in Cairo before making your return trip?" Having no real expectation of finding her parents alive, Hattie was wondering how long she herself would stay; Berry would not have expressed his grave doubts to her unless he was certain her parents no longer lived. Mainly, she wanted to arrange for a proper burial—if she could find out what happened to them—and with any luck, set a course for her future that was devoid of annoying inquisitions and hair's-breadth escapes.

The captain considered his answer while he ran his fingers up the stem of his wine glass. "The turnaround depends on a variety of factors, but usually there are a plentitude of traders seeking passage so as to bring cargo back to France or England—copies of artifacts or even the genuine article, for sale to private collections or to a museum."

Hattie felt a pang of sadness on behalf of the Egyptians, whose treasures were being transported elsewhere whilst their political situation was in too much disarray to prevent it; she knew that graft and corruption—almost a given, in the Mid-East—encouraged the authorities to look the other way.

The captain's voice broke into her thoughts. "Perhaps my visit on this trip can be arranged to match the length of your own. How long do you stay, Miss Blackhouse?"

Rather than equivocate on the subject for the entire journey, Hattie decided to reveal the true state of facts. "Unfortunately, I have not heard from my parents in quite some time; indeed, I make this journey to discover if they have met with calamity."

With a show of sympathy that also allowed him to take her hand, the gentleman offered, "Perhaps they are merely in an isolated area and must make their way to a post that allows for communication."

Hattie appreciated the theory, however far-fetched. "Let us hope so."

But Bing found this unlikely and shook her head with some determination. "No—the tomb's site is near Al Karnak," she corrected, carefully pronouncing the words. "Amenities are quite modern—there would be no impediment. Indeed, my dear brother wrote me every week." Her companion was apparently unaware that the captain had been merely attempting to offer Hattie some encouragement.

Hiding a smile at her companion's altered state, Hattie could only agree, "Yes, I'm afraid the situation appears rather grave."

The captain attempted another tack to change the subject. "The god-king's daughter," he mused aloud. "An extraordinary find—and with startling implications; if your parents do not make a reappearance, I wonder what will happen to the site? Are you familiar with their arrangements, Miss Blackhouse?"

"No," Hattie replied in a tone to discourage further questions. If he asks me about a strongbox, she thought, I will put my knife to his throat.

"You misunderstand; the Blackhouses do not own the site," Bing reminded him in the ponderous tone of one educating a schoolboy. "I imagine the Ministry will simply assign another archeological team to soldier on—the world awaits further information."

"Undoubtedly," agreed the captain. "The anonymous princess must be identified; there must be a compelling story behind her extraordinary burial. Who is believed to be her father—is it Ramesses?"

Hattie reconciled herself to yet another tedious discussion about history's giants while Bing corrected him. "Wrong dynasty—the pharaoh is believed to be Seti, instead. Or so I believe the translations indicate. Although…" She paused, her brow furrowed. "Although my dear brother found some contradictions, apparently."

"Oh?" asked the captain in an encouraging tone. It seemed to Hattie that his interest suddenly sharpened.

Bing shook her head slightly, as though trying to clear it. "He was a little vague in his last letter, but apparently he was skeptical of the dateline hypothesis, for some reason."

"Well, we can be certain the matter will be thoroughly explored by his successor," the gentleman assured her. "As long as no one is deterred by the supposed curse."

Hattie contemplated her wine glass, having noted that their host apparently knew who Bing's brother was and that he had been killed—not something one would assume was common knowledge. Pushing the glass away, she resolved to keep her wits about her.

"Did your brother recite the particulars of his work in his letters to you, Miss Bing?"

Hattie could not quite like this inquisition and could see that Bing was fast becoming fuddled. In light of this, she offered, "Mr. Bing was a *prodigious* Egyptian scholar."

But Bing had forgotten their signal and merely nodded. "He was a brilliant man. Quite fond of the Blackhouses—truly enjoyed his work." She paused. "I shall miss him acutely."

Hattie could see that the captain was winding up to further quiz Bing on this sad subject, and decided that enough was enough. Rising, she gently took Bing's arm. "We should return to our cabin, Bing—it has been a tiring day."

The captain rose also, clearly worried he had offended. "Forgive me; I was clumsy—the subject is not an easy one for either of you."

Smiling, Hattie reassured him, "Not at all, although I must confess I have little interest in the god-king's daughter. But I fear Bing does poorly and if she does not survive this night I will have to forfeit all future dinners."

They excused themselves and the captain escorted them to their cabin, Bing weaving a bit unsteadily. At their cabin door, he bowed low and expressed his pleasure in her company while Hattie assured him they would be pleased to accept all future invitations until she was forced to rather firmly bid him good night. Bing made straight for her bunk and lay with an arm across her eyes; in a matter of moments she was softly snoring.

Well, thought Hattie; the restorative does work after a fashion—Bing cannot be sick if she is sleeping. After debating the issue, she decided she should pull off her companion's half-boots but leave her in her dress clothes rather than wake her. Carefully pulling off the boots one at a time, she bent to open their storage drawer only to pause in alarm; someone had been through their things. It was nothing obvious, but she was certain, nonetheless. An inspection of the drawer only verified her suspicions—she was compelled to be tidy and knew that various items were slightly askew.

Sitting back on her heels, she tried to decide what should be done. Whoever it was had waited until both she and Bing were out of the cabin, so their movements were being monitored. Not the captain—he had been with them during the whole. Someone else, then; but perhaps on the captain's orders, she couldn't rule it out—there had been something about the way he watched her reactions, about the way he knew about Bing's brother... You are being fanciful, she reprimanded herself; pray do not start jumping at shadows.

As if on cue, there was a soft knock on the door, that indeed made her jump. Hattie stared at the cabin door and knew a moment's hesitation. Craven, she chided herself—no one would dare make an attack on a ship, you have only to scream.

Rising, she opened the door a crack to see Berry, lurking in the passageway. "Yes?" she whispered.

"If you please, you must stay inside with the door locked. As a precaution."

They regarded each other. She debated whether to ask him a few pointed questions but instead said only, "Thank you."

He didn't move. "You should lock it, please."

She nodded, and then closed the door, turning the key in the lock with an audible click. She turned and went back to sit on her berth for a few minutes but she did not prepare for bed; if only the cabin weren't so cramped—she could not be comfortable. Restless, she stood and walked the few paces she was able, and then pulled a coverlet over Bing, wishing she knew what was afoot. Whilst she was thinking, she thought she heard a noise above her. She stilled and listened, but did not hear it again.

Welcoming the distraction and the excuse to abandon the cabin, Hattie carefully unlocked the door, exited, and then locked it again behind her. Listening and holding her breath, she stood in the passageway. Again, a muffled sound from above. Walking softly down the passage, she ascended the companionway stairs and peered cautiously out on the deck. The immediate area was deserted and so she emerged into the cool night air.

The scene before her was magical; the moonlight reflecting off the waves and the colors around her muted to grays and dull greens—as though she were in another world. Aside from the occasional groaning of wood rubbing against wood and the hissing of the water in the wake, it was quiet. She stepped toward the quarterdeck, in the general vicinity of the sounds she had heard, alert to discovery and prepared to give an excuse in the event she was spotted. As she rounded the mizzenmast she heard a low grunt, and stifled a gasp as she quickly crouched down and peered around the mast's base. Before her she could make out the figures of two men, grappling in deadly earnest.

Chapter 12

The moonlight allowed for some illumination and after a startled moment, Hattie realized it was Berry, wrestling with another man she didn't recognize. His opponent was a large man and well-muscled—a common seaman, perhaps.

It was a strange scene; the men were locked together, each straining to gain an advantage in utter silence. With a soft grunt, Berry made a quick move to wrap an arm around his opponent's neck so as to gain leverage, although he was outweighed by several stone. The other, however, stymied this attempt and instead groped to find his own chokehold. Both men trembled and grunted with exertion, neither able to subdue the other. Hattie watched from her hiding place and debated whether to sound the alarm; her only hesitation stemmed from the fact that if Berry had wished to call for assistance he would have done so—there were no doubt others within a shout's distance. Before she could decide how to proceed, she observed the opponent's hand creep up to Berry's jaw and begin to push, forcing his head slowly backward despite the other's best efforts to resist.

Well—this won't do, thought Hattie. Looking about her, she grasped the nearest weapon available: a spare wooden block stored near the pin rail. Hattie was small and the block was heavy, so she swung it to one side so as to gain enough momentum to lift it above her head, then leapt from behind the mast, timing her swing so as to bring the block down on the back of the opponent's head. With a grunt, he dropped like a stone to the deck.

Inordinately pleased with herself, Hattie admired her handiwork for a moment, still holding the heavy block in the event it may be needed again while Berry bent and gasped for breath, his hands on his knees. He managed to glance up at her sideways. "I thank you."

"Is he dead?" She wasn't certain how she felt about this possibility.

Bending down, he put his fingers on the throat of the unconscious man. "No, but his head will ache tomorrow." He gestured to her. "Give me your sash."

Hattie placed the block on the deck and untied her pink ribbon sash, handing it over. Berry bent and bound the man's hands with a few practiced movements.

"Who is he?"

"No one to concern you."

Berry was in his shirtsleeves, his hair dark with perspiration and his shirt collar torn at the neck so that his throat was revealed to her interested gaze. As he recovered his breath, he stood upright and dabbed at his lip with the back of a hand—she could see that it was cut and bleeding. "You are hurt. Shall I fetch the captain?"

"No. You were asked to remain below, I believe."

"I am thankful I did not," she retorted, thinking that a small show of gratitude would not be completely out of line. "And you are mixing your accents." It was true—he was speaking with a decided accent that was quite different from his usual French one. Hattie, who had little experience in foreign accents—with the possible exception of their Yorkshire cook—did not recognize its origin.

He nodded, as though she had told him something of mild interest, and dabbed at his lip again. When next he spoke, the French accent was back in place as though it had never been gone. "You had best go below. Be certain to lock your door and do not wander about."

"Then do you believe there are more?" she asked in alarm. "Promise me you will be careful."

"I am always careful—now go."

Annoyed that he was annoyed, she retorted, "Fine," and turned to leave with a flounce, only to ruin the effect by stumbling over the wooden block.

Grasping her arm so as to steady her, he did not relinquish his hold but instead propelled her against the mizzenmast, the wood hard against her back as he pinned her with an arm around her waist. Lifting her face with his other hand, he kissed her.

Hattie had never kissed a man—indeed had never been held so, even by her father. She felt an almost paralyzing sense of exhilaration and wished she knew what she was supposed to do as it seemed clear he knew exactly what to do. As if reading her mind, he found her hands with his and pulled them up around his neck, then his arms went tightly around her waist and he was kissing her rather roughly, pressing against her in an intimate way that should have alarmed her but definitely did not.

Clinging to his neck, she responded to the movement of his mouth against hers in a way she hoped was pleasing and that certainly seemed to provoke a heated reaction. He gently pulled at her jaw so that her mouth opened, and then his tongue was touching hers and she heard a moaning sound, which she realized, with some surprise, was emanating from herself. His hand moved over her, pressing a palm gently against a breast and then drawing down over her hip to pull her even closer. I have to stop this, she thought in a haze—but not just yet.

Voices could be heard from the stern of the ship, and with some reluctance he released her. As her knees were now weak, she teetered a bit, and he steadied her with his hands at her waist for a moment, his gaze enigmatic in the moonlight while the vessel rocked in its progress through the boundless sea

"Go—quickly."

Hattie obeyed without demur, hoping no one observed her retreat although she could always claim to have wanted a breath of fresh air—and truth to tell, she needed one just now. Filling her lungs, she quietly unlocked her cabin and slipped through the door, glancing to make certain Bing still slept on her berth. After turning down the lamp she quietly prepared for bed in the dim light, thanking heaven for the captain's concoction—it seemed Bing would continue to slumber peacefully without any awareness that her charge first had been brawling and then committing improprieties on deck.

After she settled into her berth, Hattie didn't know what to think about first. Well, actually she did—but she needed to think about that later. Berry was not French. She decided she was not very surprised by this revelation; she already knew he was not whom he seemed and was only posing as her parents' agent. There had been an enemy on board, presumably the one who had searched through her things as Berry had already taken a turn and had come up empty. Hattie fingered the golden disk on its chain around her neck.

Was the captain also an enemy? She was not certain—he and Berry did not interact to any extent so it was difficult to judge. And although Berry could certainly kiss—and then some—she truly did not know whether he was, in fact, her enemy. It did seem as though he held a sincere affection for her, particularly because he had resisted it until now. Therefore, if he was bent on seduction as a means to discover her secrets, he was a very reluctant seducer. But in any event, it was clear he was not who he pretended to be, and she must have a care.

The more important question, it seemed, was why everyone was so very interested. Berry—if that was indeed his name—had hinted at a reason; with her parents' whereabouts unknown she suddenly and unexpectedly held authority over their effects, and those effects presumably were worth a fortune. But then why the interest in the disk, and in the elusive strongbox?

Fingering the coverlet, she knit her brow and thought about it. Her parents had a secret, or something that was not readily discoverable. Something that was very valuable—so valuable that people were willing to kill for it. Hattie had little doubt that the deaths were all connected in some way—and Berry had admitted these were dangerous people, whoever they were. He knew, but he didn't want to tell her. Indeed, Robbie had dropped hints to the same effect, but he didn't want to tell her, either.

And in a strange twist, no one ever had paid much attention to her but now every man jack she met was bent on beguiling her, although Berry's approach just now was much more direct. She couldn't suppress a delighted smile in the darkness, feeling a *frisson* run through her entire body at the blissful memory—she felt as though she had tasted a very potent drug and craved more of the same. For two pins, she thought, I would make an utter fool of myself and I mustn't—I must find out what is at stake, and why the disk is so important to whatever is at stake. There seems little chance that Berry will tell me, and I have to fight my inclination to trust him completely.

Unable to resist the desire to dwell on how it had felt when he kissed her, she allowed herself to do so at some length. It was intoxicating—it was wonderful—but she didn't know how she could face him again as though nothing had happened. Because it seemed evident he had no desire to be perceived by anyone—least of all herself—as a suitor; instead he had kissed her because he couldn't help himself.

Which was odd in its own way, come to think of it; she was an eligible young woman and it was clear he was attracted to her, despite the fact he wrestled to resist that attraction. If she was an heiress—well, that was all to the good. She was vaguely aware that under normal circumstances, a man who took such liberties would be expected to make an offer forthwith. But she knew instinctively that no such offer would be forthcoming and indeed—she told herself firmly—she would not accept one as she did not know the first thing about him, other than he had admittedly lied to her and he was not who he said he was; hardly points to be toted up in his favor. There was only one thing she knew for certain; this was not the last time she would be held in such an embrace.

With a happy smile, she pulled the coverlet over her head.

Chapter 13

The next morning, Hattie awoke, heavy-eyed, to see sunlight glinting in under the cabin door. She was not certain of the time but guessed she had slept late—the price of debauchery—and swung her legs over the side to assess Bing's state of health.

Her companion, however, was upright, dressed, and regarding herself in the small mirror hanging on the cabin wall with a critical eye. "You are recovered," Hattie proclaimed with some surprise. "I am so glad." This was to some extent insincere, but Hattie was encouraged to believe that Berry was the sort of man who could easily outfox a chaperone.

"Not as yet, my head aches abominably," Bing confessed.

"Shall we go discover whether there is a cure for the cure?" Hattie was in a fever to see what was happening up on deck, and in particular whether there were any other battle casualties.

Pinning her hat firmly on her head, Bing acquiesced. "I do have need for some fresh air, I believe—if you are willing, Hathor."

Needing no further encouragement, Hattie made ready to venture above decks before her companion could suffer a relapse. Although she was tempted to take the time to arrange her hair in a more becoming style, her desire to visit the scene of the cataclysmic events from last night took precedence, and so she quickly plaited her dark locks and decided a hat was unnecessary as it was only wont to blow off, anyway.

"You may wish to bring your parasol," Bing suggested as she eyed her bareheaded charge. "Your face is a bit brown, Hathor."

Upon emerging onto the quarterdeck, Hattie surveyed the immediate area, dutifully hoisting her parasol against the bright sunlight. Neither the captain nor Berry were in evidence, although a seaman was rinsing off the deck with a bucket and paused to tug at his cap. Hattie put her hand under Bing's elbow to steady her, and the two women walked over to the gunwale and considered the shoreline, barely visible in the distance.

Vague about the particulars of their journey, Hattie asked, "Where are we, do you suppose?"

Her companion considered, her chin on her breast. "Portugal, I imagine."

Hattie gazed with interest. "What will happen to Portugal, now?" The country had not fared well during the Peninsular War—after the betrayal by Spain it had been helpless when the French invaded and its losses had been staggering, particularly in those unfortunate towns between the port and Lisbon.

Bing held the brim of her hat against the sea breeze. "It is as yet unclear. The Congress of Vienna will make a determination—the recent unpleasantness has left matters in disarray."

Hattie made a wry mouth at the euphemism, remembering the Prussian Ambassador's heated criticism of the French Emperor. "More like one man has left matters in disarray."

"One man could not cause a war of such magnitude," Bing reminded her. "He has a plentitude of supporters."

"He *had* a plentitude of supporters, you mean—now that he is shown to be merely mortal I cannot imagine he would inspire the same devotion. Why, he is fortunate to have survived so as to be packed off to Elba rather than be summarily executed, as the Ambassador suggested."

"Undoubtedly," agreed the agreeable Bing. "There were many who demanded his blood."

Her childhood companion came to Hattie's mind, even though she hadn't thought of him for several days. "I wonder how Robbie does, and whether he will return to the Congress after the funeral."

Bing shot her a measuring glance from under the brim of her hat. "Perhaps he will rendezvous with you in Egypt, now that he is untrothed."

But Hattie would not be drawn on the subject, having relegated her old friend to the category of also-rans long before the passionate embrace of the night before. "Soon we will be in Cairo, Bing. I can hardly credit it."

Her companion looked out over the sea again. "I confess I am looking forward to seeing those things that Edward described in his letters—it is unfortunate that this journey is tempered with sadness."

"No need to be sad on my account," Hattie reminded her with a small smile. "You know I hardly knew them—why, your brother knew them better than I."

"Then we shall look to do your duty, rather than mourn."

"Edward was fond of them—you said so last night." Hattie had been awaiting just such an opening, as she wished to do a little probing.

Bing nodded. "He admired them greatly. They were

utterly dedicated, and not distracted by worldly gain—they made no attempt to capitalize on their own fame as many others did."

"You mentioned," Hattie added diffidently, "that he had some concerns about the dateline."

Bing raised her brows in surprise. "Heavens—did I?"

Hattie prompted, "I think it had to do with which pharaoh was the princess's father."

After hesitating for a moment, her companion confessed, "The Blackhouses were certain it was the great Seti, and so Edward deferred to their judgment, although he was not convinced."

"Were there discrepancies in the hieroglyphics, perhaps?" Bing's reticence to discuss the subject only fueled Hattie's curiosity; that, along with the fact that the captain had seemed inordinately interested last night.

Weighing her words, her companion said with an apologetic air, "Edward's correspondence always contained strict instruction that I was not to speak of these matters to anyone."

"I suppose he was afraid of tomb raiders," Hattie conceded, hesitant to press any further in the face of Bing's reluctance.

"Or rivals in their field, or even government agents— remember Egypt's rule has changed hands several times over; it would not do to unwittingly invite another such change of hands by boasting of a particular find. Edward did mention"— here Bing cast a glance over her shoulder so as to ensure they were not overheard—"that your parents were entering into negotiations with the British, unbeknownst to Muhammad Ali, the local viceroy who holds power at present."

Hattie considered this, but it didn't seem particularly alarming. "I suppose they knew the British would re-establish rule, sooner or later."

Bing nodded. "Apparently, it was extremely tiresome to have to be constantly reassessing who might hold control over the sites in Thebes—all the archaeologists had to be adept at politics even though they held very little interest in such things; deals had to be struck so as to continue the work that was so important to them."

Assimilating this information, Hattie steered the conversation back to the original topic. "Did Edward think the princess was from an earlier or a later dynasty?"

Bing lowered her voice and confessed, "That was the problem; in his opinion there was too little upon which to make a deduction—very few artifacts were found in her tomb. And the hieroglyphics were not particularly helpful with respect to her identity."

Even Hattie, who paid little heed to the particulars, knew the tombs were usually bursting at the seams with artifacts piled up for use in the afterlife. "Perhaps it had been raided already," she suggested.

"Not exactly. Edward seemed to think"—Bing took another cautious look around—"that there was a secret chamber, one that the Blackhouses knew of which supported their theory; but that he and the others on the site were not privy to its location."

Ah, thought Hattie, the penny drops; her parents indeed had a valuable secret—a secret chamber. Although why it was a secret was unclear; they had uncovered many such treasures in the past without such secretive measures. "Perhaps it is a particularly rich trove, and they didn't want to reveal it until they had concluded their negotiations with the British." She frowned even as she posited the theory aloud—this didn't make much sense either. Such a course would only postpone whatever outrage they feared from the current viceroy, not avoid it. Hattie was vaguely aware it was never a good idea to double-deal with the powerful local potentates—why, one could simply disappear, never to be heard from again. With this alarming thought, she stood very still for a moment and didn't hear Bing's response. Pulling herself together, she said, "I'm sorry, Bing, I was wool-gathering. What was it?"

"I confess I did wonder," Bing repeated, "if the cave-in that killed Edward and the others was an attempt to discover the secret chamber."

Meeting her companion's troubled gaze, Hattie shook her head in disagreement. "If Edward was anything like you, it seems very unlikely that he would flaunt my parents' wishes in such a way."

"That is true," Bing conceded. "He would defer to them, despite his own curiosity."

Hattie put a hand on Bing's at the railing. "Perhaps we shall discover what happened to Edward as well as my parents—solve both mysteries at once."

But Bing only shook her head a bit sadly. "I don't believe it is much of a mystery, Hathor; cave-ins are an unfortunate hazard of tunneling. I am reconciled—he died doing that which he most loved."

Hattie said nothing, not wanting to share her concerns with Bing, who was not aware of Berry's hints nor of the deadly scuffle on the deck the night before. She had little doubt that Edward's death was yet another suspicious one connected to the new excavation. Reminded, she asked, "What did Edward think about the curse?"

Bing gave her a look. "Edward was a scientist, Hathor; there are no such things as curses."

"But everyone seems to think there is, Bing—and it does seem that a great many have died, one after the other."

Bing rested her chin on her chest. "The natives are credulous, of course. It comes from centuries of tradition steeped in superstition; but as Edward would say, superstition is a crutch for the fearful."

Gazing out over the horizon, Hattie voiced aloud a thought she had entertained last night, when she was thinking about all the things she needed to think about. "In a way, the curse is almost helpful—no one would interfere with the site if they feared the wrath of the gods."

"Someone—unfortunately—was not afraid of the gods," Bing pointed out. "And your poor parents suffered for it."

"True—although I suppose it works both ways; someone may believe that it would best please the gods to kill those who desecrate the tomb."

Bing sighed. "If that is indeed the case, then it seems unlikely we will ever know the truth of what happened to your parents."

The two women stood in the sun for a few minutes, watching the distant shoreline as the boat heeled with the wind. I believe we will discover the truth, thought Hattie. Berry knows the truth—or most of it—and as much as he would like to winkle information out of me, I think I could do some winkling of my own; he is smitten, I believe. She took a glance around the deck, hoping to spy him.

"Your parasol, Hathor," Bing reminded her gently. "You will be mistaken for a native, else."

Chapter 14

H attie noted that the brisk sea air had brought a bit of color to the other woman's pale cheeks.

"Are you able to contemplate a bite to eat? I am afraid you will blow away in the breeze, Bing."

Her companion considered the suggestion without enthusiasm. "I shall make the attempt, I suppose. It is so lowering to be felled by such an embarrassing weakness."

"You shall simply have to stay on in Cairo and never board a ship again," Hattie teased. "I imagine there are plenty of excavations where they'd welcome another pair of hands."

"The excavation sites are upriver, at Thebes," Bing reminded her.

"Then gird your loins," Hattie advised with a smile. "The transport of necessity is by waterway."

"I'd rather not think of it," the other replied, and they made their way to the companionway stairs to forage for a meal.

Upon entering the officer's galley they met the captain, who was leaving but did not hesitate to turn back so as to join them. "Miss Bing; I trust you are feeling more the thing."

Bing nodded graciously. "Indeed, I am, Captain, and I thank you for your restorative, which appears to have turned the trick. I shall attempt some tea and toast."

The three had just settled into the wooden benches when Berry made an appearance. Although Hattie had been concerned about controlling her reaction when next they met, she needn't have worried—instead she felt a resurgence of that sense of exhilaration and met his eye without a flicker as he bowed in greeting. Noting his cut lip and a bruise over one eye, she asked with feigned concern, "Why, Monsieur Berry—I believe you have injured yourself."

As he seated himself across from her, he nodded in acknowledgment. "I am a clumsy fellow—I ran up against the mizzenmast last night."

Struggling to keep her countenance, Hattie dropped her gaze to her plate.

"The ship does roll about so, it is a small wonder you lost your footing," Bing offered with sympathy as tea was served. "Do you require medical attention, Monsieur Berry?"

"I have been attended to in the most satisfactory fashion," Berry replied. "And what of you? How do you go on, Mademoiselle Bing?"

"I am recovering—I am fortunate the captain shared his remedy."

"As are we all," Berry agreed.

Not to be outdone, Hattie turned to Captain Clements. "Do you experience any problems from the sharing of such close quarters? I imagine fights must break out between the men from time to time."

If the captain found the question odd, he gave no indication, instead reassuring her, "We do have a brig, but fortunately there are few problems—only the occasional contretemps. Nothing to cause concern, Miss Blackhouse."

But Berry was not so sanguine, and offered a caution. "The close quarters may inspire a different sort of problem and you must have a care, mademoiselle; sailors are rough men, unaccustomed to well-bred young women. You would not want to risk being accosted on deck."

Bing was shocked. "I am certain no one would dare, Monsieur Berry."

"Unimaginable." Hattie managed in a stifled tone.

"Egypt is another matter, however," the captain warned. "The tenets of civilized behavior are often disregarded, particularly in the remoter areas." With a proprietary gesture, he covered Hattie's hand with his own large one. "Promise me you will be very careful."

Hattie smiled to reassure him. "I will. And Monsieur Berry has agreed to provide an escort, which is much appreciated."

"*D'accord.*" Berry's gaze rested for the barest moment on the captain's hand on her own, and Hattie casually withdrew it; no need to instigate another brawl.

But the other man continued to evidence a proprietary interest in Hattie, leaning so as to place his arm across the back of the bench behind her. "Where will you travel after Cairo, Miss Blackhouse? Perhaps I will delay my return so as to provide an additional escort—I can't think of a more agreeable duty call."

But Hattie didn't wish to be constantly sorting out her suitors, and so answered vaguely, "I suppose that depends—I shall first speak to my parents' solicitor and discover from him what is best to be done."

It seemed to Hattie that the captain's gaze sharpened. "Well then, be aware that I stand at the ready to assist you in any way necessary."

"Thank you—I am truly grateful for so many supporters." Not so much supporters as importuners, she thought with a twinge of annoyance—although she could not claim to dislike Berry's importunings—hopefully she was slated to receive another dose very soon. She addressed Berry so as to divert him; he had watched her exchange with the good captain with a noted lack of enthusiasm. "Do you have any suggestions as to where we should stay in Cairo when we make port?"

The gentleman bowed his head. "It would be my pleasure to arrange for rooms at the Hotel Corsica, which caters to European visitors."

"Ah—the Hotel Corsica; a fine place. Will Mademoiselle Leone be joining you, monsieur?" The captain's question directed to Berry seemed a little pointed.

There was the barest hesitation before Berry replied. "I am not yet privy to Mademoiselle Leone's final plans."

The captain leaned in toward Bing and Hattie, cocking an eyebrow with a conspiratorial air. "A dear friend of his." He made it clear there was more to the relationship then mere friendship.

"Indeed," Berry agreed, meeting Hattie's interested gaze. "A dear friend from my hometown—in France."

"How fortuitous," she responded in a neutral tone. "France is a fine place of origin."

The captain chuckled. "You don't know the half of it."

"Shall we take a turn on deck, Hathor?" Bing had apparently decided to call a halt to the competition for Hattie's attention.

"Of course." Hattie rose immediately; contrite that she had been so busy enjoying her unspoken conversation with Berry that she had forgotten her companion's precarious state of health. "If you will excuse us, gentlemen." Bestowing a dimpled smile on both men, Hattie took Bing's arm as they exited the galley to reemerge into the bright, breezy sunlight on deck.

"I feared fisticuffs would soon break out," Bing confessed as they walked the deck, "and I'd as lief not have Monsieur Berry secured in the brig."

But Hattie disagreed in a thoughtful tone. "I don't think so, Bing—I didn't sense any real rancor; it was as though they were both playacting."

"Indeed?" Bing raised her brows, thinking about it. "How odd."

"Yes," Hattie agreed, and decided to keep her new-hatched theories about Berry and the captain to herself, for the time being.

They came to the stern and turned to make another circuit around the deck when Bing observed, "Here's one who wishes to speak with you uncontested. Shall I allow it?"

Hattie looked up to see Berry approaching in a purposeful fashion, his hands clasped behind his back. "If you would, Bing," and thought her a very satisfactory chaperone.

And so it came to pass that once again she leaned on the railing beside Berry, the sun and the breeze only adding to her delight in this turn of events while her cooperative companion found something of interest to view from the opposite deck. It soon became evident, however, that a light flirtation was not what the gentleman had in mind. Meeting her eyes very seriously, he spoke without preamble.

"Mademoiselle Blackhouse, I must beg your pardon, and assure you the events of last night will not be repeated. You are without protectors at present, and I should not have taken advantage of you in such a way."

Primming her mouth, Hattie replied, "I can only agree—I have little experience in such pastimes and felt I was at an *extreme* disadvantage."

Looking out over the sea, he suppressed a smile. "Hattie—allow me to make my apology."

"I beg your pardon," she said gravely. "Pray continue."

He bent his head for a moment, then added, "It would be best, perhaps, if such an opportunity did not arise again."

"Yes," she sighed with some regret. "It would be best, I suppose."

"I meant no insult," he explained, watching her. "The opposite, in fact."

She met his gaze in all sincerity and smiled. "I know it; we shall cry friends and not speak of it again."

Nodding, he looked away toward the sea again. Five days, she thought, keeping her expression carefully neutral—five days before he is seeking more kisses—six at the most. She had noted during his carefully rehearsed speech that he was unable to keep his gaze from resting on her mouth. Hiding a smile, she thought of it as an interesting paradox—she knew next to nothing about him but nonetheless, felt she knew him very well indeed.

He added suddenly, "Miss Leone is not what she will appear to be."

"I am unsurprised," she responded mildly. "No one is, apparently."

Responding to her tone, he turned to her. "I must ask again that you trust me; you will come to no harm at my hands."

She arched a dark brow. "No, I hold no grudge against your very capable hands."

A smile played around his mouth while he bent his head to chide her, "I thought we weren't to speak of it again."

"Your pardon," she offered, contrite. "I forget myself."

They stood together for a moment, his gaze stubbornly fixed on the deck. Since he seemed unable to move away from her, she asked, "Whose secrets do you hold? If you hold my parents' secrets, then why can you not tell me of them?"

"Hattie," he said softly, the brown eyes raised to hers. "It is best you not know, believe me."

"I would like to judge for myself whether it is best," she countered. "Were my parents double-dealing? Is that why they were killed?"

Ah, this hit home and his eyes widened in surprise. "What?"

Watching him, she revealed what she had discovered. "They were negotiating in secret with the British, I am told. I imagine Muhammad Ali would have been most displeased with such a development, if he found out about it." Belatedly, she realized her source had been Bing's Edward, and perhaps she shouldn't be giving away state secrets—or at least not until she knew what was what.

Nodding, he dropped his gaze again. "It is possible," he admitted in a neutral tone.

I did not tell him what he feared I would, she thought in surprise, and thought back over what she had just said. It was the reference to double-dealing—I startled him, at first; but why? With whom else would they be double-dealing, if not the British?

Berry lifted his head. "Once in Cairo, I would ask a favor; I would ask that you accompany me to question those who may have information but are reluctant to speak."

She blinked, but could see no harm in it and indeed, would look forward to such an outing in his company. "Willingly. Because I would have their sympathy?"

He tilted his head to the side in a now-familiar gesture. "That. And remember that you appear to them as the god-king's daughter."

This seemed altogether fanciful, and she voiced her

skepticism. "Truly? They will think I am some sort of reincarnation?" On the other hand, she was unfamiliar with local beliefs; perhaps they were indeed a credulous people, as Bing had suggested.

"Any advantage should be taken," he replied.

With an effort, she refrained from making yet another saucy remark, and merely nodded.

Chapter 15

H attie stood with Bing in the spacious lobby of the Hotel Corsica while Berry arranged for the transfer of their luggage, currently contained in a donkey cart outside.

Leaning in toward Hattie, Bing noted, "I must say it is useful to have a gentleman's assistance, Hathor."

"You will have no argument from me, my friend—it was a good thing the resourceful Monsieur Berry maneuvered his way onto the ship." Not to mention she had noted with amused delight that the aforesaid gentleman had begun to waylay Hattie with increasing frequency so as to be able to touch her. He couldn't help himself, poor man; it was that forbidden fruit effect. For her part, Hattie was content to treat him with an arm's length, casual friendliness and await the inevitable heated embrace that would put an end to the delicious tension that was building between them.

At midday, they had disembarked from the peaceful confines of the *Sophia* and had plunged into the chaotic sights and sounds of Cairo. Donkey-boys, beggars, and guides clamored for their attention as Berry ably procured a transport cart and handed them in, speaking in Arabic to the driver while his hand held Hattie's as though he had forgotten to let it go.

"Hold on to your reticule," he cautioned, tucking this accoutrement under her arm with a solicitous gesture.

"And ignore the requests to throw coins or we may be swarmed." He then sat across from her, knee touching knee. "Patience is necessary—you will find little that is done well or efficiently."

It was definitely not London or Paris; a slow progress was made to the hotel in the clogged and busy streets that twisted and turned with no apparent logic. The houses that lined the streets were high and narrow, with upper stories that projected outward. The heat was oppressive, and Hattie noted that most of the narrow streets were roofed with matting to provide a measure of shade. Hawkers shouted at them and brandished silks, brass objects, and smoking paraphernalia that did not bear close scrutiny. Caged birds called, donkeys brayed, and blocked cart drivers shouted at each other, making conversation impossible. Hattie caught Berry's gaze upon her and mustered a small smile, but in truth it was a bit daunting. I hope I can acclimate to the heat and dust, she thought, and stayed beneath her parasol with no urging from Bing.

By contrast, their hotel was an oasis of quiet and calm, and Hattie breathed in the scent of blue lotuses while they waited on the marbled tile floor for the arrangements to be made. Bing was gazing about her with extreme interest, her sharp features alight. "Quite satisfactory," she pronounced. "And so wonderfully warm."

To each his own, thought Hattie, who for her part was hoping the city was suffering from an unusual heat wave. But there was no denying that Bing's color was much improved and she offered, "You are finally back on *terra firma*, poor Bing."

"It is amazing how quickly the discomfort disappears; I own I am eager to reconnoiter, now that we have arrived."

Berry approached with the keys to their room, which he distributed to the ladies, his fingers lingering on Hattie's in the process. "The porter will deliver your trunks to the room—do you think we can plan on meeting for dinner in the hotel restaurant after you have settled in this afternoon?"

"We can," agreed Hattie. "Unless you would like to escort me to visit my parents' solicitor this afternoon? I confess I am eager to meet with him as soon as may be." Now that they were here, she was impatient to take action—not to mention such a visit would provide further opportunities to build upon that delicious tension that crackled between them.

But he declined with a shake of his head. "It will be more *serviable* to meet him in the cooler morning, which is when most business matters are handled." He then added in a neutral tone, "I'm afraid it would be for the best if you do not mention that you travel with me."

"Such a shame that the two of you do not get along," Hattie noted, eyeing him.

"*Quel dommage,*" he agreed, refusing to rise to the bait. "But I will provide an escort to his office, if you will permit."

"Thank you. I suppose the morning is soon enough." He took her hand briefly as they parted, and ran his thumb over its back.

Hattie and Bing ascended the main stairway and found their room, which was well-appointed and spacious—the walls white-washed in the manner of all the buildings in the area. Across the room, French doors opened to a small balcony and Hattie went out to lean on the railing and view the busy street below. Everything was so different—the heat, the noise, the manner of the people milling about— Syrians, Egyptians, Greeks. She looked down upon it in wonderment. "Come see, Bing—it is extraordinary." Her companion joined her and they contemplated the chaos below them. Teasing her, Hattie asked, "Is it worth the miserable voyage?"

"Absolutely," said the redoubtable Bing. "I have always longed to make this journey, but never thought to have the opportunity."

Yes, thought Hattie as she looked out over the noisy throng. It has not been easy for either one of us to be the ones observing from a distance, sharing only vicariously in the excitement. Spying a small clothing establishment across the way, Hattie asked, "Should we journey over to the shops?"

"We should," said Bing agreeably. "I believe it is time to cast off my blacks."

The next half hour was spent rummaging through cottons, silks, and linens in the small stall that was stacked to overflowing with clothing items. In dire need of hot weather clothes, Hattie considered some pretty gauze blouses and lightweight skirts and as she held up a blouse to gauge for size, she noticed that a man in a turban was narrowly watching her from the back entryway. Uncowed, she met his gaze with her own level one and he immediately turned and disappeared out the back. Reminded that perhaps she shouldn't be making her presence quite so obvious, she signaled to Bing that they should complete their purchases. They had no local money, but the proprietor indicated in an obsequious manner that English funds were acceptable and that it would delight him beyond measure to wait upon them. Before the transaction was completed, however, Berry appeared and smoothly interceded with the result that the proprietor returned some of their coins with gestures that were meant to be interpreted as apologies for a mere misunderstanding.

Taking up their packets for them, Berry remarked with

polite diffidence, "In the future, it may be best not to wander without an escort, mademoiselle."

"I did have a qualm," Bing confessed, "but as it was only across the way I thought there would be no harm done."

"My fault entirely," volunteered Hattie in a cheerful tone, anticipating the effect her new clothes would have on Berry. "I commandeered poor Bing when she would much rather be taking in the sights."

Bing confessed, "I do hope to visit the Great Pyramids whilst we are here." They waited for a dray to pass before crossing the busy street, and Berry placed his hand on the small of Hattie's back, where it remained as they followed Bing toward the hotel.

Berry offered, "The hotel can make arrangements for a tour of Giza—I believe they are held nearly every day."

The prospect did not excite Hattie, who never could muster much interest in the subject that had served to captivate her parents at the expense of herself. The events of recent history, by contrast, seemed much more compelling—particularly as the world had just survived a bloody war. "Were the pyramids damaged in the Battle of the Pyramids?"

"Not at all," Bing replied. "The battle did not actually occur at the Giza site—Napoleon called it such so that it would seem more historic."

Hattie found such a deception rather juvenile, and expressed her disapproval. "It seems so—so *pushing*; to be so preoccupied with establishing one's place in history—rather like the pharaohs and their grandiose tombs. It speaks of a full measure of self-absorption."

"Indeed; and I imagine Napoleon is very much vexed about the forced curtailment of his plans," Bing replied in a dry tone. "A man such as he does not concede easily—wouldn't you say, Monsieur Berry?"

Berry had listened without comment to their conversation as he held the hotel door for them. "I would," he agreed. "A foe *formidable.*"

"Did you serve in the Coalition, monsieur?" asked Hattie, curious as to his allegiance and hoping for a hint of his mysterious origins.

"I did," he answered. "Shall we look to sit at eight o'clock?"

But Hattie would not be put off. "On whose side did you serve?" She could hear Bing's small sound of dismay at such indelicacy.

"The winning side," he explained patiently. "*Naturellement.*"

Chapter 16

The next morning saw them arrive at the solicitor's office, situated on the second floor over a busy apothecary shop in the El Khalil area of Cairo. Hattie ascended the steps with Bing while Berry explained that he would take coffee at a nearby café and wait while Hattie conducted her business. Hattie found that she was anxious to finally address Mr. Bahur, who could hopefully cast some light on the uncertainties she faced; she would very much like to obtain some advice that was untempered by whatever motivations were driving all the others.

They entered an outer antechamber manned by a young clerk who looked up in surprise from his cluttered desk. Bemused, he leapt up and stumbled over a stack of files as he introduced himself to Hattie. Doesn't often entertain young women, she thought, hiding a smile. He took her hand reverently and upon hearing her name exclaimed, "Why—how fortunate that you are here in Cairo, Miss Blackhouse; you must be wondering what on earth has happened to your books. I'm afraid the fault is mine—well, not entirely—but I will willingly shoulder the blame."

With a hurried movement, he turned to clear several stacks of rolled documents from a small table and indicated an unlabeled package of moderate size that had rested beneath them.

"My books?" asked Hattie, at sea. "Which books are these?"

"From your parents," the clerk explained. "They wanted them delivered to you but unfortunately the man at the post labeled them 'Coventry' instead of 'Cornwall' and they were returned last week—I was so annoyed when they arrived with the 'Improper Address' notation. I have not yet wrapped them up anew and I do apologize for the delay—unforgivable."

"Pray do not concern yourself," Bing soothed. "We have been traveling and would not have known the difference."

But Hattie wasn't paying attention as her gaze was fixed on the package which, she imagined, was the approximate size of a strongbox. What to do? She couldn't carry it away; Berry would guess in an instant and she needed to think this over. Dimpling at the clerk, she asked, "Will you store them here in your office a bit longer? I will send someone for them shortly—there is so little room at our hotel."

"Certainly," the young man agreed, eager to do whatever she bade.

Hattie leaned in toward him. "Tell no one," she instructed in a low tone. "They are a gift." She did not explain for whom and fortunately the clerk did not presume to ask.

They stood in the anteroom while the young man went in to announce them to the solicitor. Hattie glanced briefly at her companion in the ensuing silence. "Pray do not mention the books to anyone."

"I wouldn't think of it," said Bing.

The door to the solicitor's office was flung open in a dramatic manner and a tall, thin man dressed in a very fine suit of linen stared at them. It was apparent to Hattie that beneath his implacable façade he was suffering from a strong emotion. "Miss Blackhouse," he said in a quiet tone. "I cannot tell you how pleased I am to finally behold you."

"Sir," responded Hattie, sketching a bow. She couldn't help but note the man had a recent scar that ran from the corner of his eye down his cheek; she had little doubt as to who had bestowed it.

"Won't you come in? Your visit is fortuitous—we dispatched an agent to seek you out in England only to discover that you were not at home." He said it as though annoyed that she had inconvenienced him, and Hattie had to tamp down a hostile retort. Apparently, everyone else had converged on Cornwall but—for once in her life—she was not there; it would be ironic if it weren't so ominous.

The solicitor addressed Bing rather abruptly. "You are the young lady's guardian?"

Hattie forestalled Bing's answer, not appreciating the man's patronizing attitude. "No, sir; Miss Bing is my companion."

The man made a gesture toward the door. "Then I am afraid I must ask you to wait without, madam. The matters upon which we speak are privileged."

Hattie nodded at Bing, who shot her a glance that promised reinforcements if reinforcements were needed; apparently she had sized up the solicitor and had also found him off-putting. I should find out how much Bing is paid, Hattie thought as the woman departed; and double it forthwith.

Hattie was then seated while the solicitor shuffled some documents on his desk, gathering his thoughts in a cool manner despite the heat that seemed to radiate from the white plastered walls. Hattie could only be grateful for her gauze blouse and light muslin skirt, newly purchased. I don't see how anyone becomes accustomed, she thought; one constantly feels like a damp washrag.

The man raised his eyes and smiled a dry little smile that did not reach his eyes. Rather than wait for him to speak she said into the silence, "I imagine if you had any information about my parents I would have heard."

The man spread his hands. "Yes, of course—I am terribly sorry, Miss Blackhouse, but I fear we must assume the worst. It has been several months, and if they were able, they certainly would have contacted me."

"A search has been mounted?"

He pressed his lips together and again, she held the impression he was disguising his extreme displeasure. "I assure you, I am not the only person who has been assiduously attempting to locate them, but to no avail."

"I would like to visit the site in an attempt to trace their movements." The words came out almost without conscious volition, but Hattie realized she had been anticipating such a journey all along. The tedious god-king's daughter was to have yet another pilgrim—there was truly no help for it. Remembering Berry's suggestion, she offered, "Perhaps those who were reluctant to speak to the authorities would be more willing to speak to me."

With almost grudging approval, the man nodded slowly. "A very good idea, actually. On my end, however, I will need some information to begin the proceedings that will allow the authorities to release your parents' effects to you."

Hattie shifted in her seat and reflected that once again she was to be fending off questions about her parents' effects— and from their solicitor, of all people. Warily, she replied, "So soon? I always assumed missing persons could not be pronounced dead for years."

He made a vague gesture with his hand. "There are exigent circumstances which allow the procedure to be expedited—when there are minor children, for example."

Hattie corrected him, "I am turned eighteen, and not a minor."

His vague gesture was replaced with a sharp one of annoyance. "Miss Blackhouse, may I remind you this would be in your best interests? I would not be doing my job unless I move quickly to help you make all necessary arrangements in this difficult time. I owe it to your parents."

Hattie did not argue further, feeling she oughtn't defy him on this—and at least he wasn't quizzing her about the strongbox, which ironically appeared to reside in his antechamber. "And I do appreciate your efforts, sir. Do I need to sign any papers?"

Mollified, he moderated his tone and re-aligned the ink-well on his desk with careful fingers. "I understand you are in possession of a password—a password that is necessary to obtain access to the safe deposit boxes."

There was a small silence while Hattie knit her brow and stared at him. "I am not certain I understand you."

The man stared in return, his voice once again sharp. "Surely you were given this information?"

Shaking her head she disclaimed, "No, I am afraid I was informed of no password."

The solicitor's eyes narrowed as he watched her closely. "Did not your parents send you correspondence? And this was not mentioned?"

Hattie met his gaze, unblinking. "I did receive the occasional correspondence, but I was informed of no password."

The opaque eyes continued to study her and she had to suppress a sudden impulse to call out to Bing for reinforcements. Steady, she thought; you must sort this out on your own. You do not know whom to trust—even Berry, who watches you and remembers that kiss. Lifting her chin, she met the solicitor's gaze with her own level one.

"I must insist," the man said with restrained menace, "that you turn over any correspondence of recent months."

"Perhaps the letter was lost in the mail," she suggested with a hint of steel. "Or was sent to their solicitor in England."

"An unlikely possibility," he ground out. Hattie had the impression he was struggling to refrain from leaping across the desk to strangle her.

Striving to appear unafraid and unconcerned, she waited. "Is there anything else that is needful at present?"

With an obvious effort, he pulled himself together and rose. "Allow me to draw a draft for your expenses. Wait here and I shall return shortly." He then left the room and Hattie waited, the voices from the shop below floating up through the louvered windows. Impossible not to think of the letter her mother had sent four months ago, the text memorized word-for-word. "*My dear Hathor,*" it had said—her mother did not use her nickname, "*I trust this letter finds you well. We are in the process of archiving the tomb of Seti's daughter as you may have heard. I have discovered a disk that depicts Hathor and I thought you might like to keep it about you. It has great significance and is very valuable, so please do not misplace it. Use it in the event you ever need to identify yourself to Mr. Bahur, our solicitor in Cairo. Very truly yours, Mother.*"

Hattie was careful to resist the urge to pull the disk from where it was hidden under her blouse and examine it yet again, in the event she was being watched. On one side of the disk was a crude figure of Hathor; on the other were engraved markings—not hieroglyphics, at least as far as she could tell. She hadn't known what they meant and still did not—only that every instinct told her not to present it to this man, just as her instinct had told her not to confess its existence to Berry. I do not know enough, she thought; and I cannot like how events are unfolding.

Returning with a draft on the bank in hand, the solicitor handed it to her, and she nodded her thanks and stood to leave. "Where do you stay in the city, Miss Blackhouse?"

She almost didn't want to tell him, but decided she was being fanciful. "The Hotel Corsica."

"Good," he nodded with approval. "An excellent establishment—if you have need of anything please do not hesitate to contact me." After a small pause, he then added, "If my manner was a bit brusque I must beg you to forgive me—I am over-anxious about your parents."

Not believing this change of tack for a moment, Hattie smiled her dimpled smile and sincerely hoped she would never have need to speak to him again as long as she lived. "Of course—I am sorry I am unable to be of further assistance." With an effort, she refrained from fleeing, but instead walked from the room at a dignified pace.

Chapter 17

Exiting into the clerk's antechamber, Hattie rejoined Bing and resisted the urge to depart with all speed, instead pausing to bid a friendly farewell to the young man who hovered, awaiting an opportunity to take her hand yet again. As Hattie descended the steps to the first floor she looked immediately for Berry, who stood on the crowded walkway out front, waiting for her with a watchful eye. Taking his proffered arm, she offered in a dry tone, "Such an amiable creature—it is a shame his face is disfigured."

As they began their progress down the bazaars he took a sharp look around. "What did he say?"

Glancing up at him sidelong, she quizzed, "Oh—so now I am to tell you?"

He rendered a small smile. "Yes."

She allowed her exasperation to show. "Why? You tell me *nothing.*"

Tilting his head, he checked to ensure that Bing was not within earshot and then closed his arm so that her hand was pressed tightly to his side. "What would you like to know?"

"What is your true name?"

He considered the question in silence and she was curious to see what he would say, as he was making his professed attempt to be honest with her. "It is not Berry."

"I am unsurprised, my friend. Can't you say?"

With sincere regret, he met her gaze with his own. "No. I cannot."

While she was preparing another, less controversial question she was hailed from the crowd. "Miss Blackhouse! I beg a moment—please."

She turned in surprise to see that she was approached by a stout Egyptian man wearing a white linen suit and a red fez, vigorously waving at her.

"Mr. Hafez, the Minister of Antiquities," Berry said in her ear.

She smiled in greeting but said in a low voice, "Friend or foe?"

He shook his head. "I cannot say," and Hattie was left to wonder if this was because he truly didn't know or because he didn't wish to tell her.

Stopping before her, the panting man took her hand in both of his. "Miss Blackhouse—I am truly honored to make your acquaintance. I asked at the hotel and I took the liberty of searching for you."

Unfortunately, the man's hands were damp and Hattie hid a twinge of distaste. "How may I be of service, sir?"

Flourishing a handkerchief, the minister paused to recover his breath, mopping the perspiration from his brow. "A regrettable business—may I beg a moment of your time?"

After introductions were performed, they adjourned to a nearby café where lemonade was procured for the ladies. Hattie was then required to listen patiently while Hafez expressed his sincere admiration for her parents and his gratified feelings upon making her acquaintance. He then concluded, "I am sorry to intrude, Miss Blackhouse, but I am at a loss and I am hoping you may be of assistance."

Deeply regretting the interruption of her conversation with Berry, Hattie tried to urge the talkative man to the point. "Do you wish to speak of my parents' disappearance?"

The other sighed hugely, his massive chest rising and falling so that Hattie feared for his buttons. "Indeed. I have secured the site, but am now at a loss. Have you had any communication with them that would shed light on what has happened?"

Hattie did not answer the question directly, but instead shook her head. "I have just come from their solicitor's office and he has already quizzed me on that subject at length, I'm afraid."

Crestfallen, the gentleman emanated another huge sigh and shifted his over-large frame in the small café chair. "It is a true mystery," he noted sadly. "Such wonderful people."

Witnessing his severe disappointment, Hattie was struck by a thought. "Do you report to Muhammad Ali—is it he who holds authority over the site?"

"Indeed," he nodded, spreading his hands. "Although it is a delicate business, at present. There are vying concerns..." His voice trailed off.

Hattie nodded in turn and was forced to reconsider her half-formed theory—it would seem that if her parents were killed for double-dealing with the British behind Ali's back, his minister would probably not be chasing her down in the street, obviously distraught and eager to unearth the particulars. Perhaps her theory was not a valid one, then.

"An unsettling situation," the minister mused as he sadly studied his hands. "Most unfortunate."

Hattie noted that Berry offered no contribution, and it occurred to her he rarely did—choosing always to listen, instead. In the absence of any guidance from his corner, she decided to test her other theories. "Did any artifacts go missing along with my parents?"

Shocked, Hafez assured her, "Your parents would never steal the artifacts, Miss Blackhouse—unthinkable."

"You misunderstand," Hattie quickly corrected him. "I wondered if perhaps theft was the object and my parents were casualties of a random crime."

Straightening up, it appeared the minister was affronted by the implied insult. "The site is very secure—more secure than most. I have my best men standing guard—the Blackhouses deserved no less—and there have been no reports of attempted theft."

"I understand," offered Bing to soothe him, "that the princess's tomb has a dearth of artifacts to begin with."

The minister turned in his chair and regarded Bing for the first time. "That is true," he admitted, showing some surprise that she would be aware. "And as it does not appear the tomb has been raided, perhaps the princess's gender and age would explain the lack of riches."

"Although I do believe there were several Isisian pieces of exquisite workmanship." Bing apparently felt a need to mitigate the perceived slight against the anonymous princess.

"Indeed, fair lady; I have heard the same from those on site." Recognizing a fellow enthusiast, the minister smiled upon Bing, and then saddened again. "But by all reports the Blackhouses have vanished without a trace and the status of the tomb is in limbo. I am nearly beside myself"—he turned to Hattie in apology—"which is why I must press you, Miss Blackhouse; if you have any information—even if it seems of little importance, I must ask that you share it with me."

Hattie knit her brow in puzzlement—not only from the startling discovery that anyone would describe Bing as a "fair lady," but also from the complete absence of any information surrounding her parents' disappearance. "It does seem very strange that no one has come forward—they were very recognizable people, after all. Surely some-one must know something."

The minister leaned forward. "Perhaps you can be of influence, Miss Blackhouse."

This was what Berry had intimated—she could make a personal appeal for information as the bereft daughter. "Yes—I will help in any way I can."

The party sat in silence for a moment, Hafez drumming his fingers on the table, deep in thought. "Your ring," observed Bing. "Is it a sacred scarab?"

"Yes." He took it off and handed it over for her inspection. "A cat's eye sapphire, recovered from the statue of Osiris in Abu Simbel."

Bing examined it reverently and Hattie decided her conversation with Berry could wait; Bing had found an unexpected admirer. Feigning interest, she listened with half an ear as the two discussed the artifacts found in the main temple at Abu Simbel, many years ago. Across the narrow street she noted the man in the turban from the day before, leaning in a doorway and smoking, watching her. Hattie turned to Berry and indicated the man with a tilt of her head. "Have you an acquaintanceship with that gentleman?"

Light brown eyes met hers. "Which gentleman is that, mademoiselle?"

Hattie turned but discovered that the turbaned man had disappeared. "Ah—he has left. Perhaps his name is not Berry, also."

"I would not be surprised. You were going to tell me of your conversation with the solicitor."

"Which conversation is that, monsieur?"

But he was in no mood for teasing. "These are dangerous people," he reminded her quietly. "Make no mistake."

Suddenly exasperated, she retorted, "But I am not to know who they are or why they are dangerous or what any of this has to do with me. I will hear no more of your dire warnings, if you please." Angrily, she turned a shoulder on him.

Bing glanced at her in surprise and Hattie realized she had spoken out too loudly. Subsiding, she refused to look at Berry and tried to pay attention to the tiresome details under discussion—for the love of *heaven*, what difference did any of it make? It was thirty centuries ago—let the poor girl molder in her tomb and have done. Realizing that Bing was hastily gathering her things in preparation to depart, she was ashamed of herself for interrupting her companion's *tête-à-tête* with her new admirer and so to repair this lapse she asked, "Will you visit the pyramids, Bing? Perhaps Mr. Hafez can make a recommendation."

"Assuredly," the minister beamed as he contemplated Bing. "I will insist upon organizing a private tour for you—I can see to it that you will receive every consideration. Would tomorrow be too soon?"

"I'm afraid I am too fatigued," confessed Hattie, who had never been fatigued in her life. "I intend to catch up on my correspondence tomorrow in my room."

Bing firmly delivered her regrets. "Thank you, Mr. Hafez, but I am a companion to Miss Blackhouse and I cannot leave her unattended."

Taking her cue, Hattie urged, "Please go ahead, Bing. I will stay indoors and do some reading—I truly do not intend to go out tomorrow." Definitely nowhere with any overly secretive and extremely vexing persons who did not hail from France; that went without saying.

Bing was thus persuaded and despite her annoyance with him, Hattie shot an amused glance at Berry as her companion took the minister's proffered arm when they began to head back to the hotel. He leaned down to remark, "Here is an unexpected turn of events."

Hattie unbent enough to comment, "Perhaps I shall be called upon to chaperone my chaperone."

"She would tell him nothing she shouldn't?"

Thinking it over, Hattie realized there was every possibility. Setting aside her pique, she conceded, "Perhaps. Edward relayed some information in confidence."

"You might wish to caution her, then," he advised, his expression unreadable.

Hattie eyed him. "Are you saying the Egyptian minister is another to be included in your lengthy list of dangerous people?"

"At the risk of incurring your wrath again, I will only say it is best to remain cautious."

Hattie made a sound of extreme impatience, but said nothing further. She regretted losing her temper with him and knew she was on edge because she wasn't certain what to do; she had been pinning her now-dashed hopes on her parents' loathsome solicitor and to add to her dilemma, the mysterious strongbox had apparently made an appearance.

"What is it?" he asked softly, watching her.

"Nothing," she replied, and wished it were true.

Chapter 18

"We may have solved the problem of what is to be done with you, Bing."

Her companion, always straightforward, did not pretend to misunderstand the reference. "A very nice man—we have a common interest, is all." Hattie could not help but note that the other's cheeks were a bit pink.

They were preparing for bed in their chamber after spending a satisfactory afternoon exploring the bazaars and making a few frivolous purchases. Berry had been in dutiful attendance and had taken every opportunity to guide Hattie with a hand on the small of her back on those occasions when Bing was unable to observe such a maneuver. There had been no mention of the solicitor, her missing parents, or the tedious mummy and as a result of this combination of happy events Berry was now back in her good graces.

"Are the plans to see the pyramids in train?" Hattie had a keen interest in the excursion; she gauged that with Bing in distant Giza she would hopefully soon feel more than Berry's warm hand on her back. It has been seven days since his apology on the ship and she was aware, in the way that women are, that his self-imposed restraint was fast coming to an end.

With a brisk movement, Bing shook out her coverlet.

"Yes—we are to meet downstairs tomorrow morning. You are most welcome to join us, Hathor, if you change your mind."

"Heavens, Bing; I would be bored beyond imagining and therefore likely to cut the visit short—a most unsatisfactory gooseberry."

"Mr. Hafez and I have no need for a gooseberry, Hathor." Bing was very much on her dignity as she turned down the lamp.

Resisting the temptation to tease Bing about her new beau, Hattie instead adopted a thoughtful manner as she lifted the coverlet to climb into her bed. "It does not appear that the minister is aware of Edward's secret chamber—did you note?"

Bing nodded in the dim lamplight. "Yes. Although recall that Edward was not himself certain of its existence."

"Unless…" Hattie added slowly. "Unless Mr. Hafez was probing to see how much we knew." She cast Bing a covert glance.

Bing stood for a moment, thoughtful. "It would be best to be circumspect, Hathor—a good point."

After debating for a silent moment, Hattie decided that in all good conscience she should give her companion some warning. "Monsieur Berry seems to believe there are dangerous forces at work, and that we must be very careful."

But the revelation did not alarm Bing, who only nodded in agreement as she climbed into bed. "I would not be surprised if that was indeed the case. Wherever there is treasure there are those who would do evil." It was her companion's turn to render a covert glance. "A provoking man, Monsieur Berry."

But Hattie only laughed as she plumped her pillow. "Come, Bing—you are as aware as anyone it is my own wretched temper at fault; Monsieur Berry is anything but provoking."

"I see," replied Bing in a level tone.

Hattie sighed, wrapping her arms around her knees as she sat in her bed. "I don't know whom to trust in this business, and it puts me on edge."

"No blame for it—what with all the talk of hidden treasure and ancient curses."

"And the odious solicitor—don't forget him."

"Indeed." Bing hesitated, then added, "In turn, I must mention that I am not certain Monsieur Berry has been entirely forthright with us."

You don't know the half of it, thought Hattie. Aloud, she replied, "Not to worry, Bing—I am aware that the mysterious Monsieur Berry has not been forthright. He has admitted as much to me."

"I wondered if perhaps he works for the Prefect of Police."

Hattie lay down and studied the ceiling in the darkness, her arms crossed behind her head. "You believe he is a law enforcement officer?"

"It is only an impression—but there is little that he does not notice."

Hattie thought this over, but was met with the undeniable fact that Berry could not work for the French Prefect because—unbeknownst to Bing—Berry was not French. Hattie's working theory was that he was some sort of spy— he and the captain, both—only it was unclear whose interests he represented; one thing was for certain, he was definitely not English. "An intriguing idea," she responded, and decided all puzzles could await the morning—she was tired.

She awoke some time later and wondered if it was morning already. The room was enveloped in darkness, however, with the lamp still burning low. Hattie realized she had been awakened by a soft sound and, lying still, she heard it again. Suddenly wide awake, she carefully raised herself on her elbow, her eyes straining into the darkness. In the dim light she could make out a figure crouched down near the wardrobe toward the foot of her bed and her mouth went dry. Craven, she thought—take hold of yourself. "You there," she said loudly, reaching around for something to use as a weapon. "Identify yourself."

Several things then happened in rapid succession; the figure sprang upright and, after a moment's hesitation, made straight for Hattie, who screeched in alarm and scrambled to the other side of the bed. Her attacker was revealed to be an Egyptian man in native garb, who reached across the bed to grasp her arm roughly while Hattie unsuccessfully twisted to avoid him. He dragged her across the bed while Hattie furiously punched at him with her free hand until Bing's voice rang out. "Halt," she commanded. "I am armed and I will shoot."

It was unclear whether the intruder spoke English, but he ignored Bing and wrapped his arms around Hattie, wrestling her toward the door. Hattie sank her teeth into his wrist just as a loud report sounded; Bing had fired. The intruder yelped, although Hattie wasn't certain if he had been shot or merely bitten, and Hattie pulled herself free long enough to leap toward Bing who stood unflinching, holding her pistol on the intruder. The balcony doors were suddenly flung open and the turbaned man appeared, hesitating in the dimness as he took in the scene. Hattie gasped to Bing, "Don't shoot the new one," just as the original intruder decided a retreat was in order. He ran at the turbaned man, knocking him back, then leapt over him to disappear through the balcony doors, the turbaned man up again and hot on his heels.

Hattie stood with Bing, her heart hammering in the sudden silence, and before either could speak the door to the room burst open and Berry appeared in his shirt sleeves, his own pistol drawn.

"They both went out the balcony," Hattie pointed.

Berry went to peer over the balcony into the night as he secured his pistol into his belt. Turning to them he said, "Stay here until I return—do not leave." Alarmed voices could be heard in the hallway as the two women nodded. It seemed to Hattie that Berry's gaze lingered on her *dishabille* just before he leapt over the balcony railing, hanging for a moment on the wrought iron supports before jumping down to the street below. Hattie stepped over to watch his figure disappear around a corner but Bing drew her back with a hand on her arm. "Best we lock these doors, Hathor."

Once inside, Hattie regarded Bing with approval, the blood still coursing in her veins from all the excitement. "Did you shoot him?"

"No; I merely wanted to frighten him away."

"You are amazing." Hattie was all admiration.

"Not at all," Bing disclaimed. "Are you hurt, Hathor? Come over to the lantern so that we can assess."

A group of guests were huddled outside their broken door, and Hattie decided she should pull on her robe, although she couldn't help but be pleased that Berry had been given an opportunity to glimpse her pretty nightdress. A proprietor from the hotel pushed through the guests and approached them with concern. "Ladies," he said in heavily accented English. "What has happened?"

"An intruder," said Bing succinctly. "Routed out the balcony."

Both the hotel proprietor and the crowd expressed their dismay and outrage at such a turn of events, and the door's broken lock was examined. "I will post a guard," the man announced. "Rest assured you will be undisturbed the remainder of the night, and tomorrow we will repair the door."

"Thank you," said Hattie, and the room eventually

cleared, the spectators murmuring among themselves in the manner of people who did not yet wish to relinquish their shock and outrage.

Bing asked, "Is there anything missing, Hathor? Jewelry, perhaps?"

As Hattie owned little jewelry, an inventory took only a moment. "No. Nothing appears to be missing." How fortunate that she had left the package at the solicitor's—it seemed beyond coincidental that this raid took place after her meeting with Mr. Bahur, who had made it clear that he was aware she was withholding information—information that he desperately needed. I should share my conclusions with Berry, she thought, although if he hasn't reached the same conclusions on his own I wash my hands of him.

Perched on the foot of Bing's bed, she settled in to wait for Berry's return. "And who was the other gentleman?" asked Bing as though she was only mildly curious.

"I have seen him speaking with Monsieur Berry," Hattie explained. Not exactly true, but she'd rather not confess to Bing that the man had been monitoring her movements for two days.

After an hour, Berry tapped at the door and the guard allowed him in on Hattie's nod.

"You are unhurt?" he asked, assessing her with a brief glance.

"Yes." Little doubt that she would have bruises on her arm tomorrow but, she reflected with satisfaction, the intruder in turn would sport teeth marks so she felt she had won the encounter.

"Is anything missing?" His gaze was on Hattie, intent.

Hattie shook her head and Bing offered with some severity, "I am not certain the motive was robbery; I believe he had fell intent—he was attempting to seize Hathor and force her out the door."

Berry's eyes flew to Hattie's for verification and she could sense his surprise. Whatever the concerns were that had prompted him to post a guard to watch her movements, he had not anticipated abduction.

"Did you catch him?" asked Hattie.

Berry shook his head in chagrin. "He was very elusive."

Not a straight answer, noted Hattie; naturally. There was no point in asking any further questions—she had gone this route too many times before.

Berry indicated he needed to speak to the authorities and assured the ladies they would be safe if they remained in the room. After they agreed to meet upon the morrow, he took his leave with a last, enigmatic glance at Hattie, which she could not interpret.

Bing surveyed the chamber, her hands on her hips. "I will pull a chair against the door, Hathor, just as a precaution."

Hattie teased, "He wouldn't dare try again—he would be shot through."

Reminded, Bing searched for the bullet and used a hair pick to pry it out of the plaster, where it had lodged. "I hope we will not be charged for the damage."

Hattie crawled back into bed, although it seemed unlikely she would sleep for the remainder of the night. "It was certainly not our fault, Bing—although I wouldn't mention that it was Monsieur Berry who broke down the door." Thinking on it, Hattie decided he had made a very dashing appearance as he burst into the room to her rescue. She had noted with interest that his hastily clad shirt revealed hair on his chest—a bit darker than his hair color. Flinging back the coverlet, she decided that the room was over-warm and restlessly tried to find a more comfortable position.

Chapter 19

T he next morning, slivers of sunlight filtered in through the closed louvers as Hattie opened her eyes. The events of the preceding night came flooding back and she sat up, sleepy but determined to seek out Berry to discuss the solicitor's role in her attempted abduction. With some regret, she realized that Bing was now likely to cancel her visit to the pyramids and therefore there would be no opportunity for a private *tête-à-tête*. A shame—she was certain the man was nearly to the breaking point.

After casting a glance at her sleeping companion, Hattie decided to exit the bed and begin dressing in the hope that her movements would awaken Bing. Unfortunately, this gambit did not succeed and so Hattie was forced to drop her hairbrush with a clatter on the tile floor.

Bing responded sleepily, "You needn't be quiet, Hathor—I am awake."

With complete insincerity, Hattie replied, "I am so sorry, Bing—you must be tired."

But apparently Bing had her own motivations and was not loath to rise. "I will nap later; let us discover if there is any news from last night."

A short time later, the two women descended to the dining room for breakfast. Bing alerted the front desk that they were out of the room so that the door could be repaired and, after inquiry, discovered there was no further news about last night's intruder; the proprietor had not contacted the authorities on Berry's assurance that he would do the honors.

Doubtful, concluded Hattie—Berry is about as likely to hand this over to the Egyptian authorities as he is to tell me from whence he hails or for whom he acts. Further inquiry revealed that Berry had left the premises, and had left no message. Deflated, Hattie passed a desultory hour with Bing at the breakfast table before Hafez made his appearance, expecting to visit the pyramids.

"I must beg your pardon," Bing explained, "but we have experienced untoward events and I fear I must postpone our visit."

Upon his exclamations, Hattie had to sit through yet another recital of the intrusion, all the while keeping an impatient eye on the door. While she could concede that Berry may have other concerns that were more pressing than waiting attendance on herself, he must be aware she was in a fever to speak to him—among other fevers best not examined too closely; mainly she was longing to have him maul her about again.

"It is of all things alarming," the minister pronounced in dismay after Bing concluded her tale. "You are to be commended for staying with Miss Blackhouse today in her distress."

Hattie blinked, as the man must be blind to think she was distraught as opposed to merely bored. "Pray do not stay here on my account, Bing," she offered, trying not to sound as though she were pleading.

"I cannot be easy, Hathor—we shall stay close to home today."

Crossly, Hattie surmised that the fact Bing's new admirer

was also close to hand made the decision all that much easier. I am slated to play gooseberry, she thought; a pox on the intruder for upsetting my plan to negotiate a surrender with the weakening Monsieur Berry.

With a small bow, the minister gallantly offered his protection and support. "May I entertain you ladies in some way? Perhaps a game of cards?"

"There is a chessboard in the lobby," Hattie suggested with some hope; it would provide a lengthy distraction and Bing did play, although Hattie had a gift for the game and regularly beat her.

"Only two can play," Bing pointed out.

"I shall keep score," offered Hattie promptly, "being as how I am distraught."

"There is no score to keep," noted Bing, giving her a look.

"Then I will watch and learn," countered Hattie. "And procure the refreshments."

Bing surrendered to Hattie's machinations and the minister was escorted to the chessboard, which was set up near a large window in the lobby, the morning sunlight splashing across the game table. As Hafez and Bing were seated, Hattie decided to perch upon the window seat where she could keep a weather eye on the front door without making it too obvious that this was her intent.

The mechanical fan slowly turned overhead as the players set up the pieces, and Hafez asked, "Did the intruder come away with any personal items, Miss Blackhouse?"

For the love of heaven, Hattie thought; not another one. "No—nothing was taken." To turn the subject and boost Bing's stock, she added, "Miss Bing fired her pistol at him and he retreated in disarray."

While Bing blushed and disclaimed, Hattie listened to

Hafez's professions of admiration and wondered why he had asked the question—perhaps he was yet another searcher for the mysterious strongbox, which she should probably try to examine before any further ruckuses ensued. With an inward sigh, she recognized that she would be forced to trust someone soon and very much wished to follow her inclination to trust he-who-was-not-named-Berry. Although perhaps the minister could be trusted—presumably he sought only what was best for her parents and for Egypt. Berry did not seem to think this the best tack, but then again, Berry may be attempting to throw dust in her eyes. Reminded, she asked, "Are you aware of the tragic news with respect to Madame Auguste, Mr. Hafez?"

Taking his gaze from the board, the minister looked up at her in surprise. "No—what is the news?"

"I'm afraid she died recently in Paris—rather suddenly."

The minister stared at her in dismay and Hattie decided his surprise was genuine. She continued, "I am so sorry—I understand you were acquainted with the lady and her late husband."

"Yes, indeed—a tragedy—a terrible tragedy." He uttered the words in sincere sorrow and dropped his gaze, much affected. "Such fine people."

"Who has replaced Monsieur Auguste as your Ministry's liaison with the Blackhouses?" asked Bing. Hattie thought it a good question, as whoever was willing to replace the decedent would be very brave indeed, given all the deaths piling up.

Heaving a huge sigh, the minister replied, "No one—he was irreplaceable."

As this seemed overly dramatic, Hattie offered, "At least no one is needed just now, while the dig is at a standstill."

But the man disagreed, turning to her to explain. "Oh no,

Miss Blackhouse; in his absence there are competing interests who are all bringing pressure to bear. If only he was still with us—he excelled at negotiation."

Hattie was going to inquire as to the nature of the negotiations when she sensed a presence next to her and looked up to behold Berry, who had materialized at her side. She was certain he hadn't entered via the front door but it hardly mattered—he was finally here and at long last, was regarding her with an expression of undisguised warmth. Unable to suppress a smile, she decided that there was nothing like an attempted abduction to remind a gentleman of opportunities wasted. After greeting him in a distracted fashion, the chess players settled back into their game and Hattie sidled close to Berry so they could converse unheard—and so her arm could brush up against his.

"Do you play?" He gestured toward the board.

Dimpling up at him, she answered with some pertness, "Very well. And you?"

He tilted his head and echoed her words. "Very well."

"Perhaps we should play each other, then."

"You would have the advantage—I would be unable to concentrate." His gaze rested on her mouth and held such a measure of meaning she had to look away for a moment so as to control her unbridled delight; it appeared a glimpse of her nightdress had created an impatience for further intimacies—and not a moment too soon.

"Are you recovered?" He brushed a covert finger across the back of her hand.

With a *frisson* of anticipation, she could feel her color rise. "Completely—a few bruises, is all."

Smiling down into her eyes, he suggested in a low voice, "Then perhaps we could walk in the courtyard and leave the players to their game."

The hotel had four wings that surrounded a central court-yard; surely there could be no objection to an unattended stroll so close to hand. "Let me inform Bing." Having relayed the information to her compliant companion, she took his arm.

"You will need your parasol, I think," he warned. "It is quite hot."

Pleased by his protective attitude, she assured him she would return in a moment, and ascended the stairway to the second floor. Walking swiftly down the hall to her room, she inserted the key and entered to walk across to the closet where her parasol was housed. With a gasp, she drew up short. Berry stood on her balcony, leaning on the rail and smiling at her through the open French doors.

She had to laugh with delight at the feat. "How on earth did you do that?"

Tilting his head, he disclaimed, "I prefer not to disclose my secrets."

Inferring that he had leapt between balconies, she was impressed. Nevertheless, he shouldn't be here and if he were caught she didn't like to think of the scandal—not to mention Bing would not be so compliant in the future. "I believe you are uninvited," she chided in a teasing tone, smiling so that he knew she wasn't offended.

Instead of heeding her, he approached to stand very close. "Send me away, then." Placing his hands at her waist, he pulled her to him and bent his head to gently kiss her mouth.

Her pulse beating erratically, Hattie hoped they couldn't be seen from the street, although she was too paralyzed with exultation to do anything about it. It was clear he had seized upon this opportunity to take advantage—now that Bing was otherwise occupied—and she struggled with her conscience for a moment. It wasn't a fair fight, with his warm, probing mouth upon hers—and her conscience didn't win. Only for a few moments, she promised herself; then we will descend to the courtyard for a decorous stroll.

Sinking into the bliss of sensation, she pressed her hands against his chest as he deepened the kiss, slanting his mouth against hers and pulling her closer to him with one arm while the other hand rose to caress the side of her face. As though she had done so a hundred times, her arms went around him and she was beyond concern—it was so natural and right, as though they had been slated to be together from the first—the attraction that drew them together was elemental; unstoppable.

With escalating heat, he broke away from her mouth to kiss the side of her face, her throat, her neck—no easy feat as he was so much taller. Surrendering to the heady sensations, she raised her chin to allow his delightful mouth full access to her neck, feeling his fingers move along the base of her throat with a feather-light touch.

"Daniel?"

Hattie froze in horror. Berry paused, then straightened up and turned toward the sound without any show of discomfiture.

"Do I interrupt?" The young woman who watched them from the balcony next door was amused. She was blondly beautiful, tall, and dressed in the first stare of fashion.

"Mademoiselle Blackhouse, allow me to introduce Mademoiselle Eugenie Leone."

Hattie wished the ground would open up beneath her. "How do you do?" she stammered instead.

"Not as well as you, I think. When you have a moment, Daniel." With a twinkling eye, the other woman disappeared from view.

Mortified, Hattie turned to gaze up at him, and he laid a gentle finger on the tip of her nose. "I should go," he said softly, his tone tender.

"Yes." This much seemed evident.

She had the impression he wanted to tell her something, then thought the better of it. "May I exit through the door?"

Still struggling to recover her equilibrium, she agreed, "That would be more in keeping, I suppose."

They walked across the room, his hand once again resting on the small of her back. "If you would return to Mademoiselle Bing, I will be there directly."

"Certainly," she replied, trying not to betray her continuing embarrassment.

She detected a gleam of amusement in the brown eyes as he paused to gently kiss her mouth. "We will continue our discussion at another time—yes?"

"We shall see," she equivocated, not wanting him to believe she was as malleable as she had proved thus far. He chuckled as he made his exit, not deceived by her show of coyness.

Hattie closed the door behind him and leaned against it in acute distress. To be discovered in such a compromising position—she held her breath for a moment to see if she could hear raised voices next door, but heard nothing. Mademoiselle Leone is not what she seems, he had told her, but one certainly could believe they were on intimate terms if she was looking for him in his room—and she had called him "Daniel," which was equal parts interesting and infuriating, as Hattie had never been offered his name, and certainly one would think she had earned the right. Although it probably wasn't his true name, which was apparently as much a secret as the wretched mummy's. I don't understand any of this, she thought a bit crossly—and it is *so* annoying that we are constantly being interrupted. Brought up short, she took herself in hand; you have no business allowing such liberties—exercise some restraint, for the love of heaven.

She then ruined the effect by wishing she had at least one low-cut gown in the manner of Mademoiselle Leone's—Hattie's décolletage was just as impressive.

Chapter 20

The new arrival joined them at breakfast the next morning, and Hattie was given an opportunity to study the unflappable Mademoiselle Leone, who was entirely French, with a vivacious and charming manner. She also made a point of openly flirting with Berry, which Hattie took in good part as the other girl was witness to Berry's preferences, and could be forgiven for her pique. If the newcomer thought to get a reaction out of Hattie she was to be disappointed, particularly because Berry's hand kept finding hers under the table. But when the gentleman bent his head to Hattie his murmured words were far from lover-like: "Did you mention our concerns to Mademoiselle Bing?"

Hattie responded in the same low tone. "Yes. Bing will release no secrets."

"*Eh bien*, what is it you two speak of?" Eugenie interrupted with a pretty pout, tapping her silk fan on Berry's wrist. "Napoleon's horse?"

Berry turned and responded with a few rapid words in colloquial French that Hattie could not follow but which caused Eugenie to subside into silence, pouting. Interesting, thought Hattie as she turned to speak with Bing so as to cover the awkward moment. I believe Eugenie works for Berry—or at least she answers to him, and I believe he wishes me to be aware of this; I wonder what her role is in these events. For that matter, I wonder what my role is—other than to produce the missing strongbox and bear a striking resemblance to the god-king's daughter. She met Berry's glance for a moment. And to convince this gentleman that a bachelor's lot is inferior to other options available.

"Mademoiselle Bing," said Berry, "I wonder if Mademoiselle Leone and I may be allowed to escort Mademoiselle Blackhouse to the British Consul General's offices today; if we are to travel to Thebes there are certain arrangements that must be made and I believe it will expedite the process if the Blackhouse daughter is present."

"Wouldn't you rather visit the French consul?" asked Hattie. Considering he was pretending to be French, he should at least make the effort.

But he explained patiently, "It would be best if you were the supplicant—your heritage is a powerful influence."

Bing saw the wisdom of this. "Very well—if Miss Blackhouse has no objection."

Hattie very much appreciated that Bing always made it clear that Hattie decided her affairs for herself. "Where is the consulate located?"

"In Old City, by the Nile—it is probably best to go as soon as we can make ready so as to avoid the midday sun."

"Willingly," agreed Hattie, who then had another notion. "As I will be taken care of, Bing, perhaps another attempt to visit the pyramids is in order—could you send a note 'round to Mr. Hafez?"

Bing was enthusiastic and expressed her desire to make the visit even if Hafez was unavailable. "I asked the desk clerk, who tells me there is nearly always a daily group making the tour and that I may join in with no difficulty."

"Who is this Mr. Hafez?" asked Eugenie, her porcelain brow knit.

Hattie explained, "The Minister of Antiquities—he and Miss Bing have found in each other a kindred spirit."

In reaction, the other girl seemed surprised and cast a swift glance at Berry, who did not meet her gaze. "I see," she offered in a doubtful tone.

"Where do you hail from, Mademoiselle Leone?" This from Bing, whom Hattie suspected was attempting to turn the subject from her relationship with Hafez.

"Martinique," the young woman replied, her blue eyes guileless.

Intrigued, Bing raised her brows. "Indeed? I understand the Empress Josephine hailed from Martinique. Are you acquainted with the family?"

"Indeed," the girl replied in an arch tone, and Hattie entertained a suspicion that she was mocking Bing, which seemed rather unkind.

"And you are acquainted with Captain Clements, I understand." Bing persevered with what to Hattie seemed admirable patience.

"*C'est vrai*," the beauty agreed, laughing at the memory. "He was so kind as to abduct me, once; but as I was very much in need of an abduction, I forgave him."

"Admirable," offered Bing in a neutral tone, and asked no further questions.

But Hattie was made of sterner stuff and took up the mantle. "And how are you acquainted with Monsieur Berry, mademoiselle?"

Her eyes dancing, Eugenie turned to him and asked, "Shall I say?"

"No," he answered without hesitation.

"I cannot say." She smiled and shook her golden curls. "But be assured it is nothing *scandaleux*." Slyly, her eyes slid to Hattie, who could feel herself color up and did not dignify the implication with a response.

"Mademoiselle Leone will accompany us to Thebes," Berry announced as though the girl was not trouble personified. "She has never been."

"No, and I look forward to it above all things." Smiling up at him, the Frenchwoman wound her arm around his in a provocative manner.

"It will be a new experience for Miss Bing and myself, also." Hattie was unaffected by the other's attempt to get her goat—this particular goat was hers. She could almost feel sorry for the girl; it must be very annoying to a beauty of Eugenie's caliber to have to cede the field.

But Eugenie's beautiful brow puckered in confusion. "Surely you have visited Thebes before?" She glanced at Berry in puzzlement.

Wondering why the woman would seek verification from Berry, Hattie assured her, "No—I have never been." She tamped down the resentment that always threatened to rise when she thought of her long exile in the wilds of Cornwall—there was no point to it; her parents were no longer persons to be resented—they were persons to be recovered and buried.

"I believe," Bing said into the silence, "that Mr. Hafez intends to accompany us, also."

"*Très bon*," murmured Eugenie, examining her nails with a satisfied smile.

"We shall have quite a group, then." Hattie wondered crossly if every stray guest at the hotel was going to latch on to their expedition; every addition undoubtedly meant fewer opportunities for Berry to kiss her neck—not that she should allow such liberties in the first place—but it was all very annoying.

"Shall we meet in the lobby in an hour's time?" asked Berry, rising.

Taking their cue, the breakfast party broke up and Hattie retreated with Bing to their room to prepare for their respective outings. Hafez sent an acceptance with gratifying promptness and Hattie teased her, "Pray do not elope with him, Bing—I insist upon standing up with you at the church door."

Bing displayed her dry smile as she pinned her veiled hat carefully to her head. "I do not think it is I who is slated to receive an offer, Hathor."

Disclaiming, Hattie teased in a light tone, "Alas for any such hopes; the beautiful Mademoiselle Leone has entered the lists."

"You may be certain of him," Bing assured her with a nod toward the mirror. "His gaze is drawn to you, especially when you are unaware."

Finding this revelation very satisfactory, Hattie said only, "It is early days yet, Bing—we shall see."

Taking up her parasol and her notebook, Bing made ready to depart. "I hope to return for dinner, Hathor, if all goes as planned."

"I shall hear of your adventures at that time, then." Hattie closed the door and prepared for the proposed outing to the consulate, trying to decide if she could pretend she forgot her kid gloves, which were uncomfortably hot. As she was thus engaged, there was a soft knock at the door. Smiling, she took a quick assessing glance in the mirror, pinched color into her cheeks, and opened the door with her best smile.

Instead of the expected visitor, however, she beheld a message boy from the front desk. "Miss Blackhouse? You have a visitor at the desk who begs a moment of your time."

He handed her a card upon which was inscribed a name Hattie did not recognize. She debated for only a moment, and decided there was no harm to it; her attacker could not possibly have come to call upon her and she would certainly be safe in the hotel lobby.

Accompanied by the boy, she descended to the desk only to recognize the young clerk from the solicitor's office waiting at the desk for her and smiling nervously. "Miss Blackhouse," he stammered. "I hope I do not intrude."

"Not at all," she assured him, offering her hand. "How very pleasant to see you again." She hid a smile—he had taken pains with his appearance and was dressed in what she imagined was his best suit of clothes.

Indicating the wrapped parcel on the counter, he offered, "I took the liberty of bringing your books."

As she had already indicated she was not looking to house them, Hattie correctly surmised this was an excuse to call upon her. Unsure of how to handle such earnest devotion, she was loath to snub him—he was far too young, being approximately her own age. "Does your employer know of your errand?"

"No," the young man admitted. He leaned toward her to confide, "He has been out of reason cross ever since your visit, and is often from the premises."

"I have done you a favor, then," observed Hattie, and he laughed as though she had said something very amusing.

Making a visible effort, the young man gathered up his courage. "Perhaps—perhaps you would be available to go out walking this evening, Miss Blackhouse."

Anticipating just such a question, Hattie shook her head with feigned regret. "As tempting as the invitation is, I'm afraid I am constrained by my parents' disappearance—I cannot be seen to participate in such an enjoyable pastime."

His face fell but he nodded in understanding. "I hadn't thought—I beg your pardon."

"It is quite all right," she said sincerely. "I do appreciate the offer."

There was a pause while the clerk came to the realization he would have to withdraw. "Perhaps some other time—you have my card? Please do not hesitate to contact me if any assistance is needed."

"I will indeed," Hattie agreed, and threw him a bone. "I imagine I shall visit your offices in the near future, to address this difficult situation." She sincerely hoped not; the solicitor was what Robbie would have deemed a curst rum touch.

Plucking up with this thought, the clerk bowed his way out and Hattie was left to eye the package, debating what to do with it. She could check it at the desk, but she then decided that as her things had already been thoroughly searched—and more than once—there was no harm in secreting it in her room. That way, at her first opportunity she could open it and see what the fuss was all about.

After placing the package in the bottom of her wardrobe amongst her shoe boxes, she fetched her hat and her parasol and returned to the lobby to meet up with Berry and Eugenie, now assembled and waiting for her. As she greeted them and reluctantly pulled on her gloves, Hattie noted that the two were never found in idle conversation with each other, in rather the same way Captain Clements and Berry never made idle conversation. They are all in this spying business together, she thought, and need not be convivial;

151

it must be rather a relief—not to have to wear a polite mask with each other. Indeed, she had the impression that Berry was carefully monitoring what Eugenie said to Hattie, as though ready to rebuke her at a moment's notice.

As they exited through the lobby doors, the ladies immediately hoisted their parasols against the bright sun and Hattie adjusted the straw brim of her hat so that it sat lower on her face. The maneuver also allowed an opportunity to take covert inventory of the Frenchwoman's attire—Eugenie held a silk-embroidered parasol and the frivolous confection that passed as a hat had nothing to do with blocking the sun and everything to do with complimenting the contours of her lovely face. *She will stop traffic,* thought Hattie with sincere envy. *I shall watch and learn*—although to his credit, Berry appears unimpressed and once again has his hand on my back; he will leave a permanent print there if he is not careful.

Even though it was morning, the heat was already oppressive as they threaded their way through the crowded street. Berry procured a transport cart and they were underway, headed to Old City where the consulate was located.

Eugenie waved a languorous fan and addressed Berry. "Have you enough money about you, Daniel? We shall need it for our journey, *n'est-ce pas?*"

"I have."

Unfolding her wrist with a flourish, the girl displayed a soft bundle of bills in her hand. "As do I."

Hattie stared in surprise that Eugenie would brandish such an amount. Amused, Berry took it from her. "I will keep it, if you please." He glanced at the other girl with a shake of his head. "Try not to bring attention to us, Eugenie."

She laughed behind her fan, clearly enjoying herself. "It was too simple, Daniel—I could not resist."

Hattie gazed out at the Saladin Citadel in the distance, struggling to keep her countenance. Eugenie was a pick-pocket, then; a commendable trait in a cohort, one would think. "Must we pay a fee to travel down the Nile?" Hattie wondered at the reference to needed funds.

"There is no fee *comme tel*," Berry answered carefully, "But the journey will depend on securing cooperation from those who will expect to be compensated."

Hattie was unsurprised, considering there was no strong central authority to oversee such things. "Bribery, in other words. Is it so corrupt, then?"

He shrugged. "At present, the local authorities hold sway, but the situation will probably not survive the year and everyone seeks to make a profit while they may."

"Because once the British regain authority, graft will be discouraged," Hattie concluded. "The rule of law will be enforced."

"Perhaps French laws will be enforced, instead," Eugenie offered with a small smile from beneath her parasol. "Just because you are English, you should not make such an assumption."

Hattie lifted her brows in surprise at the pointed observation—which seemed to have no particular point. "The French? Certainly that seems unlikely, Mademoiselle Leone— the French government is in as much disarray as is Egypt's."

"*Quand même*, one never knows," the other replied, and turned to gaze at the scenery.

Chapter 21

The British consulate was located in the heart of the Old City district, the white stone edifice dominating the busy promenade where hawkers worked in abundance, hoping to sell all variety of goods to the British tourists who visited the building. After Berry handed her down from the transport cart, Hattie paused to take in the interesting sights and review the wares on display—maps of the excavation sites in Thebes and Abu Simbel as well as trinkets guaranteed to bestow good luck on their purchasers. With a smile, she admired a group of crude brass figures representing the goddess Hathor while the vendors redoubled their efforts to convince her to buy. She lifted her head to convey her regrets but before she could speak, one of them started and backed away from her, staring in amazement. "*Dgahtr af,*" he muttered, then turned to his colleagues in alarm and repeated the words, gesturing toward her. The other vendors paused in their efforts and a sudden, profound silence fell as they all stared in amazement at Hattie, some making a sign with their fingers as they backed away.

Berry firmly took her arm and led her up the steps to the consulate. "Come along, Mademoiselle Blackhouse."

A low murmuring broke from the crowd as they walked up the steps to the consulate. "They have seen the likeness of the god-king's daughter," Hattie deduced as she hurried beside him. She was surprised by the strength of the vendors' reaction—surprised and a bit shaken, truth to tell.

"Yes—and they are probably selling them as well. Try to refrain from sending forth a curse, as I cannot answer for the consequences."

Appreciating his attempt to make light of the situation, she tried to match his easy tone. "Would that I could."

As he held the door, she crossed under his arm and he remarked, "There is no question that you can bewitch, mademoiselle." Pausing, she met his gaze and they shared a mutual reminiscence of stolen embraces.

"*Allons*, you two," prodded Eugenie crossly. "It is no time for the sheep's eyes."

Once inside, they were met by a soldier who ushered the party into a marble-floored anteroom where a clerk presided at an imposing desk, the atmosphere suddenly very British in direct contrast to the disorganized chaos outside. The clerk rose as Berry presented Hattie. "I am the Blackhouse agent, and this is Mademoiselle Blackhouse, here to arrange a search for her parents in Thebes."

His words had an immediate effect, and the clerk nearly goggled as he reverently took her hand. "Miss Blackhouse—it is an honor. Please accept my"—the clerk caught himself— "sincere hope that your parents will be rescued."

"Thank you," said Hattie, her conscience stung by the implied condolences. Perhaps she should make an effort to appear more grief-stricken and less sheep-eyed.

"Allow me to inform the undersecretary that you are here; I am certain he will wish to speak with you immediately." With a respectful gesture, he indicated they were to enter an adjacent waiting room and be seated, and refreshments were promptly offered. He then hurried away, his footsteps echoing importantly on the marble floor.

"I can see now why we do not apply to the French consulate," remarked Hattie in a wry tone. "I am a princess and a legacy, combined."

"'Legacy'—I do not know what this means." Eugenie pursed her full lips in puzzlement.

Hattie explained, "I am a famous daughter."

Eugenie's reaction was to smile in her rather annoying, condescending way. "*De vrai*; you are indeed." She then glanced at Berry, who made a gesture with his head toward the door, as though calling Eugenie to task.

An older gentleman, very distinguished and diplomatic in manner, entered the room and immediately approached Eugenie to bow over her hand. "Miss Blackhouse."

"You mistake—this is Miss Blackhouse," Berry corrected him, indicating Hattie. Eugenie giggled and simpered foolishly behind her fan in a manner that was very unlike her, provoking a sharp look from Hattie as she took the gentleman's hand.

Introductions were made and the undersecretary said all that was proper about Hattie's tragic situation. Hattie noted, however, that his eyes kept straying to Eugenie, who used her own eyes and fan to advantage. I wonder what our object is here, Hattie thought; whatever it is, this poor man stands no chance.

Upon being informed of the planned trip up the Nile, the undersecretary assured Hattie he would do everything in his power to offer aid. "Regrettable business." He sadly shook his head. "To have disappeared without a trace."

Berry pressed the point. "The Minister of Antiquities will accompany us; he reports that his own attempts to obtain information at the time of the disappearance were met with resistance—brigands, I understand."

The undersecretary frowned in disapproval. "Is that so? I'll admit that lawlessness has been a recurring problem in the area—not unexpected, considering the treasures being unearthed. I can ask for an increase in security personnel at our embassy's facility in Al Karnak in anticipation of your visit—indeed, if you'd like, personnel can be directly assigned to your party."

But this was not, apparently, the solution which was sought. "An excellent suggestion," Berry bowed in appreciation. "However, perhaps posting British guards at the tomb site would be most helpful—there would be little question of loyalty to Mademoiselle Blackhouse."

"True." The man nodded, thinking. "I have already heard concerns that the Egyptian guards look the other way in exchange for bribes. Very good—I will see to it; there can be no objection—not with Miss Blackhouse on site—the local authorities must defer in this matter." Upon voicing this resolution he was rewarded with a warm smile from Eugenie, which caused him to lose his train of thought.

Berry ruthlessly drew him back. "We sail on the *Priapus* tomorrow. If Mademoiselle Blackhouse could be issued a safe passage, under the imprimatur of the Consul General, it would ensure the utmost cooperation of those on whom we must rely."

The man nodded, impressed. "Another excellent suggestion, sir; allow me to arrange for it now, before you depart." Rising to leave the room, he threw Eugenie a glance and left the door ajar. That lady, nothing loath, rose and stretched like a cat then wandered out the door toward the antechamber.

Speculating, Hattie glanced at Berry, wondering what he was about. "You are very thorough in your preparations."

"Your safety is of paramount importance." She had the impression he was listening, but there was only silence from the antechamber, or at least as far as Hattie could tell.

After a pause, she ventured, "Why a safe passage? Is it what it sounds?"

He brought his attention back to her. "Yes—it is a diplomatic document that allows the bearer free passage without need of a passport or other identification. It is merely a precautionary measure."

If Hattie wondered why someone as well-known as herself, armed with a passport and bearing a famous resemblance to the entombed princess, would need such a document, she kept the thought to herself.

The undersecretary returned with a formal-looking parchment but Eugenie was nowhere in evidence. "Here it is; the safe passage. Shall I make it out?"

"No need—I will see to it." Berry gave it a glance and deposited the folded document in an inner pocket.

They conveyed their gratitude and the official said all that was proper as he ushered them back into the foyer where Eugenie was now deep in conversation with the desk clerk, who had the look of a man who could not believe his good fortune. She is a handful, thought Hattie—lucky for him, she is not Berry's handful. The undersecretary cleared his throat in disapproval and the man snapped to attention. Farewells were said all around, the undersecretary murmuring something to Eugenie that made her laugh. He then smiled with kindness as he bowed over Hattie's hand. "I shall hope you discover only good news, Miss Blackhouse."

Hattie returned his smile even though they were both

aware of the unlikeliness of this. "If nothing else I shall discover the Egypt they knew."

"Perhaps you will carry on their work," he suggested kindly. "It is in the blood, after all."

Definitely not in my blood, Hattie thought as she made an equivocal answer and they parted. As they were escorted toward the entrance, Berry asked, "You have no interest in Egyptology?"

Hattie shook her head without shame. "Absolutely none. My knowledge of the subject is only slightly more than yours—which is nearly nonexistent." She had the satisfaction of hearing him chuckle and looked up to him with a twinkle.

When they emerged into the sunlight, a roar erupted. Startled, Hattie was met with the sight of a large crowd gathered at the base of the steps with all eyes fixed upon her. Holding out an arm to halt her progress, Berry ushered her back through the door and into the foyer. "It would be best," he informed the astonished footman, "if a covered coach could be sent to the back entrance, with some out-riders." Acutely embarrassed, Hattie stood with Berry and Eugenie while the sound of many murmuring voices could heard—the words *dgahtr af* discernible above all else.

"You are *la héroïne*," noted Eugenie in surprise, as though it was hard to credit. "Why is this?"

"My parents distributed a likeness of the god-king's daughter and used me as a model," Hattie explained. "I'm afraid the locals have gained the wrong impression."

"*Extraordinaire*," the other agreed in wonderment. "They are indeed foolish, no?"

"Come," said Berry, indicating the footman who beck-oned to them from the back entrance.

"*J'ai la clef,*" said Eugenie to him in a low voice as she walked past, her tone triumphant.

"Which key is that?" asked Hattie as they crossed the hallway, distracted by the clamor and wondering what was meant.

Eugenie paused. "*Que?*"

"Didn't you say you have a key?" asked Hattie in French. She had a solid knowledge of the language, her governess having been an avid Francophile.

"No, no," Eugenie laughed. "Instead, I said we were brief—*nous étions bref.*" She smiled indulgently. "Your French is only fair, *n'est-ce pas?*"

"*Mais oui,*" agreed Hattie with a smile, wondering with alarm why Berry would wish to steal a key to the British consulate.

Chapter 22

B ing returned just before dinner, exhausted but very much satisfied with the sights she had witnessed. "Marvelous," she pronounced, her face burnt from the sun as she unpinned her hat and dusted it off. "Would you mind, Hathor, if I have a tray sent up to the room? With Mademoiselle Leone present, there can be no objection to your dining under Monsieur Berry's auspices."

"I am willing to stay and hear your tales of the crypt," Hattie offered. "There will be plenty of opportunities to dine with our companions when we travel up the Nile."

"Best not to allow Mademoiselle Leone a clear field," Bing opined with a knowing air as she unlaced her half boots. "Men tend to lose their bearings around women of that stamp."

This was undeniably true, as Hattie had witnessed first-hand at the consulate. In fact, she would not be surprised if Eugenie's role was to cause certain hand-picked men to lose their bearings. The list would not include Berry, but as Hattie would rather be in his company anyway she did not demur. "I shall come hear of your adventures after dinner, then—in the meantime I'll go down and arrange for your tray."

"Something substantial, if you please," directed her

companion, lying back on her bed with a happy sigh. "I confess I am sharp-set."

After having arranged for a tray of cold meats and soup for Bing, Hattie joined Berry and Eugenie in the dining room for dinner. With an apologetic smile she announced, "Bing sends her regrets—she is exhausted from her tour."

"A shame." Berry pulled out her chair, his fingers brushing Hattie's shoulders as she was seated.

Aware that she should not feel quite so gleeful at the prospect of further improprieties, Hattie nevertheless could not contain a sidelong glance at Berry to gauge his reaction to the loss of her chaperone. His manner was all that was correct and polite, but she was not fooled; the emotion was there, simmering just beneath the surface. I am beyond redemption, she thought without remorse; but it is such a sweet, sweet surrender.

All thoughts of heated embraces, however, were replaced by abject surprise as Hattie spied a familiar figure approaching the table. "Why, Robbie," she exclaimed.

With a familiar gesture, Robbie leaned to take her hand, smiling at her reaction. "Hattie, you devil—I have finally managed to track you down, and no thanks to the management here, who seem to suspect I am some sort of burglar."

"Robbie—I must own I am astonished. You remember Monsieur Berry, my parents' agent?"

Berry had stood to shake hands and Robbie greeted him before his gaze rested on Eugenie. "Ah—Mademoiselle Valérie."

"Leone—Mademoiselle Eugenie Leone," she corrected him with a beguiling smile.

"I beg your pardon—my wretched memory." He seemed amused for some reason as he took her hand.

Hattie offered a place at the table, ashamed of herself for

feeling a bit disappointed that Robbie had chosen to make an appearance at this particular juncture; it was just as well, she told herself firmly—you are nothing less than a hoyden. "Do join us, Robbie; have you eaten?"

"No; I am just arrived and set out to find you first thing—Lord, Hattie, you gave me a turn."

But Hattie was unrepentant and lifted her chin. "Turnabout is fair play, my friend. How does your superior?"

Unable to suppress a grin, he confessed, "Fit to be tied; that's how he does—I expect to be summarily fired at any moment."

Hattie shot him a look from under her brows. "If you expect me to feel sorry for you, Robbie Tremaine—"

Berry interrupted the exchange before it escalated into fisticuffs. "Please accept my condolences, Monsieur Tremaine."

At the reminder, Robbie assumed a grave expression and thanked him in a sincere tone before seating himself between Hattie and Eugenie as they signaled that an extra setting should be brought. Hattie could not help but note that he wore no black mourning band—although she wasn't certain of the protocol, as the dead woman was not yet his wife. Deciding there was no point in putting off the topic, she added, "Yes; I am also sorry to hear of your loss, Robbie."

The newcomer poured a full measure of wine into his glass as he made a wry mouth. "It is insult upon injury, I'm afraid. The prefect questioned me very closely—in this type of situation the men in the dead woman's life are always scrutinized."

Outraged on his behalf, Hattie exclaimed, "Surely they do not suspect you?"

He shrugged. "It was irksome to be questioned but it could not be helped—I'll admit I departed before they were quite done with me, so I have an ulterior purpose in coming to track you down—I figured you'd need some help over here."

"Your help will be much appreciated," Hattie assured him politely, aware that the gentleman seated across from her refrained from comment.

"It is a shame I must offer you my condolences, Monsieur Tremaine, before I have had the chance to offer my congratulations on your engagement." Eugenie's beautiful face was solemn, as was her tone, but Hattie noted her eyes were dancing. Her acquaintanceship with the other woman was not longstanding, but it was long enough to know this was not a good sign.

"I thank you," Robbie replied, matching her tone. "How does your sister; must I offer condolences also?"

Eugenie laughed and shrugged her pretty shoulders. "*Eh bien*; she is alive and well, to everyone's astonishment."

As though suddenly aware he was leaving Hattie out of the conversation, Robbie turned to her. "What has happened, Hattie—is there any news of your parents?"

"We travel to Thebes tomorrow—and I have been to visit my parents' solicitor."

Robbie's interest sharpened. "What did he report?"

Hattie shook her head to convey her regret. "He was disappointed I could not produce correspondence from them which might have been helpful."

Artlessly, Robbie shrugged a shoulder as he dug into his beefsteak. "He should not have been surprised—they never corresponded with you very much."

"No," she agreed, a bit stricken by the bald statement.

Between bites, Tremaine looked up to her. "Did the solicitor give you funds? Have you enough to mount a search?"

"Yes," Hattie assured him. "In fact, he wanted me to take

control immediately, even though we are not yet certain they are no longer alive—it was a little strange." Prudently, she didn't mention the contretemps about the password— although now that Robbie was here, perhaps he should be the person she trusted with the golden disk, instead of Berry. She wanted to trust Berry, but the fact that he had stolen a key to the consulate gave her pause.

"Are you certain you have enough money, Hattie? If you are in need I can stand the ready."

Although he meant well, Hattie was a bit embarrassed by his heavy-handedness. "Thank you, Robbie, but my parents have provided a bank account for which I am the sole signatory—indeed they have been surprisingly generous."

A small silence greeted this remark, and Hattie thought they all seemed struck by this arrangement—which certainly wasn't that unusual, after all. Robbie addressed his plate again and replied, "That is to the good, then. Where is Miss Bing this evening?"

"Suffering from happy exhaustion in our room. She visited the pyramids today with the Minister of Antiquities, and took to her bed upon their return."

"Mr. Hafez?" asked Robbie, his interest piqued.

"Yes, Mr. Hafez." Hattie was reminded that Robbie's late bride's late husband—honestly, it was all so very confusing— had worked with Hafez. "Do you know him?"

"We met briefly when I visited the site with Madame Auguste. Has he cultivated an acquaintanceship with you?"

Hattie found the choice of words strange, and wondered if Robbie was another who didn't trust the seemingly innocuous official. "I suppose you could call it that—he and Bing discuss treasures from Abu Simbel and compare cat's-eye sapphires."

"Interesting." Robbie finished up his beefsteak and began in on the stewed figs.

"It is of all things *incroyable*," offered Eugenie, miffed.

"Never say you are not included in such discussions, Mademoiselle Valérie," Robbie teased with a grin.

"Leone," she corrected him again. "You confuse me with another, *n'est-ce pas?*"

"Undoubtedly," he agreed, his blue eyes amused as he drank his wine.

Hattie decided she felt as though she were a child at a table with adults, trying to follow along in the conversation. To turn the subject, she described that day's visit to the consulate and the procurement of the safe passage, leaving out those incidents of theft which seemed extraneous to the story.

"A good idea, monsieur," Tremaine turned to compliment Berry in a sincere tone. "I am dashed grateful that you've been seeing to Miss Blackhouse in my absence."

Berry studied his wineglass, his fingers showing white where they were pressed against the stem. "I am happy to be of service."

Hurriedly, Hattie sought to change the subject and found an object to accomplish this aim. "Why, here is Mr. Hafez, now."

The minister approached in a distracted fashion, perspiring with the effort of moving his portly frame with as much speed as he could muster. "Miss Blackhouse—forgive my interruption but I am afraid I have most disturbing news."

Alarmed, Hattie bade him to sit but he declined, saying, "I am afraid I cannot stay. But your status must remain unsettled for the time being; I regret to report your parents' solicitor—Mr. Bahur—has been killed."

Hattie stared and was aware, for reasons she could not state, that this was not news to Berry. "Why—how terrible," she exclaimed, thinking of the earnest clerk—her would-be suitor—and hoping he would not suffer any hardship as a result. Oh, she thought suddenly—oh, God in heaven—the parcel. "Do we know what happened?"

Mopping his forehead with his handkerchief, the minister lamented, "He stayed late at his offices last night and was assaulted—the premises ransacked. It will be nearly impossible to piece together the contents so as to discover what is missing, if anything."

"A tragedy," said Eugenie, placing a slender hand on the minister's sleeve. For the first time, Hafez seemed to notice her. "Mademoiselle Leone," offered Hattie in introduction. "And I believe you have already met Mr. Tremaine."

"How do you do?" he bowed to Eugenie, then nodded to Robbie. "May I leave a note for Miss Bing, Miss Blackhouse? I fear I will be busy on the morrow and cannot escort her to the *Priapus* as planned."

"Please—I shall see to it that she receives it."

After he performed this service, Hattie noted that her fellow diners seemed disinclined to discuss this latest development, which seemed a bit odd, and so she ventured, "I had no idea that Cairo was such a dangerous place."

"I will book a passage to Thebes tomorrow," Robbie announced, and placed his hand over Hattie's on the table to reassure her. "Rest easy, Hattie; I will see to your safety."

"I appreciate it, Robbie." Hattie slid her hand away, fearing Berry's wineglass would be snapped in two.

The dinner party broke up and Hattie slowly ascended to her room, thinking about Robbie's arrival along with this latest death and hoping that her poor clerk would not meet a similar fate. There seemed little doubt that someone sinister was after her parcel—after all, nearly everyone she met coveted the miserable strongbox; whatever could it contain to inspire such bloodlust? Hopefully, even if he were questioned it wouldn't occur to the clerk to mention the parcel, as he believed it to be an innocent set of books. I must discover what is inside, she thought, and that will determine what I am to do.

Deep in her abstraction, she didn't realize Berry had followed her down the hallway until he appeared at her side. "*Bonne nuit,*" he said, taking her hand and holding it in his.

"*Bonne nuit,*" she replied, smiling despite her worries.

"Come—walk with me." There was a world of promise in the invitation; the brown eyes intent upon hers.

Feeling reckless, she took his arm. "Only for a few minutes," she warned, thinking of her chaperone, who undoubtedly had the lamp lit against her return. After escorting her to the far end of the hallway, Berry then led her down the servants' stairs and into an alcove located beneath the stairway that afforded some measure of privacy. It was dimly lit by a sconce burning on the wall, and Hattie's heartbeat accelerated in pleasurable anticipation—at long last they would be alone and undisturbed.

Turning to take hold of both her hands in his, he bent his head and confessed in a low voice, "I seek a private moment with you, Hattie—as of tomorrow we will not have many opportunities."

Anticipating a declaration, she met his gaze, enrapt, then heard whispered voices approaching. Berry drew her back into the shadows and they beheld Robbie and Eugenie, arm in arm, coming to the back stairway in a breathless hurry. Robbie paused to kiss his companion thoroughly and Eugenie wholeheartedly complied, giggling when he released her. They then ascended upward, presumably to the privacy of a room.

Hattie stood with Berry for a moment in the ensuing silence. "That was not well done of you," she said quietly.

Chapter 23

There was a pause. Berry did not deny the machination, but said only, "He was not unwilling."

"I should go." She turned to leave.

His expression intent, he caught her arm to stop her. "Look, I am sorry; I was angry because he pretends that you belong to him."

She lifted her chin. "I belong to no one."

His jaw clenched, he lowered his gaze to the floor and did not respond. Half hoping for an argument, Hattie saw she was not going to get one and to cover her disappointment, she explained in a constrained voice, "He is my oldest friend and I will not allow you to disparage him. His family"—she paused; you are not going to cry, she assured herself—"his family allowed me to join in with them."

He raised his gaze to hers. Gently, his fingers touched her arm. "Forgive me," he said. "Please."

"What is it?" she demanded angrily, trying to control her emotions. "What is it about women like her that makes men behave like imbeciles?"

Tentatively, he raised his hand and drew a finger along her cheek, gauging her reaction to his touch; she did not flinch. "It can be useful; men cannot resist beautiful women. Most men," he corrected.

"You are not helping," she said crossly, refusing to meet his eyes.

"It is a powerful weapon." His hand moved from her cheek to stroke the hair back from her temple with a gentle thumb. "I am something of an imbecile, myself." Thus encouraged, his hand then came to rest on the nape of her neck and he began to apply gentle pressure, pulling her toward him as he leaned down, his eyes meeting hers as his mouth descended, watching for an objection.

I will let him do his penance, she decided as she lifted her face to meet his kiss—it is only sporting. As the kiss deepened, his arms came around her and the heat leapt between them—it seemed that every time he kissed her, matters escalated more rapidly—and she lost her will to resist just as rapidly. Making a soft, surrendering sound in her throat, she responded to the openmouthed kiss, wondering what it would be like to be abed with him in the way Robbie and Eugenie were undoubtedly abed—to feel his skin beneath her mouth and hands. After he caressed the contours of her breasts, one arm came around her waist while his mouth and tongue moved down her neck; he tugged at the neckline of her blouse to kiss the upper globe of her breasts with increasing urgency. More thrilled than scandalized, she pressed against him and gave in to the sheer pleasure of it until suddenly a small alert sounded in her mind. With a quick movement, she grasped his wrist and twisted away. He was removing her necklace; he had broken the chain and was in the process of pulling it off.

There was a long pause while they stared at each other, breathing heavily. "Give it to me." Her voice was icy.

Holding her eyes with his, he did not relinquish it. "I cannot."

They stood, unmoving for a frozen moment while Hattie felt as though her breast was suddenly numb with misery. "If you do not give it back to me"—her voice broke and she struggled on—"I *swear* I will never speak to you again." It would have been more forceful if she weren't going to cry, but there was nothing she could do—her heart was broken and her throat was thick with misery. As she took a shudder-ing breath, the bitter tears came.

His gaze did not waver but he turned his wrist and poured the necklace into her hand. Clenching it, she wept while they stood, silent. Unable to look at him, she wiped away tears with the palm of her free hand. "Go away."

"Hattie," he said gently. "I must see what it says."

"No," she managed between sobs.

"Please do not cry—it is important or I wouldn't ask."

"Important for whom?" She tried to sound angry but was mainly sick with despair.

There was a pause. "Everyone. Everyone in the world."

This seemed overdramatic, and she stifled a sob and met his eyes. "That is *nonsense*. And why should I trust you?" With a mighty effort, she tried to put a stop to the waterworks. "I wish you hadn't been so—so *duplicitous*. I'd so much rather you had simply coshed me and stolen it." Pretending as though he was enthralled and nibbling on her neck—oh, she was a complete and utter *fool*.

"I had little choice—you told me you did not know of the disk."

Stung, she retorted, "And why should I tell you anything? Because you pretend to admire me?" Unable to stop a renewed rush of tears, she covered her eyes in shame with her free hand, the other wrapped tightly around the broken necklace.

Taking her carefully by the shoulders, he moved her into a loose embrace that she did not resist. "I do admire you, Hattie."

"You don't have to pretend anymore—is *stupid* Eugenie your *stupid* mistress?"

"Hat-tie," he remonstrated gently near her ear, emphasizing each syllable. "She is nothing to me."

"Are you married?" Hattie asked, her voice muffled by his waistcoat.

"No. As I told you before—it is the truth."

Lifting her head, she looked out toward the hallway and took a deep, shuddering breath in an effort to regain her composure. "You seem to be suffering under a constraint of some sort."

He did not deny it. "That is not the constraint."

"Then what is this about? Why do I feel as though I am being treated like a child?" Unable to control it, she bent her head into his chest and began to weep again.

In response, he cradled her head in his hands and placed his forehead against hers. "You are tearing my heart out."

"Good," she retorted.

He came to a decision. "I will tell you what this is about but you will not thank me."

Raising her face to his, she declared with some defiance, "I have no intention of ever thanking you for anything."

"Your parents were aiding Napoleon."

She stared at him while he watched her. It took several seconds to assimilate what he had said, it was so outlandish. "Napoleon Bonaparte?"

"The very same."

Frowning, she scoffed, "That is absurd."

He tilted his head. "I'm afraid it is irrefutable."

Stepping back, she sought to think without the distraction his nearness provided. "Why would you say this? They were English—why, they had no French connections at all."

His gaze held hers. "It is believed they were beholden to him when they were first given permission to excavate in Egypt."

Knitting her brow, Hattie thought about this shocking revelation while he watched her with a grave expression. Unfortunately, she could see all too well how such a thing could come to pass—her parents cared for nothing but their all-encompassing pursuit, and when they had first begun, Napoleon held Egypt. They were not inclined to be loyal to their country if circumstances didn't warrant—after all, they had abandoned their only child in pursuit of their life's work—small wonder if they abandoned their country, too. "Infamous," she breathed in acute horror.

"Yes," he agreed in a grave tone. "Infamous."

But it made little sense—even if the bargain had indeed been made, long ago. "Surely there was no reason to continue—whatever it was they did for him—after he lost Egypt to Nelson."

Moving his hands gently on her arms he explained, "A portion of their finds—and their earnings—went to finance his war effort. It still does."

God in heaven—all this time—it was almost unthinkable. Casting about for an argument, she returned to her original point. "But surely that stopped when he was exiled to Elba—there is no longer any war to fund."

But he could offer no comfort and said quietly, "There is a persistent belief that Napoleon will escape Elba and attempt to return to power."

Staring at him, Hattie wondered how many more shocks

she would be required to absorb this night. The very idea was unfathomable—not with everyone sick of war and the Congress working to restore some order. "And you believe such a thing could happen?"

He ducked his chin for a moment, weighing what to tell her. "I am afraid such an attempt is inevitable. Your parents were asked to secretly store weapons and treasure toward his planned escape before they disappeared."

"The secret chamber," she breathed in dawning comprehension. "Edward was looking for the secret chamber and was killed for his troubles." She looked up at him, her heartache forgotten in the press of other disasters. "Did you know of it?"

He bowed his head. "I knew it existed—I am afraid I encouraged Monsieur Bing to discover its location."

"Oh," said Hattie, acutely dismayed. "Don't tell Bing."

He continued, "Your parents were shocked by his death; it is what caused their change of heart, I believe."

This was of interest, and Hattie grasped at it. "They repented of their treachery?"

Reluctant to disillusion her, he shook his head. "I'm afraid it was not that simple. They began to make overtures to the British, believing the British would soon control the site. They were hedging their bets."

Hattie thought this over. "And someone must have found out."

"Yes—someone must have found out. And those who work for Napoleon could not take the chance your parents would reveal what they knew to the British—just as they could not take the chance that Edward would discover the chamber."

She met his eyes. "And what is your role?"

He shook his head slightly with regret. "I cannot say, Hattie—you mustn't ask."

Exquisitely frustrated, she stared at him. "Why? Are you in danger? Am I? I don't understand."

He cradled her head so that his thumb caressed her cheek. "The less you know of this, the better—believe me."

Stepping back from his embrace, she crossed her arms before her, in part to guard herself from him because she was very much inclined to seek out the comfort of his embrace and she needed to think. "You must see that I have no reason to believe you—you stole the key to the British consulate and you were trying to steal my necklace."

But he was unrepentant. "You had the disk but did not tell me—I could not rule out the possibility that you were aware of its significance."

"I am *no* traitor."

He tilted his head. "I could not be certain—and you were not honest with me."

Eyes flashing, she retorted, "That's rich, coming from you." With a monumental effort, she barely refrained from stamping her foot.

He stood silent while she tried to calm herself; it did appear as though he had a point—and that he had been acting in a consistent manner throughout, now that she knew his motivation. With a deep breath, she controlled her temper and asked, "How did you know I had it?"

"When the intruder came in—I saw it."

She made a wry mouth. "And here I thought you were admiring my nightdress."

"It is a most excellent nightdress." His gaze rested ever so briefly on her breasts.

As she had already determined that he was very much

attracted to her breasts, she was unsurprised by this lapse. With a mental shake, she took herself in hand and returned to the point of the conversation. "Why is the disk important— how did you know of it?"

"I eavesdropped on your parents," he admitted without a flicker of guilt. "You must let me examine it, Hattie—I believe it holds a clue."

Torn, she unfolded her hand and looked at her necklace. "Why should I trust you?"

He thought about it for a moment. "Because I love you."

Chapter 24

O ff balance, Hattie dropped her gaze and stammered, "I thought as much." She had little doubt his declaration was sincere—he was mixing his accents again.

"I will not allow you to be harmed, Hattie; but it is very important that I see it."

Opening her hand, she lifted it to him. "I will allow you to copy it, but I would like to keep it, if I may—they gave me so little."

Taking it from her hand, he held it up to the light of the sconce. "Warn me if anyone comes."

This seemed unlikely, as there was little pedestrian traffic at this back stairway, but she willingly kept a look-out. "Should I fetch paper and a pen?"

"No."

To be useful, she explained, "The figure is of Hathor on the one side."

"That may be of significance—what does she represent?"

Hattie tried not to blush. "Fertility."

She watched him turn the disk over and study the markings on the other side, unable to glean anything from his expression. "Do you know what it means?"

"It is in a Napoleonic cipher that should not be difficult to translate." He lifted his gaze to hers. "Did you show it to the solicitor?"

"No—he made me uneasy."

He returned to his scrutiny. "Someone else was made uneasy."

She decided she may as well ask. "Did you kill him?"

Glancing up, he was almost amused. "No." Relinquishing the necklace back to her, he instructed, "You must secret it on your person in a way that it is not visible to any—not around your neck."

She nodded.

He was very serious. "You must tell no one you have it—no one at all. Do you understand?"

This seemed evident, and nodding again, she ventured, "Do you think it would be best if you carried it?" Perhaps she was being foolish, if it was so very dangerous.

But he shook his head. "It is safer with you."

Because, of course, he could be killed if anyone thought he held the information—so many others had been killed and now it made complete sense. It was probably why he memorized the markings instead of writing them down. "You will be careful?" He was secretive to the point of exasperation but if he were killed she didn't know how she would cope, the wretched man.

"I will."

Finished, he handed her the necklace and they faced each other again. Suddenly shy after his declaration of love, Hattie looked away. "I should be going—I wouldn't want to come in so late that Bing shoots me by mistake."

Staying her with a hand on her arm, he sought permission, this time. "I would like to kiss you, if I may."

"I have no other jewelry to wrest."

With a small smile, he bent in and whispered, "Nevertheless."

The kiss was soft and chaste—as though he could not be

gentle enough. It made her want to cry again but instead, when he drew away she whispered, "I know where the strongbox is."

She had shocked him, and felt a sense of accomplishment—he who was so unshockable. His hands found her arms and he squeezed them gently. "Hattie," he said with quiet intensity. "Tell me."

Lost in his eyes she paused, wondering if she was being foolish, trusting him because he said he loved her and it was so very nice to be loved. "Why did you steal the key from the British consulate?"

He didn't miss a beat. "I must discover how much is known."

"Aren't your interests the same as England's?" She realized the thought had been niggling around the corners of her mind ever since their visit—perhaps he and Eugenie served the enemy; he was pretending to be French and Eugenie seemed genuinely French.

Patiently, he explained, "I believe you know what this business of mine is—in this business, it is best to trust no one. Many have died as a result of trusting an ally who was not, in fact, an ally."

This made sense, she supposed. "The British do know something. Robbie—is Robbie in your business, also?"

"Perhaps," was all he would say.

"Robbie asked me if I knew of a strongbox."

His brows drew together. "Did he indeed?"

"I'm not certain it is a strongbox," she clarified. "I haven't opened it up yet—but it seems likely."

"No, it is not a strongbox; but I would very much like to see it immediately."

"As you wish." She hoped she wasn't being an imbecile, herself. Glancing up at him as they made their way up the stairway she took a quick breath. "I would rather Bing didn't know about my parents."

With emphasis, he met her eyes. "Do not tell anyone of any of this, Hattie—even Mademoiselle Bing. I will have your promise."

"Not to worry," she assured him in an ironic tone. "You have it."

As they hurried down the hallway toward her room she observed, "It hardly seems fair—I am expected to tell you everything, yet you tell me nothing in return."

"Believe me—you are better off."

She subsided and they walked together for a few steps in silence. "I have a sister," he offered.

Smiling, she turned to regard him, walking sideways to keep up with his long strides. "Do you? Older or younger?"

"Younger. She is wed, and has a little boy."

Delighted with this insight, she replied, "How lovely."

Taking her hand, he lifted it to kiss her knuckles. "Perhaps you will meet them soon."

Their eyes met, and she thought—yes, I would very much like to meet them and I don't very much care where they are, as long as I am with him; I sincerely hope he is what he seems and is not my enemy.

Once in her room, Hattie tiptoed past the sleeping Bing and carefully lifted the parcel from the interior of the wardrobe. With some stealth, she carried it out to the hallway where Berry took a quick look around and then pulled her into his adjacent room and shut the door behind them. I am lost to all propriety, she thought without much regret, and wondered if she had the wherewithal to resist a seduction if he were bent on such. However, it seemed that the pleasures of the flesh were the last thing on the man's mind as he deposited the package on the bed, turning up the lamplight to scrutinize it carefully. "How did you come to have this?"

Thinking about it, Hattie replied, "I'd rather not say. But I believe it was sent to me by my parents and misdelivered."

As he unwrapped the parcel, she watched over his shoulder, holding her breath. Beneath the wrapping was revealed a brass casket of some sort, bound in twine. With a pocketknife, he sawed at the twine and opened the casket to reveal a wooden object—a board of approximately ten inches by five, mounted on short wooden legs. Berry sat back on his haunches and made a sound of satisfaction. "The senet board."

Knitting her brow, Hattie remembered Bing's reference. "A game board? For the love of heaven; all of this trouble for a game board?"

Handling it gently, he picked it up and examined it. "There should be playing pieces." Carefully, his long fingers palpated the base of the board.

Hattie picked up the brass casket. "Could this be them?" Lining the floor of the casket were small flat disks, each about the size of a ha'pence.

Berry plucked one out and examined the engravings on it next to the lamplight. "Hieroglyphics," he pronounced, frustrated. "I cannot translate."

"Can you tell me the significance? Or why my parents would send it to me, of all people?" Aware he may not wish to tell her, she couched the words respectfully and considered leaning over so that her breasts brushed against him, but it turned out that such tactics were unnecessary.

"They put together a map to show the location of the secret chamber in the event they were stricken with fever or injured—any variety of things that could happen in this part of the world."

"Murder," Hattie added succinctly.

"Murder," he concurred. "Only three knew of the secret chamber at the tomb—your parents knew and Monsieur Auguste knew, also. There had to be a map as a precaution, and the map had to be stored at a distant place—to avoid the illness or other catastrophe that would have taken their own lives."

"And implausibly, they were all struck down—it is enough to make you believe in the curse."

He glanced at her. "Your parents' death was a means to ensure they did not negotiate with the British by offering to reveal what they knew of the secret chamber."

"And Monsieur Auguste?"

With a shrug, he conceded, "I have investigated and as far as I can tell, his death was a coincidence—he was indeed killed by brigands. It must have been a terrible blow to those who frantically seek the secret cache."

"So instead, they frantically seek me." Small wonder every stray spy was visiting Cornwall—Hattie hoped they hadn't alarmed the neighbors.

"Yes." He bent his head, thinking. "I must have this translated."

"Mr. Hafez?" suggested Hattie.

"No," he said immediately, meeting her gaze in all seriousness. "He is not to know of this, Hattie."

"Is he an enemy?" Hattie thought of poor Bing.

But as always, he would allow no insights into what was apparently a complicated maze of allegiances. "I cannot say—trust no one."

"We can trust Bing—she may know the translation."

He leapt upon this idea. "Excellent—let us ask her."

"Now?" Hattie asked doubtfully.

"We sail tomorrow," he pointed out as he rose to his feet. "There may not be another opportunity."

So it came to pass that Hattie stood beside Bing's bedside, holding up her robe and gently shaking her awake. "Bing, Monsieur Berry is here and requires your assistance."

Sleepy, Bing sat up. "Certainly," she said, and pushed her arms through the robe. If Hattie wondered what explanation Berry would offer for his strange request, she hadn't long to wait.

"Mademoiselle Bing," he began with respectful deference. "I'm afraid there are those who would take Mademoiselle Blackhouse's inheritance from her." As he produced the senet board Hattie could hear Bing's reverent intake of breath. "I believe this board contains a map which her parents created to show where it was hidden, but I am unable to translate the markings on the playing pieces."

"Interesting." Bing lifted a disk between her thin fingers, examining it closely. "Normally these are players—rather like chess pieces."

"These are easier to engrave," Berry suggested.

"Undoubtedly." Bing moved to hold the piece next to the bedside lamp, her brow furrowed with concentration. "This one reveals a measurement—Egyptians measured in cubits of approximately 15 inches." She lifted another. "This one also—only it contains a different measurement."

Watching her, Hattie asked, "If it forms a map, how do we learn the manner in which the measurements are applied and in what order?"

"I imagine the board is instrumental in that respect." Berry indicated the surface of the board, which contained a grid of small squares.

Bing carefully examined the board, and then examined the

disks. "I believe there is a correlation to the squares engraved on each disk, but I'm afraid it will take me some time to puzzle it out."

Berry thought about it, turning over a disk in his hand. "Shall we copy the engravings onto paper so as to allow you an opportunity to translate? Only do not arouse suspicion and do not describe the senet board." He added with some emphasis, "To anyone."

"I wouldn't think of it," said Bing, unable to refrain from running her fingers gently along the smooth wood of the board. "Only imagine what this board has seen."

"Have you a hiding place for it? It may be best if you keep it, rather than Mademoiselle Blackhouse."

Bing thought for a moment. "My hat box; I shall place it under my sun bonnet."

"Excellent." Berry stood and bowed. "I must leave, but I thank you for your assistance."

Nodding her head, Bing was as dignified as though she was in a drawing room and not abed in her robe with her hair plaited down her back. "You are most welcome."

They watched as he let himself out, off—Hattie surmised—to conduct a search at the British consulate.

"Here's an interesting turn of events." Bing gave her a shrewd glance as she looked about for paper and pen.

"Are you uneasy, Bing?" Hattie was trying to decide if she was uneasy, herself. She had a lot to think over.

"No," said Bing in her forthright manner. "He will never act to your detriment."

Hattie hovered for a moment on the verge of confiding in Bing, but decided the news was too cataclysmic—it would be a simple leap to guess that Edward's death was no accident and there was no point in reopening that terrible wound.

Instead, while her companion scratched the markings on a sheet of paper, Hattie made ready for bed, her mind filled with what she had learned this night and the journey to come the next morning. Her relationship with Berry had coalesced, no question. A shame it was not unadulterated happiness—she still didn't know who he was or whom he served. And she felt a cold knot of despair when she contemplated her parents' treachery; he had wanted to spare her the knowledge and in some small corner of her mind she wished he had—the sheer weight of it was so daunting. I wonder how many know, she thought in shame, and then remembered that many of those who knew had died. Perhaps Berry could arrange matters so her parents' duplicity would not be made public; otherwise, no matter where she went, the Blackhouse shame would follow her. The best thing to do, she realized, was to change her surname. On this hopeful note, she slid into the bed.

Chapter 25

H attie stood on the deck of the *Priapus* and watched the teeming city of Cairo recede from view. A good riddance, she thought; perhaps she would develop a fondness for Egypt in the more rural areas where the excavations were located, but she could not say that she held any fondness for Cairo. Although it was here that Berry finally abandoned his mighty resistance—she had little doubt an offer of marriage would be made once the urgent matters were settled, and she would accept him with a whole heart. She didn't want to dwell on the unfortunate fact she knew next to nothing about him—including his name—so she did not. Like Bing, she was certain he did not serve the enemy, although she hoped she would not be called upon to stake her life on it—literally. The fact that he had been monitoring her parents and going to such lengths to thwart the planned escape from Elba all pointed to his role as an ally.

With one hand shading her eyes from the sun, she stood at the rail and glanced around at her surroundings. The *Priapus* was a Nile river *dahabeeyah* that carried twenty passengers in ten cabins, all traveling to the ancient city of Thebes where the barge would dock for a matter of days, allowing the passengers to explore the famous sights.

"At least on the river, the heat is not quite so unbearable," Hattie remarked to Eugenie, who stood close by.

"No. Although my hair, it does not behave as it ought." Eugenie indicated Bing, standing at a small distance and deep in conversation with Hafez. "Will they make a match of it, do you think?"

Remembering Berry's cautions about the minister, Hattie said only, "Perhaps—they are certainly very compatible."

Eugenie slid her a glance, the girl's blue eyes very bright. "If they marry, would you stay in Egypt with them?"

"No thank you—I prefer a cooler clime." Surely Berry must abide somewhere cooler than here—for the love of heaven, *anywhere* was cooler than here.

Eugenie raised one delicately arched brow. "Now that Monsieur Tremaine has suffered the death of his bride, perhaps he will return to cool England also."

The observation was laced with innuendo, but Hattie decided two could play at this game. "He does not appear overly bereaved," she returned, and arched her own brow at her companion. After a startled glance from Eugenie, the subject was mutually dropped. Hattie was not so untutored as to think that Robbie meant anything serious by Eugenie, and she had already deduced that he must have offered for Madame Auguste on orders from his grey-eyed spymaster so as to secure the woman's safety. Unfortunately, the ruse had not intimidated the enemy, who had not only silenced the woman but had implicated Robbie in her murder for good measure—these were indeed dangerous people.

"Have you any suitors back home?" Eugenie's gaze was amused, but if she thought to needle Hattie by making an oblique reference to the kiss she had witnessed, she would be disappointed; Hattie was not one to be needled.

"Not a one," Hattie confessed with a smile. She threw in for good measure, "My last suitor married my last companion."

The other girl threw back her lovely head and issued a genuine laugh, which made Hattie like her better. She then clucked her tongue in sympathy at such a turn of events. "*Mal chance*—bad luck."

Shrugging, Hattie was philosophical. "I should not have made a good curate's wife, I think."

"Certainly not," agreed Eugenie with a toss of her curls. "The holy men, they are never very good in bed."

Deciding it would be best not to ask the basis for such a conclusion, Hattie only smiled and the two women stood for a moment in silence, watching the crew as they efficiently performed their tasks on the deck below. "Daniel is not about." Another bright glance from under Eugenie's lashes.

"Perhaps he is tired." Hattie wondered what his search had turned up, if anything. She was suddenly struck with how odd it was that Berry did not work for the British and apparently did not trust the British, but had nonetheless maneuvered to get British guards posted at the tomb.

"I think not—he is indefatigable." Eugenie preened in a self-satisfied manner, implying a carnal relationship.

Nothing daunted, Hattie agreed with her own knowing smile.

Rather than annoyance, the other accepted the riposte with another trill of genuine laughter. "You are not at all English," she declared, quirking a corner of her mouth.

Thinking of her parents' shame, Hattie almost wished she weren't. "And you—are you truly from Martinique?"

"*Mais oui*; although I am from everywhere, now."

"I envy you," Hattie said sincerely. "I have always longed to travel."

Turning, the other girl regarded her. "*Quant à ça*, you have never been to Egypt?"

Hattie confessed, "I have never been anywhere. Except Paris, just now."

"It was unnatural, yes, for your parents to behave as they did?"

Thinking this was not a subject she wished to discuss with Eugenie, Hattie simply replied, "They were dedicated to their work." Thinking of their dedication reminded her of the golden disk, now firmly pinned to the inside of her shift. My wretched legacy, she thought with a twinge of revulsion. I don't know why I longed for them so much—the god-king's daughter was welcome to them.

Eugenie turned to view the shoreline as they passed. "*Voyons*; Saqqara is next, I think."

Hattie stood on tiptoe in an attempt to view the ancient site as it came into view, but couldn't see over the wheel-house. "I cannot see—I shall have to walk to the bow."

Eugenie smiled as she rested her gaze on the men below once again. "Indeed; you are *très petite*. Go, then."

Berry does not mind that I am petite, thought Hattie as she made her way to the bow. And Eugenie is a minx; I wonder what her task is—he would not have brought her along, otherwise. Leaning over the rail, the weak breeze stirred her curls as Bing came to stand beside her.

"Saqqara," Hattie pronounced—although she wouldn't have had a clue if Eugenie hadn't told her.

"Necropolis for Memphis, the ancient capital," agreed Bing with satisfaction. "And I'm afraid you will be quite brown, Hathor."

"I left my hat somewhere," she confessed. "How does Mr. Hafez?"

"I am making casual inquiries about ancient Egyptian measurements."

Hattie was impressed. "Excellent sleuthing, Bing."

But her companion pursed her mouth for a moment, troubled. "Did Monsieur Berry indicate who would do such a thing—purloin your inheritance? Your parents certainly would not have stood for it."

This was a good question, and of course Bing was unaware that her parents were capable of much worse. Stammering a bit, Hattie equivocated, "Monsieur Berry does not know the nature of the trove, Bing—only that there is one. Perhaps they were merely secreting funds because they could not visit their banking house regularly."

"The whole thing may be a fish tale—a feint," Bing warned. "Edward said your parents greatly enjoyed a joke; pray don't get your hopes up."

Hattie smiled to show she was not upset about the fanciful loss of her fanciful inheritance. "Even if that is the case, it is an interesting puzzle, and will keep us occupied for the journey."

Bing nodded, somewhat reassured. "I will go below, if you do not mind, and make a note of what I have learned."

"I will be down in short order to fetch my parasol." Although truth to tell, Hattie much preferred the sun on her face—here was one advantage Egypt had over Cornwall. Standing again at the rail, Hattie leaned over to watch the barge cut through the wide river and then saw Robbie appear in her line of sight, smiling and holding her hat in one hand.

"Is this yours, Hattie?"

"It is—thank you for fetching it to me." She dutifully tied the broad ribbon under her chin as he came to stand beside her, resting his elbows on the railing so that his height was nearly level with hers. "Don't lose it in the river as you did at Truro."

"Unfair," she laughed. "Your wretched brother James threw it in."

"As I recall, Papa gave him a whipping as a result."

"And well deserved."

They stood together in companionable silence, watching the water. "Would you jump?" he teased.

Assessing the distance, Hattie considered. "It is a longer drop than from the bridge on the River Fal—I'm not sure I would. You?"

"Without hesitation." He shook his head in a mock reprimand. "Fie, Hattie—you were always so fearless."

"I've grown old and decorous," she agreed in a grave tone. Berry would jump, she thought. He has already jumped to and from the balcony with little effort—and if he jumped into the Nile I suppose I would jump right in after him. She wondered if Berry could swim and guessed that he could; I would like to swim with him, she thought, and felt a heat that had little to do with the hot sun.

Glancing toward the stern, she spied Hafez walking with Eugenie. He appeared to be explaining something to her whilst she paid rapt attention and clung to his arm. Ah, she thought; here is her task—my poor Bing stands little chance, although I truly do not think her heart is at risk. Thinking to tease Robbie, she indicated the couple with an arch look. "Best look lively."

He glanced at her warily, trying to gauge the tenor of her remark. "I have no interest there—far from it."

"Oh," she said easily, looking back at them. "I was mistaken, then."

Robbie noted in a neutral tone, "She seems very friendly with Monsieur Berry."

"Yes," Hattie agreed. "It certainly seems that way."

Robbie bent his head for a moment and contemplated his hands on the railing. "I wanted to mention something to you—now, don't fly up in the boughs, Hattie—but perhaps you should keep him at arm's length, so to speak."

Hattie feigned ignorance. "Monsieur Berry, you mean?"

Meeting her gaze with his own, he nodded. "His manner toward you borders on the proprietary, sometimes."

She teased, "He is French, after all—perhaps it comes naturally."

"Perhaps," he agreed, treading carefully. "But you are such an innocent, Hattie—I only wanted to mention it, so that you are made aware."

Not so very innocent, thought Hattie, hiding a smile—and shockingly ready to be made less so. "Do you think him a fortune-hunter, then?"

"No—not at all. It's just that we know so little about him."

She gently pointed out, "He was my parents' agent, Robbie; and it does appear they trusted him completely."

Nodding his head in acknowledgment, her companion nonetheless cautioned, "I know. But I must stand as your protector on this journey—you have no one else, after all."

"Then you should not goad me to leap into the Nile, if you please."

He laughed, and they were easy again. Until, that is, he asked in a causal manner, "Have you had an opportunity to ask him if he is aware of a strongbox?"

Hattie only shook her head whilst grinding her teeth.

Chapter 26

That evening, their party dined with three other passengers to make up the table of ten. Mr. Canton was a jovial Englishman in the best tradition, who took Hattie's hand with great interest. "Are you related to the famous Egyptologists?"

"I am," she replied, and hoped her smile didn't wobble. "I am their daughter."

"What a happy chance, to have met you—I am financing a dig in Abu Simbel and I follow their work with great interest."

Apparently he had not heard the latest news and so Hattie only nodded, trying to decide whether she should explain that they were missing or put if off and hope it needn't be revealed—in the end she decided to put it off.

"Do you join them?" the gentleman asked, clearly presuming that this was the case.

Unsure of how to respond, she temporized, "I hope to."

Bing came to her rescue by interjecting smoothly, "What dig do you finance, Mr. Canton?"

"The Temple of Amenophis," he explained. Somewhat abashed, he added, "I've made precious little profit, but I find the subject fascinating."

"An expensive hobby," nodded his fond wife, who sat by his side and methodically buttered her bread.

The gentleman explained, "The authorities hold you

hostage—charging fees or requiring concessions that are nothing short of extortion. It hardly matters, though—I live to see what is under the next sand dune."

"I completely understand," said Bing. "I follow the subject very closely, myself."

The two enthusiasts compared notes for a few minutes while Mrs. Canton and Hattie smiled at each other in the manner of those who did not share the call. While she listened absently, Hattie thought about how Napoleon had used his authority to extort her parents' support for his ambitions. Perhaps they were without a choice in the matter—like Mr. Canton—and had to do as they were told. Or perhaps it had been a small matter, at first, and then they had been unable to disentangle from the web, once they were caught up. Impatiently, she discarded the attempted excuses—treason was treason and was not to be condoned, no matter the devotion to one's work.

To her other side was Mr. Smithson, a short, spare man who was revealed to be a vicar from Shropshire. He listened in a friendly fashion but had little to offer by way of conversation. "Are you interested in Egyptology, Mr. Smithson?" Hattie asked, to draw him out.

"Very little, I'm afraid—I was to travel to the Holy Land but my tour was canceled; I thought I may as well sail up the Nile, as I was stranded in the vicinity."

"A different sort of holiday than you expected," Hattie noted with a smile.

But the gentleman was philosophical. "It is always interesting to learn new things—we never know why we are led."

"I suppose that is true." Indeed, Hattie's temper had led her out the window at the Prussian embassy in Paris, and her life had changed irrevocably as a result. As they ate their repast, she noted some constraint between Canton and Hafez, and overheard the latter's pointed remark, "Very altruistic people, the Blackhouses—greed was never a motivation."

Hattie could feel herself color up and briefly met Berry's eyes across the table. She surmised that Canton intended to take artifacts back to England, which naturally put him in the minister's black book. Still, all parties were civil in discussing the upcoming ports of call.

"Do you stop at Thebes?" Canton asked Bing, his fellow devotee.

"Yes—we will visit the Blackhouses' latest excavation."

"Ah—the tomb of the god-king's daughter; best beware of the curse," he warned, half-serious.

"Bah—we fear no curses, do we, Monsieur Hafez?" asked Eugenie, who prettily sought his confirmation that he would protect her from all enemies, real or imagined.

"There are times," the minister admitted with a huge sigh, "that I do indeed feel cursed."

He was probably thinking of Monsieur Auguste's untimely death; or perhaps his country's crumbling infrastructure, or the loss of priceless artifacts to entrepreneurs like Canton, or even the missing strongbox—it was enough to make one feel quite sorry for him. Hattie wondered what information Eugenie had been dispatched to beguile from him.

Into the small silence, Berry addressed Robbie in a deferential manner. "Mademoiselle Blackhouse tells me that she has a long friendship with your family, Monsieur Tremaine; it is fortunate that you are at hand to assist her."

"We've grown up together," the other agreed. "Why, just this afternoon we were reminiscing over some childhood misadventures." Robbie turned to smile warmly across the table at Hattie, but she was already warmed by Berry's attempt to extend an olive branch.

"Where was this?" asked the vicar, and a comparison of Cornwall and Shropshire ensued, during which Hattie shot Berry a grateful glance and in this brief exchange she was given to understand he would speak to her privately before the evening concluded.

Thus it was with some impatience that Hattie sat through a discussion extolling the merits of the tedious New Kingdom and the equally tedious Middle Kingdom until Mrs. Canton finally tugged on her better half's arm and insisted they retire before she fell asleep on the tabletop. With good humor, the dinner party broke up and Hattie felt free to tease Bing as they walked out on the deck, "Mrs. Canton had best look to her husband or you'll have another one hanging on your sleeve."

Bing rendered her dry smile at the jest. "A common interest, is all."

But Hattie found it amusing in the extreme. "Honestly, Bing—had I know it would be so alluring to the opposite sex, I would have paid more attention to the museum exhibition in hopes of securing a beau."

Bing smoothed her gloves and said only, "I have no fears on that front, Hathor."

They took a turn around the deck, Hattie lifting her face to feel the cool breeze. "Thank heaven there is a breeze at night, Bing—we can open our porthole and be more comfortable." Their stateroom was more spacious than on the *Sophia*, but Hattie continued to dislike the feeling of being enclosed in a small space. "Where do you suppose we are?" Pausing at the railing, they viewed the shoreline that would reveal an occasional cluster of lights in the darkness, evidencing small outposts. Toward the shallows, a random lit lantern would reveal a fisherman on a small wooden vessel, his spear poised to stab the fish attracted by the light. The air was close and heavy, and smelled of rich, wet earth.

"Asyut, perhaps," guessed Bing. "It is difficult to discern with so few landmarks along this stretch of the Nile."

"If I may be of help, ladies," said Smithson from behind them. "I have just returned from the wheelhouse and the captain informs me we come to Girgeh within the hour."

"Excellent," said Bing with a nod. "I believe we are ahead of schedule."

She and the vicar moved toward a hanging lantern to examine his map, and Hattie leaned on the railing with her forearms, listening to their voices and the lapping of the water against the hull. Berry materialized beside her with gratifying promptness, and taking a quick glance about, lifted her hand to kiss the knuckles.

"*Bonne nuit,*" she said with a delighted smile.

"*Très bonne,*" he agreed, his gaze on her upturned face. Everything has changed, she noted with a jolt of pure happiness; he no longer attempted to shutter his emotions when they were alone.

"What did you discover at the consulate?"

"Hattie," he remonstrated, his head bent close to hers. "That is not very romantic."

I should tell him that I love him, she thought with some nervousness, gazing into the brown eyes that held such tenderness. He told me, and it is only fair. However, as she had never said the words before she felt ridiculously awkward and could not quite bring herself to do it.

The moment passed and he indicated Bing. "Any progress with the senet board?"

"Now who is unromantic?" she teased, and ran her fingers

lightly across the back of his hand, which caused a gratifying intake of breath as he moved closer to murmur in her ear.

"Do not, I beg of you—I do not dare kiss you for fear Monsieur Tremaine will call me out."

Hattie had little doubt who would prevail should such an event occur, but instead said with mock severity, "It is just as well—I have decided there will be a price for these kisses I have given so freely."

Chuckling, he turned and leaned back against the rail, looking down upon her. "I will pay any price," he declared, which she considered a very satisfactory answer.

"You must tell me something about yourself—that is the price."

He smiled, glancing up at the stars. "What is it you wish to know?"

She shrugged lightly in her best imitation of Eugenie. "I don't know—anything you are willing to tell me, I suppose. Do you like dogs?" Hattie had never owned a dog but she adored the Tremaines' dogs.

Eyes gleaming, he brought his chin down. "I have four dogs."

Very pleased with this bit of information, she laughed, "Four? Isn't that excessive?"

"No." He smiled back at her. "They hunt with me."

"Oh." She considered. "Are they allowed in the house?"

"They are not small," he explained. "I do not argue with them."

Laughing, she had to quieten when Bing and the vicar looked up from their conversation.

"So now I have told you four things," he noted, his gaze focused on her mouth.

"I believe that only counts as one," she disagreed in a pert tone.

199

"Four," he repeated firmly, leaning in to whisper next to her ear. "I shall keep an account."

Hattie's compliant chaperone had apparently decided enough was enough and she returned to her charge's side. "Shall we play cards?" Bing asked. "It would be a means to pass the time."

"Certainly," agreed Berry, and Hattie was given to understand that a game of cards was not the true object of this request.

"What shall you play?" asked Smithson hopefully. "I am rather fond of cards."

Without missing a beat, Bing invited the vicar to join them and they made their way to the dining room. After having determined that they would play whist, the four settled in while Hattie hoped the vicar would not stay long—she was tired from her late night the night before.

As the cards were dealt, Berry said, "You are a military man, I believe." Hattie looked up in surprise; Smithson did not appear so to her.

"Indeed," the other agreed. "I was a chaplain with the 3rd Division on the Peninsula."

Berry nodded. "You saw heavy action, then."

"Yes," the man sighed. "Unfortunately my services were much in demand."

The players took up their cards. "You were under the command of Le Marchant?"

"No," the other corrected, "General Picton—and Colonel William Merryfield was my commanding officer."

Berry is testing him, thought Hattie as she studied her cards. Because in his mysterious business, you do not trust anyone and the good vicar suddenly seeks our company.

"Was the 3rd Division involved in any of Wellington's

great victories?" asked Bing. "I'm afraid I must profess some ignorance."

"I had the honor of meeting the Iron Duke at Salamanca," Smithson replied, "and heard his stirring exhortations before the coming battle. A great man—one could sense it immediately."

"*We few, we happy few, we band of brothers,*'" quoted Bing, impressed. " '*For he today that sheds his blood with me shall be my brother.*' How fortunate, to take part in such events."

Making a discard, the other shook his head. "I'm afraid I shall not '*stand a tip toe when this day is named.*' War is a terrible thing—thank heaven it finally came to an end."

"I beg your pardon," said Bing, a trifle mortified.

"Oh dear—I meant no rebuke," the other explained hastily. "There is no question that this was a just war, and well fought by the Allies; I only regret the necessity."

Hattie noted that the other man did not inquire after Berry's service, probably because Berry was, to all appearances, French and there was every likelihood the two men fought against each other—good manners precluded such a pursuit. I wonder for whom he fought, if anyone, Hattie thought, watching Berry from beneath her lashes. And if he also saw heavy action or if he merely lurked behind the scenes as he does here.

They played for an hour and then Smithson stood to take his leave, thanking them for allowing him the pleasure. "A very amiable man," pronounced Bing, watching him leave. "It appears he has hidden depths."

But Berry was not interested in pleasantries, and dealt another hand so that it appeared they continued to play. "You have made a translation?"

"Yes—as you say, I believe it is a map. The disks are marked with a pair of numbers that correspond to squares on the board, rather like 'four across and two down.' When they are laid out in order on the board, the measurements upon them explain the direction and how many feet to travel to follow the map."

"Excellent," Berry said with approval. "You have done extraordinary work."

But Bing made a gesture of regret. "Unfortunately, there was one additional safeguard made to ensure the secrecy of the clues. One cannot ascertain where the map begins or ends without some sort of starting point and a reference to a compass of some sort."

The other two stared at her. "It does not explain which way is north?" asked Hattie.

Bing nodded. "From what I can understand, the disk at the center of the puzzle must be replaced with another to ascertain this information—and the location of the missing disk is disclosed upon the false one."

"Well then, Bing; where is the missing disk?" asked Hattie impatiently.

"It is affixed on the princess herself," explained Bing in a regretful tone. "Inside the sarcophagus."

Chapter 27

*T*he *hundred-gated Thebes,*'" quoted Bing in reverent tones as she stood on the deck, shading her eyes against the bright sun. "Sacred city to countless generations of the ancients."

The barge had docked at the wooden quay the night before and its passengers now prepared to disembark onto the embankment, which was enclosed by a gated palisade hewn from new wood. Observing it, Hattie noted, "It seems the dock here is more secure than the one in Cairo."

"Of a necessity," explained Hafez, who stood beside them. "Visitors must now register upon arrival and no one may depart absent a search of the vessel. Fortunately, the river is the only practical means of transportation and this allows us to control the comings and goings. We must do what we can to prevent the further depletion of my country's treasures."

With a nod of her head, Bing indicated the west bank on the opposite side of the wide river, the ruins of the Necropolis near the shore and the famed barren cliffs rising starkly in the background. "Edward said it was helpful that the only entrance to the Valley of the Kings is narrow—any other entry or exit is nearly impossible."

Hattie held the brim of her straw hat pulled low over her eyes, and tilted her head back to contemplate the famous Necropolis across the Nile. That morning she had noted with some alarm that she was indeed so brown that she could be mistaken for an American Indian; it came from walking on the deck in the hopes of meeting up with Berry. Poor Bing, on the other hand, was deprived of her sun bonnet as it served as the hiding place for the senet board. "The tombs are beyond those cliffs in the back?"

Hafez nodded. "And within them—as Miss Bing indicates, there is a single narrow entrance to the Valley." Leaning over, he pointed to explain the location on the opposite shore and Hattie was impressed—despite herself—by the sheer history of it.

Turning her gaze to the east bank, where they were now docked, Hattie asked the minister, "And Thebes is on this side?"

"Thebes is actually on both sides of the river; the town and the principal temples are on the east bank—where we are—and the west bank consists of the Necropolis and the tombs. Most of the government offices are here on the east bank, and I shall register with the local authorities so that they are aware of our presence." On a somber note he added, "Ever since your parents disappeared there are additional precautions—the authorities wish to be informed of all visitors."

Reminded, Hattie turned back toward the Valley of the Kings. "Where is the new tomb? Is it located near the tomb of Seti?"

"The princess's tomb is the one nearest to the entrance— closest to the river. It was discovered almost by accident—a pile of rubble obscured the entrance and the tomb is not a large one. It is presumed that Seti's tomb is nearby, but it has yet to be discovered."

"Her tomb is most unusual," noted Bing. "The queens and princesses were normally buried in the Valley of the

Queens, which is opposite to the Valley of the Kings and nowhere near as grand."

Hafez agreed. "It is theorized that Seti the Great could not bear to have his beloved daughter so far removed from him in death."

How gratifying—to be a cherished daughter, Hattie thought with a pang, then quickly diverted her thoughts by looking about her for Berry; they had made a plan to rifle the sarcophagus and secure the missing disk first thing this morning. Hopefully it would be apparent upon opening; Hattie was uneasy with the idea of disturbing the mummified princess. However, instead of Berry she observed the Cantons, coming their way to bid them goodbye before they caught another vessel for Abu Simbel, further up the river.

Shaking hands, Mr. Canton said in his hearty manner, "Good luck, Miss Blackhouse—perhaps we shall return to Cairo together at the conclusion of our respective visits."

"I would enjoy it very much," said Hattie politely.

With a meaningful look, the bluff man added, "Our oldest son is a likely lad—perhaps you will permit him to call upon you once you are back in England."

"Frederick," remonstrated his embarrassed wife. "I beg your pardon, Miss Blackhouse—pay no attention to my husband's schemings."

The man laughed good-naturedly. "Can't blame me— imagine sitting down to the Christmas goose with the Blackhouses—I couldn't ask for more in life."

Hattie laughed also, to show she wasn't offended. Best not to mention she had never sat down to the Christmas goose with the Blackhouses, either—Christmas was instead a merry affair spent at the busy Tremaine household with Robbie and his family. Hattie had a strong premonition, however, that her next Christmas would be spent elsewhere—the exact location as yet unknown. With defiance, she lifted her face to the sun, unable to suppress her happiness. I decided to seize hold of my life, she thought, and instead my life seized hold of me.

As the Cantons waved and left them, Berry joined the party on deck. Watching him, Hattie thought he seemed a bit preoccupied. "Is all in train?" she asked in a low voice as he stood between Hattie and Bing. They had decided that Bing would distract the minister once they were at the tomb so that she and Berry were left in the inner chamber with the sarcophagus. As an excuse, Hattie was to pretend to sketch the interior, which was truly a deceit—Hattie was no artist. Berry had at first been reluctant to allow her to participate in the tomb-raiding scheme but she had insisted. "It is my inheritance, after all," she had said in front of Bing, and so he had been outmaneuvered.

"Yes—do you have your sketchbook?"

It was actually Bing's sketchbook as Hattie would have scorned such an accessory, but she nodded nonetheless. Glancing around to see that no one was within earshot, she asked a question that had occurred to her last night. "Did you have an opportunity to translate the Napoleonic cipher on my disk? Perhaps it is a second source, so to speak, and we needn't disentomb the miserable princess."

"Yes—but it was not helpful; the words on your disk refer the reader to the senet board, and since we are already aware of the senet board's existence it proved of little help." Bending his head, he met her eyes and addressed her in a very serious tone. "Now that we are to travel on land you must stay close to me at all times. Do not speak to any strangers—I will have your promise on this, Hattie."

Hattie nodded, her expression somber for a moment—it was easy to forget that opposing forces were intensely interested in the secret chamber and by extension, in what she knew.

Reading her thoughts, he added. "You will be kept safe. I will see to it."

Eugenie drifted up beside them in a cloud of perfume and Berry gave her a severe glance. "You must not cause trouble, Eugenie—I will send you home."

"Bah," the other girl exclaimed in disgust. "Who would believe such a rich man would have such a cheap watch?"

"Did you return it?"

Her pretty bosom rose as she sighed with regret. "But of course—I do as you say."

Hattie inferred that Mr. Canton had been her unknowing victim and was intrigued. "How did you manage to get close enough?"

Eugenie gave her an arch look, the implication of which Hattie found a bit shocking but Berry forestalled any further explanation. "You are not getting close enough where you need to." He threw a meaningful glance back at Hafez, who was standing next to Bing and conversing with her in an animated fashion as he gestured toward the landmarks on shore.

Eugenie pouted and protested, "What am I to do?" She shook her head in exasperation. "A very strange man, that."

Hiding a smile, Hattie suggested, "You can lead a horse to water but you cannot make him drink."

"*Eh bien*," Eugenie nodded her head emphatically. "He does not wish to drink the water."

"Make him thirsty," Berry ordered her.

Eugenie tossed her head toward Hattie. "Perhaps this one should make the attempt—if she is so *irresistible*."

"I cannot hold a candle to Bing, I'm afraid," Hattie demurred. She could almost sympathize; it must seem incomprehensible to the beautiful girl that both Berry and Hafez had other preferences.

"Go," directed Berry. As Eugenie turned with a flounce to join Bing and Hafez, Berry asked Hattie, "Where is Smithson? He could be of use."

Hattie blinked, as this seemed a *non sequitur.* "How so?"

"There is an attraction, there," he explained, as though to a child.

Hattie stared at him. "Bing and Smithson? For the love of heaven—that woman is a *siren.*"

But her sally earned her only a perfunctory smile as he watched the others. Deciding she may as well ask, Hattie ventured, "What is Eugenie supposed to discover?"

Having no real expectation he would tell her, she was surprised when he replied, "There are the French, there are the British, and then there are the minister and his allies."

So—another potential enemy. "Perhaps he merely seeks to secure his country and its treasures against the others." In Hattie's opinion, Hafez truly did not seem to represent a hazard.

"He is dangerous because he is uncertain—I believe it was he who sent the man who was in your room that night."

Hattie blinked. "Why—I assumed it was the French; after all, it is the French who seek the cache."

"No, it was not the French who sent the intruder," he said with certainty. "Which leaves the minister, in league with your parents' solicitor." He paused. "And possibly Monsieur Auguste, when he yet lived."

Hattie looked at him in alarm. "If that was the alliance, then Hafez is the only one left alive. It is indeed ominous—small wonder if he is nervous."

Berry nodded. "Which is why he is dangerous."

"I don't understand," she said, thinking it over. "Why don't you believe it was the French who came after me...?"

"Hush, Hattie. Tell no one." The words were barely out before Robbie joined them, his gaze meeting Hattie's with a warning at finding her deep in conversation with Berry. He casually took her elbow to turn her toward himself. "Hallo, Hattie; monsieur."

After greetings were exchanged, Robbie deliberately addressed only Hattie. "Should we tour the Necropolis, Hattie? Although I'll wager it isn't half as fearsome as the Devere family cemetery was on a certain occasion."

"Don't remind me," she laughed. "But I am slated to tour my parents' last excavation with the minister this morning."

"Perhaps I shall join you, then."

"Please," Berry interjected. "I am certain the minister would be grateful for any assistance."

"Indeed," agreed Hattie, thinking this was the last thing they wanted but willing to cooperate if Berry didn't mind. "Do join us, Robbie."

Berry expressed his desire to make final arrangements and then excused himself, and Robbie's gaze held a gleam of amusement as the other man left. "For all of his sobriety, I believe he has a *tendre* for you, Hattie—have a care you do not trifle with his heart."

"I am no trifler," she protested in a mild tone, and left it at that. Robbie would discover soon enough how matters stood and it would be his turn to suffer a shock. Thank heaven for his faux betrothal; in retrospect, the late Madame Auguste had done her an enormous favor—Hattie would have never climbed out the window, else.

Chapter 28

A short time later, the party assembled on the gangway to disembark for the tomb. Hattie noted that Robbie was not present, and asked Berry in a low aside, "Confess; what have you done with the poor man?"

"I imagine he has been delayed." He met her eye. "He is a thirsty horse."

Sighing, she shook her head. "Poor Eugenie is doing yeoman's work—I hope you are paying her well."

But Berry was unsympathetic. "It is no hardship for such as she." Taking her arm, he led her down the wooden planks to the embankment. "He will want to join up with us, so we had best go quickly."

Accompanied by Bing and Hafez, they hired transport across the river in a *felucca*, one of the small sailing vessels that ferried residents and visitors alike across the Nile. Hattie had remembered her hat, and the veil attached to it fluttered in the breeze as the waterman navigated the boat to the west shore of the river, using the current to make the crossing as he skillfully plied the rudder. As they approached the opposite shore, Hattie contemplated the barren cliffs and thought, we are finally to meet—the princess and me—and at last I will see one of the famed Blackhouse excavations; I wish that I could muster some enthusiasm for either. She glanced at

Berry to find his gaze upon her, and she had the brief impression he was worried, even though he gave no outward sign. With a pang, she remembered that her own petty concerns were as nothing compared to his concerns, which were to avert the next war. She smiled in encouragement and saw his face soften as he moved to sit beside her.

"When we pass through the town, it would be best to keep your veil over your face—I would like to avoid attention."

"Shouldn't I speak to the native workers—appeal to them?" It seemed unlikely that she could obscure her identity if this was the plan.

"Not today," he explained. "I must make some inquiries, first."

She nodded. "What are we to do once we find the secret chamber?" It had occurred to her that if he didn't quite trust the British or the Egyptians, he was running out of candidates with whom to secure the cache—certainly they were not going to carry it away themselves.

"We shall see," was all he said, and she shot him a look so that he was aware she knew he was withholding information from her.

"It is a delicate business," he explained by way of apology. "We must await events."

I trust him—I do, she thought, as she looked away toward the approaching west bank. But I cannot help but wish that I had more answers and fewer questions.

Once landed, they procured a transportation cart that was little more than a wagon with benches lining the interior. The carts served as the principal means of transportation for tourists and were commanded by local boys who were constantly flicking their sticks over the backs of the placid donkeys with little perceivable effect. A slow but steady progress was made past the Colossi that guarded the Necropolis and then they entered the Valley of the Kings, the winding dusty road all that was left of the watercourse that had existed unnumbered years ago. The legendary valley was a fantastic sight—devoid of any life form, the landscape consisting entirely of rubble and rock as far as the eye could see. The entrances to several tombs could be observed in the distance, marked by crude scaffolding and equipment at each site. The area had attracted European interest when Napoleon, fresh from his conquest of Egypt, had sent French explorers to conduct a survey of the area and as a result of this heightened interest, at least twenty more tombs had been recently discovered. As there were over three hundred known pharaohs, it seemed likely that many more would be unearthed; there was an intense worldwide interest in the excavations and Egyptian-themed furniture was all the rage—everywhere except the Blackhouse manor in Cornwall, which Bing had learned to her disappointment.

They soon pulled to a stop; as Hafez had indicated, the tomb of the god-king's daughter had been discovered by accident and relatively close to the narrow entrance to the Valley of the Kings, cleft in the bedrock. The unlooked-for presence of the princess lent credence to the theory that there were more tombs in the immediate area—including that of the great Seti himself—and the find had inspired other Egyptologists to carefully survey the area for clues. They could be seen scattered along the high cliffs, wearing broad hats and tapping the rocks and crevices with long slender poles, their native guides alongside them. Hattie contemplated the topography, and decided it was an excellent place to store weapons and treasure that may be needed at a moment's notice—the area was desolate and yet was relatively close to the river.

The entrance to the hillside excavation was cordoned off and manned by two armed guards who were seated in the shade of a small makeshift awning. While the ladies remained in the cart beneath their parasols, Berry and Hafez approached the guards and presented their *bona fides*. The moment that the gentlemen made reference to Hattie became evident as both guards looked her way with interest.

"I am infamous," Hattie remarked with a sigh.

Bing could not disagree. "It is a compelling story and some curiosity is to be expected. You are a sympathetic figure."

Hattie remembered what had happened outside the consulate. "I hope they do not recognize my supposed likeness to the princess—they will expect me to raise the level of the Nile or some such thing."

"They do not appear credulous," Bing remarked. "And they wear British uniforms."

The two men returned to escort the ladies to the tomb, having secured the permission of the guards. Hafez was red-faced and unhappy and the nature of his complaint soon emerged.

"…it is an insult and I shall make a complaint through diplomatic channels."

Berry soothed him, "I imagine there is a concern for Mademoiselle Blackhouse's safety—it is unknown as yet what has happened to her parents, or who was responsible."

"Nonetheless," the other exclaimed angrily. "I should have been consulted."

"Why, what has happened, Mr. Hafez?" Bing touched his sleeve in sympathy.

"The consul has stationed British guards here in place of the usual ones." He bowed his head to Hattie in apology. "I mean no offense to you, Miss Blackhouse—but it must be

213

remembered your parents had no claim to the tomb itself, and neither does the English king."

"I quite understand," she soothed, and did not look at Berry. "It is indeed an affront to you, and you are ill-served."

Her mild outrage seemed to mollify the minister. "Exactly so—an affront."

"I can't imagine the soldiers would think to countermand you—after all, you serve the viceroy." Unspoken was the addendum that as matters stood, it was not a calamity, perhaps, to ingratiate the British.

On reflection, Hafez appeared to come to the same conclusion. "True," he agreed. Drawing a sigh, he shook his head. "I must apologize; I am beset by troubles and should not have lost my temper."

"Small blame to you," offered Bing. "It is as though your poor country is the prize in a tug-of-war, and you are merely a bystander."

Only the stakes are not at all like the children's game, thought Hattie. Too many have died, and I imagine more are slated to die before it is all over. Gazing around her at the tombs, she wondered if anything had changed over the millennia, and very much doubted it. It seemed there would always be conquerors and those who resisted them—and the bloody havoc that was the certain result.

"Shall we go inside?" Berry was apparently not as interested in human nature and its historical ramifications as he was in securing the missing disk from the body of the mummified princess.

The gentlemen assisted the ladies up the crude wooden steps that had been applied to the hillside to expedite access to the tomb. A narrow entryway hewn into the rock was revealed at the crest, and several wooden signs were posted;

one contained a warning in several languages, including English. Normally, the tomb entrances were fashioned on a downhill slope but this one was unusual in that it was located on a hillside. As a result, the rubble of the excavation had been cleared out a smoot hole to the side of the entry and a long cascade of discarded rocks and rubble sloped down the hill.

One sign warned of severe penalties for trespassing and another indicated the tomb was presumably that of Seti's daughter. Hattie found it unfair that history defined the princess only by whose daughter she was—the slight was one well familiar to her. "Isn't there a record of her name somewhere?"

"Seti had many daughters and her name is as yet unknown," Hafez explained. "We are hopeful that soon we can make a determination based upon the hieroglyphics in the chamber. What we can translate, however, refers to the pharaoh's 'hidden treasure.' It is possible that the description is actually a form of her name but we are not yet certain."

"A devotion that transcends time," Bing observed. "Most touching."

Hafez gestured to another wooden sign, this one written in Arabic. "A warning to tomb raiders of the terrible punishment that will be imposed," he explained. "It also warns of the curse—and those who have died—for added menace. The thieves are almost impossible to thwart, but we must make the attempt—otherwise, if there are rumors of treasure the guards will be attacked."

At the mention of the curse, Hattie was suddenly reminded that this visit could not be an easy one for Bing. Taking her companion's hand, she offered, "If you'd rather wait outside, Bing, I will wait with you."

But the other woman only shook her head. "No, Hathor—Edward lived for this and he died for it, also. I hold no resentment, and would very much like to see what is inside."

Berry lit a lantern, and the party stepped inside the tomb of the god-king's daughter.

Chapter 29

H attie could immediately sense the antiquity of the place, the indescribably musty smell that resulted from centuries of isolation and airlessness. The dancing lantern light revealed a narrow entry hall carved from the rock that slanted downward for perhaps two dozen yards or so, and then made an abrupt turn to the left, presumably into the burial chamber. The men were forced to bend over to navigate the low-ceilinged entry hall and no one spoke at first, the weight of history having put paid to any trivial thoughts. Hattie grazed her hand along the wall as she walked and then withdrew it, thinking of the countless hands that had done the same.

They confronted the burial chamber at the end of the entry passage, and Hattie saw that the excavators had mounted the stone door to the chamber onto a wooden frame with leather handles so that it could be slid aside more easily. Hafez did the honors, and the group entered the chamber, where the ceiling was higher and the men could now stand erect.

Once within, Hattie paused and the others were also silent as they gazed around the sanctuary, the men holding the lanterns aloft. The soft light revealed a chamber perhaps fifteen feet by thirty, the room dominated by a free-standing sarcophagus that stood at the far end. Hafez swung the lantern to illuminate the walls and Hattie could hear Bing's delighted intake of breath. The chamber was bordered at the bottom by a pattern of brightly colored lotus blossoms and palm leaves, and the upper walls revealed illustrations and hieroglyphics, the vibrant hues presumably chronicling the life of the decedent. Bing walked toward one, leaning to scrutinize it with her hands clasped behind her back. "Horus," she pronounced, "—borne on the horns of the bull, Apis. And here is Priapus, being carried in triumph to the underworld."

"Preserved in the same condition as the day they were drawn," agreed Hafez with reverence. "It is of all things remarkable."

"Are there illustrations of the princess?" asked Hattie, trying to make sense of the fantastic renderings that covered the walls.

"None that are labeled as such," Hafez explained. "Although oftentimes in these tombs the deceased is drawn in, consorting with the gods."

"Edward believed there was no likeness portrayed," Bing noted. "He was greatly disappointed."

Looking about her, Hattie realized the sarcophagus was the only remaining artifact in the sanctuary. The heavy reliquary was not gold-gilt as so many others were; instead it was plainly decorated, of carved rose-colored stone.

"Unusual," mused Bing as she walked to stand beside it. "The sarcophagus is alabaster, which was used at a later time, not at the time of Seti. And it seems a bit plain for a beloved princess; perhaps there was a reason for haste, or there was fear of contagion."

"Perhaps," the minister agreed. "Or tomb raiders have stripped whatever precious metals and gems adorned it—I'm afraid we will never know its original condition."

"She has lain here for so long," said Bing in a quiet tone, standing in contemplation of the stone sarcophagus. "It does give one pause."

"It was built to withstand eternity." Hafez indicated the drawings on the ceiling with his hand, tilting the lantern's shield so as to provide illumination. "The Book of Heavens often decorates the ceiling—it depicts the journey of the sun god through the darkness. The emphasis is upon the eternal, not the worldly. It is ironic that the Book of Heavens looks down on the tomb raiders, who will gladly risk eternal damnation for worldly goods."

To cut short such tedious philosophizing, Hattie produced her sketchpad and pretended to begin a sketch of the ceiling, hoping Bing would take her cue and create a diversion.

Alive to her role, Bing turned to the minister. "Edward mentioned in one of his letters a trap door near the entry, but I did not notice one. Do you know of it, Mr. Hafez?"

Hafez turned to stare at her, much struck. "Did he? Why—I have never heard of such a thing."

"I have my parasol," Bing indicated, brandishing it. "Shall we do some prodding?"

While the minister indicated an eager consent, Hattie demurred, "I shall stay and sketch, I believe." Hafez was too distracted to think of chaperoning duties and in short order she was left alone with Berry in the burial chamber. Wasting no time, they both leapt to the sarcophagus, Berry testing the weight of the lid. "It is heavy," he warned. "Step back and mind your fingers."

Straining, he pressed upward with his palms and shifted the stone lid to one side while Hattie held the lantern aloft. A dark cavity within the sarcophagus was revealed, and Hattie felt a moment's qualm at thus desecrating a grave site. I beg your pardon, she offered; but it will only be for a moment and the stakes are quite high.

With the lid balanced off-kilter, Berry took the lantern from Hattie and lowered it into the sarcophagus, Hattie, on tiptoe, leaning in to see. It was completely empty.

Berry cursed softly and fluently in his own strange language.

"I don't understand," said Hattie in bewilderment. "Who would take her? Who else would know of the disk?" Nonplussed, she looked across at him, and saw that he was frowning, thinking.

"I know not."

Hattie was doing some thinking, herself. "Even if the disk were the object, there seems little point in taking the entire mummy."

When he did not respond, she tried to find some encouragement to offer. "I suppose we could make a hit-and-miss attempt, to guess which way is intended to be north on the senet board—there are only four possibilities."

But he was not to be consoled and bent his head between his arms in frustration. "You are assuming it is that simple— the reference may not be to points on a compass."

Gauging the level of his frustration, she inquired softly, "Is there so little time, then?"

"There is little time," he agreed, his jaw line rigid.

Ominous to think the Corsican Monster would soon make another attempt at world domination, but she did not doubt Berry's mysterious sources and stood in sympathetic support while he contemplated this latest catastrophe. "Surely no one else knows of the senet board," she consoled him, "—even if some unknown rival has secured the disk."

He looked at her but she could see his mind was elsewhere. "It makes little sense."

After waiting for a few moments in respectful silence she ventured, "We'd best put it to rights. I imagine Robbie will appear in short order."

The topic, however, seemed only to exacerbate his foul mood as he shoved the lid back into place with an angry gesture. "You must not allow him to touch you."

Hattie was surprised. "Does he touch me?"

"Yes." The syllable was bitten off. "He does." He aligned the lid so that it was straight and wouldn't look at her.

"I love you," she said simply, the words echoing in the stone chamber. "You have no reason to be jealous—he is like a brother to me and nothing more."

He was not happy with his own loss of composure, she could see, but he seemed unable to stop himself. "It is you who were jealous of Madame Auguste," he reminded her.

This, of course, was undisputable, and seemed as though it had happened a hundred years ago. Calmly, she replied, "That was before I met you—when I just wanted to marry someone and start my life. I love you. I will never love another."

They faced each other in the flickering light across the empty sarcophagus for a long moment. "Good," he said.

Chapter 30

Voices could be heard echoing in the entryway; Bing and Hafez speaking to Robbie with Bing's level of volume raised so as to give them warning. Berry moved quickly to stand by the door while Hattie went to the opposite corner with her sketchbook. She made a half-hearted attempt to sketch the bull, but an observer could be forgiven for thinking her rendering nothing like the original. The bull's name was Apis, Bing had said, so she dutifully wrote the name down so as to give more credence to her questionable endeavors. It was undoubtedly some god who turned into other things—as did the Greek gods, who were constantly causing problems for humankind by such maneuvers. A ridiculous religion, truly, that tried to convince one that one's king was, in fact, a god. Wellington had famously said that no man is a hero to his valet and it could be presumed that the pharaoh's servants were very much aware their master was not, in fact, a god—it was only a farce to enforce a hidden agenda. Her hand stilled. A farce, she thought, gazing up at nothing in particular. Why, I believe that is the solution to this puzzle.

Distracted, she didn't even notice that Robbie had come into the chamber until he was next to her. "Hattie," he apologized with some ruefulness. "I'm afraid I overslept."

Aware that he had placed a hand beneath her elbow, she carefully withdrew it—no point in inciting fisticuffs—not with Berry in his current mood. "Small matter, Robbie—we are only just getting our bearings, and Bing and Mr. Hafez are looking for hidden trapdoors."

"Capital," he said with some enthusiasm. "Perhaps there is one in the entryway." He looked about. "I need some sort of a prod."

"I have a knife," offered Berry, and pulled one out of his boot.

"Excellent," said Robbie, taking it. "But what will you use?"

"I have another," said Berry, and pulled a wicked-looking, narrow dagger from a sheath at his waist, which earned him a long look from Hattie. She wandered after the two men as they exited into the entry hall to discuss who would cover which area. Both then knelt to prod the packed earth with their knives, moving along slowly, foot by foot. Robbie would occasionally direct Berry, who would obey him in his best imitation of a subservient. Her mind filled with her new theory, Hattie squeezed by them so as to rejoin Bing but she took the opportunity to run a caressing hand down Berry's back as she passed him by—it seemed like years since he had held her in his arms, and she was growing impatient.

She found Bing and the minister near the entrance, discussing the likeliest location for a hidden underground chamber. Hattie explained the search that was underway in the entry passage and with much enthusiasm, the minister took Bing's parasol and went to their aid.

When he was out of earshot, Bing pounced on Hattie. "Well?"

"Nothing—no mummy in the sarcophagus."

Shocked, Bing's brows drew together. "How extraordinary. And it seemed so promising."

"I don't know, Bing—I am thinking there never was a mummy to begin with."

"Are you indeed?" asked Bing, crossing her arms. "Well."

Hattie explained, "Remember what Edward wrote—that he thought the find was inconsistent with what my parents believed?"

"He did," Bing agreed. "But he deferred to your parents and kept his doubts to himself."

In a low tone, Hattie continued, "Don't you see? If my parents determined this was the tomb of Seti's daughter, no one would dare question it. Not even Edward, who could see for himself that this was actually—I don't know—probably only some sort of minor official."

Bing considered, one hand on her chin. "It is true the sarcophagus does not match the dateline. But to what end, Hathor?"

Brought up short, Hattie tried to think of a non-treasonous explanation to relate to Bing. "Perhaps to have a secret place to store something valuable? Museum pieces," she suggested vaguely, "—or something."

"But why wouldn't Mr. Hafez be aware of this deception, if this were the case?"

"Perhaps they didn't trust him." Glancing at her companion, she then suggested, "Or perhaps they were doing something unlawful."

"Unthinkable," Bing protested. "On the other hand, Monsieur Berry warned us not to speak of the chamber to Mr. Hafez."

"It does not look well for Mr. Hafez," Hattie agreed tentatively. "Say nothing as yet—allow me to speak to Monsieur Berry about it."

And so Hattie waited in a fever of impatience while the men made their painstaking way to the end of the entry hall with nothing to show for it. Dusty and disappointed, they conferred about what should be done next and came to the conclusion they would make inquiries among the locals to determine when and where Hattie's parents were last seen. As little could be accomplished during the midday heat, they agreed to return to the *Priapus* until the afternoon, and make some inquiries at the government offices at that time.

As they descended the stairs, Hattie murmured to Berry, "I must speak with you."

"With pleasure," he responded, but his gaze was on a fine horse that was tied under the shade of the guards' awning—apparently Robbie had managed to come by it somehow between the barge and the tomb.

"Beautiful animal," Robbie agreed as they all walked over to admire it. "A party from the French embassy came to meet with the minister, and I explained that he was here and borrowed the horse to fetch him back—I confess I forgot to mention it, in all the excitement."

"Very good," said Hafez, but it seemed to Hattie that the minister was less than enthused about the coming meeting.

Berry drew a casual hand over the animal's glossy neck but Hattie knew that the news of the visitors was no ordinary happenstance—she could sense it in his posture. He was wary; and she surmised it meant more enemies among them—apparently they were plentiful in this god-forsaken place.

After the men had discussed the horse's finer points with the guards, Robbie mounted up and the rest of the party loaded onto the cart to make the return journey. Bing, bless her, turned her back on Hattie to engage Mr. Hafez in conversation so that Hattie could speak in a low voice to Berry. "Tell me about these Frenchmen from the embassy—what have they to do with all this?"

But he remained unwilling to give her any insights, and only said with all seriousness, "You must not ask questions, Hattie; I cannot answer them."

She took this in good part, mainly because she was bursting to tell him her news. "Well then, I have some answers for you, for a change." At his look of inquiry, she said without preamble, "I think it is all a feint—a farce. I don't believe there was a mummy—it was all to allow the storage of the weapons without remark, and to create a curse so as to keep the curious away."

He listened without reaction, his gaze scanning the horizon. "Why do you believe this?"

"Edward had some doubts, but no one would question my parents' conclusions—do you see? They were the experts and so could create whatever reality they wished. It explains why there are few artifacts and no references to the princess—in actuality, it was probably only a minor find— perhaps not even a tomb at all but an adjunct of some sort."

Berry turned his head to her, considering. "But if that is the case, why does the false disk refer to the princess in the sarcophagus?"

But Hattie had already considered an explanation and was unable to suppress her excitement. "I imagine Bing made an assumption—the clue probably did not specify the sarcophagus, but the god-king's daughter, instead. Bing assumed it meant the mummy—"

"But it actually referred to you," Berry concluded for her, his own eyes mirroring her excitement. "I think you may be right—there must be a clue on your golden disk that is not apparent at first. Do you have it?"

She made a subtle gesture toward her breast. "It is pinned to my shift."

"Lucky disk," he said with a smile.

"When are we going to be alone?" she demanded in annoyance. Honestly; it had been far, far too long.

"Soon," he soothed. "But let us stay focused on the task at hand, if you please. Wait for word from me in your cabin— above all, do not show the disk to anyone."

"What will you be doing?" she asked with some impatience. She couldn't imagine what could be more important than an immediate examination of the golden disk or an equally immediate examination of her anatomy.

"Listening."

"Oh." She had forgotten that the new visitors from the French embassy were apparently a cause for concern. "May I do anything to assist? Perhaps I could listen, too—they would not guess I was spying."

Bringing his face very close, he locked his gaze upon hers and said in all seriousness, "Hattie, you must stay well out of it, and do as I ask. It is very important that you do not travel about alone, or speak to anyone who is here—anyone at all. Wait for me to accompany you, always."

"I will," she agreed, resenting the implied rebuke when all she had done was offer assistance. "You have already warned me, remember?"

"It is of extreme importance." After a pause, he continued in a more conciliatory tone, "There is much you do not understand, and I am not at liberty to explain. I must ask that you trust me. Can you do this?"

She nodded, chastened, but felt much better when he clasped her hand, hidden between the folds of her skirt, and they remained thus most of the way back to the river.

Upon arrival back at the *Priapus*, they were met by the sight of several horses tethered to the palisade, along with the one Robbie had borrowed. Hattie noted with interest that Berry's assessing gaze rested on them, and she teased, "So—it appears the dogs have horses."

"They do," he confessed, and rested his gaze on her lips. "More than a few."

She primmed her mouth to keep from laughing and said with mock severity, "That only counts as one piece of information."

"We shall see," he said with meaning, which brought the color to her cheeks just before they approached the gangway. Hattie noted that Robbie stood on deck, watching them approach, and accompanied by several other men in French uniforms. With some surprise, she recognized Monsieur Chauvelin among them, the Baron's henchman whom she had met at the Prussian embassy, back when this strange sequence of events first began. Dropping her gaze, she murmured to Berry, "The second from the left—he broke into the townhouse in Paris and I had the felicity of shoving him down the stairs."

Berry, though, did not seem overly surprised by this revelation and in reply simply said, "Say nothing, Hattie, and go straightaway to your cabin."

Further discussion was curtailed as they came to the gangplank, the assembled Frenchmen openly watching her, every step of the way, as she came on board. Embarrassed, she lifted her chin and ignored them as Robbie strode toward her, sunburnt and dusty from his ride. "Come, Hattie, let's go inside and call for lemonade—it is dashed hot."

But Bing intervened, "I'm afraid I must insist Miss Blackhouse lie down in her cabin—I believe she feels a bit faint."

As Bing was well aware Hattie was not a fainter, she inferred there was an ulterior purpose and thus did her best to appear wilted. "A good idea, Bing." Smiling weakly at Robbie, she demurred, "I will meet up with you in a bit, Robbie."

However, Monsieur Chauvelin moved to impede her progress, stepping forward to make a polite bow. "Ah—we meet again, Mademoiselle Blackhouse. Monsieur Hafez, I confess I had the honor of meeting this young woman in Paris; a true pleasure."

Thus reminded, the minister dutifully introduced the gentlemen to the ladies while the Frenchman held her hand overlong, and she sensed that his intent was to make her uncomfortable. But Hattie was not one to be intimidated, and only nodded politely as she resisted an urge to snatch her hand away. A bully, she thought with some disdain; and undoubtedly here hoping to find the strongbox and thus the weapons and the treasure. For two pins I would give it all to the poor beleaguered Egyptians, who surely deserve it more. Hard on this thought she felt Bing's hand on her elbow, urging her toward their cabin. Willingly, she allowed herself to be steered, wondering how soon she could retrieve the disk and study it. The sooner they could solve the puzzle, secure the trove, and be away from all this unholy scrutiny, the better.

"Monsieur Berry asked that I escort you directly to your cabin," Bing noted in an apologetic undertone.

So; I am to be sequestered well away from whatever intrigue is going forward, Hattie thought. Aloud she said crossly, "I have half a mind to climb out the window again."

"I cannot swim," Bing replied with much regret.

Chapter 34

That afternoon, Hattie, Bing, and Berry accompanied Hafez to the government offices, Robbie having decided to enlist a translator and return to the site for another search, as there were rumors of a hidden map. No point in asking whether they should take Robbie into their confidence; it seemed clear that Berry would play his cards very close to the vest.

On the other hand, there was no need for the rest of them to accompany the minister when he went over to register the *Priapus*, but Berry had deftly arranged for it and Hattie surmised that this meant that Berry was monitoring Hafez—who according to Berry, was operating under some sort of duress—and keeping her close at the same time. It did seem that Berry's manner was more preoccupied, and Hattie wondered what he had learned while eavesdropping on the contingent from the French embassy.

Hafez also announced that he would make another attempt to discover which of the workers from the worker's village had helped with the Blackhouse excavation in their final days—or at least the days that they were last seen alive.

"I believe you have already performed this task," Hattie commented to Berry as they were jolted along in the transport cart to the government compound. "And with precious little to show for it."

But he shrugged and expressed his support for such a plan, "It does no harm to make another attempt, now that some time has passed. The minister has more authority than I, and we cannot overestimate the impact your presence may have."

"The bereft daughter," she noted with some irony.

"Burial rituals are important to these people; it may overcome whatever fears they have of speaking out."

Hattie shifted her gaze to Hafez, who was listening to Bing with only half an ear as the cart made its slow progress. The French visitors indeed had wrought a change in the minister, who appeared distracted and was perspiring more than his usual. Thinking on it, she commented in a low voice to Berry, "All in all, perhaps it would be for the best if the secret chamber remains undiscovered; if no one can find it, no one can put it to its evil use."

But Berry could not agree. "Such a trove will be very useful to whoever finds it—the weapons and the treasure will be an enormous advantage in the coming conflict."

Hattie remained skeptical that the conflict would actually take place—although perhaps she was being naïve—and shook her head slightly. "It seems almost unimaginable that anyone would support Napoleon again—not after all that has happened." Mainly, she didn't want to think about Berry fighting in another war; there seemed little doubt he would wind up in the thick of things.

"It would be a grave mistake to underestimate him; there are many who only await a chance to support him again, and he is a very dangerous man." Berry turned to check on their progress and Hattie understood that the subject was closed. I should not tease him about it, she thought—he may regret that he told me about Napoleon's plans in the first place and so I mustn't vex him.

The government compound was home to the local authorities who monitored and protected the historic sites as well as enforced the laws. The compound was located near the ruins of the huge Hypostyle Hall, which had served the same purpose forty centuries earlier. By contrast, the visitors' building was foursquare and simple, with large archways that opened on to a veranda so as to access the river breeze. Several Egyptian officials processed paperwork behind ancient wooden desks while a number of civilians sat along the benches in the shade of the building, most of them elderly men passing the time by observing any visitors and conversing with each other in a desultory manner. As the stone walls made the interior relatively cool, it was with some relief that Hattie waited within for the gentlemen in her party to conduct their business. Hafez was treated with the deference due to his position, and Hattie could see Berry's point; it seemed likely that more doors would be opened to the native minister in their quest for information.

Unable to resist, Bing wandered over to one of the open-air arched doorways to gaze upon the famous ruins next door, and Hattie strolled toward the west side of the building so as to feel the breeze from the river. In doing so, she passed by several of the old men seated on the benches.

"Halima," cried one in surprise as she walked past. He then added an unintelligible sentence in Arabic, addressing her with some excitement.

I am definitely too brown, Hattie thought in amusement, and faced him to smile and spread her hands so as to indicate he had mistaken the matter.

The old man regarded her, the emotion in the rheumy eyes fading. "Your pardon," he said in halting English, shaking his head. "There are times I forget how the years have passed."

"No matter," she said with a smile, and made as if to move on.

Bing appeared in an archway to ascertain her whereabouts and then indicated with a gesture, "I shall be just over here, Hathor," before she ducked outside again.

"Hathor?" asked the old man in surprise. "Can it be that you are little Hathor?"

"My name is Hathor," Hattie disclosed, thinking to humor him. She had little experience with the elderly, but she understood that sometimes their minds drifted.

Scrutinizing her, his grizzled face broke into a delighted grin that revealed yellow and broken teeth. With some satisfaction he nodded. "It is indeed you—the Blackhouse girl."

Hattie stared. "I beg your pardon?"

Pleased with his role as the bearer of information, the old man continued, "You stayed here—with Halima and the soldiers. It was when I worked here—oh, many years ago. You would not remember; you were very small—hardly walking." He indicated with his hand.

Hattie blinked, completely at sea. "Truly? I never knew I had been in Egypt; my parents never mentioned it."

"You stayed here, with Halima. And the soldiers, who guarded you." He paused, and nodded. "Yes; many soldiers."

Enrapt, Hattie stepped toward him. "Who is Halima? Did she care for me?"

Enjoying her attention, the man displayed his broken teeth again. "Yes, she was your nursemaid, your *amah*—a beautiful girl. While you learned to walk she would hold both your hands over your head." He demonstrated with a gesture, rocking back and forth, smiling in remembrance. "She delighted in you."

Hattie smiled in delight herself, fascinated by this

glimpse into her childhood. "How extraordinary—how long was I here?"

The old man tried to remember, raising his eyes upward in calculation. "A month—perhaps longer."

"That long." Hattie was amazed; her parents must have left her behind with this Egyptian girl while they went on an excavation—the surprising fact was that they had taken her to Egypt at all, especially as an infant.

"Yes—it was a sad day for many of us when your parents came to claim you. Halima wept for days, but she was set to wed one of the soldiers. We told her she would soon have children of her own to make her smile again." He beamed, misty-eyed. "Little Hathor—how wonderful that you have returned to us for a visit." Shaking his head in apology, he confessed, "I was confused—I thought you were Halima."

But Hattie's smile had faded, and she could hear her heartbeat in her ears. This man had mistaken her for her former Egyptian nursemaid and Hattie could not be said to resemble either of her fair-skinned, thoroughly English parents. Had her father fathered an illegitimate child?

She was dimly aware that Berry touched her arm. "Hattie? Come away, now."

But Hattie was staring out the archway, unseeing. Her parents had been married from the first—they had been married years before she was born. This visit to Egypt would have been around the time of—she closed her eyes with the effort to remember—their dig at Rashid.

"Let us go outside." There was an edge to his voice—almost a desperation. With a firm grip on her arm, he swung her out through the archway and onto the deserted veranda.

She looked up into his face without seeing it because a black, black thought was hovering around the edges of her mind and she refused to give it entry. Impossible to believe her father, devoted to his wife, would father a child on a local girl. Even more impossible to believe they would bring a baby with them to Egypt, especially on one of their earliest excavations. Indeed, it must have been just when Napoleon had begun his campaign—about the time her parents had made their bargain with the devil. Their bargain.

Hattie stood very still and the black thought could be refused entrance no longer. She remembered Eugenie's sly comments and the scrutiny of the Frenchmen today. She had been heavily guarded when here as a baby, when the French had held Egypt—no, not exactly the French—it was Napoleon who held Egypt. She swayed slightly, and through the roaring sound in her ears she heard Berry speaking intently to her as he supported her in his arms, although she could not comprehend what he said.

Suddenly she was furious, and lashed out at him, hissing through her teeth, "You *knew*."

"I love you, Hattie." He pulled her close.

"I was a joke," she rasped out into his shoulder, clinging to him so as to remain upright. "They named me after Hathor, the goddess of fertility—they said I was the daughter of the god-king—it was all a joke to them and nothing more." Maddened by the horror of it all and perilously close to hysteria she gasped, "Oh, God."

"I love you, Hattie," he whispered. "It does not matter."

She pounded her small fists against his chest, emphasizing the words. "You knew this—*everyone* knows—"

"No." He took her hands and folded them into his, against the chest she had been abusing. Pressing his cheek against hers he spoke gently into her ear, "Few know. You must hush, Hattie; we will marry and I will send you to my sister's home until this is over and then I will come for you."

She drew back to gaze at him in scornful amazement, her heart still beating in her ears. "You speak *nonsense*—utter nonsense."

"It does not matter, Hattie." He was in agony—she could tell—but she couldn't find any comfort for him, having none.

"Of course it matters," she bit out. She then ruined the effect by resting her forehead against his chest and closing her eyes, wishing she could crawl inside him.

She was vaguely aware that Bing was standing in the archway, taking in the strange tableau without comment. "I will take her home," Berry said in a tone that brooked no argument.

But Bing did not move. "Hathor?" she asked quietly.

"Please go, Bing." Breathing in Berry's scent, she didn't move while he held her tightly. She was a bastard—and not just any bastard, but the bastard of her country's greatest enemy. And the people everyone assumed were her parents were base traitors; in truth, she was hard-pressed not to howl in despair.

Hattie wasn't certain how long they stood thus, but eventually her practical nature reasserted itself and with an effort, she stood upright. He immediately tucked her under his arm and led her across the way to a café, not speaking. Clinging to his side, she was content to allow him to navigate across the dusty road and once at the counter, he ordered a brandy and held the glass to her mouth until she drank a healthy swallow, then downed the remainder himself. Gasping, she felt the burning sensation in her midsection and the world came into focus again.

"Look at me," he commanded.

It was not easy—she was ashamed and had been avoiding his eyes. But she gazed at him for several long moments, and then nodded, to show him she was recovered.

"There's my girl," he said quietly.

"I would like to speak to the old man," she replied.

Chapter 32

"Who is he?" Berry asked as they returned to the visitor's building, his hand firmly under her elbow.

"He worked here, and remembered I was here as a baby. He—he remembered my nursemaid. Apparently, I resemble her."

He asked nothing further but stood nearby as she approached the old man again to address him in as level a voice as she could manage. "I am so pleased that you told me of my visit when I was a child. I would like to speak with Halima, if I may—only think how surprised she will be, to meet her charge from so many years ago."

But the man was regretful and shook his head. "Halima followed her new husband to France—we have not heard from her in many years."

Hattie regarded him for a moment, her heartbeat returning to normal. "Do you have an address, perhaps? Or the town's name?"

He shook his head and spread his arthritic hands in regret. "I am sorry."

As they left, Berry assured her, "If she yet lives I will find her; an Egyptian woman living in France—it will not be a hardship."

But Hattie had been thinking it through, her brow knit.

"I don't know—if she has a family and has made a new life, it may not be for the best." She took a long breath, feeling the knot of sick misery lessen a little. "It was just a thought."

He tucked her hand into his arm and they stood together for a few moments in silence. "What would you like to do? Return to the barge? Sit and rest?"

Lifting her face, she caught view of the enormous ruins of the Hypostyle Hall. "I would like to walk for a while, I think."

And so she walked with him among the giant columns that bore testament to a once mighty civilization, standing timeless and unchanging amidst the uncertainties of the present. I was never very interested in any of this, she thought. But I should have been—it is my heritage, or at least in part. There is something very comforting in it; the concerns of the temporary inhabitants seem of little importance against the backdrop of millennia—of the countless generations who have lived and breathed and borne life's heavy blows.

"At least it all makes sense, now." They had not spoken in some time.

He drew a long breath. "I had hoped to spare you this."

Absently, she ran a palm along the raised relief on an ancient column. "No, it is for the best—don't you see? Only think of how wracked you have been, worried that I would speak to someone and find out—it would have eaten at you." She slanted him a sidelong glance. "There should be no secrets between us, my-friend-who-is-not-named-Daniel."

Placing his hand over hers on the column, he did not take the opportunity to divulge his secrets to her, and she did not press him. There was now no doubt in her mind that his allegiances—whatever they were—came second to his allegiance to her. "Who knows of this?" she asked, wishing no one did.

"Very few—it was kept very quiet so that his wife would not learn of it; there had been problems caused by other infidelities, and recall that Josephine could not conceive."

Hattie slowly shook her head. "Such goings on—I thought he was devoted to the empress."

His mouth curved into a small smile. "You are naïve, perhaps."

"Another thirsty horse," she observed in a dry tone, amazed she could see the humor in it.

"It is a common failing—particularly among men of power; often it presents a weakness to be exploited by their enemies."

Which is why women like Eugenie are so useful, Hattie concluded. I suppose if they are beautiful and there for the taking, there is little hesitation. Immediately, she shied away from the thought—she didn't like to think that Halima was like Eugenie.

Berry took her arm again as they walked through the southern colonnade, the shadows stretching across the pathways before them and the gravel quietly crunching beneath their feet. "I will contact Captain Clements; he will marry us and see that you are safely delivered to my sister."

There was an edge of determination to his tone that she sincerely appreciated. With a soft smile, she looked up to him and was relieved that she retained her composure; that her mouth did not tremble. "You must see that I cannot marry."

"I see no such thing." His voice was like steel.

Lowering her gaze, she squeezed his arm, gently. "I imagine you have prospects, and a fond family. I will not offer them false coin."

"You are a Blackhouse, Hattie. Nothing less."

Her mouth twisted into a wry smile. "After their treachery is revealed, I imagine that will be of little comfort."

He was silent a moment and she took her courage in both hands and lifted her face to his. "We can be together, nevertheless."

He did not change his pace or the tempo of his words but she was aware he was very unhappy with her. "You will never say such a thing again. Do you understand?"

"Be reasonable," she gently pointed out. "I cannot marry anyone, even if the secret is kept. It would be—it would be dishonorable. And it is you that I love. I would not change anything—anything at all—if it meant I would not have met you."

"You will speak no more nonsense," was all he said, and she allowed the subject to drop. It was only a matter of time—he was a thirsty horse, himself.

She turned the subject to something more productive than the dashing of all her dreams. "I examined the disk, and I have an idea—if you can find me a stick I can show you."

They sat on a stone bench and she bent down to draw in the dirt. "I think the disk does indeed contain a clue—we were distracted by the cipher on the one side, but I think the true meaning is in the figure of Hathor." She duplicated the stick-like figure of the engraving.

"Her arms and legs," he agreed. "I see."

She continued to scratch in the dirt. "A compass, perhaps? And there are three stars on her crown; it is the only adornment in the engraving so it must mean something."

"Yes. Do you recall this motif anywhere in the chamber?"

"I wasn't paying much attention," she confessed. "But Mr. Hafez was referencing the ceiling as the Book of Heavens, so perhaps there are stars on the ceiling."

"Very good—you should be in my business," he said with approval.

She dropped the stick and sat back with a shake of her head. "No thank you—there are too many hazards for my taste, and no one says what they mean."

"It brought me to you," he pointed out. Taking her hands in his, he looked into her face; the brown eyes—usually so shuttered—alight with tenderness. "I knew you belonged to me the moment I saw you."

But she could only chuckle. "That is an out-and-out falsehood, my friend; you were horrified that you were attracted to me."

"No—you mistake. I was *boulversé*, not horrified. I am not one to allow my desires to lead me, and it took me some time to be reconciled."

She lifted his hand to kiss it. "I was *bouleversé*, myself."

"So I understood."

She laughed, and felt much better. He had tested her, that first night, by calling her the god-king's daughter, to see if she knew—but how could she? She had been sequestered in the wilds of Cornwall and cut off from civilization—apparently by design. There is that, she acknowledged—I inspired my real father to place me with famous parents, ones that he believed would grant me an exceptional life—so at least the attempt was made. I imagine the largesse I have received over the years came from a different source altogether—it is such a shame that he is a bloodthirsty tyrant, and if I ever met him I would feel obligated to shoot him through the heart. "We should probably return," she noted, relieved that her sense of perspective continued intact. "I have kept you from your listening duties."

"I have already heard enough," he admitted.

She eyed him as they hailed a transportation cart but he offered nothing more. "If it is possible," he suggested as he handed her in, "see to it that Mademoiselle Bing does not accompany Monsieur Hafez in his travels tomorrow."

This seemed significant, and Hattie paused in alarm. "Is she in danger?"

"No—but I imagine he will seek to disappear and it will aid him in this endeavor if he is unattached."

"It is he who is in danger," Hattie concluded, remembering the deaths of his two allies, and his uneasiness this day, after the visit from the loathsome Monsieur Chauvelin.

"I should not be surprised," was the only answer she was given, which was answer enough.

Back on board the *Priapus*, Hattie separated from Berry so it would not be as obvious that they had been alone together, and made her way to the cabin. The French visitors were not in evidence, and neither was Robbie. It was rather quiet, as the other passengers were presumably preparing for dinner.

Bing was sitting on her berth, ramrod straight and hiding her agitation with only moderate success. Hattie took the woman's hands in hers and said immediately, "I am so sorry, Bing. What must you think of me?"

Bing's sharp eyes searched her face. "Is he married, Hathor?"

"No. He is an honorable man." Hattie struggled with an explanation for her behavior, but nothing came readily.

"Is it your parents?"

Hattie gave up the attempt, and said only, "I am afraid I cannot speak of it, Bing."

Bing nodded. "We shall say no more, then. If I am needed to perform a service, Hathor, you have only to ask."

"You are beyond marvelous, Bing." Hattie's voice quavered with emotion; truly, it had been a tumultuous, miserable day.

Her companion responded to this accolade by indicating

Hattie should sit while she took up a brush. "Your hair should be redone before dinner, I believe."

It was exactly what was needed; Bing rhythmically drew the hairbrush through Hattie's long, black locks while she closed her eyes and thought of nothing at all. Eventually, she opened her eyes and noted, "Monsieur Berry has the impression that Mr. Smithson is smitten."

The brush paused. "Does he indeed?"

"Perhaps you would condescend to spend some time with the poor man," Hattie teased. "Unless you believe Mr. Hafez would come to cuffs with him."

"I am not here to entertain gentlemen," Bing said with some severity, and resumed her task.

"I don't know, Bing—best strike whilst the iron is hot." Inspired, she added, "I may not be a charge upon you for much longer."

"I must say I am not surprised, Hathor." Bing was pleased; Hattie could hear it in her voice. Hattie hoped that Berry lived far enough away so that the truth of her position as a mistress and not a wife would never be revealed. Although she imagined Bing would not be shocked—she seemed impervious to shock. Which reminds me, thought Hattie; I must speak to Eugenie.

By the time the dinner bell rang, Hattie had recovered enough to present her normal face to her fellow diners although she could feel Berry's concerned scrutiny. How wonderful it is to be loved, she thought—it requires one to be brave for the sake of the other. Subtle as a serpent, Hattie announced her intent to visit the Necropolis on the west bank the following morning, then noted to Smithson that she had heard there was an impressive Coptic chapel located quite near the ruins, if he would like to join in the excursion.

Having obtained the vicar's assent to this plan, she felt she'd done a good night's work—if Hafez wished to extract himself from their group he would have no impediment.

After the meal, the men reviewed a map of the area while Hattie took the opportunity to invite Eugenie to take a stroll on deck. "I must ask a favor from you, if you do not mind."

"What is it you wish?" Eugenie's rosy mouth was sulking as they paused at the railing to look out over the darkened Nile. "I have been warned by someone that I am not to tease you."

Hattie said with all sincerity, "I do not mind when you tease me, Eugenie—truly. But I am in need of some advice."

Eugenie eyed her with suspicion. "What sort of advice?"

Now that the moment was here, Hattie found it more difficult than she had anticipated. "Well—I suppose you could say—advice about men."

With some amusement, the other sought clarification. "Men, or what men do in bed?"

"What men do in bed," Hattie admitted, her cheeks reddened.

"*Bien sûr*. After all, you need no advice about men." A hint of resentment could be discerned in the other's tone.

Hattie confessed, "I have no one to ask—about what is pleasing, I suppose."

The other woman chuckled, and replied with some cynicism, "One need only be female and be present to be pleasing."

Thinking that this was not going well, Hattie nodded and decided not to press the issue, turning to view the river instead.

Watching her, Eugenie relented. "Do you know how it all comes about, at least?"

"Yes," said Hattie. "That is, I believe so," she qualified.

And so Eugenie patiently explained the finer points of

lovemaking while Hattie listened, equal parts shocked and fascinated. At one point she interrupted, "But, how can one make such an overture—wouldn't he find it very strange?"

"There will be no protests made, believe me. And you must talk—praise, inquire, praise even more—although some men do not wish to talk," she amended. "They are the least pleasing."

"It all seems rather awkward," Hattie admitted, grateful for the breeze on her cheeks.

But the other disagreed, shaking her curls. "When your heart is involved, it is simple—there is no awkward." With a raised shoulder, she added, "Now go away, if you please. You make me feel *très ancien*."

Chapter 33

The next morning dawned clear and hot as Hattie, Robbie, Bing, and Smithson prepared to cross the Nile so as to explore the Necropolis of ancient Thebes. Hafez was not in evidence and despite keeping a sharp eye, Hattie had yet to catch a glimpse of Berry this morning. In truth, she was rather surprised that Robbie had volunteered to come along; he was not one to be interested in ruins and she imagined that he would have his own mysterious errands to complete elsewhere—he also seemed rather preoccupied, now that the French visitors had made their appearance.

"The Ramesseum, or the Temple of Medinet?" asked Bing, referencing her guidebook as they strolled to the river bank. "Where should we like to start once we are across?"

"I must defer—I am afraid one ruin is very like another to me," Smithson admitted with a small smile.

"The Ramesseum," Robbie decided. "I mentioned to some friends we may make a tour this morning."

"You have acquaintances among the locals?" Hattie regarded him with an amused arch to her brow, well aware that this was a fish tale—she could read him like a book. Hopefully, whatever scheme he was hatching didn't involve yet another suitor for Bing—it was already hard enough to keep track.

"Friends who are with the British consul's office," he explained in a casual manner. "I met them when I was last here."

"With your bride," added Hattie, ruthlessly needling him. Robbie met her gaze, a playful light in his eyes. "As a matter of fact, I did meet my bride at the British consul's office."

"Such high romance," she remarked, and quirked her mouth.

"Indeed." He then grinned in a way not at all in keeping with a bereft bridegroom.

Shaking her head in amused disapproval, Hattie resolved to get the full story from him before the outing was over—she had been distracted by other matters, otherwise she would have done so before now. How extraordinary that Robbie's strange betrothal had slipped so much in significance, the other matters being much more compelling—to the good and otherwise.

"Are you betrothed, Mr. Tremaine? My congratulations." The vicar offered his hand as they waited for the ferry.

Taking it, Robbie explained with a rueful smile, "I'm afraid the engagement was short-lived." There was a pause, and Hattie had to bite her lip.

"Hard luck," said the other. "Better luck next time." Smithson's gaze rested for the briefest moment on Hattie.

But I will never be a bride, thought Hattie, watching the ferry's approach and pretending not to notice the byplay. With sad resignation, she examined this aspect of her life now that she was coming to terms with the cataclysmic news of yesterday. As a little girl, one never pinned one's hopes on becoming a mistress, but an adjustment was now necessary, given the circumstances. Fortunately, she knew down to her bones that Berry loved her and would treat her well— hopefully till death did them part. Still, she decided not to dwell on it until she became more accustomed to the idea.

They were ferried across the river to the opposite shore with several local residents, two goats, and a thin little dog Hattie leaned down to pat, thinking of the four dogs with whom Berry didn't argue. The man was going to be tiresome about trying to marry her—she could sense it—and he was one who did not give up easily; they were very similar in nature, the two of them. But while his dogs may not care about the circumstances of her birth, his sister certainly would and Hattie knew she must remain resolute. I wish I knew where they lived, she thought; perhaps it is in some corner of the world that has never heard of the Elban prisoner. Unfortunately, this seemed unlikely.

With a smile, Robbie leaned back on the bench and watched her with the dog. "What is my mother planning to do with Sophie's pups?"

Hattie ceased her attentions, but the dog pushed its muzzle into her hands, insistent, and so she began to stroke it again. "It was too soon when I left; but last time she took them to church in a box and they were all claimed in short order."

"She'd probably rather keep them, knowing Mother."

Hattie laughed, and agreed. "But your father will be firm, being as he always complains that the place is already a menagerie."

Robbie chuckled, and looked out over the broad river. "I will check for letters tomorrow, although the post is unreliable here. Are you homesick for England, yet?"

"I miss your family," she replied truthfully. Henceforth she would never long for a place, only for a person.

Bending beside her to run his hand along the dog's back, he added, "We will have to tell everyone about your sad news, unfortunately. I wish we had more to tell."

"I sometimes wonder if we will ever find out what

happened to them." If indeed her parents had been killed for double-dealing, it seemed unlikely the dark deed would ever come to light, which—all in all—may be a good thing; one less unsavory connection to face down, and any crumb of comfort would be appreciated at this point. It was hard to believe that as late as last month she had been chafing about the sameness of her days.

"We will." Robbie's hand covered hers on the dog, and his voice was gentle. "We will find them, Hattie. Someone must know something."

Hattie nodded, then casually removed her hand and sat up again. She would have to let Robbie know there was to be no future between them, although it may be an awkward conversation as she was not at all certain he saw himself as a potential suitor. Nevertheless, the conversation must take place; he-who-was-not-Daniel was a possessive man.

Once they reached the west bank, they disembarked from the vessel and hailed a cart to take them to the massive ruins on the river bank. Fortunately, at this hour in the morning there were long shadows in which to linger as they mingled with other tourists to view the mortuary temple dedicated to the god-king Ramesses. Bing served as their guide, pausing before the landmarks to recite from her guidebook as Smithson listened attentively. Hattie and Robbie were content to trail behind and soon were out of earshot as Hattie twirled her parasol to and fro out of boredom, wishing Berry were there. "I confess I am not very interested in all this."

"I toured it last time I was here," Robbie acknowledged. "Dashed dry stuff—once is more than enough."

She eyed him sidelong from under the edge of her parasol. "Why, Robbie Tremaine; you were falling in love and should remember it with great fondness."

Shaking his head at her sauce, he admitted, "I imagine you are already aware there were other forces at work."

"Such as?"

He squinted into the distance, deciding what to say. "She held important information and our people were negotiating for it. She demanded protection, and fancied me above the other potential candidates—I never meant to marry her, of course."

"Unfortunately, someone was not very impressed by your gallant gesture, my friend. What sort of information did she have that called for such a heroic sacrifice?"

Choosing his words carefully, he explained, "Her husband worked closely with the find, and there were concerns that— along with your poor parents—some inventory was missing. She intimated that she was aware what had happened to it."

"I see—she was leveraging whatever information she had in exchange for protection." Hattie turned her head to pretend an interest in the pylons while she assimilated the almost unbearable fact that Robbie knew the truth about her parents—knew and was trying to spare her. It was a sweet gesture, and greatly appreciated, but the shame was oh, so humiliating. I shall never become accustomed if I live to be a hundred, she thought, her cheeks aflame. I wonder if I can convince Berry to take up residence somewhere outside the bounds of civilization. With an effort, she kept her voice even. "Did you discover what she knew, if anything?"

"Unfortunately not," he replied in a neutral tone. "But with any luck we can uncover the truth."

"I hope so." She tried to sound sincere, so as not to reveal that she would be acutely shamed by the truth.

Tilting his head back, he considered the massive ruins around them. "And then you and I will gladly put Egypt behind us and return to a more hospitable climate, devoid of dust."

"And dull ruins," she added.

"And dull ruins," he seconded. "Although Miss Bing and Mr. Smithson seem very keen." The other couple had their heads together, discussing something in the guidebook.

"Very keen," agreed Hattie, and they exchanged a significant look in the manner of childhood playmates who could communicate without speaking. "And pray do not be inspired anew by the ruins and make an offer for Eugenie this time around—your poor mother would take to her bed."

Making an attempt to disclaim, he met her eye, saw that she knew more than he would like, and so changed tactics. "She is a merely a means to pass the time, Hattie—for God's sake, you should not be speaking of such things."

Remembering her frank speech with Eugenie the night before, Hattie could only hide a smile. "I beg your pardon, Robbie; I shall say no more."

And no more was said on the subject, as instead Robbie nodded in the direction of the central courtyard. "Here are some gentlemen from the consul's office who seek an opportunity to speak with you."

Hattie turned to see two men, their hands clasped behind them, strolling in their direction as though the meeting had not been pre-planned with Robbie. God in heaven, she thought in dismay; pressure is being brought to bear—a pox on Robbie for forcing me to sort out my allegiances.

Robbie took her hand in the crook of his arm in a gesture of support. "They have some questions about the missing artifacts, Hattie—I am afraid it is very important."

It always seems to be, thought Hattie with extreme annoyance; but at least I am no longer playing blind man's bluff.

Robbie introduced her to Mr. Drummond, a grey-haired man with a neatly trimmed beard who had the felicity to be the high commissioner for the British consulate in Luxor. "Miss Blackhouse," he said, bowing over her hand. "Such a pleasure to meet you; I followed your parent's endeavors very closely."

Yes, thought Hattie, I imagine you did—and with considerable dismay. Drummond's associate was also introduced, and for the second time in two days Hattie was surprised to behold a figure from her short-lived visit to Paris; she was certain that the quiet man who accompanied the British high commissioner was the same man who posed as a hackney driver, in league with the grey-eyed spymaster. Assessing him under her lashes, Hattie concluded that she was not mistaken—the gentleman was definitely in the same line of work as Berry. He had the same air—that of an eagle masquerading as a dove.

"Would you mind if we walked with you?"

"Certainly, sir." She smiled in what she hoped was a manner appropriate for a concerned daughter who was unaware her parents were base traitors and the world was on the brink of exploding yet again. With Robbie beside her, the party began to walk along the outer walls of the courtyard, Bing and Smithson up ahead. Hattie no longer twirled her parasol but gripped the handle, wary.

"Terrible news about your parents," Drummond began in the awkward, bluff manner of an Englishman who was more comfortable with action than words. "Rest assured—we are moving heaven and earth to ascertain what has happened."

"I would that I could be of more help," she confessed, and hoped she wouldn't be compelled to lie outright to them— she much preferred pound dealing. But she needed to be careful—Berry didn't trust the British, for some undisclosed reason. Neither did she, come to think of it—and they owed her a reticule.

"Of course," Drummond acknowledged with a regretful tilt of his head. "Mr. Tremaine has mentioned that you were—unfortunately—not in your parents' confidence."

"No, and in fact I rarely heard from them. I understand"— she paused delicately—"that there are some concerns about missing inventory on the new site. I sincerely hope my parents were not involved in any wrongdoing."

"It may be nothing, Hattie," Robbie quickly assured her.

Drummond nodded in agreement. "We are carefully reviewing their last actions—or at least their last known actions—for any clues. I understand their agent—Monsieur Berry, I believe—travels with your party; has he offered any insights into their disappearance?"

So—here it was. She thought of the River Fel near the Tremaine estate, and how the spring bluebells swayed in unison when the breeze came through the lea and she concluded: I am English to the bone, come what may—even if I have not a drop of English blood in me. On the other hand, I will not betray what I know or suspect about Berry himself; not until I've had a chance to confer with him. "Monsieur Berry is also chagrined and wishes I had more information than I have." I hope, she thought, that I never have to choose which allegiance is paramount.

They walked a few more paces, the men thinking over what she had told them while Hattie felt as though the disk secreted next to her skin was burning a hole in her dress.

The erstwhile hackney driver spoke for the first time, his manner deferential. "Has Mr. Hafez offered a theory concerning your parents' disappearance? He is believed to be the last person to have seen them." There was the slightest edge to this observation.

She met his eyes, her own widened in surprise. "I was unaware of this. Are you—are you implying—"

"The best people are conducting the investigation, Hattie, believe me." This from Robbie, who squeezed her hand to reassure her. "But Mr. Hafez is a high official and the situation is delicate—we can't be accusing him as though he were a criminal."

And Berry believes Hafez is going to make a discreet exit this very day, thought Hattie, and he doesn't seem to think it a bad idea, either. Curse *everyone* for making this so difficult; I don't know what to reveal and what to keep secret. Hesitating, she offered, "I must say it appears unlikely that Mr. Hafez is a suspect; he seems to have been plagued by all sides on account of my parents' disappearance." Thinking to offer a scrap of information, she added, "Indeed, a contingent from the French embassy was putting him through his paces just yesterday."

Mr. Drummond nodded his head toward Robbie. "Yes— we are aware. We are cooperating with the embassy staff here, as it would benefit all parties to secure the site."

There was a small pause. "And discover what happened to my parents," Hattie prompted.

The man hastened to assure her, "Of course, of course—a terrible business."

Thinking to throw out another fact so as to assuage her conscience, she offered, "Monsieur Berry wishes to escort me to the worker's village tomorrow in the hope that I may evoke additional information—he believes that I would be a sympathetic figure."

"A good plan," agreed Drummond. "There has been precious little cooperation among the locals."

"I will join you," offered Robbie.

This was actually a welcome offer; presumably Robbie would report back to these British men who theoretically held her loyalty even though Berry held her heart. "Please," she smiled, to impress upon the other gentlemen that she was nothing if not cooperative. "I would appreciate your support, Robbie."

But the associate unexpectedly spoke up, his expression grave. "I am not so certain of the wisdom of this—perhaps it would be best if Miss Blackhouse avoided those areas which are not secure."

A bit surprised, Hattie glanced at him and wondered if he didn't wish them to discover the truth—which seemed unlikely. On the other hand, the warning seemed sincere, and for a brief moment she was reminded of the warning given by the Comte, that first night in Paris.

"Do not be concerned—it is more likely they will prostrate themselves," Robbie observed with his ready grin. "They believe she is the mummy, reincarnated."

"Nonsense," offered Drummond with bluff gallantry. "Miss Blackhouse could never be confused with a dried-up relic, princess or not."

"As you say," the associate agreed politely, and Hattie had to refrain from giving him a sharp look; there was a thread of awareness in his response that she could not like. I wonder if he knows, she thought in dismay, and tilted her parasol so as to conceal her heightened color. I truly am not going to be able to bear this—this wondering if everyone I meet might know my terrible secret. Subdued, she tried to turn her mind from the difficulties that lay ahead, and instead focused on the amusing tale Robbie was relating to the others.

Chapter 34

After dinner that evening, Hattie remained at the table with Berry, hoping to have a chance to speak with him privately. She hadn't seen him before dinner, and neither Hafez nor Robbie had joined them. The other passengers had gone above for a walk on deck, Bing joining them after Hattie met her chaperone's eye. Eugenie had originally stayed behind, but at a similar glance from Berry she sighed, much put-upon, and then had flounced off to join the others. Apparently in Hafez's absence the woman was at loose ends; Berry's strictures against thievery no doubt put a damper on her activities.

"I was quizzed by a representative from the British consulate today," Hattie confessed, "and I wasn't certain what to say."

Berry was leaning back in his chair and nursing a glass of red wine, his long legs stretched out before him. "Did you mention the senet board or the disk?" He asked the question as though it made no difference to him either way.

She arched a brow, amused by his cavalier attitude. "I did not. Should I have?"

He tilted his head in the familiar gesture. "I would rather you did not—not until we are certain of the secret chamber and can secure it against all others."

Eying him, she challenged, "You do not feel I can trust the British consul?"

He swirled the wine, his gaze on the glass. "It is best to be cautious."

"The representative—a Mr. Drummond—has an associate who rather reminds me of you. And I met him before in Paris—although he thinks I am unaware; he was working with the British spymaster and posing as a hackney driver."

This seemed to catch his desultory attention and he looked up at her, the expression in the brown eyes intent. "Describe this gentleman for me, if you please."

Frowning in concentration, she made the attempt. "He is so ordinary as to be hard to describe—middling height, rather nondescript with dark hair; perhaps thirty-five."

"A scar across the back of his hand?"

She thought, then confessed, "I'm afraid I didn't notice."

He made no response and appeared to be unconcerned, lowering his gaze once more to his wine glass. Watching him, she added, "He wanted me to know that Mr. Hafez was the last person to see my parents—I think he was trying to warn me."

At her unspoken question, his eyes met hers. "I must disagree—Monsieur Hafez was not the last person to see your parents."

She decided that she may as well ask. "Do you know who was?"

"You must not ask me—not yet," he replied gently.

Sitting here with him in the nearly deserted dining room, Hattie thought about who he was, and who she was, and how complicated everything had turned out to be. "Will you ever tell me anything?" It was not asked in an accusatory fashion—she was genuinely curious.

"I will tell you that I look forward to spending the day with you tomorrow," he responded, turning the subject with a half smile as he drank his wine.

"I'm afraid Robbie is to accompany us," she cautioned—it was nothing more than he deserved, maddening man.

"Is he?"

If she expected a show of disapproval she was to be disappointed. "I told Mr. Drummond of our plans about going to the worker's village on the morrow—it seemed the least I could do—and Robbie offered to come."

Something in her voice caught his attention, and he set down his glass and said gently, "Hattie, if you wish to tell them anything—anything at all—I will not prevent you. I only ask that you give me warning."

Nodding, she added, "You see—I have decided I am English, after all."

"It is a fine thing, to be English," he agreed, his gaze back on his glass. "I have known many brave Englishmen."

Deciding she'd rather speak of lighter subjects, she teased, "Speaking of which, Mr. Smithson spent the day with Bing."

"That is rare courage, indeed."

"That is not what I meant—I think perhaps you had the right of it." It was on the tip of her tongue to suggest her companion and the vicar might make a match of it, but she decided not to raise such a sensitive subject—he had not reintroduced the topic of their mutual future and she wished to give him more time to be reconciled to the hard truth before it was raised again.

His long fingers played on the stem of his glass. "Will you wear your yellow dress tomorrow?"

Disproportionably pleased by the question, she smiled. "I will if you would like."

"Yes, I would like." His unreadable gaze rested upon her.

She shook her head at him with a small smile. "You are in a strange mood tonight, my friend."

He continued to finger his glass, a gleam in his eye. "I visited the tomb today."

Staring at him wide-eyed, she breathed, "Did you find it?"

Amused, he chided, "Come now, Hattie—in the daytime? But I did note there are three stars in the corner of the chamber's ceiling."

With an effort, she attempted to control her excitement. "Where?"

Taking a quick glance around, he sketched with a finger on the table, using a candle holder as a reference. "Here is the sarcophagus; here is the entrance; here are the stars."

Frowning, Hattie thought about it. "Then the chamber is in this direction." She laid a finger on the tablecloth. "We need only the exact measurements from Bing."

"Very good," he said, impressed. "You have a good mind for maps."

"It is like chess." She glanced up to catch a speculative look in his eye, quickly extinguished. Oh, she thought, a bit stricken—an inherited trait, apparently.

The light mood vanished and she could feel herself blush as he smoothly continued, "It is only a matter of finding the appropriate time to unearth the chamber."

Entertaining an unthinkable thought, she cautioned, "I will accompany you, you know; do not even consider leaving me behind—not after all this."

"Hattie." He leaned forward. "Be reasonable."

"I am past being reasonable," she retorted. "It would be *horrendously* unfair."

"I will think on it," he temporized, in the tone of a

parent who has no intention of giving in to the importunings of a child.

Before the argument became heated, they were interrupted by Robbie, who pulled up a chair beside Hattie and signaled to a servant to bring him something to eat. "Robbie," asked Hattie in a pointed tone, "do you remember when we had to crawl down the abandoned tin mine at the Tor?"

"Couldn't forget—we were filthy." He turned to Berry to explain. "One of my sisters fell in."

Hattie pressed her old playmate. "Was I afraid? Did I falter?"

"Pluck to the backbone," Robbie pronounced, picking up her wine glass and drinking from it. "Why?"

She crossed her arms, annoyed. "Just to show I don't scare easily."

He considered. "Unless you're closed in somewhere—that scares you."

"That is neither here nor there," she said hastily.

Berry brought the discussion back to the matter at hand. "I understand you will accompany us to the worker's village tomorrow, Monsieur Tremaine."

"Yes—I thought to support Hattie." The two men exchanged a look by which she was given to understand any information discovered would not necessarily be good news. It didn't matter; she wanted only to resolve all mysteries so that she could leave this place and move forward into her future, wherever it was. And prevent another war, for good measure.

"Mademoiselle Bing should stay at home, I think," Berry suggested. "It would be best if you were to appear vulnerable and bereft."

"I will notify her," Hattie agreed, wondering what he was up to; he knew better than most that she could no more appear vulnerable and bereft than she could fly to the moon.

"Have you seen Mr. Hafez?" Robbie asked, taking a quick look around. "I am to arrange for a meeting with Mr. Drummond but he has not left word of his whereabouts."

"He did not join us for dinner," Hattie volunteered.

"Perhaps he has been detained," suggested Berry in a neutral tone. Hattie shot him a look but he did not meet her eye. Maddening man, she thought again, and watched him drink his wine, her gaze on his throat as she wondered in exasperation when he was ever going to kiss her again—there would be no opportunities tomorrow, certainly. When he lifted his eyes to hers, she was made aware he knew exactly what she was thinking.

"We must be patient," Berry said aloud, setting down his glass.

"Well, I hope he makes an appearance soon," said Robbie, oblivious to any byplay. "I need to buttonhole him."

"The sooner the better," agreed Hattie with fervor.

Chapter 35

T he next morning Hattie, dressed in yellow, stood before
two Egyptian men who sat on a crude bench before a
small market stall, smoking hookahs and regarding her with
unreadable dark eyes. Berry addressed them in Arabic, but
the two men made no reply. With a gesture, Berry indicated
Hattie and said something further. One of the men took one
last draw on the hookah, and then stood to disappear behind
the fruit stalls.

Berry turned to report to Hattie and Robbie. "We are
looking for a certain man—it may be a few minutes before
he is located."

Hattie tried to avoid eye contact with the remaining
native, who drew on the smoking tube and continued to
regard her unblinkingly. "Who is the man we seek?"

"One of the porters who was with your parents on the
site. I have indicated that you particularly desire to speak
with him."

Hattie nodded. "And what are my lines?"

"Appeal to his chivalry, perhaps—that you are now alone
in the world and need his help. You seek to bury your parents with the rituals of your religious beliefs."

"Be careful you don't offend him," warned Robbie. "They
are sensitive about certain protocols—keep your veil down."

"Unless it is necessary to lift it," suggested Berry. "We shall see."

Hattie sincerely hoped she would not have to offer a glimpse of the god-king's daughter to obtain assistance; she wasn't certain how one would go about it. They were once again on the west bank, only this time they had traveled past the ruins and into the small cluster of white-washed huts nestled against the hills that provided housing for the native laborers who worked the excavations. The accommodations were very basic, and the open air market seemed to serve as a general meeting place—although it seemed unnaturally quiet for a market, and around her Hattie observed turbaned men and veiled women watching them from shadowed doorways. She lifted the hem of her best yellow from the dusty pathway and was regretfully aware the dress would be the worse for wear after this excursion. It was more an evening dress than a day, but if it was favored by Berry, she would wear it morning, noon, and night with pleasure; she was pleased to think that he took notice of such things.

The man returned, and gestured silently for them to follow. Berry indicated Hattie should proceed, and she stepped between the stalls to follow the Egyptian, unable to resist glancing behind her to confirm that Berry followed.

"I will stay close," Berry assured her quietly so that Robbie would not overhear. After several twists and turns, they arrived at a makeshift café—hardly more than a lean-to—which consisted of a curtained doorway dividing a kitchen from a small dining area, the floor nothing more than hard-packed earth as the flies buzzed in circles in the center of the room. At one of the crudely-built tables sat an Egyptian man, his gaze resting for only an instant upon

Hattie before he watched Berry come toward him. He did not look at Robbie.

Berry indicated that Hattie should stand slightly behind him. "He will not speak directly to you, because you are a woman. You must not address him, but communicate only through me."

Hattie thought the protocol ridiculously stilted, so she cut to the heart of the matter. "Tell him I have come to bury my parents."

Berry translated, and the man sat for a moment, expressionless, and then spoke in Arabic. Hattie had the impression he knew English, but was using the translation process to stall and so put them at a disadvantage.

Berry turned to her and translated, "Have they no son?"

Hattie was sorry to discover that this was the wrong thing to say to her, and raising her veil, she advanced on the seated man, her eyes flashing and her heart beating in her ears. "No, and they did not have a daughter, either. You are going to tell me what you know or by *heaven* I will not be answerable for the consequences."

"Hattie—for God's sake," warned Robbie, startled.

But Berry said nothing as Hattie leaned over the seated man, pointing a finger in his face and hissing through her teeth, "How *dare* you insult me?"

Berry said something, but Hattie knew he was not translating.

The man's liquid dark eyes rolled from her to Berry as he stammered in English, "Please—they have been buried. The prayers have been said—Christian prayers."

Surprised, Hattie straightened slowly. "Where?" she demanded.

Shaking his head, he disclaimed in genuine fear, his arrogant pose completely vanished. "I cannot say—it is worth more than my life."

"Your life is worth nothing unless you tell me," she countered in a grim tone. "Speak."

His eyes slid to Berry again, and he made what sounded like a plea in Arabic. In response, Berry shrugged.

"You are a coward, in a country of cowards," Hattie bit out in disdain. "You allow foreigners of every stripe to come in and plunder your treasures, afraid to speak out or defend yourselves. Your mighty ancestors must weep in the afterlife, ashamed of the lot of you."

The man spoke rapidly to Berry, who nodded in acknowledgment and then took Hattie's arm to gently draw her away. As she turned, she could see that perhaps a half dozen other men were now crowded into the adjacent kitchen, staring at her in amazement from behind the lifted curtain. Now I've torn it, she thought, forcing herself to calm down; I hope Berry does not have to carry me out of here.

"It is best to go, now," Berry suggested, as a rising crescendo of murmuring voices could be heard. With his hand firmly on her arm, they ducked out the doorway and walked with a rapid progress back toward the market street, Robbie following close behind with his hand resting on the hilt of his pistol. As the hushed voices surrounding them became louder, Hattie saw faces suddenly appear in windows and doorways to look upon her; saw children pulled in from their play by anxious mothers who held their veils up to cover their faces. I am not afraid of any of you, she thought in defiance, and lifted her chin to stare them all down.

They made it to the waiting cart without incident and once safely away, Robbie explained to Berry in an apologetic aside, "She's always had a temper, I'm afraid; especially on behalf of others."

"He was so condescending, Robbie," Hattie hotly

defended herself. "If I were a man I would have knocked him down."

"If you were a man he would have knocked you right back, Hattie; try to remember the situation is a delicate one and we are seeking a favor—we need to find the missing inventory."

"It couldn't be helped," she insisted, crossing her arms. "I cannot say I am sorry for it."

Berry, who had been watching the exchange without comment, interrupted to point out, "He told me where your parents are buried."

Hattie and Robbie interrupted their quarrel to give him their full and silent attention.

"There is a Christian graveyard—on the east bank between the Embassies, which is used to bury foreigners who die while visiting. Your parents are in unmarked graves on the site."

Hattie stared at him for a moment, her brow knit. "And who buried them there?"

Berry shrugged. "I imagine it will not be difficult to find out."

Robbie added with some satisfaction, "And whoever buried them may know how they died, and why—or at least know someone else who knows."

Berry deferred to Robbie with a respectful gesture. "Exactly. You may wish to cross the river straightaway to see what can be discovered at the cemetery before others hear of this episode—I imagine word will spread very quickly. If you'd like, I can see Mademoiselle Blackhouse safely home."

"An excellent idea." With an easy movement, Robbie leapt down from the cart to trot toward the quay—all the while assuring Hattie over his shoulder that he would report back to her as soon as he knew anything.

In the ensuring silence, Berry then gave a direction to the driver, who stirred the recalcitrant donkey into action once again. Hattie regarded him as they resumed their progress. "You already knew this."

"No," he admitted. "But I am not surprised."

Her temper having now cooled, she assimilated the Egyptian's revelation and its implications. In a subdued tone she offered, "I imagine they were murdered by the French— upon orders by my"—she couldn't quite bring herself to say it and amended—"the prisoner."

"Or someone acting for him," Berry agreed, watching her with open sympathy.

Arching an eyebrow, she tried to make light. "Small wonder, then, that the porter didn't know what to tell me."

Berry tilted his head. "It was a terrible dilemma for him."

"What was it you said?"

"I reminded him that you were the daughter of the god-king, and should not be crossed."

"Yes." She dropped her gaze to examine her hands in her lap, trying to control her emotions. "Well, it certainly turned the trick."

Leaning forward, he placed his hands over hers. "Shall we visit their graves together?"

She nodded, grateful for his support. "I should buy markers, I suppose. Although—although perhaps it is for the best that no one knows where they rest." She wiped away tears with the flats of her fingers.

"I believe," he suggested gently, "that more brandy is needed."

Looking up at him with a small smile, she confessed, "I never had spirits until you and your brandy."

"Well, you shall have them again, I think."

They came to a stop before a modest establishment whose

sign proclaimed "The Osiris Inn," and he dismounted to hand her down from the cart and escort her inside. The innkeeper, a bald, stout man with an elaborate black mustache, observed their approach from behind the desk and showed no sign of welcome or even of interest; Hattie had the fanciful impression that if the earth had suddenly opened up and swallowed them, his impassivity would continue undisturbed. The man must have some sensibility, however—there was a small golden icon hanging on the wall behind him, the type one saw in an orthodox church. If Hattie thought it a trifle odd that the Osiris Inn boasted such an icon, she made no comment. Berry made an inquiry and the man indicated they were welcome to step into the dining parlor, a thankfully cool room that was empty of any other guests. It was an odd hour, Hattie surmised, and the luncheon crowd had not yet arrived.

As they were seated, drinks were served and Hattie tentatively sipped the concoction, which was the color of raspberries. "Oh—it is good; rather like negus punch."

"Passion fruit, with *vodka*," Berry informed her with a warm smile, touching her hand on the glass. "Do you like it?"

"I do," she said, although there was a strong, tangy under-taste. "Is *wod-ca* a form of brandy?"

"The spirits are from a different source—the taste is not as strong."

She nodded, and drank so as to match him in sophistication—it appeared he was a man who was accustomed to drinking spirits so she had best acquire a taste for them, and truly the drink was rather good. It was such a comfort to put the events of the morning behind her and sit with him—just the two of them, for once—in this quiet and peaceful place. A benevolent feeling of warmth was making its way down her veins as she felt all her concerns dissolve away. "What have you done with Mr. Hafez? Smithson will carry off the palm with the poor minister all unknowing."

He regarded the linen tablecloth for a moment, deciding whether to tell her. "Mr. Hafez would rather not be found, at present."

"Does he yet live?"

He was amused. "Yes, he lives."

"It is not such a strange question," she pointed out in her own defense. "Given recent events."

"No—it is only that you are so *sangfroid*." He lifted her hand to turn it over and kiss her wrist, his mouth warm on her skin. "You continually surprise me."

Her pulse leapt at the contact, and she was reminded that he hadn't kissed her since Cairo and that this lack should be remedied as soon as humanly possible. "Do you remember what we spoke of—that which you said I wasn't to speak of again?"

"We will not speak of it," he said firmly, and motioned to the mustachioed gentleman for another round of drinks.

She subsided, castigating herself for raising the issue too soon—he was not yet ready to face facts. She sincerely hoped he wasn't going to avoid making love to her in some misguided attempt to change her mind; at the moment she was fighting a very strong urge to crawl onto his lap. After she downed another half-glass of the punch, she asked, "If there is another war, will you fight?" She knew she should not be asking him such a thing but found that she was having trouble monitoring her words.

Tenderly he placed a hand against her face, the palm completely covering her cheek. "I am very careful, Hattie."

"I know." She leaned into his hand. "Sorry. Sometimes I worry."

"You needn't," he said gently. "I will always come home to you."

It was shaping into her worst fear—that after having the ground cut out from beneath her with respect to every other constant in her life, she would lose him, too. Stop being maudlin, she commanded herself—you are not one of those women. Mustering a smile, she teased, "And where is home?"

"Wherever you are," he answered easily.

Shaking her head, she pronounced, "You are the most complete hand—I can never catch you."

"Not true—I am well and truly caught." Rising, he came around to help her to her feet, his hands beneath her elbows. "And here is Monsieur Smithson."

To Hattie's surprise, Mr. Smithson indeed stood beside her, smiling happily. "My best wishes, Miss Blackhouse."

"Thank you," she replied, and hoped he wouldn't notice that she was a bit unsteady on her feet. "It is indeed a relief to know at long last."

"Shall we begin?" asked Berry.

Glancing up, Hattie noted that the innkeeper stood within the room at a small distance, his expression wooden. Before she could gather her wits to make an inquiry, however, the vicar opened his Book of Common Prayer and intoned, "Dearly beloved..."

Chapter 36

Ooooh no," said Hattie in an ominous tone. "I will not hold—forever hold my peace." She then ruined the effect by hiccupping.

Drawing her arm firmly under his, Berry said to Smithson, "Continue, if you please."

Nonplussed, the vicar addressed Berry with an apologetic air. "If the lady has an objection, I'm afraid I must desist."

"The lady has no objection—do you, Hattie?" Berry said in a tone that brooked no argument.

"I do have an objection," insisted Hattie, who wondered why the room was so warm. "I told him not to marry me—I am going to be his mistress, instead. You are here under false pretenses." She smiled so as not to hurt the clergyman's feelings.

The vicar stared at her, his brows elevated. "But—my dear, if this man wishes honorable matrimony—"

"There would be nothing honorable about it," Hattie explained kindly.

"Hush, Hattie," said Berry, his other hand caressing hers on his arm. To Smithson, "Please proceed."

"Please do not," objected Hattie with a great deal of firmness. "I am sorry for the incon—for the conven—for your trouble."

As Smithson closed the book in some confusion, Berry drew his pistol with a smooth movement and held it at arm's length, pointed to the vicar's head. "You will proceed."

Smithson gaped, speechless.

"Now look what you've done, Daniel—or whatever your name is," Hattie said crossly. "A man of God, for the love of heaven."

"Proceed," said Berry, his voice like steel. The innkeeper stood and observed as though the events unfolding before him were completely routine.

Ashen of face, Smithson nevertheless stood upon principle. "I'm afraid I cannot proceed without the lady's consent."

The pistol did not waiver. "Consent, Hattie."

She stamped her foot. "I will not. You have run mad."

"My arm grows tired." Berry cocked the hammer back with a click.

Hattie hit upon an impediment. "You don't have a ring—it doesn't count unless there is a ring."

"Yes it does. Tell her." He gestured with the pistol.

Swallowing, Smithson explained, "Monsieur Berry is correct—technically it makes no difference."

"I am trying to protect you," Hattie said in an exasperated stage whisper to the vicar. "Look *alive*."

Staring down the barrel of the pistol, the officiate tried a different tack. "If I may inquire, Miss Blackhouse, what is your objection?"

Drawing her brows together, Hattie thought about it carefully—although it was hard work to concentrate. "I love him too much to let him marry me." Realizing this did not sound like a plausible objection, she added, "It is a long and *sordid* story."

The barrel of the gun within inches of his eyes, the vicar

offered, "He does seem very sincere in his affections, and if you love him—"

"He is not what he seems," she hinted darkly. "And for that matter, neither am I."

"Hush, Hattie. Give the man your consent."

"I don't know where the dogs live," Hattie explained to Smithson in a wistful tone. "I don't even know his name."

"Dimitry," Berry said.

Enrapt, Hattie turned to him, smiling mistily. "Oh— Dimitry. That is a fine, fine name."

Berry lowered the gun and with his free hand, cradled her face and kissed her. She had forgotten how wonderful it was to be kissed by him, and clung to his neck because her knees had suddenly gone weak. He lifted his face and said to her, "I love you, Hattie. Do you love me?"

Gazing into his eyes, she nodded.

"Then do this for me." His gaze held hers. "Please."

"I do," she said, and he smiled broadly then kissed her again, very thoroughly.

The vicar could be heard, speaking with some amusement. "I'm afraid we are not yet at this point in the ceremony."

With some reluctance, Hattie disengaged from Berry but staggered a bit after losing his support. Discerning yet another impediment, the vicar asked with some delicacy, "Is the lady, er—impaired?"

"Proceed," commanded both Berry and Hattie at the same time and in the same tone. With no further ado, Smithson saw to it that they were wed.

The papers were signed and witnessed, with Smithson enjoined to secrecy. "Although Bing would not be surprised," Hattie informed him in a complacent tone. "She saw it from the first."

"Yes," agreed the vicar with a smile. "But mum's the word—I understand in the present situation it would be best to keep this happy news *sub rosa.*"

He thinks we are keeping it quiet because my parents are missing, thought Hattie, and couldn't restrain an inappropriate giggle. Small influence matters of mourning would have on the determined Monsieur Berry, or whatever his name was—her name, now. With this thought, she paused and tried to gather her wits. I should discover what the date is, she thought muzzily, and write it down somewhere.

After they said their thanks and farewells, Berry steered her into a well-appointed room, where he shut the door and resumed the kiss that had been interrupted by the ceremony, his mouth urgent upon hers and his arms holding her tightly against him. After a very satisfying space of time, she broke away to protest, "I am a drunken bride—and your fault entirely."

"Nonsense; you are enchanting," he murmured as his mouth traveled down her neck, his hands busy loosening the lacings down her back. As her yellow dress collapsed around her feet he steadied her arm. "Step out, please—we don't want it to be wrinkled."

She obeyed him, asking with some surprise, "Are we truly going to do this now?"

He laid her dress carefully over the back of a chair. "Yes, we are. Don't be afraid, Hattie—if the way you kiss me is any indication you will have an easy time of it."

"I am not afraid," she assured him, her hands caressing his chest. "I asked Eugenie about it."

He laughed aloud, and kissed her. "Pay no attention to anything she said."

"She said when the heart is involved, it is simple."

He paused, and kissed her mouth again. "There are times when Eugenie surprises me." He gently slid his fingers beneath the straps of her linen shift so as to peel them off her shoulders, leaving her breasts exposed. He then made a sound in his throat that she interpreted as a compliment of the highest order.

"You have been impatient to see this," she teased, pleased by his reaction.

While she watched in fascination, he leaned in to kiss the hollow between her breasts as he began unbuttoning his shirt. "I will show you how patient I can be. Come, we will lie down."

He swung her up in his arms and laid her upon the simple bed, murmuring endearments in French and in his own undecipherable language as he divested them of any remaining clothing while trailing kisses across her collarbone and then downward to the peak of a breast, which made her gasp and arch against him in surprised pleasure. His warm hands stroked and caressed her hips as he fitted his body atop hers, necessarily arching due to the difference in height. Overwhelmed by the sensation of skin upon skin, she explored his body tentatively, then with more boldness as she assessed his increasingly heated reactions to her touch.

"*Zhena*," he breathed.

"What does that mean?" She gasped against his mouth, her fingers digging into his shoulders.

"Wife," he muttered with his mouth buried in the side of her throat. "*Zhena*."

"Dimitry—" she whispered, and then found she was no longer able to create words, English, French, or otherwise.

Chapter 37

The news that Hattie had discovered her parents' final resting place was the central topic of conversation at the dinner table on the *Priapus* that evening. That the discovery paled in significance to other discoveries experienced that day only compounded Hattie's headache. Nevertheless, she was expected to be a tragic figure and accept sympathetic overtures when she would so much rather be accepting her new husband's overtures. Or taking a tincture; one or the other.

"I found their graves—or at least I'm fairly certain," Robbie reported. "The groundskeeper said there were no records with respect to them—which is apparently not as unusual as one would think. He recalled that they were buried at the request of the British consul, but Mr. Drummond has no such recollection and he can't imagine who would make such a request without having him informed; it was no secret the Blackhouses were missing and there was an intense interest in their fate."

Frowning, Bing suggested, "Perhaps the man is mistaken—it was some months ago, after all."

But Robbie was not dissuaded. "He seemed certain—he explained that he remarked on it in particular because they were a married couple; usually those who end up at the foreigner's cemetery are without family."

"Was he aware of their identities at the time?" This from

Smithson, who had done a credible job of pretending nothing untoward had taken place amongst the other diners this fine day. For her part, Hattie had to resist the temptation to hold a glass of ice water to her aching head or sit and stare in bemusement at Dimitry. Eugenie was right—the process had been blissfully simple. Twice.

His expression skeptical, Robbie responded, "He claims he was not aware who they were, although this seems unlikely to me—especially when it became common knowledge that the Blackhouses were missing."

"Did he mention the cause of death?" asked Bing with a sympathetic glance at Hattie.

"'Accident,' but nothing more specific than that."

The diners sat in silence for a moment, assimilating what they had heard. Smithson ventured a theory. "A tragic accident—perhaps a cave-in caused by a worker's carelessness. In a panic, they were buried and nothing was said so as to protect the miscreant."

"It is a good theory," agreed Dimitry.

Bing covered Hattie's hand with her own. "We will visit tomorrow, if that is agreeable, Hathor."

"Yes, Bing." Hattie wished Bing wouldn't speak quite so loudly; particularly because she was remembering that Dimitry didn't trust anyone at the British consul's office, and she would realize why this was important if only her head didn't ache so. Among other places that ached. She slid a glance across the table at her new husband and found his gaze brimful of sympathetic amusement.

"I'm sorry for it, Hattie—this day has been hard on you," offered Robbie.

"Very hard indeed," she agreed in a grave tone and couldn't resist another glance at Dimitry.

Robbie continued, "Mr. Drummond awaits your instruction—if you'd like them to be disinterred and transported home, he assures me the British government will see to it."

Thinking on it, Hattie shook her head, and then wished she hadn't. "I think it best they remain where they are; this was more a home to them than Cornwall."

"Fitting," agreed Bing. "They find eternal rest among the very ancients they studied."

"You will go home, now, yes?" Eugenie could barely conceal her relief.

"Not just yet; I have much more to learn." This time she refrained from glancing at Dimitry, which was just as well—it hurt her eyes to look at him sidelong.

Her smooth brow puckered, Eugenie glanced to Dimitry. "No? But you know of your parents, now—there is no reason to stay."

As if on cue, their party was joined by Captain Clements, who bowed to the ladies and was met with their exclamations of surprise and pleasure. "Here's a charming group— Miss Bing, Miss Blackhouse, Miss Valérie."

"Leone," Eugenie corrected him with much amusement.

He sank his grizzled head in mock chagrin. "I beg your pardon—how I could have misnamed such loveliness is a mystery."

"*De rien*," she smiled, and indicated he was to sit beside her.

Hattie watched the other woman interact with the captain and concluded—now that she was aware of such things— that Eugenie's heart was involved.

The captain was introduced to Smithson and Robbie and after the men had exchanged pleasantries, Clements turned to Hattie and asked how her visit went. With a monumental effort, Hattie related the discovery of her parents' grave site yet again, resisting an urge to press her fingertips to her temples in the process.

"I am sorry to hear of it," the captain said with respectful sympathy. "And even though it was not entirely unexpected, there is an end to hope—which is not an easy thing."

"You have the right of it, sir," she agreed, and was aware that all trace of flirtatiousness had been erased from his manner toward her; that he knew about her marriage seemed evident, and she imagined he heard nothing about her parents he didn't already know. He and Dimitry must have already shared this information, which was impressive as she had been with Dimitry for all but an hour this day. Obviously they had a network of people supporting them here, whoever they were.

Even with the windows opened, the dining room felt uncomfortably close and Hattie was considering a strategic retreat before she disgraced herself when Bing—with an assessing eye on her charge—put a stop to any further discussion in her brisk manner. "Would you like to retire, Hathor?"

"I believe I could use some air, Bing." And an opportunity to speak to Berry—Dimitry, she corrected with a soft smile, remembering how he had responded when she whispered his name while they were abed. As she rose she gave him a glance to indicate she wished to speak with him, and then made her way out to the deck with Bing, stepping carefully so as not to jar her poor head.

The cooler air felt much better, although there was little breeze tonight, and Hattie walked over with Bing to lean on the railing, wishing she could lay her forehead on the cool wood and close her aching eyes. "Perhaps," her companion offered with some delicacy, "—perhaps with this discovery today all matters have been resolved for the best."

Bing was referring to the suspicion that her parents had been involved in purloining artifacts—if only that were indeed the case; a bit of theft was nothing as compared to a bit of treason. "Yes, I suppose. Although Monsieur Berry tells me he believes he knows the location of the secret chamber, thanks to you." With any luck he would respond to her unspoken message and make an appearance soon—why on earth does anyone drink this vile stuff, she thought crossly; the repercussions surely outweigh the benefits—although I suppose I wouldn't have married him sober, so there is that.

"Then perhaps any scandal—if there is one—could be scotched."

Bringing her mind back to the topic, Hattie agreed. "That is to be devotedly hoped for." Poor Bing—she was worried about Hattie's reputation and Edward's legacy and possibly Smithson's reaction; she was unaware that her parents' misdeeds would pale in comparison to other cataclysmic events if the Elban prisoner was to march again. And in such a case it seemed unlikely that the salacious circumstances of her birth could be kept quiet—it would be a disaster in every respect, although she supposed she should be more concerned about the fate of the world than her own paltry troubles.

Dimitry joined them, and with a dry smile Bing found something of interest to view on the shoreline so as to allow them to stand together at the railing undisturbed.

Looking up into his eyes, Hattie smiled a smile full of warmth and knowledge and he reciprocated with a tender smile of his own. They stood together in silence for a moment, relishing the sensation, while Hattie forgot about her aching head and every other unsolvable problem.

He offered in a sympathetic tone, "You are a bit green, I think."

"No longer," she teased, arching a dark brow.

His white teeth flashed in the darkness. "Hattie—you shock me."

"I am not going to your sister's," she said without preamble. "Tell the captain to go away."

He tilted his head. "Do you not think I would rather you were here with me?"

"But it is so unfair," she protested, then remembered not to raise her voice or suffer the consequences. "I have been so very useful."

He ran a caressing hand over hers. "You have indeed—but it is necessary; I cannot conduct my business properly if I am worried about you."

She paused, and reflected that—in theory at least—she was now enjoined to obey her husband, which was a novel idea to someone admittedly as headstrong as she. To take her mind off this inconvenient tenet, she asked, "Why did you insist on British guards but at the same time you do not trust the consul's office?"

"That is impressive," he conceded, his eyes alight with admiration. "But I cannot say."

After deciding with some reluctance that he had the right of it—it was time to relinquish the field—she asked quietly, "You will be very careful, Dimitry?" Aware that she sounded fretful and clinging, she explained with an apologetic air, "My head hurts and I am past being brave."

"I love you." He lifted her hand to kiss it, even though Bing could probably see the gesture. "I will be careful."

In an attempt to take advantage of his soft mood, she wheedled, "May I stay a few days longer? Think of poor Bing and her new romance—it is the least you can do after encouraging her other beau to vanish. And perhaps we can find another free afternoon." This said with a meaningful look.

"Unfair," he protested, without giving her a straight answer. "As for now, we need to speak to Mademoiselle Bing, to obtain the measurements."

"Are you going to the tomb tonight?" She was torn because she wanted to accompany him but she was very much afraid she would have to stop to be sick along the way.

"No more *vodka* for you," he teased, again without answering the question, which gave her leave to believe he was indeed planning such a visit.

"Will you at least tell me if you find the secret chamber?"

He leaned in to whisper near her ear, his breath warm against her skin and evoking delightful memories. "Perhaps."

"You are beyond exasperating, husband." She fingered one of his buttons, deeply affected by his masculine nearness and *longing* to be abed again.

He laughed again—gratifying, how she had never heard him laugh before today but now he could not seem to stop. "And you are adorable—particularly when you are explaining to the priest that you would rather be my mistress."

"I do prefer marriage, thus far." She dimpled up at him. "And don't call him a priest—he's likely to be offended."

"My mistake—although I think there is little I can do to redeem myself."

She could only agree. "I can't imagine a bridegroom has ever held him at gunpoint."

"No—only angry papas, perhaps."

She laughed with him, even though the effort cost her. Although she was unwell, she was determined to stay with him until they were forced to part. Moments like these were precious; she was soon to be packed off to some unknown place—somewhere where there were priests. I am unafraid, she thought; I would follow him anywhere, and after all that I have weathered these past few days, I am ready to rebuild somewhere peaceful—surely there are no more shocks to be sustained.

"Shall we speak with Mademoiselle Bing?"

"Yes," she agreed easily, determined not to cling and complain as he led her toward her companion.

Chapter 38

The following day Hattie and Bing made their visit to the foreigner's cemetery, a bleak enclosure located in the area behind the government compound on the east bank. The cemetery was no larger than the one at the church in Cornwall, only it was many levels more forlorn—consisting of grave sites that were nothing more than gravel and sand; as there were undoubtedly few visitors, there was little point to more than a cursory maintenance. Fortunately, due to its proximity to the Nile, there were several spreading willow trees that provided a measure of welcome shade and made the entire aspect a little less desolate.

As had been arranged, the two women met Drummond from the British consulate at the gate, and Hattie looked for his associate, hoping to verify the scar across his hand for Dimitry. The other man was not in evidence, however, as Drummond offered his sincere apologies for the consul's failure to be made aware of the burial. "We believe their deaths were an accident, and those who may have been involved were too frightened or too remorseful to come forward."

Frightened, concluded Hattie—the porter at the worker's village was too frightened to tell her where they were until she did a little frightening of her own. Aloud, she assured him, "It makes little difference, Mr. Drummond—at least the mystery is solved." And she privately held out cautious hope that no one would ever discover their misdeeds or their infamous bargain to take in an inconvenient child from the wrong side of the blanket. That she was someone lesser than she thought she was still stung, and it was fortunate that Dimitry had provided her with another role altogether to ease the shame of it.

Footsteps could be heard on the gravel path and the three looked to see another man approaching. With no little surprise, Hattie observed Baron du Pays, the French vice-consul whom she had last seen in her drawing room in Paris. Not a fortuitous turn of events, she decided—that he should reappear at this juncture and in this place. She dipped a graceful curtsey to hide her concern.

"Mademoiselle Blackhouse." He greeted her, the pale eyes assessing her behind a cool facade. "We meet again— much to my delight." He did not relinquish her hand and continued, "I deeply regretted the circumstances which required your immediate departure from Paris."

"It was a sudden decision," she agreed. "You are acquainted with Mr. Drummond?"

"Of course—we were reacquainted last night," the Baron said with a show of affability, "—and shared the latest news from the congress over an excellent bottle of port."

"What is the latest news?" asked Bing with keen interest. "We have not been able to keep up."

The Frenchman shook his head in consternation. "Prussia seeks Saxony; Austria insists on Italian territory and Tallyrand—who was the Emperor's man—now represents the new order and happily pits each participant against the other like the puppet-master he is. Almost, one cannot blame him—the situation is ripe for exploitation."

"If they are not careful, the former emperor will be emboldened," warned Drummond as he nodded in agreement. "There is far too much uncertainty."

Bing displayed mild alarm at the tenor of the conversation. "Surely no one believes Napoleon will escape his captivity? Why, I understand both French and English ships guard the harbor."

"Never underestimate the audacity of the man," cautioned Drummond with a grave expression. "It cannot be an easy thing to be demoted from Emperor of Europe to Emperor of Elba."

Her color high, Hattie changed the subject and made a gesture toward the cemetery, hoping to hint that the others should take their leave. "We have discovered my parents' graves, Monsieur le Baron, and I have come to pay my final respects."

To her chagrin, the Frenchman only used this announcement as an excuse to take her hand again. "I have heard the sad news; my sincerest condolences, Mademoiselle Blackhouse—a deplorable attack. I hope you will allow me to advise you in this difficult time?"

"Thank you." She did not mention she was just as likely to take advice from the Elban prisoner himself.

The Baron continued, "And recall we had made plans to tour the sights in Paris which—regrettably—had to be canceled. Now that your sad charge is completed, perhaps I may be allowed to raise your spirits by taking a tour of Thebes. To this end, you and Mademoiselle Bing"—here he bowed toward Bing—"may be more comfortable at my consulate's guest quarters. I can send servants to transfer your belonging this very afternoon, if that is agreeable."

"Mr. Tremaine," murmured Bing behind Hattie.

Hattie demurred prettily, bringing her dimples to the fore.

"I will discuss this idea with Mr. Tremaine, but I must warn that it is unlikely he would agree to such a plan—he has stood as my escort and advisor on the journey and I imagine he would like to keep me close to hand. I do thank you for the invitation, however."

Taking the refusal in good part, the Frenchman bent his head in acquiescence but persisted, "In any event, please assure me you will dine with me this evening—along with Monsieur Tremaine, if he will join us; I assure you my chef does not disappoint."

"With pleasure," Hattie agreed, feeling she had no other polite option. To rid herself of him, she decided stronger tactics were needed. "If you gentlemen do not mind, I feel I should reflect and pray by my parents' graves for a time."

Bowing, the two men took their leave but invited the women to tea at the British consulate after their visit. After making an equivocal response, Hattie reached to push open the wrought iron gate with some impatience. "God in heaven, Bing—he makes my skin crawl. Think of a plausible excuse to forgo dinner, if you please."

"Perhaps you should make him aware that your feelings are otherwise engaged," Bing suggested as they entered the cemetery.

"I don't think that it would much matter to him." And there was something else, she thought with a small frown; I wasn't paying attention and he said something important— now, what was it?

She paused before they headed toward the far corner of the cemetery and turned to Bing. "You will not be insulted if I send you away, Bing; I'm afraid there may be equal parts praying and cursing and I'd rather not have a witness."

"Small blame to you," was her companion's only brisk

reply. "I shall take a tour of the Temple of Karnak while I have the chance." Bing indicated the nearest set of ruins, which, to Hattie, looked very much like any other set of tedious ruins. To each his own, she thought as she made her way over to the two unmarked mounds, the cemetery quiet and the occasional stirring of the willow branches in the breeze the only movement. Dry-eyed, she contemplated the raw, graveled graves for a moment, unable to muster up much grief. You have gotten off lightly, the both of you, she thought with some bitterness. No one will know of your perfidy, and as for me—I will have to bear this terrible burden you have placed upon me, this secret that makes me ashamed to show my face and ashamed for the honorable man I married—

"Miss Blackhouse."

Hattie looked up in surprise at hearing the whispered voice, and beheld Drummond's associate, standing against the willow tree at a small distance, his hat in his hand—she had not heard him approach but this was not surprising, as he was some sort of hackney driver *cum* spy. Before she could fashion a response he continued in a low tone, "I must apologize for this intrusion but I must take the opportunity—I have been commissioned by a certain gentleman to speak to you."

Wondering for a startled moment if he referred to Dimitry, she decided this seemed unlikely. "Which gentleman is that, sir?"

"The eighth of August."

Hattie stared at him. The date was her birthday. The gooseflesh rose on her arms and the nape of her neck, and she bowed her head to contemplate the graves, her mind racing—this must be the reason Dimitry didn't trust the British consul; apparently it was infested with Napoleon's supporters.

The man's voice continued, "The gentleman sends his sincere desire that you depart from this area with all speed and return to your home in England—it is not safe here. I have been commissioned to make immediate arrangements."

"I see." It was an echo of the comte's warning—only at that time she hadn't realized her true heritage; hadn't realized that she was regarded as some sort of perverse princess by those who sought to destroy England even as they urged her to return there, to a corner in Cornwall that was well away from the anticipated destruction. Furious with her parents— all of them—Hattie could hear her heartbeat in her ears and had to caution herself to keep her composure, not to let this man know that she would not fall in with their despicable scheme. Instead, she should find out what she could and tell Dimitry, although he almost certainly already knew who this man was; it must be the reason he had shown such an interest in him.

The man bowed. "That is all. I am sorry to have disturbed you at this difficult time."

"Wait." Hattie turned to him, trying to think of something she could ask that would assist Dimitry.

Shaking his head with regret, the associate cautioned, "I can answer no questions."

This seemed evident; she was not going to discover anything of interest because this man was probably as maddening as Dimitry when it came to withholding information. In fact, he and Dimitry were probably sworn enemies, which meant she had one more worry to add to all the others as she was forced to leave the arena—

Suddenly, Hattie was struck with the realization that—all in all—she held the whip hand in this situation and there was no reason she shouldn't put her miserable heritage to good use. Lifting her chin, she commanded, "I will return a message to the gentleman."

Surprised, the man considered this for a moment as he met her gaze. "Say it, then."

Returning her gaze to the graves she continued in a level tone. "I travel with a man—Monsieur Daniel Berry. I have married him in secret."

She could sense his surprise, although she did not look at him. "You have *married* the Count Leczinska?"

The Count? Dimitry was a Count? Was there no end to the irony? In her best imitation of a countess, Hattie continued smoothly, "Yes—Dimitry; I wasn't certain you were aware of his true name. As I said, he is now my husband." If nothing else, she could keep him safe; based on the strange respect they all afforded her it was unlikely they'd murder her husband. And besides, she thought a bit grimly; it was past time to call in a favor from at least one of her miserable parents.

But the associate was plainly confused. "Surely you do not request that he be allowed to leave with you? The work he does for the gentleman cannot be duplicated by any other." His tone was respectful but held an underlying thread of scorn, the scorn that warriors reserve for fearful women.

Hattie stood very still for a moment, then by sheer force of will overcame the paralysis that had settled within her breast. With some steel she said quietly, "I only ask that the message be relayed; I do not ask for your opinion."

"Your pardon; I shall do so." He hesitated for a moment, then pointed out, "The desire is that you return to the English countryside—it would be best to avoid Poland at this time."

"I shall consider your advice," she replied through stiff lips. "You may go."

Hattie stood silently for some time, staring at her erstwhile parents' graves without truly seeing them. Why is it, she thought, that just when I am coming to grips with the latest crisis, another one presents itself? Although to be honest, she couldn't be overly surprised; Dimitry had been willing to marry her, after all, and in the back of her mind she had wondered—and more than once. He pretended to be French, and hid his true nationality. He had searched the British consul's office, and inveigled a safe passage document from them—only the one, as though he wished to assure his own escape, should it be necessary. He worked closely with her parents who were themselves working for the enemy, and knew of the missing disk and the senet board when everyone else thought it was a strongbox. And then, most damningly, he had summoned the hackney driver that first night in Paris—the hackney driver who was a double agent for Napoleon, posing as an Englishman. Too many things didn't add up, and she had been foolish to turn a blind eye. Small matter to him that she was illegitimate—she was the daughter of the emperor, god-like to his followers. And Poland had been Napoleon's ally in the war. With some bitterness she acknowledged that she had been a bit dazzled and—truth to tell—starved for affection in pretending that all of this was not as ominous as it actually was. Love was truly blind—or at least it was overly optimistic and now she had yet another competing allegiance to sort out, because she loved Dimitry, and he was her husband.

After taking a steadying breath, she left the graves without a backward glance and went to find Bing.

Chapter 39

H attie walked out the gate and toward the ruins where Bing was seated, watching for her. The movement helped—with each step Hattie felt less frozen with horror and more inclined to turn over various options in her mind. When she arrived to stand before her companion, she had decided on what she hoped was the best course. "If you don't mind, Bing, I would like to visit the Coptic chapel across the river; I would like to arrange for prayers to be said."

"Very well, Hathor." If Bing thought it strange that Hattie sought prayers from a foreign church, she made no comment. Perhaps she believes I am hedging my bets, she thought—I only wish I could.

As her companion rose to her feet, Hattie added in a low tone, "I am concerned that we may be followed. Keep a sharp eye out, if you please."

Bing paused for only a moment, then took Hattie's arm as they headed to the river, giving her charge a quick, assessing look. "For whom do we watch?"

"Anyone who in turn appears to be watching us—I am afraid I do not know more." They walked in a leisurely fashion to the quay and boarded a *felucca* while Hattie remained silent, her mind busy, thinking. She finally emerged from her reverie to remark, "It is so difficult,

Bing, when you cannot go back, nor around, and your only choice is straight forward."

"I know exactly what you mean," agreed her companion with a nod. "One is called upon to marshal one's courage, whether one wishes to or not."

Hattie watched the waterman maneuver their vessel across the Nile and thought, I am heartily tired of being buffeted by shocking news, and I wish so much weren't at stake. But I do trust Dimitry—against all reason, even if he serves the enemy. Besides, she thought fiercely, if he wishes to do me harm, I may as well let him—life would hardly be worth living. "On the way to the chapel we will make a stop so that I may leave a message for—for Monsieur Berry."

And so it came to pass that Hattie stood before the inn-keeper at the Osiris Inn, who gazed at her from behind his desk with no sign of recognition. "Hallo again; I must speak to—to Dimitry, and as soon as possible. I am not certain where he is or how to send for him." Her eyes strayed for a moment to the icon on the wall. "I shall return in an hour."

If Bing thought the entire situation strange, she made no comment and asked no questions, instead accompanying Hattie to the chapel in supportive silence. That is the difference between Bing and me, thought Hattie, hiding a smile; I'd be demanding answers and throwing things. Forced to possess her soul in patience, Hattie spent the greater part of an hour sitting in the Coptic chapel beside Bing, contemplating the gilded altarpiece. "Do you think we were followed, Bing?"

"I do not believe so, Hathor—although many of the children look alike."

"No," said Hattie. "It would have been a man. Or more than one."

"Who is Dimitry?" asked Bing deferentially.

"Monsieur Berry is Dimitry," Hattie replied absently. "Has it been an hour?"

But before her companion could consult her watch, Dimitry himself slid into the pew beside Hattie. With a glance that did not conceal his concern, he assessed her quickly and she felt a pang that she had alarmed him, then caught herself—he deserved every moment of anxiety visited upon him, the wretched, *wretched* Pole.

"What is it, Hattie?" he asked, and Bing moved away to light a candle, although Hattie knew she wasn't popish. Small matter, she thought; I would light a candle myself if I thought it would help.

Taking a breath, Hattie confessed, "I may have torn it, Dimitry, but I am not certain, and I need your advice."

He watched her profile for a moment, his own expression grave. "Tell me."

With a mighty effort, she kept her voice level. "Mr. Drummond's associate—the one with the scar—"

"Yes," he said.

"He works for Napoleon."

"Yes." He waited, knowing there was more to come.

"He seems to think you do, also."

There was a pause. "What did he say to you?"

She bit her lip for a moment, then decided there was nothing for it. Unable to face him, she continued to speak in an even tone, looking toward the altarpiece. "He carried a warning from—from the prisoner, who wishes me away from here and back to Cornwall."

He was quiet, and she concluded after a breath, "I'm afraid I mentioned that we had married."

"Did you indeed?"

"I wasn't thinking—I am worried that I caused you trouble, by telling him."

"No matter, Hattie." He took her hand and after the barest hesitation, she folded her hand around his. Perhaps she could rehabilitate him—he needed only to see the error of his imperialist ways; surely there was hope for it, he was a good man—he *must* be.

Suddenly, she realized what had caught her attention. "I think that the Baron du Pays—from Paris—remember? I think he killed my parents. He let slip that they had been attacked, but everyone else thinks it was an accident."

"Yes, although the assassin was Monsieur Chauvelin."

She looked up at him. "I see. I confess I am not surprised; he's a nasty piece of goods. The Baron is here—do you know?"

"Yes."

She assimilated his quiet comment. "He wanted me and Bing to stay at the French consulate, but I declined the invitation."

They sat together for a moment or two. "I don't know what to do," she confessed, clinging to his hand and wishing the two of them could walk away from all of it, forever.

But Dimitry began giving instruction in a low voice. "It is important that you be away, and quickly. You must return to the *Priapus*; I will see to it that the others from the consul's offices are kept busy this afternoon. A boy with a boat will ask for you; you will leave with him. Take no luggage, and Mademoiselle Bing must stay behind to say you are ill in your cabin. The boy will take you to Clements's ship. Tell Mademoiselle Bing you will need at least five or six hours' head start." He squeezed her hand. "Do you understand?"

"Yes." She took a ragged breath. "You should leave with me." Turning to meet his eyes she continued, "I cannot allow you to go through with this."

He tilted his head to touch her forehead with his, the same gesture as the night he took her necklace—the first time he told her that he loved her. "I am not your enemy, Hattie. Can you trust me?"

"I don't know," she answered, trying to control a quaver.

"I have not lied to you since Paris," he continued in an intense tone. "I swear it, Hattie."

"When will I see you again?"

He squeezed her hand. "I know not. But you will be in my heart, every moment."

Ducking her chin, she nodded, miserable.

"I will go; wait another half hour before you leave and do not hurry."

Unable to speak, she nodded again and he was gone. Examining her hands in her lap, she decided she had little choice—she was married to the man and she loved him. She could report to the British consul, but that course seemed fraught with peril since Drummond's associate was an enemy agent and therefore she probably shouldn't trust Drummond—or anyone else there, either. She could apply to Robbie, but he would presumably turn the matter over to the authorities, unable to believe they couldn't be trusted. I hate Egypt, she thought bitterly—it has brought me nothing but heartache. Unbidden, she remembered her unconventional wedding and the blissful afternoon abed with her new husband. It doesn't matter, she thought with defiance—I *still* hate Egypt.

Hattie raised her head and signaled to Bing, who dutifully approached and slid in next to her. "Bing, would you mind if I borrowed your pistol?"

"Not at all, Hathor." Bing calmly fished in her reticule, and then taking a look around, slipped it to Hattie, who studied it for a moment. "Do you require instruction?"

"Yes, to refresh me; Robbie taught me but it was some time ago."

"It can fire two rounds before it must be reloaded." Bing gave an impromptu lesson and Hattie listened carefully, hoping that it wasn't a grave sin to be exchanging firearms in a church. Hattie then slipped it into the glove pocket sewn into the seam of her dress. "Now I will astonish you and tell you that I have married Monsieur Berry."

Bing raised her eyebrows and considered this bit of news. "My best wishes, Hathor."

Taking her companion's thin hand, Hattie explained, "I am sorry I did not invite you, but I was not invited, myself."

Bing glanced at her in alarm. "Never say he took advantage of you?"

Definitely, Hattie thought, but instead she said, "No, of course not—Mr. Smithson did the honors, and you may tell him I give my permission to tell you the story—it is a round tale."

"Well," said Bing, leaning back into the pew. "That is a wrinkle."

"Brace yourself; there are more shocks to come."

"We are leaving posthaste," Bing guessed.

"You are half right. I am leaving whilst you defend the fort." She recited Berry's instructions while Bing put her chin to her chest and listened.

Unable to make an adequate explanation to her companion, Hattie offered, "I am *wretchedly* sorry, Bing—apparently there are dark forces at play."

Bing sighed. "Perhaps the treasure is indeed cursed."

No, thought Hattie; the only curse at work here is ambition—ambition and greed. "I would suggest you think twice before reposing your trust in the Baron du Pays or in anyone at the British consulate."

"Heavens," remarked Bing in a dry tone. "You alarm me, Hathor."

"I am alarmed, myself," Hattie admitted. "I am sorry to leave you to make the explanations."

"Never fear—I shall think of something. May I suggest there has been an elopement?"

Hattie considered. "Best not. I'm not certain it is meant to be common knowledge, and I would not be surprised if Monsieur Berry remains here."

"I understand," her companion replied, but it seemed to Hattie that this was unlikely.

"I am so sorry, Bing."

"Hathor," said Bing, taking her hand with all sincerity. "I have never experienced such an adventure in my life, and I owe it all to you. I would not have missed it for the world."

Hattie faced the altarpiece again. "Don't make me cry, Bing—if I start I won't stop."

"Very well," said Bing briskly. "Shall we go?"

Chapter 40

L ady, lady—come look."

It wants only this, thought Hattie in annoyance as they made their way to the quay to secure passage by *felucca* back to the *Priapus*. A vendor had blocked her progress, imploring her to examine his wares which consisted mainly of very poor replicas of the Temple of Arum.

"Lady," the man implored, closing his fingers around her arm with one hand as he gestured with the other toward the makeshift table.

He was a bit too aggressive and Hattie pulled her arm away. "No," she said firmly, but he only grasped both her hands in his and began to pull her into the crowd. Now thoroughly alarmed, Hattie crouched and pulled back with all her strength, her feet sliding over the gravel path as she turned to call for Bing. Instead, a rough-hewn sack was lowered over her head and she could feel an unknown accomplice pin her arms down from behind. She shouted, only to feel a hand cover her mouth over the sack as she was lifted off her feet. Struggling, she was powerless to raise much of a resistance but as she kicked out she made contact and had the pleasure of hearing a man grunt as she was hustled away. She fought to breathe, and thought she could hear Bing shouting from a distance.

Her abductors slowed, and she could hear them speaking in Arabic to one another as she was lowered with relative care onto a hard surface. She was finding it difficult to breathe through the sack and just as she began to fight panic, the sack was slid off her head. Panting, she squinted against the sunlight and saw three men crouching in a cart around her while a fourth acted as the driver, urging the donkeys to move along. One man grasped her hands as another brandished a length of rope to bind them. Gauging her moment, Hattie struck both her hands up in a blow to his chin, then scrambled toward the side of the cart. Exclaiming in annoyance, the three pulled her back but not before she implored the startled faces who lined the streets, "Help—get help!"

This time, she was firmly pinned on her back on the floor of the cart by the others whilst her hands were bound. The vendor leaned in so that she could feel his breath on her face, and said in broken English, "Lady—quiet please."

In response she screamed as loudly as she was able, and he quickly put his hand over her mouth. Just as quickly, she bit down hard on his hand and between the three men, they managed to insert a gag into her mouth. For the remainder of her journey she lay on her back, fuming, while the men kept a careful watch around them. Trying to breathe evenly, she assessed the situation. Not good, she concluded— although it appeared they were instructed not to cosh her, which was a hopeful sign. For a wild moment she wondered if the prisoner was behind this abduction but rejected the idea—there would have been no need to have the associate warn her off. For the same reason, it seemed equally unlikely that the associate had masterminded this insult; his manner toward her had been deferential. The baron, then, she guessed; unhappy that she had not willingly come to the

French consulate. Or Drummond, perhaps—but to what end? None knew she intended to slip away except Dimitry and Bing. Frowning, she gave it up and awaited events—she had every confidence that Bing would marshal her allies; she had been warned about the British consul but she would certainly seek out Robbie and with any luck, find Dimitry—perhaps even return to the Osiris Inn. Hattie had only to be patient, matters were not as grim as they seemed, and she had Bing's pistol.

The cart finally came to a halt and the sack was once again shimmied down over her head. The vendor counted under his breath, and the three lifted her and unloaded her out the back. Kicking and twisting furiously, Hattie hoped that since it was still daylight she could draw enough attention so as to allow her rescuers to trace her. Or perhaps she could hold the pistol to a hostage and parlay her way out—unless they never unbound her, which seemed a likely possibility, given her attempts at escape. She would wait and reassess her strategy; perhaps it would be best to feign passivity, although she wasn't certain she could do such a thing.

After having been deposited on a chair, the sack was removed. Her hair tangled around her face, Hattie gazed in bemusement at Hafez, the Minister of Antiquities who regarded her with a solemn expression. They were in a rude hut, barely big enough for the number of people crowded inside.

"Forgive me, Miss Blackhouse," the minister apologized, bowing. "I am down to my last bargaining chip, I'm afraid." He carefully untied the gag and Hattie's captors, observing this, stepped back a cautious pace.

"What is the meaning of this—this *outrage*?" Hattie asked in an ominous tone. In truth, she had quickly grasped the meaning of this outrage upon being confronted with the minister; it appeared Hafez was afraid he'd be summarily murdered by Chauvelin—as had his other allies—and had decided he'd use her as a hostage until he could come to terms with his enemies.

Hafez spread his hands. "You will come to no harm if you cooperate—my assurances on it."

She tossed her head to clear the curls away from her eyes. "I wish that I could say the same for you—you will be made to pay for this, and pay dearly."

Hafez moved to twitch the curtain back and peer out the door as he mopped the perspiration from his brow with a handkerchief. "I would point out that you are in no position to make threats, Miss Blackhouse."

"Shame on you," pronounced Hattie with disdain. "You backed the wrong horse; then you and your cohorts turned coat and scurried over to the British. Did you think Napoleon's people would overlook your double-dealing?"

Annoyed, he allowed the curtain to fall back. "You must calm yourself, Miss Blackhouse—I ask only that you sit quietly."

As this seemed unlikely, Hattie eyed him with skepticism. "What is it you hope to gain? You cannot imagine to survive—your cohorts certainly didn't. You would be better served to seek my favor, and ask that I intercede for you."

He approached to stand before her in a manner meant to intimidate. "It is none of your concern—stay quiet."

Hattie curled her lip in scorn. "My only consolation is that Bing is not here to see this."

Fast losing patience, Hafez leaned over to put his finger in her face, warning, "You will stay quiet, or I will gag you again."

So that he would not think she had been cowed, Hattie lifted her chin and looked around her. She was in the worker's village, in one of the huts hidden away in the maze of other huts, which meant she may be difficult to find. Possessing her soul in patience, Hattie tried to sit quietly in the hope that they would unbind her so that she could summarily shoot someone.

After about an hour, murmuring voices could be heard outside the curtain, the general tone evidencing concern. The curtain twitched aside and the faces of several native men were revealed, one asking a question.

"Get help," Hattie implored in an urgent tone, wishing she knew some Arabic.

Hafez stepped to the curtain and angrily gestured the men back. "Gag her," he instructed the vendor of trinkets.

And so the gag was reapplied while Hattie sat and seethed, waiting for she knew not what.

Finally, as the light began to fade, noises and voices outside the hut signaled the approach of a sizable party. Hafez gave an instruction in Arabic to her captors, then passed outside the curtain. The vendor stepped forward, drew his pistol, and held it to Hattie's head. They cannot mean to kill me, she assured herself, but found that the proximity of the barrel caused a curious sensation in her midsection. The curtain parted and Hafez reentered, accompanied by the baron and an escort of several native men.

Upon seeing her situation, the baron paused upon the threshold and spoke in French. "Surely there is no need for such measures?"

"There is every need," Hafez insisted. "I cannot trust you."

The Frenchman considered Hattie's situation with a frown. "No—you would not dare."

Hafez cocked his head. "It is not I who would have to explain to him that she was dead due to my carelessness."

Ah, thought Hattie, enlightened; the fact that the baron was another Napoleonite came as no surprise at all—he seemed well-suited for treachery.

Conceding, the Frenchman spread his hands in a conciliatory gesture. "What assurances can I give, then?"

"You will assure me that no harm befalls me, the artifacts are returned to the ministry, and no one speaks of any of this. I can guarantee that nothing is ever said to the British authorities." He emphasized the last, as apparently this would be the main reason for his assassination by his former allies.

"And the weapons?"

Hafez said emphatically, "I don't care what happens to the weapons—take them with my blessing."

Nodding, the baron rested his pale eyes upon Hattie while he thought this over. "Agreed," he said. "Now, unbind her." To Hattie he said in English, "I am sorry for this, Mademoiselle Blackhouse; please be assured it is none of my doing."

Once the gag was removed, she replied coldly, "I insist that I be returned to the *Priapus* immediately." As Hafez's man continued to hold a pistol to her, she commanded, "Call him off."

But the baron spread his hands in apology. "I regret that is impossible at the moment; Monsieur Hafez feels it necessary to have you along as a guaranty." With a gesture, he indicated she was to be untied.

"Along where?" asked Hattie, with a sinking feeling.

"We visit the tomb—Monsieur Hafez knows the location of some articles that are of extreme interest to me."

So—the secret chamber was the object, although this made little sense; if Dimitry was working with the enemy, he now knew where it was and presumably had already been to visit it last night. With a leap of her pulse, she held out cautious hope that this meant her husband was not aligned with this villainous crew, which would be the first piece of good news she had heard this entire miserable day. Once unbound, she calculated whether it was the moment to use the pistol and decided against it, as the vendor still held his own weapon upon her. Instead, she rose to her feet, dusted off her skirts and announced, "I am going nowhere but back to the barge."

But Hafez was unimpressed by her bravado and replied with some menace, "You will come quietly or I will have you bound and carried again, Miss Blackhouse."

In response, Hattie made a dash toward the door but was grasped and pulled back just as she threw the curtain aside. Outside, there was a small throng of men who watched her recapture with no little uneasiness, murmuring among themselves. "Stop them," she pleaded as she was forcibly wrestled back inside, but no one stepped forward and despite her struggles to resist she was dragged back to the chair, seething with impotent rage.

The baron watched her desperate movements with an avid expression, which she recognized as being grounded in lust, now that she was familiar with such things. "She is very like him," he commented in French to Hafez.

Utterly furious, Hattie spat into his face and in response, the Frenchman struck her across the cheek with the back of his hand with such force that she stumbled back against those who held her.

"No need for that," Hafez chided—he was alarmed because there had been a collective gasp among the Egyptians when the blow landed.

But the baron was unrepentant as he wiped his face with a handkerchief, his cold, hooded gaze upon Hattie. "She must learn who is her master—regrettable but necessary."

But Hafez could not agree with such a strategy, and warned, "You will gain a powerful enemy."

"On the contrary—after my services to him in this matter I imagine that he will be so pleased so as to bestow her upon me; it is not as though she is legitimate, after all."

Hafez made no comment, but his expression conveyed his skepticism that such a thing would ever come to pass. Hattie was skeptical herself, having now determined who would be the beneficiary of the business end of Bing's pistol.

As her captors once again bound her hands, the murmuring outside became louder, and a shouted question could be heard.

"What is it?" asked the baron, with an irritated glance toward the curtained entry. "What do they want?"

Hafez made a gesture of impatience. "You have stirred the bees—they are ignorant and believe she is the reincarnation of Seti's daughter. Fool! You should not have struck her; I will speak to them."

He stepped outside the curtain and could be heard speaking in Arabic to the throng, his voice conciliatory. The baron took the opportunity to step over to Hattie, and ran a hand slowly down the side of her face, although his gaze was on her breasts. "I regret that my action was necessary, my dear. We shall come to terms—never fear."

While Hattie bit down hard on the rag in her mouth, the vendor gestured nervously with the pistol, indicating the older man was to retreat. Acquiescing, the Frenchman stepped back, holding his hands up in a gesture of cooperation. One of the black-clad native men stepped forward, crouching before her to check her bindings. He raised his face to hers and Hattie found that she was looking into the eyes of her husband.

Chapter 41

A stonished, Hattie quickly lowered her gaze as Dimitry stepped back. He was dressed in the native *gallibaya* and sported a neatly trimmed beard which, coupled with the *tarboosh* headdress, obscured his appearance. Nearly light-headed with relief, Hattie awaited events.

Hafez returned, and announced that it would be best to conclude their business as quickly as possible before the crowd was stirred into action. "They are unhappy with what they perceive to be a grave insult."

"Very well," replied the Frenchman with a wary glance toward the doorway. "Let us go, then."

Once again, Hattie was loaded onto the cart while the native bystanders watched and muttered in an ugly undertone, rising in volume so that those who served Hafez and the baron were forced to wave their weapons in a threatening manner so that they stayed back. She noted that the crowd had increased, and wondered if she should struggle against her captors so as to incite a possible riot—the circumstances seemed ripe for it. Watching Dimitry from the corner of her eye, she decided she'd best not attempt any heroics for fear he had a plan that would be disrupted—but on the other hand, it may be to the greater good to disrupt Dimitry's plan, depending on his allegiances. On the horns of this particular dilemma, she finally decided to hold her powder—a melee might jeopardize his plan and it did seem more and more likely that he was working against the enemy, hence the disguise.

Thus, as evening fell she began the slow journey to the tomb of the god-king's daughter, keeping her chin raised and refusing to look at anyone although she could feel the scrutiny of many watching eyes as they passed through the narrow streets. The donkeys trod methodically and the wooden wheels churned on the rough gravel as they made their way into the sacred Valley of the Kings, the cliffs around them as indifferent to the schemings of men as they had been forty centuries ago. Hattie flexed her hands, which were beginning to go numb; I suppose this is what it felt like to be riding in a tumbrel, she thought, and then quickly banished the comparison from her mind.

Upon sighting their approach, the British guards at the tomb drew their muskets and waited at the ready while Hafez approached them. Hattie watched while the minister made gestures and discussed the situation—it was unclear what possible explanation would be proffered for her own state of capture, and it seemed to Hattie the guards remained uneasy as they lowered their weapons and allowed them to pass.

Once again, Hattie climbed the wooden steps at the entrance to the tomb—only on this occasion she was bound and gagged, with Hafez's men firmly holding her arms on either side with their pistols trained upon her. Despite her perilous situation, she tried to puzzle out where the secret chamber should be and frowned, realizing it made little sense—the chamber should open off from the entry hall, but she remembered no door or other opening along the stark walls in the entry hall.

Several of the men lit lanterns and as the party ducked into the entryway, Hafez began to negotiate with the baron about how many men were to accompany them inside. This seemed understandable; Hattie easily surmised that if it weren't for the fact that Hafez was holding her as hostage, his life wouldn't be worth much once the secret chamber was revealed—the baron and his cohorts had proved to be ruthless killers in pursuit of this particular goal. In the end, Hafez brought two men into the tomb to guard Hattie while the baron brought only one—Dimitry—and he was allowed in only after he had relinquished his pistol. Her relief at this arrangement was short-lived, however; Hattie saw the baron give her husband a significant look in the dim light—one that indicated a covert plan. With a sinking heart, Hattie realized that Dimitry appeared to be aligned with the despicable baron—even though this was hard to imagine. She then reassured herself by remembering that whatever his motives or allegiances, Dimitry could not be pleased with the other man's actions toward her—he who had raged when Robbie negligently touched her hand; she could only hope he was playing a deep game, and wait to see what developed.

At a location nearly halfway down the slanting floor of the entry hall, Hafez paused and spoke in Arabic to the vendor who escorted Hattie. The man stepped forward to thrust a staff into the dirt at the base of the stone wall, and grasping the staff with both hands, he began to apply leverage on the length of wood, working it back and forth into the hard-packed dirt until it could be heard to scrape against a plate of some kind, approximately a foot beneath the surface. The man leapt up to apply his full weight to the staff, and with a groaning noise, a portion of the wall began to move. As they watched, the contours of a door were revealed where some of the seams between the bricks became more pronounced. Pressing his hands against the left upper corner of the hidden door, the servant slid it back on oiled hinges, and a dark recess could be seen within.

Despite herself, Hattie was fascinated and stepped forward with no coaxing from the men at her sides to enter the secret chamber. The flickering light of the lanterns revealed muskets—hundreds of them—stacked up against the walls, and other treasures carefully lined up on lengths of burlap—golden figures, decorated jars and caskets; mainly small items, which she imagined could easily be smuggled out. Hattie reviewed them in silence, no longer intrigued; this was no treasure hunt—instead it was a means to war.

The baron stepped in and took a careful review of the items assembled. "And where is the Glory of Kings—the *Shefrh Lelmelwek*? I do not see it."

Hafez scanned the interior himself, which was not difficult, as it was perhaps fifteen feet by twenty. "It must be here—I have seen it myself; perhaps it was moved."

"You assured me it was here." The baron's voice held a hint of accusation.

Hafez stepped through the length of the chamber and scrutinized the assembled items with increasing desperation, searching through the dully glimmering gold. "It was here—as late as last week; I swear it."

In two strides, the Frenchman took Hafez by the shoulders and shoved the heavy man with some force against the wall, causing several muskets to clatter to the stone floor. "You hope to gain leverage to protect yourself; you know the emperor desires the sword."

"No," Hafez insisted in a strangled voice, his breath coming in rasps. "Take your hands off me or she will suffer for it." His face mottled, Hafez's eyes rolled toward Hattie, and in response the nervous vendor drew the hammer back on the pistol beside her ear. God in heaven, she thought, and struggled to remain calm.

The baron looked toward Hattie and loosened his grip but did not release the minister, instead warning in a voice filled with menace, "You have one minute to tell me where the sword is; the emperor wishes to have it when he returns in triumph and I will not disappoint him." The minister was roughly shaken to emphasize the last few words.

"I don't know, I tell you—it was here—I swear it."

While the assembled men stood in a tense standoff, Hattie heard a whizzing sound near her ear, and the vendor beside her first grunted, then made a horrendous gurgling sound as a plume of blood sprayed across her face. She gasped as the man sank to the ground, a familiar thin blade lodged in his throat.

Almost before she could process this development, Dimitry was upon her other guard, twisting his arm behind him with a quick movement so as to grasp his pistol, and then holding the man before them like a shield, the pistol to his head.

Hafez stared at the fallen man in horror, the pool of blood widening at his feet. "Let us start afresh, shall we?" said the baron coolly, as though nothing untoward had occurred. "Where is the sword?"

Hafez swallowed, aware that he no longer had any leverage. "I will find it, I swear—"

"Unfortunately there is no time and I have little patience."

Desperate, Hafez suddenly shoved at the baron and broke for the door, but with an almost causal air, the Frenchman drew his own weapon and shot him in the back, the large man collapsing in the doorway as he desperately clawed at the ancient stones for a moment, then lay still. Almost immediately, Dimitry discharged the pistol he held on his own man, who slumped to the floor. In the ensuing silence, acrid smoke drifted in the glow of the lanterns as Dimitry bent to retrieve his blade from the fallen vendor's throat and Hattie stood in shock, contemplating the carnage around her.

"Hafez? Monsieur le Baron? What goes forward—I heard a shot." Within moments, Drummond's associate appeared in the entry hall outside the room, and dispassionately reviewed the bodies on the stone floor for a moment. His gaze then rested on Hattie, and with a sound of dismay, he stepped over the body of the minister to pull out his handkerchief and wipe the blood from her face. "Good God—what is the meaning of this? Unbind her immediately."

"I regret to say it was necessary—she was inciting a response among the natives." Hattie noted with surprise that the baron was apologetic; it was clear he deferred to the other man.

The associate produced a knife and cut her bindings himself. "I do beg your pardon, Miss Blackhouse."

But the associate's deferential attitude had given Hattie an idea—after all, there was no point in having the blood of a ruthless conqueror in your veins unless you put it to good use. As soon as her gag was removed, she rubbed life back into her wrists and announced coldly, "When my father hears of this, there will be no corner in hell for any of you to hide." With a deliberate movement, she lifted her skirts to step over the fallen minister and exit the tomb.

They all stared at her in dismay, but the associate reluctantly stepped before her to block her retreat. While she glowered up at him from beneath her brows he said in a placating tone, "I assure you, madam, that you will suffer no further indignities. However, I'm afraid I cannot allow you to leave just yet—there are some questions I am compelled to ask."

Hattie raised her chin and crossed her arms, her gaze on the stone wall. "I will answer no questions; I demand that I be let go *immediately.*"

"I believe you mentioned your marriage, madam."

"What?" exclaimed the baron, astonished. "Married to who?"

The associate turned his head to regard the Frenchman. "You did not know of this?"

"*C'est pas vrai*—it is nonsense," the other insisted. "She has no husband; perhaps she seeks to throw dust in your eyes."

"She claims to have married Count Leczinska."

There was a long, silent pause while the baron considered this revelation. Hattie was impressed; the man's gaze never traveled to Dimitry, standing silently behind her. "Impossible," he finally pronounced. "Perhaps it was a ploy to take her to his bed."

The associate shrugged. "Perhaps—but it is inconceivable either way; he would never marry her without the emperor's consent and he would never be mad enough to seduce her."

The two men turned to consider Hattie, who stared at the wall, stone-faced, and wished she was anywhere else or at least that she knew her lines—she would have given anything to have a quick conference with Dimitry.

"Perhaps," suggested the associate, "you could explain yourself a bit further, madam; it is possible—although I am loathe to suggest it—that you have been ill-served by the count."

"I have been ill-served by no one but yourselves," Hattie retorted, her low voice echoing off the walls, "—and by *heaven*, my father will hear of it."

"We shall say no more," the baron hastily assured her. Then, to the associate, "Better that we discuss the matter with Leczinska at a later time, perhaps."

But the associate was not so certain and regarded the other with a grave expression. "I wonder," he mused in a somber tone, "—if the count is who he says he is."

Chapter 42

The baron frowned. "Why—what do you mean, monsieur?"

The associate took a long breath. "I have heard rumor that *Le Sokol* has taken an interest in our little endeavors, here."

The Frenchman's surprised dismay was palpable in the silence that followed this suggestion. "What have you heard?"

His gaze thoughtful upon Hattie, the associate replied, "Little—of course. But the rumor persists."

The baron began to pace in agitation, his arms crossed. "This is indeed serious. Would you recognize him? Do we have a description?"

"No. I have never seen him—few have." The associate added in a bitter tone, "Unlike the emperor, who was forced to make his acquaintance when retreating from Moscow."

"I know of it—such an insult!" the baron exploded in anger. "And the loss of so many good men—"

"He has much to answer for," agreed the associate. "And I would very much like to speak to the count, if only to lay these concerns to rest."

Hattie could see that the baron had been given pause and was weighing his options. With a rush of exhilaration, she suddenly remembered the icon—the Russian Orthodox icon, perhaps—that hung on the wall at the Osiris Inn, and her gaze slid over to Dimitry, who had listened to the discussion with apparent indifference. They didn't know she had Bing's pistol and if she shot one of these men, Dimitry should be able to handle the other, certainly; he had already demonstrated his competency in such maneuvers. Fingering the pistol in her pocket she waited, equal parts relieved and nervous, aware that she should not upset any plan and alert to any signal that may be given.

The associate turned to address her again, "Do you know of this, madam? Please understand your supposed husband may represent a grave danger to your father, and it is best that you tell us what you know."

Hattie crossed her arms and replied coldly, "All I know is that I have been insulted in every way possible and I shall take great pleasure in seeing to it that the appropriate punishment is meted out."

Any potential response was not to be heard, however, as suddenly there were crashing sounds outside, answered by gunfire and alarmed voices from the Egyptian guards who manned the tomb's entrance.

"Wait here with her," the associate directed tersely, and ducked out the door.

Immediately, the baron turned to Hattie and indicated Dimitry. "Have you indeed married this man?"

Hattie stared at them both with icy disdain. "I have never seen him before in my life, and you are a fool to believe that other fool."

More crashing noises could be heard, and distracted, the baron stepped to the chamber's doorway to peer up the entry hall. With a swift movement, Dimitry was upon him, knocking his head with a quick crack into the stone doorway. As the man slumped, Dimitry instructed her, "Turn aside, Hattie."

As she obeyed, she heard a grisly cracking sound that she could easily interpret as the breaking of the man's neck. Dimitry then gave a soft command in his own language and to Hattie's astonishment, the guard whom he had supposedly shot scrambled to his feet and departed swiftly out the door, leaping nimbly over the minister's body.

"Come, Hattie." Dimitry hoisted the dead baron over his shoulder. "Fetch the lantern."

Although she had many, many questions, Hattie held her tongue and lifted the lantern to light the way to the rear burial chamber. "Quickly," he urged in a quiet tone as he hurried into the room, bent over to avoid scraping the doorway lintel. "We will hide you in the sarcophagus, and I will return later to retrieve you." He then suited word to action and strained to shove the lid aside on the stone sarcophagus.

Aghast, Hattie felt it was time to make her feelings known. "You cannot mean to stuff me in there with him."

"There is no time to argue—I will see to it the lid is not sealed so that you will have air to breathe and you will not be as fearful."

So; at least he remembered her dread of enclosed spaces. There was nothing for it—she would do as she was told. She watched him unceremoniously dump the body into the receptacle, then he lifted her by the waist to set her inside, on top of the lifeless baron. "I have hidden the sword within; do not hurt yourself on it."

Hattie was having trouble keeping track of all the variables. "You are stealing the sword?"

Despite the exigent circumstance, she could see that he smiled, as though at a private joke. "I know a man who deserves it more than Napoleon."

Reminded, she told him, "I have Bing's pistol."

He met her eyes, his own very serious. "You must not kill the other man—Drummond's associate. I need information from him."

She nodded, rather flattered that he believed her capable of successfully shooting someone in the first place. While he gently pressed down on her shoulders, she swallowed hard and obligingly lay back; trying to assure herself that after everything she'd been through, surely she could manage an hour or so in a stone sarcophagus. Dimitry shoved the lid back, leaving it misaligned so that it didn't close completely. She heard his footsteps quickly recede, and Hattie was left in the pitch darkness atop the still-warm body of a dead man.

Straining her ears, she listened for a few moments but could hear nothing. Small surprise, the walls in these tombs were typically five or six feet thick; composed of limestone. She began tapping one of her feet on the end of the stone enclosure. There were twenty-six tombs discovered thus far—more or less. Her breathing sounded unnaturally loud in the silence. The Great Seti's tomb had not yet been found and perhaps it was not nearby, since this tomb was a false one; there was no god-king's daughter, after all. Instead, the queens and princesses were in the Valley of the Queens, several miles away. It had been sheer foolishness to believe that the ancients would make an exception for a mere female and construct her tomb where only the god-like pharaohs were allowed—the Blackhouses liked their little joke.

Hattie wondered how many minutes had gone by—the body beneath her was beginning to grow cool. Bing must be worried, although nothing seemed to discomfit Bing. And Dimitry was someone else—someone other than the someone else she already believed him to be. It was dizzying—truly; one needed a playbill to keep track of all these tangled identities, the associate included. Dimitry should be careful not to talk in his sleep although of course, she'd be the only one listening—that is, if they managed to survive this and go home to the place of priests and icons and dogs and horses.

Wriggling, she lifted her knees to her chest and placed her feet on the bottom of the sarcophagus lid. Pushing as hard as she could, she moved it aside enough so that she could squeeze out. Cannot do it another moment, she thought in a panic. Sorry, Dimitry.

Breathing in the musty air, she tried to calm down and get her bearings; it was inky black and impossible to see her hand in front of her face. She carefully crawled out of the sarcophagus and once on her feet, leaned in to carefully feel around until she seized upon the stupid sword; it was probably best to keep it with her, so that the prisoner never got his hands on it—one needn't be superstitious to err on the side of caution. She debated for a moment whether she should search the dead baron for any additional weapons. No—she decided; cannot do that, either.

Groping carefully with one foot tentatively in front of her, then the other, she made her way forward until she came to the wall. She then used her free hand on the roughened brick to find her way to the doorway and as soon as she passed through, she could feel the air stirring slightly and imagined the darkness was not quite as absolute. I have no idea what I am doing, she admitted—I only know I cannot remain in here. Unfortunately there was nowhere to go other than out the entry; she could no more hide in the weapons chamber than she could stay in the sarcophagus—she would go mad.

Sword in hand, she carefully advanced up the slanted floor of the entry hall until she could hear voices before her, and soon thereafter could make out a square that was a lighter shade of darkness representing the tomb's entrance. She sidled along the rough stone wall, straining her ears.

"...revealed themselves?" It was the associate, sounding harried.

"No, monsieur; they stay hidden." Dimitry, she thought, at his most servile.

"Mere troublemakers, perhaps. Keep watch, and everyone fire at will." He paused. "Where is du Pays? We must secure the girl."

Dimitry offered, "Shall I fetch him here, monsieur?"

In an impatient tone, the other man replied, "I will fetch him instead; he'd better not be offering her insult, back there."

Oh-oh, thought Hattie, in a panic—I cannot let him find me here—I will tangle up Dimitry's plans if the stupid associate seizes me again. For a moment, she considered returning back to the hated burial room but figured she could easily be discovered and so instead, she gripped the sword between her teeth and dropped to her hands and knees to scramble through the rubble-smoot as quickly as she was able. Biting down against the pain of crawling over the rubble, she emerged out the opening on the side of the sloping hill, panting, and then carefully skittered down the cascade of discarded rocks and debris feet first, scraping her hands and the backs of her legs in the process.

After she landed in an ignominious heap at the bottom of the rubble pile, Hattie examined her cut and bleeding hands for a moment whilst she caught her breath, then rose to her feet. By the light of the half moon, she began to circle around the narrow valley in front of the tomb to where the entrance road was, careful to stay out of the sight-line of the men above who defended the tomb and holding the sword by her skirts. She formed a vague idea of escaping to a safe place—perhaps the Osiris Inn—to wait for Dimitry; above all, she could not allow the associate to seize her so that Dimitry was stymied again.

Because she was keeping a sharp eye on the tomb's entrance, above and to her right, she nearly ran into Smithson, who was carrying a large clay water jug. "Why, Mrs. Berry," he whispered, bowing. "How very nice to see you again."

Chapter 43

H attie could not have been more astonished. "Why, what is toward?" she whispered.

In response, the vicar placed the jug on the ground and drew her beside him as they walked away from the tomb, at a right angle from the entrance. "Miss Bing and I are creating a diversion, along with the two British guards," he explained in a low voice.

"I see," said Hattie, who didn't see at all. "Am I to be rescued?"

"Mr. Tremaine has ridden to fetch the British soldiers at the consul's Office and our task is to keep those in the tomb pinned down until reinforcements arrive to surround them. We are trying to confuse the enemy and convey the impression there are more than four of us."

And I imagine this is why the guards are British, Hattie thought as Smithson directed her behind a large boulder and instructed her to stay down; in the event they would be needed for a skirmish such as this one.

"That is a fine sword you have there."

For the first time, Hattie examined it by the moonlight. It was rather shorter than other swords she had seen, with a strangely-shaped hilt that was hooked at a right angle; a fearsome object. "It is the *Shefrh Lelmelwek*."

It was clear her companion was not up to speed. "That is nice," he observed kindly. "Now, cover your ears." Smithson aimed his pistol carefully and fired on the clay pot, which exploded with a loud crash.

Exclamations could be heard from the tomb as fire was returned in the direction of the smashed pot, and Hattie was all admiration. "Joshua's strategy at Jericho."

"Gideon against the Midianites," he corrected her with a small smile, referencing the Bible story of the outnumbered Israelites. "And it continues to be a useful ploy."

"I have escaped," Hattie pointed out modestly. It seemed the good vicar was unaware such heroics were no longer necessary.

"Mr. Tremaine believes there are other forces at work here, left over from the recent war," Smithson explained. "He wishes to take all these men into custody so as to sort it out."

Hattie nodded, thinking hard—here was another dilemma in what was apparently a never-ending series of them; Drummond must be unaware that his associate was the enemy's point man in Egypt, and Dimitry said he needed information from the man—probably the particulars about Napoleon's planned escape from Elba. With this in mind, it seemed she should try to work against any rescue of the associate by the British, and trust that her husband was indeed this mysterious *Le Sokol* person, working for the Allies and not against them.

Her thoughts were interrupted by another crash from the other side of the tomb. "Bing," she deduced with a smile.

"Miss Bing," Smithson agreed as he fired another round into the shards of the broken pot, drawing more fire upon it. "She raised the alarm when you were taken and then it wasn't difficult to trace you here—the natives were up in arms and showed the way. Indeed, many are here in the valley, but Mr. Tremaine didn't think it wise to enlist them to assist us."

Ah, thought Hattie; here is a task that is exactly suited to me and to no other. I suppose I am not slated to go off and hide somewhere until it is safe—that is not who I am and not who I ever was; I had almost forgotten, I was so thrown off by all of this.

Just then, she heard a gunfire report from the tomb, followed by a loud pinging noise as the bullet hit her boulder. She gasped, and the vicar calmly advised, "Best stay down, Mrs. Berry—the ricochet is unpredictable."

As she crouched beside Smithson, Hattie thought through her plan; if those in the tomb were pinned down until the British arrived, Dimitry would have little chance of securing Drummond's associate for himself. A means to allow them to escape was necessary—some type of diversion, and she had the very solution here at her fingertips. "I am going to retreat a ways," she informed the distracted Smithson, gripping the sword as she crept away from the barren area that stretched out before the tomb. The moonlight aided her endeavors as she circled around, and soon she could hear the murmuring of many voices as she traversed the boulders and gravel that littered the landscape. I wore the wrong shoes for this, she thought, ruthlessly pushing the remaining pins back into her tangled hair. As she scrambled over a final mound of rocks to reach the road, she came upon the group of native men, conversing in low tones and watching the gunplay in the distance. Edward had said that superstition was a crutch for the fearful, so it was time to inject a healthy dose of courage into the proceedings. Drawing herself up, she advanced toward them, holding the sword aloft and trying to look warrior-like.

Upon viewing her approach, the men stared in astonishment, several steepling their hands before them and bowing with deep respect. Hattie stood among them and indicated with the sword. "Does anyone speak English?" She was met with only silence. "Does anyone speak French?" she asked in that language, and several men indicated they did. "Good." In her best portrayal of a reincarnated princess, she gave instruction, "We are going to put a stop to this sacrilege—I need a contingent of men to approach the tomb with me. We will need a torch, and something to hold as a white flag."

Hattie noted they all stared at her as though she were mad, but there was nothing for it; she needed to warn Dimitry that she was out here, that the British reinforcements were on the way, and that his time to secure the associate was running short. Hopefully they would not shoot her outright—there was enough moonlight to reveal that she was female and wearing a dress that had once been a pretty sprig muslin but which was now considerably the worse for wear; it would be a tragedy beyond bearing if Dimitry were to shoot her by mistake.

"This is a sacred place," she explained in a firm tone. "There is to be no more violence—I assure you, they will not shoot me." They nodded in agreement and she looked upon the intent faces, realizing there were some who stood in superstitious awe and some who merely listened to an English girl with a plan, which was just as acceptable to her. I have no desire to be the god-king's daughter, she thought; I am Hattie-with-an-as-yet-unknown-surname and no one, not my parents or the prisoner himself, can take that away from me.

Without asking for volunteers, she held the sword and began to walk in the direction of the tomb. Two or three men immediately fell in beside her, one holding his *kaftan* above his head, the white cloth signifying a parlay. Hattie did not turn but she could sense the others join in, so that there was soon the tramping of many feet behind her.

Taking a deep breath, she shouted as loudly as she could, "Parlay!" and advanced to the base of the tomb's hill, hoping her last moments on earth were not to be spent in wretched Egypt at the wretched, faux tomb of the *wretched* god-king's daughter. There was a profound silence as all gunfire ceased.

Upon seeing her advance, one of the British soldiers who had been lying prone behind a boulder rose and ran to her. "Miss," he panted, "You must take cover."

"I cannot," she explained. "In fact, I think I am the only person who can resolve this stand-off."

"It is too dangerous," he said firmly, taking her arm. "Come with me."

"They will not shoot me; instead I believe there has been a misunderstanding."

As there was indeed now only an eerie silence, he glanced between her, the group of men behind her, and the tomb. "Who are they? Mr. Tremaine seems to believe they are enemy forces."

She shook her head at him. "No—I believe it is only Mr. Drummond's associate from the consulate, and his men. Mr. Tremaine was mistaken." I hope, she thought, that I am not making a catastrophic mistake, here. She continued to stand at the base of the tomb, her escort in a silent group around her and the British soldier at her side. Peering up at the tomb's entrance, she was unable to make out any figures in the shadows. "Sir, you must desist," she shouted. "There has been a misunderstanding and the British soldiers from the consulate will be arriving in short order." Hopefully Dimitry understood her message—that is, if he hadn't suffered an apoplexy upon beholding her before him instead of safely tucked away in the sarcophagus.

"Where is Monsieur le Baron, madam?" The associate's voice could be heard, and Hattie gauged that he sounded a bit apoplectic, himself.

"He is unwell," she shouted, which was more or less the truth. "I believe we are working at cross purposes and it would be best that you descend so that we can sort matters out."

"I wish," his voice rang down, "that you had heeded my original request, madam."

"I am not one for heeding requests, I'm afraid. Now, will you desist?"

There was a small silence. "Yes; I will require assurances that those on the ground will cease fire."

"They will do so." She smiled to herself; apparently he believed he was outnumbered, thanks to Gideon.

In the silence of the cease-fire, Hattie could hear footsteps approaching and turned to behold Bing, coming to join her. "Thank you for fetching reinforcements, Bing. I must report that the baron is dead, as is Hafez, and Monsieur Berry is disguised as an Egyptian, so pray do not shoot him."

Bing assimilated this report without a blink. "Very good."

With a smile, Hattie indicated the sword. "Edward's sword, Bing."

Reverently, Bing grasped it, and turned it one way and then the other. "Bestowed upon the pharaoh himself by the gods."

Truly, it almost made one believe it—standing in the barren, surreal valley; the moonlight glinting off the mythical object. Bing paused for a moment. "I am not a fanciful person, Hathor, but I almost feel Edward's presence."

Hattie gently squeezed Bing's arm in silent sympathy as the two women contemplated the priceless object. "Take it, Bing; it is Edward's, by all rights."

But the moment had passed and Bing regarded Hattie with her dry little smile as she handed it back. "No thank you, Hathor; the gods did not bestow it upon me."

Hattie nodded, her emotions mixed. It seemed that no one would discover the Blackhouse perfidy, nor the true cause of Edward's death. Perhaps it was for the best—lives other than her own were affected, after all. And as long as the scheme to arm the deposed emperor came to naught, there was no harm done.

The two women looked up to observe the associate and his men making their way warily down the makeshift wooden steps. Now that she knew it was he, Hattie easily spotted Dimitry, his gaze meeting her own, even in the darkness and across the distance.

Hattie stepped close to her companion and looked up into her face. "I may be required to leave forthwith, Bing. I do not know yet where I will live, but I will write you the moment I know and you must"—Hattie emphasized this last—"come visit me at your earliest opportunity. I will have your promise."

"You have it," Bing assured her.

"I know Robbie will see you safely home."

But Bing needed no such assurance. "Not to worry, Hathor—Mr. Smithson and I have come to an understanding."

Hattie could not resist smiling upon the other with delight. "Who would have imagined all this when we left Cornwall, Bing?"

"Not I, certainly," her doughty companion admitted. "I shall think of you often."

Hattie's smile faltered. "I may not be able to come visit you in England for a while—I'm afraid it is rather complicated."

Bing's shrewd eyes met hers. "If I may be so bold, Hathor—we each make our own way; one's heritage matters not a whit next to one's legacy."

While Hattie stared at her, Bing nodded sagely. "Now, allow me to go inform Smithson that he is not to shoot Monsieur Berry."

A fter conferring with the British soldiers, Drummond's associate approached Hattie and quietly drew her aside. "I'm afraid I must depart straightaway and I insist that you accompany me, madam—I have learned to my dismay that you cannot be trusted to do as you are asked."

"Unfair," Hattie pointed out. "It all depends upon who is doing the trusting."

She could see he was amused, despite himself, and his gaze rested on her cheek, which should sport quite a bruise by now. "I am sorry you were injured—du Pays will answer for it, believe me."

Prudently, Hattie made no rejoinder, thinking here was another man who had best be careful lest he incite Dimitry's hair-trigger jealousy.

Hard on this thought, Dimitry himself joined them, shaking his head in chagrin. "I cannot find *le baron*—perhaps it would be best if the young lady was safely delivered to the British consul's office; in this way she would remain under your safekeeping and none need know of your role."

But the associate disagreed as he looked toward the valley's entrance where the British reinforcements would soon appear. "I'm afraid I cannot allow such a course—she may reveal too much and my mission would be compromised."

"I am not going to compromise your tedious mission," Hattie retorted, thinking she should work toward whatever Dimitry's end was. "I ask only to be left unassaulted for a space of ten minutes at a time."

The associate gently took Hattie's arm and guided her further away from the others. He motioned to Dimitry. "My horse, please—quietly."

Uneasy, Hattie waited for instruction from Dimitry but he was fetching the associate's horse without demur. Should she protest? Surely she should not simply allow the enemy to spirit her away. Hattie pulled her elbow from his hand, "I will go nowhere with you—I demand to be returned to the *Priapus* immediately."

The associate placed a propelling hand at her back, polite but firm as they melted away in the darkness, Dimitry following with the horse. "I must disappoint you, I'm afraid, but I can assure you there will be no more ill treatment—there is a transport ship leaving tomorrow and you will be very comfortable."

Wishing she had some direction from her exasperating better half, Hattie asked him coldly, "Leaving? Leaving for where?"

"The Cote d'Azur."

Although Hattie was unfamiliar with this destination, it sounded dauntingly French. "I am going nowhere without my husband," she declared, hoping said husband would feel free to contribute at any time.

As the associate watched Dimitry tighten his horse's cinch, he addressed her in a serious tone. "I am afraid I have grave doubts about your new husband, and until I can make some inquiries it would be for the best if you are away from the area, as was requested." He placed a faint emphasis on the last words.

Hattie responded with equal impatience. "You must see that I have no reason to trust you more than I trust my husband."

Taking the proffered reins from Dimitry, he attempted to assure her. "I give you my word you shall come to no harm, madam—but I cannot allow you to remain here. I would rather not bind you to the saddle, but I shall take whatever measures are necessary."

As he gestured to her, Hattie glanced to Dimitry and saw him shake his head slightly.

Responding to the instruction, she backed away from the associate. "You do not dare lay hands upon me."

"With all due respect, I must." With some determination he advanced on her.

Holding him at bay with the sword, she pulled Bing's pistol from her pocket and leveled it at him. "Stand back."

The associate paused in surprise, then changed tack, his manner now conciliatory as he spoke in a gentle tone. "Be reasonable, madam—I sincerely believe your so-called husband is duping you for his own purposes; you will soon see."

Hattie did not falter. "You will come no closer."

The man spread his hands in a disarming gesture. "Come—I will prove to you that no true marriage took place."

"You would not succeed," said Dimitry.

The associate paused for a long moment, then turned to face Dimitry, and the two men took the measure of each other. Then with a lightning-quick movement the associate pulled a knife from his belt, but Dimitry was faster and leapt to grasp the other's arm with both hands, staying the descent of the knife. The associate's free hand clutched at Dimitry's, the scar plainly visible, and the two strained for an advantage, their hands locked together.

"Step back," Dimitry said softly, and Hattie realized he

was speaking to her. She obeyed, but continued to hold the sword and the pistol before her. If things did not look well for Dimitry she would shoot, needed information or not. Such a strategy was unnecessary, however. The associate's arm began to tremble with exertion and then the knife fell from his hand and clattered to the ground where Dimitry kicked it aside. The two men broke apart and squared off, circling, but with no hurried or overt movements. It was a strange and subdued form of fighting, as though each knew what the other would do and so all inefficient movements were not even attempted. Occasionally, one or the other would make a quick strike that was always parried by his adversary, their actions quick and deft. Soon it became apparent that the associate was on the defensive, his face wet with perspiration and his jaw set in an attitude of endurance—on an elemental level Hattie knew Dimitry was enjoying this demonstration of his mastery over the other man while she watched.

Finally, with a quick movement Dimitry successfully closed on his adversary and the two grappled until Dimitry secured his throat in the crook of his arm, squeezing while the associate gasped for breath and his face empurpled. After a few seconds he dropped to the ground, unconscious.

Her husband roughly turned the man over and pulled his arms behind his back. "I will need your sash."

"You should be better prepared," she chided. "I am running out of ribbon."

"If you had more ribbon I would use it to bind you to me," was the mild reply as he quickly secured the man's hands.

"I am sorry, Dimitry—I couldn't stay there, truly."

He was philosophical as he gagged the man with a length of linen torn from his *gallibaya*. "It is of no moment—you did well to have us out before the soldiers come."

"Will you kill him?"

He glanced up at her, amused. "Perhaps not; we shall see." He said a quiet word in his own language and his cohort from the tomb materialized at his side. Hattie realized her heroics with the weapons had been unnecessary—nothing had been left to chance. After hearing an instruction the man nodded, then hoisted the associate over his sturdy shoulder to disappear into the darkness.

Dimitry placed a gentle hand under her chin to examine her cut lip. "Are you all right?"

"A few cuts and bruises," she admitted. "I will recover."

"Come with me and we shall recover together." He took the sword from her and slid it through his corded belt, then turned to fetch the horse.

"Truly? I can come with you?" This seemed too good to be true.

Lifting her at the waist, he placed her atop a large rock. "Quickly, now." He mounted the horse and held out his hand to her so that she stepped onto his stirruped foot and was launched up behind him, her petticoats bunched up so that her lower legs were exposed. She clutched at his waist while he wheeled the animal around and urged it forward, kicking it into a gallop so that the gravel flew and Hattie held on for dear life. "Where do we go?" she gasped in his ear.

"Hold on," was his only response.

Hoping he could see the road well enough in the moonlight, she decided she'd rather not watch and instead closed her eyes, clinging to him with her cheek pressed against his back. She gauged that they headed toward the entrance to the valley at what seemed to be an impressive clip for a few breathless minutes. Then he placed a hand over both of hers at his waist to hold her secure as the horse suddenly bounded up a hill on the side of the road near the entrance. Gritting her teeth so that she didn't cry out in alarm, Hattie hung on until the lunging animal reached the crest and then— finally—their headlong dash appeared to be stayed for a moment. The horse's sides heaved as it caught its breath, and Hattie peered out from behind Dimitry to view the desolate valley stretching out below them. With his gaze fixed upon the narrow entrance, he absently picked up one of her hands to kiss it.

Into the silence Hattie said, "Bing knew—she knew all along."

He was unsurprised. "Her brother was no fool; I imagine he told her." His hand caressed hers at his waist. "It did not matter to her, Hattie. Do you see?"

"No, it did not matter," she agreed with her newfound confidence. "But it makes me wince, nevertheless—it is too new a wound, I suppose."

"A wound that will heal, *dorogoy*."

She sighed. "Do you truly think so? I have my doubts— such a secret is bound to come out—there will never be an end to it."

He tilted his head, his gaze upon the road. "Then you must mount a defense; when anyone hints at it, you must arch those brows of yours and pretend to be flattered and amused by such a report. You must neither deny nor confirm."

She thought about it. "I suppose it is my only choice, other than to drum my heels and howl."

"If any offers you insult, I will introduce them to my blade," he promised.

She was all admiration, thinking of the slain man in the tomb. "You are indeed handy with your blade."

"*Bestard*; no one shall threaten you and live." One of his hands moved to clasp her hand at his waist again.

Smiling, she brushed her cheek against his back, pleased to have inspired such devotion, however bloodthirsty—and equally pleased that he had reverted to his own accent, which she viewed as a high compliment. "I made use of the wretched sword, did you see?"

"I did. I will remove a gold ferrule from the grip so that your wedding ring can be fashioned from it."

"An interesting conceit," she acknowledged with amusement.

"It is only fitting—I am wed to the daughter of the god-king."

She laughed so that he had to warn her to hush as he maintained his vigil. I will come about, she thought as she squeezed him in affection; now that I've remembered who I am.

Chapter 45

H attie knew when Dimitry spotted the approaching British troops by the sudden tension in his torso, and tried to hide her apprehension. "Is there to be more racing?"

"Hold on very tightly," he instructed. "You have done well."

She realized he was waiting until they were spotted, outlined at the top of the hill in the moonlight; apparently he meant to lead the soldiers away from wherever the associate was being transferred. "Robbie will be frantic," she pointed out with some concern. "He will not realize it is only you."

"That is to be hoped," he replied, unsympathetic.

"Dimitry," she gently rebuked him, "I cannot do this to him."

"It cannot be helped." He gathered up the reins. "Too much is at stake."

"Surely Robbie can be trusted with the truth?"

Briefly, he laid a hand on hers at his waist. "He comes with Drummond—and the others. How can one be told without the other? I cannot chance another situation where a weapon is held to you."

Reluctantly, she saw his point; she was indeed a powerful bargaining chip—and for either side in this battle behind the scenes. "And you are not certain of Drummond?"

"I do not believe he is aware of the truth," he conceded. "But I will not take that chance."

Subsiding, she waited in tense silence. A party of perhaps fifteen mounted men filed into the valley, then made haste toward the tomb. They were almost past them when a rider pulled up his mount in surprise, and Hattie fancied she could recognize Robbie. A faint shout, "Hattie?" confirmed her surmise, but Dimitry had already wheeled around, urging his horse down the other side of the rocky hill. Burying her face in his back, Hattie concentrated on hanging on while the horse slid in a mad scramble down the slope, its haunches tucked beneath it and stones skittering away to either side. Once away, they rode in a straight line to another cliff, and Hattie realized there was a tomb entrance at the base, sloping downward into the recesses of the hill. Almost before they were stopped, Dimitry wrapped an arm around her and swung her down just before he leapt off.

"Stay quiet, please," he warned in a low voice, and led her quickly into the entry. The horse balked for a moment, its ears forward and its eyes wide at having to confront the narrow, dark tunnel, but Dimitry spoke to it in his language and tugged on the bridle until suddenly the resistance was gone. They stood packed together in the tunnel, waiting— the scent of overheated horse mingling with the now-familiar musty scent of the ancient tomb. In a few minutes their pursuers could be heard over the sound of the horse's breathing, the rocks and gravel clattering as they rode in haste up the valley floor.

"Quickly, now," said Dimitry, and led her outside to mount up again. This time he circled around the base of the hill, heading toward the valley's entrance. Despite the darkness and the uneven ground, only once did Hattie fear they would go down—but the horse regained its footing and they continued on. They slowed once the cliffs rose up on either side, signaling their proximity to the cleft in the rocks that provided entry to the Valley of the Kings. Dimitry shifted in the saddle and whispered, "They will have left a guard, as there is only the one way out. I will indicate you are injured—you must say nothing and stay at a distance."

She nodded, and he dismounted and led the horse a few hundred yards toward the entrance. As he had predicted, a single mounted guard watched their approach, his pistol trained on Dimitry. "Halt," the man called. "Come no closer."

In response, Dimitry raised his arms to show he held no weapon, then jerked his head toward Hattie and spoke at length in Arabic.

"Are you injured, miss?" the man called out. "I cannot understand what this fellow is saying."

Mentally apologizing for the deception, Hattie only bowed her head. Dimitry continued to speak volubly in Arabic, and the soldier sheathed his pistol and held up a palm to him, indicating quiet. "All right, all right—let me see." He kicked his horse toward Hattie, but as he passed Dimitry he was suddenly seized by his right hand and pulled off the horse with a quick movement. After a brief scuffle, the soldier found himself looking into the barrel of his own pistol while Dimitry instructed him to raise his hands. Dimitry then backed toward the soldier's horse and removed its bridle, slinging it over his shoulder as he came back to mount up before Hattie.

The soldier watched him from the ground, his hands raised, and Hattie could see him calculating his opportunity to make a rush to save her. As she could not allow him to be injured in such an endeavor, she said calmly, "Pray do not be concerned. I am in no danger."

His face lifted to hers in surprise, the soldier replied, "Very well, miss."

Watching behind her, Hattie could see him continue to stare after them as they slipped through the opening, then she faced forward again as Dimitry once again urged the horse into a gallop.

After a few minutes of hard riding, they left the main road and headed toward the river, their pace slowing in keeping with the terrain that was getting softer as they came closer to the Nile. Finally, in a field of melons, Dimitry allowed the horse to walk for a bit and Hattie found herself taking a deep breath, relieved the mad flight appeared to be over.

"We will get off and walk, now."

"I have lost a shoe," Hattie confessed.

He chuckled. "No matter, I will carry you so we leave but one set of footprints. Don't lose the other one—we must leave no clues."

Once he dismounted, she slid off the horse and onto his back, wrapping her legs around his waist. She had been carried many a time in such a manner by Robbie, but deemed it prudent not to give voice to this bit of nostalgia. Dimitry placed a hand on the horse's nose in an appreciative gesture, spoke to it for a moment in his own language, then slapped it on its way.

"A good soldier," she commented, watching it trot away into the fields.

"Two good soldiers," he said, hoisting her up higher on his back. "I love you."

She kissed his neck as a reward for this sentiment—up to this point he had been all business.

"I wish your dress was not white."

"I beg your pardon," she said, kissing his ear. "I should have worn something more appropriate for an abduction."

He tilted his head as they trudged along because he liked what she was doing to his ear. "I would give you my tunic to wear, but then I would have naught but a white shirt."

"No matter," she said generously. "What is it we fear, searchers?"

"There will be searchers," he said with certainty.

This was of interest, and no doubt he referred to the murderous Monsieur Chauvelin and the other French soldiers—the ones who had stared at her because they knew. Of course they would search; both she and the associate were now missing under inexplicable circumstances, and no one would look forward to making such a report to the prisoner.

After a few more minutes they came to the water's edge, and Dimitry began to walk in the shallow water, splashing occasionally when the step was unexpectedly deep. This continued for several hundred yards, until they came across a dirt embankment with several fishing boats hauled onshore.

Making a sound of satisfaction, Dimitry instructed her to slide off onto the floorboards of one such vessel, then he procured a pole and pushed her out into the river shallows. Leaping into the narrow wooden boat, he then began to pole the vessel along the shore. In a quiet tone he directed, "You must lie on the floor and not speak; the sound will travel across the water."

Hattie obligingly curled up on the floorboard of the boat while Dimitry silently maneuvered the small vessel through the bulrushes. She watched that portion of the shoreline she could see from her position and after a short period of time, imagined she could hear horses and voices in the distance, although she had no point of reference and could not guess where they were. Silently, Dimity maneuvered the boat so that they were well hidden among the bulrushes that grew thick along the shoreline. Crouching down to his hands and knees, he then lay atop her, covering her white dress with his dark-clad body. As though nothing unusual were happening, he said in a low voice, "We shall wait a bit, now."

She nodded, trying to match his calm manner, and they lay thus for some tense minutes. Straining, she could hear nothing but the river insects. To calm her, he kissed the side of her face, whispering in her ear, "I am sorry I put you in the sarcophagus." He wound his arms around hers and interlaced their fingers, laying his cheek to her face as he rested the length of his long body over hers.

She whispered in return, "Then we are all even; I am sorry I disrupted your plan." As the water lapped on the hull beneath her head, she smiled, thinking the situation very satisfactory despite the perilous events of the day. It felt as though they were alone in the world with the thick, close darkness enveloping the small boat. "I do admire your beard," she whispered. "You are handsome and rather sinister, which is appealing in its own way."

"You didn't know me." He said it in a mock-accusatory manner.

"No—I'm afraid I was too busy dodging blows from the wicked baron."

"*Mudak*," he said succinctly, and she decided it was best not to seek a translation for that particular word. Instead, she whispered, "Is '*Sokol*' our family name?"

"No."

"What does it mean?"

He thought about the translation. "Falcon."

"What is our family name? Can you say?"

There was the slightest pause. "Khilkov, but you must not tell anyone; not as yet."

She repeated it, trying to become familiar with the unfamiliar pronunciation. "Is it Russian?"

"Yes." He kissed her again.

She smiled, feeling the whiskers of his false beard against her face. "It is a good name, Dimitry—and I must admit to relief; I would not have made a very good countess."

He made no response, and into the silence she sighed. "Best tell me the whole, husband."

She could feel his breath against her ear. "You are indeed a countess, and the House of Khilkov is fortunate to add your bloodstock to theirs." The words were firmly said, and his fingers tightened around hers. "I will hear no more of it."

"Yes, my lord," she teased, her tone light. There was no longer any point to being missish about her birth; she may already carry the heir to the House of Khilkov—may as well get on with it. Thinking of such things, she giggled. "Is that the mighty Glory of Kings I feel?"

Laughing softly, he pressed his hips suggestively against her. "I cannot help myself, Hattie—you feel so good against me."

"Well, I cannot be any more bedraggled than I already am," she said in an invitation, moving his hands to her breasts.

"Quiet; we cannot give our position away," he warned, but he was already turning her over beneath him and hiking up her skirts with an impatience that belied his caution.

Twining her arms around his neck, she kissed the hollow of his throat, below the beard. "I will be as silent as the stupid sarcophagus."

"I am sorry to have done it to you," he said again as his

mouth trailed along her throat and he pulled at the draw-string on his trousers. "But it seemed the best course."

"I lasted for all of five minutes—which was a major accomplishment, I think."

"This may not last much longer," he admitted, his voice husky in her neck.

And so her husband made quiet and efficient love to Hattie in the bottom of a wooden fishing boat while the crickets resonated and the eternal stars of Egypt burned overhead. It is truly not such a terrible place, she thought, arching against him and biting her lip to keep from crying out; one need only meet the right people.

Chapter 46

Dimitry was shaking her gently. "Hattie."

She opened her eyes, disoriented for a moment. The last thing she remembered was lying with him in the boat after lovemaking, content to be silent while they rocked with the current of the river. She must have fallen asleep, and now Dimitry was crouched over her, his expression intent. "I must go."

This woke her as nothing else could, and she sat up, blinking, only to realize they were out in the silent river, another boat alongside. "I will meet up with you as soon as I may."

She nodded, her breast suddenly heavy. "Good luck," she said, not certain of what one said in such a situation.

He laid a hand against her face then leapt nimbly into the larger boat that abutted theirs. In the moonlight, Hattie could make out the cohort from the tomb manning the oars and the inert form of the associate stowed on the floorboards—they had been successful in spiriting him away, then. She turned her head to observe that the innkeeper from the Osiris Inn was now doing the honors for her own vessel.

"Do I need my safe passage?" she reminded Dimitry as he placed a boot against their boat to push them away.

"It was never intended for you," he admitted.

She nodded. Apparently, the capture of the associate

had been his object all the while, and securing the treasure only a means to that end. That he had also secured a wife was an unexpected boon that had caused only slight complications—he was indeed an excellent chess player. She wondered where they would deliver the associate and decided that the less she knew about it, the better.

"Clements will see to you," he said softly as his figure faded away in the darkness, and then he was gone.

Masking her sadness, Hattie turned to face her impassive companion. "Hallo, again, sir. I believe we shall become fast friends, after all is said and done."

Wooden-faced, the innkeeper began to pole the boat. His only reaction was to indicate with a gesture that she was to lie down.

With a sigh, she complied, wondering whence she was to be shuttled now. Hopefully it was somewhere that featured a hip bath, as she had never been such a mess in her life—not that Dimitry had offered any objection when he had joined his body with hers on the floorboards. She decided she didn't want to think about him just now, and concentrated instead on the passing sky. After perhaps a half hour she could spy lanterns coming into view overhead, and propping on her elbows, she peered out and saw that they approached a small schooner, anchored in the river. As they slid quietly alongside in the shadows of the hull, a cabin porthole opened and Captain Clements's head appeared, wordlessly indicating she was to stand and lift her arms. Hattie carefully stood, holding her arms out to keep her balance, then lifted them toward him, hoping she wasn't to suffer the final indignity of the evening by falling into the Nile. The big man grasped her wrists and pulled her up so that she kicked off the hull and scrambled head first through the small opening, sustaining a few more bruises and scrapes in the process.

"Welcome aboard." With an easy movement, he set her upright on the floor within.

"I am dying for a bath," she responded without preamble.

He took her arm and steered her toward the interior of the cabin, indicating she was to sit on the low berth in the cramped quarters. "Not just now, I'm afraid. You must stay below decks and away from the windows." At her look, he offered in apology. "I can feed you, instead—will that do?"

She brushed at her filthy skirts, then gave it up as hopeless. "Do we leave immediately?"

"I await one more passenger, but we leave within the hour, regardless."

Eyeing him, she asked, "Where do we go?"

He shook his head. "I am not at liberty to say—not as yet, I'm afraid."

She gave in with good grace. "Very well then—I will cooperate if you teach me a few words in Russian."

The captain raised his bushy brows in surprise. "What makes you think I would know how to speak in Russian?"

With a shrug, Hattie offered a benign smile. "Just a thought."

He was amused. "I'm afraid you will have to take your lessons elsewhere."

She made a *moue* of disappointment. "I so wanted to surprise him."

"Instead, you have surprised me." He closed the door behind him.

After taking in her surroundings, she contemplated the undeniable fact that once again, she was uncomfortably enclosed in a small space. At least there was the porthole, such as it was. As she lifted an arm to examine a scrape on her elbow, the door opened to reveal Eugenie, looking very much put upon. "You look terrible," the Frenchwoman pronounced with satisfaction.

"If you bring a hairbrush, you may insult me all you wish."

"I am instructed to be of assistance," explained her reluctant handmaiden, pulling a hairbrush from the storage cabinet. "*Votre dragon* being absent."

Dimpling, Hattie had the pleasure of informing her, "My dragon is betrothed to Mr. Smithson."

"*Zut alors.*" Amazed, Eugenie shook her head in wonderment. "Who would think she could attract the men, that one? She is like a stick with eyeballs."

Unpinning the few pins left in her hair, Hattie noted, "I think they admire her for her mind, Eugenie."

"Bah." The woman made a gesture of repulsion. "Then they are not real men."

"Not like the captain." Hattie gave her a knowing glance as she started the long process of untangling her hair from the ends up.

But Eugenie was not to be discomfited. "Or Daniel."

"Or Daniel," Hattie agreed, thinking of the heated session on the fishing boat.

"He has left you?" It was asked with no real hope.

"Not yet, but I promise I will inform you immediately should it ever happen."

Eugenie laughed her genuine laugh, and Hattie joined in. It was into this merry scene that Robbie appeared, opening the door and standing in bemusement on the threshold. The two women scrambled to their feet, Eugenie smoothing her hair with a graceful gesture and Hattie deciding it was not worth the attempt.

"Hattie." Robbie came forward to embrace her. "Thank God."

"I am sorry to have worried you," Hattie said, disengaging from him and sliding her eyes toward the other woman with some significance—she didn't want to discuss the latest turn of events before Eugenie; Hattie had duly noted that she did not know Dimitry's true identity.

"Could you fetch me something to eat? I'm dashed sharp-set," Robbie asked Eugenie with a smile.

"Eugenie is acting as my dragon," Hattie said helpfully, and watched with interest while the other woman struggled to control her temper.

"She is not old enough," Robbie offered promptly. "I shall have to chaperone the both of you." For emphasis, he swatted Eugenie's bottom as she walked through the door, earning a wicked smile for his action.

"Robbie; I am shocked," remarked Hattie affably as he shut the door.

"I am the only one allowed to be shocked—I understand I am to wish you happy."

With a broad smile she dipped a mock-curtsey. "You may."

Brows drawn together, he stared in consternation. "How in the name of *all* that is holy did this come about?"

Hattie laughed at his professed amazement. "I fell violently in love one fine night—over the course of about ten minutes, I would gauge. It is my sincerest wish you suffer a similar fate."

Shaking his head, he smiled and embraced her again, holding her close. "Then I am indeed happy for you."

Hattie stumbled a bit, as the boat's movement could be now felt. "Oh—we are away; do you need to leave?"

"I am to travel to Cairo with you. Berry—or whoever he is—was concerned you were worried about me."

For some reason, this revelation brought a lump to her throat and she struggled not to cry.

He watched her with a thoughtful expression. "So—how much can you tell me?"

Reminded of her duties as a spy's wife, Hattie offered delicately, "I believe he is an ally, and is involved in a livelihood that is similar to yours."

"Yes." He seemed relieved, and she had to smile; neither of them knew how much to reveal to the other. "And a good thing too—he has done us a huge favor."

Tentatively, she suggested, "Drummond's associate?"

"The very same; we suffered a breach of security a few months ago—one of our men had a wife in London who was selling secrets to the enemy. They used the information to send one of their best men to infiltrate our operations on the continent; we are lucky your husband put an end to it before more information was compromised."

"A wife who was a traitor," Hattie repeated in amazement, and then thought of her parents. And—now that she knew about this twist to the story—it would not be far-fetched to conclude that this was how Napoleon's people were able to discover that her parents were secretly negotiating with the British; because of this treacherous wife. Which in turn meant they were summarily executed for their sins, with no mercy shown. "What happened to her—the wife who set this all in motion?"

"Dead."

She looked up at him, stricken by these revelations, one after the other. "Let's talk about something else, Robbie."

But he bent to reassure her in a sincere tone. "Berry seems very resourceful, Hattie; I know it's difficult, but I would have no fears on his behalf."

Unable to suppress her pride, she disclosed, "He had something to do with Napoleon's disastrous Moscow retreat, apparently."

Robbie raised his brows. "Did he? I confess I am not surprised; we believe he is a member of the Hospitallers—the Order of St. John, and they are based in St. Petersburg."

"What is that—a religious order?" She thought of the gold icon on the wall, hungry for any scrap of information he could relate.

"Well—yes, although with a military bent. They are otherwise known as the Knights of Malta—the organization includes what is left of the original Knights Templar, also. They're rather mysterious, and"—here he tilted his head and glanced at her—"they are not always aligned with our objectives, I'm afraid. But all in all, they do good work, particularly in fighting the Barbary pirates."

"I see." Indeed, this recitation seemed very much in keeping with what she knew of her new husband, and she teased, "Don't tell Swansea and her new husband that I've turned popish."

"Good God; that is the least of my troubles; m'father always assumed I would marry you. He will think me a sorry excuse."

Hattie found this piece of information very amusing, in an ironic sort of way. "Tell him it was not to be—only don't bring home Eugenie in my place; he *would* think you a sorry excuse."

He let out a bark of laughter and then admitted, "Mother would always tell him we were too familiar to marry."

"Your mother is a wise woman."

With a smile, he teased, "You'll never tell her of my engagement to Madame Auguste? Promise?"

"As long as you'll never tell her of my parents' treason."

He ducked his chin and ran a comforting hand down her arm. "Done," he agreed, his voice gruff.

"I will be very happy to shake the dust of Egypt from my sandals," Hattie pronounced with no small bitterness.

"I cannot blame you," he said quietly. "Where do you go?"

She smiled. "To his sister's." Hopefully this answer would suffice, and before any further questions could be asked, the cabin door opened to reveal Eugenie, carrying a bottle of wine and a napkin that revealed bread and dates when it was unrolled on the berth.

"I am to remind you to stay away from the windows," Eugenie said. "And there are no glasses so we must share the bottle."

"Excellent work," pronounced Robbie, and removed the cork with his pocketknife.

They settled on the berth and passed the wine bottle between them in the light of the single candle. "Easy, Hattie," warned Robbie. "You are not used to spirits."

"Only a sip," she assured him in a meek tone.

"Shall we play cards?" Eugenie asked Robbie, running her fingers along his sleeve. "We can play for Hattie's hairpins."

He laughed. "I understand you tend to fleece those foolhardy enough to engage you in cards."

"I shall be happy to fleece you, and more than once." She looked at him from under her lashes and Hattie chuckled in appreciation, which drew an admonitory look from Robbie. It is so much better to be married—to understand the innuendos, she thought. But how I wish he was here, so that I could say such teasing things to him. Stifling a pang, she reconciled herself to the sad fact that she may not see her husband again for quite some time. I miss you, Dimitry, she thought. *Please*, please be careful.

Chapter 41

H attie sat cross-legged on her berth, writing a letter to Dimitry. They had transferred from the small schooner to the *Sophia* and were currently anchored at Cairo, but were to depart very shortly for points eastward. The night before, Robbie had said his farewells before slipping away quietly so as to draw no attention. Hattie did not witness his leave-taking because she continued to be consigned to the lower deck, and as a result of the forced close quarters she and Eugenie were ready to strangle each other—although to the good, Hattie was fast learning the finer points of cheating at cards. To pass the time and to fight claustrophobia, Hattie was writing the letter and striving to maintain a light and encouraging tone. As she and Dimitry knew so little about each other's lives, she thought to relate the high points of hers up to the day they met. Unfortunately, the recitation thus far did not amount to more than a page and a half—truly, she had lived a very dull life until her trek to Paris, and then she had made up for it with a vengeance.

She was ready to be away, now that Robbie had disembarked—ready to meet her new family and begin the business of setting up her new life. And it would be a relief beyond measure to feel safe again—the small schooner had experienced a few tense moments near Helwan when local officials had boarded to make a search; apparently all vessels heading to the Nile delta were undergoing a search for reasons that were not explained but which Hattie could easily guess. Curled up tightly, she hid in a cupboard in the captain's quarters, and Robbie told her later that their unnamed vessel flew a Dutch flag and Captain Clements spoke in that language to the boarding party as he presented his passage documents. Robbie had been instructed to say nothing unless asked, and fortunately the officials were too distracted by Eugenie to make any inquiries.

"I feared her bosom was going to fall out of her dress," he confessed in amusement, "and I believe every man on board feared the same thing."

"Hoped, you mean," Hattie corrected him. "God bless Eugenie."

During their trip down the Nile, the other woman had offered one of her dresses to Hattie, who had nothing but the bedraggled sprig muslin in which she had arrived. Hattie wore Eugenie's dress now and was grateful even though it was several sizes too large and required her to lift the hem to walk.

Holding her arms over her head to stretch her back, Hattie wondered how much longer before they left for the open sea and she could go above decks and once more feel the sun. A soft knock on the door made her swing her legs over the side and straighten her skirts; Eugenie would not knock. "Come in."

The captain poked his head through the door. "Would you come with me for a moment, madam?"

Lifting the too-long skirt, Hattie followed him to his quarters where he opened the cabin door and signaled her inside, making no comment. She stood within the cabin as the door shut behind her and stared at the captain's berth, which featured the prone figure of her husband.

She stood in complete shock for a moment, then advanced carefully. He was asleep, fully clothed even to his dusty boots, one arm flung across his forehead. Moving slowly, she knelt next to the berth and leaned back on her legs, drinking in the sight of him. She had never had the opportunity to gaze upon him unabated and she took it now, loathe to wake him when he was so tired that he couldn't stay awake even while she was fetched. An almost unbearable feeling of protective tenderness rose within her breast, and she longed to cradle him against her. The lines on his face were deeper, his chin had not seen a razor for a few days, and there was dust in his dark eyebrows—she thought he was the most beautiful sight she had ever seen.

Careful not to move, she sat quietly for some time, watching him breathe as the boat gently rocked with the current. I will watch him thus for the rest of my life, she thought, and hugged the thought to herself, unable to believe her good fortune.

He stirred, and the brown eyes opened and looked into hers.

"*Dorogon*," she said softly, trying to remember the word.

With a sleepy smile, he reached to caress her face with his hand. "*Dorogoy*," he corrected in a tender tone.

She turned her head to kiss his palm. "Go back to sleep, if you wish. I do not mind."

"I have little time," he said with regret. "But I wanted to see you again." Stiffly, he rose to sit on the edge of the berth, and took her hands in his. "You are well?"

"I am perfectly well." She smiled at him from her position on the floor. "You must not worry about me—I look forward to staying with your sister."

He nodded. "Clements will be needed in Lisbon, but he will commission another to deliver you—a curé, who can be trusted completely."

"Can he deliver letters to you?"

"There are others who will see to it." It was all that he offered, and remembering Robbie's disclosures about his organization, she asked no further questions. Dimitry kept his gaze focused on her hands in his, his head bent.

"Tell me—whatever it is," she said softly, watching him. "I promise I won't have the vapors."

He lifted his head to meet her eyes. "I wrote to him."

There was no question as to whom he referred. She stared at him, speechless.

He continued in an intent tone, "I wanted to assure him that we are honorably wed—that I did not seek to take an advantage—and that there is a deep affection on both sides. I remember how I felt when the pistol was held to you; I would not wish such a feeling on anyone."

"Oh—I see," she replied, even though she didn't see at all. I wonder if I will ever understand men, she thought, genuinely perplexed—or if I will ever understand the power of love; imagine his dilemma in contemplating marriage to me, but nonetheless he moved heaven and earth to accomplish it. His devotion has more than made up for all the lack of devotion I have ever experienced. "I love you." She looked into his dear face, and meant it to the soles of her slippers.

"*Ya tebya lyublyu.*" He kissed her palms, one after the other. "I have a letter for you to give to my sister."

But the kisses had started an entirely different train of thought, and she leaned forward because the loose dress did a very poor job of covering her breasts. "Do we have so little time?" she teased in a low voice.

He put a hand on the nape of her neck and pulled her to him, resting his forehead against hers. "I am not so selfish—I am content to speak with you; to look upon you while I may."

She thought about this, fingering the button on his sleeve. "And if I insisted, what then? Would you draw your blade on me?"

Now it was his turn to think about it. "No," he decided, and lifted her chin to kiss her mouth.

Twining her arms around his neck, she pushed him back and wriggled, allowing her dress to fall off her shoulders. "Shall I lock the door?"

"He would dare not enter."

"I am not worried about the captain—Eugenie does not knock."

With a swift movement, he pulled her over so that he was now atop her, his mouth on her throat. "She will have to wait her turn, then."

Laughing, she punched his arm in mock outrage. "I thought you had so little time."

But he became serious, and paused to rest his cheek against hers. "There is indeed little time—I have never missed anyone so much in my life, and there is so much more to come."

It was nothing more than what she had thought a thousand times these past few days, but instead she stroked his hair and responded as she knew she must, "It cannot be helped, Dimitry. I would not change a single thing if it meant I was not married to you, and so I will accept whatever comes with a grateful heart."

He lifted his head and brushed his lips against her mouth, the moment of vulnerability over. "You are *extraordinaire*."

"I suppose that is true," she teased, to match his

changing mood. "Only ask the crowd at the British consulate in Cairo."

"So, you can make light of it, now." He pressed his curved nose against her straight little one as he worked her gown down her body. "At the time, it was not so amusing."

"No, it was *ridiculous*; I am the last person anyone should confuse with a goddess."

With an impatient gesture, he lifted off her for a moment to draw his shirt over his head. "The goddess of fertility, perhaps—we shall see."

With a delighted giggle, she pulled him to her.

Author's Note

Those familiar with the historical timeline will realize that Hattie should be a few years younger than she is. Historical accuracy has been sacrificed so that the story can include a romance.

About the Author

Anne Cleeland holds a degree in English from UCLA as well as a law degree from Pepperdine University and is a member of the California State Bar. She writes historical fiction set in the Regency period and contemporary mystery. A member of the Historical Novel Society, she lives on Balboa Island, California, and has four children. Find her on the web at www.annecleeland.com.